TRAITOR

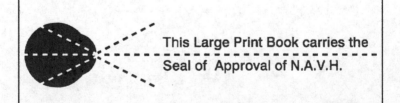

This Large Print Book carries the
Seal of Approval of N.A.V.H.

TRAITOR

A THRILLER

JONATHAN DE SHALIT

Translated by Steve Cohen

THORNDIKE PRESS

A part of Gale, a Cengage Company

Farmington Hills, Mich • San Francisco • New York • Waterville, Maine
Meriden, Conn • Mason, Ohio • Chicago

Copyright © 2015 by Keter Books, Ltd.
English language translation copyright © 2017 by Jonathan de Shalit Books Ltd.
Thorndike Press, a part of Gale, a Cengage Company.

Thorndike Press® Large Print Thriller.
The text of this Large Print edition is unabridged.
Other aspects of the book may vary from the original edition.
Set in 16 pt. Plantin.

LIBRARY OF CONGRESS CIP DATA ON FILE.
CATALOGUING IN PUBLICATION FOR THIS BOOK
IS AVAILABLE FROM THE LIBRARY OF CONGRESS

ISBN-13: 978-1-4328-4984-9 (hardcover)

Published in 2018 by arrangement with Emily Bestler Books/Atria, an imprint of Simon & Schuster, Inc.

Printed in Mexico
1 2 3 4 5 6 7 22 21 20 19 18

TRAITOR

1

Rome, 1983

The darkness fell out of nowhere. So blue and pristine just a few minutes earlier, the sky turned momentarily purple and then black, as if infused with ink. The warmth of the day, a pleasant enough one in early March, was replaced with a sudden chill. Shadows lengthened and darkened. Dim lights illuminated the street, while the beams of concealed floodlights washed over the walls. And in their glow, the magnificent structures took on the appearance of a grandiose backdrop for a play. The time was 6:02. A young man walked down the narrow street once more, tugging on his coat zipper, which was already pulled up as far as it could go anyway, and again passed by the iron gate of the American embassy. He was alone on the street, which appeared deserted for a moment. The noise of incessant traffic could be heard coming from the

Via Veneto, the wide street that the splendid façade of the embassy, located in a building that had once served as a palace, overlooked. Whipped by the cold wind, its red and white stripes glowing in the beam of a spotlight, a large American flag flew at the top of a tall pole. To the young man, the huge building, with all of its windows sealed shut, looked empty and gloomy; but he knew its rooms were filled at that very moment with hundreds of people. He retraced his steps and firmly pressed the intercom buzzer on the gate. Two security cameras installed high above him rotated silently and focused on him.

"Yes," came a metallic, nasal voice from the intercom speaker.

"I'd like to speak to someone from intelligence," the young man said in fluent English, his voice steady.

"Consulate hours are ten to two," the voice responded. "You can come back tomorrow."

"I'd like to speak to someone from intelligence," the young man repeated. "I don't require consular services and I have no intention of returning tomorrow. I'm here on an important and urgent matter."

"What's your name and what brings you to the embassy?"

"The who and why are details I'll reveal only to an intelligence representative." The young man hesitated for a moment, and then added, "It's a matter of national security."

"Come in, please," the voice instructed. A brief click was followed by the sound of a metal door swinging open. The young man walked in, and the door closed behind him. He found himself enclosed between high steel walls, the black sky visible above him. It was a small yard, measuring two by three meters. The Rome street disappeared behind the gate that locked behind him. Bright lights shone on him suddenly, and he closed his eyes for a second. "Welcome," said the metallic voice that had addressed him moments earlier. "You'll need to remove your jacket and raise your arms. We need a clear view of your hands. A security guard will be with you soon. You need to obey his instructions. Is that clear?"

"Perfectly clear."

Dressed in a suit covered by a leather coat, the guard entered the compound through a door that opened in one of its walls and passed a metal detector over the young man's body. He then slipped the metal detector into one of his coat pockets and frisked him along the length of his raised

9

arms, over his back, and down his legs. "Come with me," he said.

The young man followed the security guard into a structure that looked like a large glass aquarium. He was asked to remove his coat and take off his shoes, belt, and watch. He was then instructed to empty his pockets and pass through a large metal detector. "Where's your passport?" one of the security guards asked. "I don't see a passport here," he continued, looking at the small pile of items the young man had removed from his pockets.

"I'll show my passport only to an intelligence officer," he said.

"You won't be going any farther without a passport," the guard replied in a brusque and stern tone. "You'll be back on the street in no time."

"I left it at the hotel, but I have a driver's license in my wallet."

The guard opened the wallet, pulled out two credit cards and a driver's license, recorded the license particulars on a form he retrieved from a drawer under the counter, looked again at the credit cards, and returned them and the license to the wallet. He nodded to a second security guard, who then said: "Take your things and follow me."

They entered the embassy building

through a side door and walked down a long neon-lit corridor. There was no one else around, and their footsteps echoed down the passageway. "Wait here," the security guard said after they entered a small, illuminated room, bare and devoid of any superfluous items. It contained nothing but a metal table, two chairs, a small refrigerator that reminded the young man of a hotel minibar, an image of a bald eagle embossed on the wall, and an American flag standing in the corner.

2

Dressed in a dark suit, his graying hair a little too long and somewhat unkempt, the man who entered the room looked fifty or so. He approached the young man, who half rose from his chair, shook his hand, and, with the young man still motioning to stand, said, "Sit, sit, please.

"My name is John Roberts, and I'm the deputy consul," the man introduced himself, clearing his throat but only partially concealing the irony in his voice. He placed a writing pad on the desk straight in front of him. "And how may I help you?" he asked, his face lighting up all of a sudden.

"I asked to meet with an intelligence representative," the young man responded, inhaling deeply like someone who was about to keep talking.

"This is an embassy, and we are all State Department officials," Roberts said. "But I can assure you that whatever you have to say will be passed on to the very person who needs to hear it. Trust me, take it easy, and I'll be able to assist you. We at the consular division handle such matters routinely and in a highly professional manner. Don't worry. Would you like something to drink?"

"Cold water, mineral water if possible. Thank you."

Roberts walked over to the small refrigerator in the corner of the room and retrieved a bottle of water and a plastic cup. "Look," he said, "procedure requires us to begin with having you complete the following forms in the most detailed and comprehensive manner possible." He opened one of the desk drawers and removed a pile of questionnaires printed on greenish paper. "I'd also like you to hand over all documents in your possession — passport, driving license, student card, whatever you have . . ." He retrieved several sheets of paper from the pile and placed them in front of the young man across the desk from him. "Fill them in. No need to hurry. We'll speak afterward. I have time. You, too. Do a good job." He sighed and leaned back in his chair.

The young man reached for the pile of forms, glanced over them, and, his voice suddenly hoarse, said: "May I have a pen, please?"

14

3

An hour and fifty minutes later, Roberts collected the forms. The young man sat back in his chair and took another sip from the cup of water. He was pale and appeared extremely tired — on the verge of exhaustion. Roberts lifted the telephone receiver by his side, dialed four numbers, and said: "Bring us a pot of coffee, please. Black, strong. Yes, now." He flipped through the forms, which were now filled with tight, neat handwriting. Details upon details upon details. Names, addresses, phone numbers, names of parents, schools attended, beginning with elementary school, academic studies, places of employment, military service, acquaintances, hobbies, favorite books, membership in organizations, social activities, overseas travel, relatives and friends, particulars, names, dates. "Okay . . . ," he said, placing the forms on the desk, opening the top button of his shirt, loosening his tie, and then hesitating for a moment while glancing at the papers in front of him. "Okay, Alon, let's start talking."

"To be honest," Alon said, after realizing that Roberts expected him to say something, "to be honest, I first thought of approaching you about a year and a half ago, toward the end of 1981. As I've just written down, there on the forms," he continued, nodding in the direction of the greenish papers, "I served as commander of a small shore-located naval base, with the rank of lieutenant. The navy is a small corps, but significant nevertheless. Almost all of the Israel Defense Forces' operational plans include a naval element and perspective — troop transportation, search and rescue, intelligence and gunfire support, or even simply to be ready to counter an enemy response via the sea. Furthermore, we played a major role at that time in operations against the Palestinian terrorists in Lebanon. Naval commandos carried out operations of one kind or another almost every week, and the activities of the entire corps were focused on each one — truly the entire corps. So even the commander of a beach station was exposed to such operations, sometimes as the result of a specific mission he was required to carry out, and sometimes just to be in the

16

picture in the event of unforeseen developments.

"We believe, and justifiably so," he went on, "that in order to think big — in order to take everything into consideration, and in order to make educated decisions, one has to see the complete picture. Okay, I wasn't always aware of every detail; but for a young officer in charge of a small and pretty marginal unit, I knew a lot."

The young man paused for a moment. A tremor, unnoticeable, went through Roberts as he tried to regain the focus he had lost for a moment. He continued to listen, a look of concentration and interest on his face, while jotting down notes on the writing pad. Since the entire session was being filmed and recorded by a concealed audio-video system, he didn't have to write down every word; experience had taught him, however, that such meetings always yielded extensive information. Usually random and insignificant, the details were sometimes important, and it was good to highlight various points and references by hand — for help later when writing up the summary report. It was important, too, for the walk-in — the term used to refer to someone who knocks on an embassy door and asks to meet with intelligence officials — to know that he was being taken seriously and that his statements were being noted. And yet, something about the manner in which this session had started appeared to indicate that something important was afoot, that this guy was serious. He couldn't put his finger on it exactly. His candor, perhaps, his straightforwardness. The fact that he was proposing a simple and clear-cut deal: Invest in me now, for an extended period of time, and you'll get your money's worth in the end. I have potential. My experiences to date — military service as an officer, integration into the circle of Israeli parliamentary aides, academic excellence at university — are testimony to this potential. You will enjoy the fruits of its realization. Perhaps his self-confidence, the calculated coolness with which he was crossing the line of treason, the frozen gaze in his eyes were what caused Roberts to sit up and listen more intently, awakening in him a latent instinct of sorts, a delicate flutter, a pleasant and evocative thrill, one he had thought would never again course through him.

"One day I received a top-secret envelope," the young man continued, "the kind that has two red stripes printed in the corner — for my eyes only. As base commander, I was responsible for opening the

18

envelope, studying its contents, and keeping it in my personal safe. The document bore the title 'Large Pine — The Naval Campaign.' Drawn up by the navy's Operations Division, the document offered a detailed description of the role of all the corps' units in the upcoming war. It left me astounded. I simply couldn't believe my eyes. It was a plan for a complete takeover of Lebanon. To this end, the navy's role included imposing a siege on the Beirut port, artillery and missile fire on targets from the sea, the defense of supply routes, deployment for the purpose of facing off against the Syrian naval forces in the arena, readiness to counter efforts by terrorists to infiltrate Israel from the sea — everything, absolutely everything. I have to say it troubled me. It troubled me a great deal. I was disturbed by the divide between the declarations concerning keeping the terrorist threat away from our northern border and the megalomaniacal plans to occupy Lebanon in its entirety and take control of its capital. As I saw it, and I knew so despite my youth and inexperience at the time, someone appeared to have lost his mind. An insane plan. And in a moment of desperation I thought to myself that you — yes, you — need to know of the existence of such plans. That you would realize we had lost it. That you'd have the power to prevent us from doing something foolish."

"And . . . ," Roberts asked, "did you do anything about it?"

"I copied the order and I kept the copy in the safe of my small office on the base, too, and later I shredded it. And no, I didn't do anything, I moved on, I must have pushed it to the back of my mind; and a few months went by, June arrived and the war broke out and, you know, it was too late by then . . ." he said, his voice trailing off.

"Yes," Roberts said, "your situation in Lebanon, now, too — how should I put it — is a complex one."

The young man sitting across from him blinked and quickly ran a hand over his eyes, seemingly inadvertently.

"It's been almost two years since the war," Roberts added. "What made you decide to come to us now?"

Ashen-faced, Alon hesitated. He tried to pour some water from the plastic bottle into the cup by his side, only to sheepishly find it empty. Roberts went over to the small refrigerator, retrieved a second bottle of water, and poured some into the empty cup. Alon sat up in his chair and said: "You are the world's strongest superpower. You may

20

not know it yet, but in the not-too-distant future, less than a decade maybe, the Soviet Union will fall apart. You're focused constantly on the Soviet Union's tremendous military might, but I'm looking at its economy. The Soviet superpower's economy is rotten, sick, a wreck. The Soviet Union is going to collapse, and you will be left as the world's sole superpower. History," he declared, his eyes bright, "history is about to change, a lot sooner than most of the world thinks. And we, in Israel, need you. Your protection, your support, your guidance. You need to help us help ourselves, help us overcome our terrible fears and inclination to self-destruct. And I want to help you do so. I'm young; I'm resourceful — very resourceful, if I may say so of myself. I can go far. I'm already a parliamentary aide. I'll be a ministerial official within a year, in the bureau of one of the ministers. Within ten, fifteen years, I could be your man in the most strategic locations. I'll be there; I know it. I'm smart and ambitious. And you can assist my rise up the ladder. Guide me, wield all your powers — to the knowledge of no one, of course. Invest in me now, and together we'll go far."

The young man ended abruptly. His slim frame looked deflated. His dark eyes had narrowed, and appeared to Roberts to be slanted and cold. Roberts, too, suddenly felt exhausted by the deluge of words from the young man, who had spoken and spoken and tried so hard to demonstrate his broad perspective, his maturity, his ability to lucidly analyze global processes. He could feel the weariness spreading slowly behind his eyes. He had seen so many like him. Endeavoring. Groveling. But that same thing that had been echoing in his consciousness whispered to him to shake it off and fight through the exhaustion. Perhaps — after so long, way too long — luck had finally dealt him an ace.

There was a soft knock at the door. A young man in a suit, his fair hair meticulously combed, entered the room hesitantly. Visibly nervous, he was carrying a tray bearing a pot of coffee, two mugs, a small milk jug, and a few packets of sugar and artificial sweetener. Roberts gestured for him to lay the tray on the table, and the young man did so with somewhat shaky hands, softly mumbling, "Sir." He then exited in a hurry, taking care to lightly shut the door. Fucking cadets, Roberts thought to himself ungraciously. Brings coffee, and is slow in doing so, and is all worked up as if he's about to cross the border into East Berlin. I'm too old for this shit.

cross the border into East Berlin. I'm too old for this shit.

4

Roberts knew that this was the point at which the meeting should come to an end. The walk-in was squeezed dry. He, too, felt drained. He needed a deeper understanding of certain things. And for that he needed time. Time with himself. Time during which one's thoughts could swirl almost haphazardly in the mind, circling, crashing into one another, and then instantaneously take on form and volume. He needed to achieve a moment of enlightenment. Who was this young man? Why was he really there? What was driving him? What was his mind, as sharp and impressive as it might be, seeking? And what was his soul after? How could he be of service? What was he worth right now? What chance did he have of becoming someone truly significant in the future, someone with real and intimate access to actual secrets? How much investment, if any at all, was he worth? How long would it take to maintain and develop a relationship with him, until it stabilized? He was going to have to decide if this young man had any value.

"Okay, we need to end here now — this session, at least," Roberts said. "I will pass everything on to the relevant parties. It may take a while before we get back to you."

Alon nodded.

"I, or someone on my behalf, will contact you at some point," Robert continued. "I, or someone on my behalf, will use the name Alan Stone, okay? We won't meet with you in Israel — unless we have a special or critical need to do so. When we talk again, we'll meet at one of our embassies overseas, in keeping with the options available to you. Preferably in Europe. We won't use the word 'embassy' over the phone. It'll be enough to say, 'Our office in Rome,' 'Our office in Paris,' and so on. Got it?"

Alon swallowed his saliva and nodded, confirming he had understood.

"Repeat the instructions I have given you," Roberts said.

The young man did so clearly, his voice shaking suddenly.

"If we meet in Israel," Roberts went on, "and the chances as I've said are very slim, we'll do so in the lobby of the Tel Aviv

Hilton. If you wish to contact us, call this number." The embassy official handed him a business card bearing the name of a trading company and a telephone number in Hamburg. "Don't call from a telephone associated with you, and always identify yourself as David Mannheim. Ask to speak with Alan Stone. We'll get back to you. Be patient. It may take some time."

The young man stood up, his face blank and his eyes cold. "I appreciate the time you've given me," he said, shaking Roberts's hand. "It was good meeting with you — I hope," he added with a smile, well aware of the cliché on his lips, "that it's the beginning of a beautiful friendship."

The man who had introduced himself during the meeting as Roberts was actually William Duke. He waited for the walk-in to leave the room in the company of the security guard, stood up, stretched his aching back, ran his fingers through his hair, and returned to his office. With a brief glance at the photograph of his wife and children on the desk and a despairing look at his watch, he retrieved a yellow notepad from one of the drawers and began writing up his report on the meeting that had just ended.

1. Attached hereto are the questionnaire forms containing the complete particulars of the individual in question. See comments below.
2. Intelligent, calculating, knows what he wants, determined.
3. Appears to be motivated primarily

by money. The subject is looking for a long-term relationship that would ensure him a steady income. If he does indeed rise through the ranks of the Israeli establishment as he intends to do, his price is expected to rise accordingly. Although still early days, it's safe to assume already at this point that if his aspirations bear fruit and he truly finds himself walking the corridors of power and influence, we'd probably be happy to pay.

4. The deal the subject is offering us reflects a profound degree of cynicism, which, based on my initial impressions, forms a significant aspect of his personality.

5. The subject appears eager to be a part of "something" bigger than himself — a great nation, an all-powerful organization, and the like. Dime-store psychology aside, I direct your attention to the matter of the subject's father and his abandonment of the family during the subject's early childhood (see questionnaires), with all its emotional and financial implications.

6. The subject makes a point of stress-

ing that his approach to us doesn't conflict with his country's best interests, both due to the fact that we are allies and because he views us as the "responsible adult" with the power, diplomatic wisdom, and international standing to know what's best for his country; more so than its leaders themselves. It's important to preserve and develop this line of thought.

7. The subject's current value is marginal. Our prime interest is not the military intelligence to which he has access in the framework of his service in the reserves, although we may be pleasantly surprised. And the political information to which he is privy as a parliamentary aide won't offer much more than our embassy staff can obtain openly. Nevertheless, a position in the bureau of one of the government ministers — if he is able to secure one — may offer some real potential.

8. His true value, therefore, lies somewhere in the future. There's no guarantee that the subject, of all people, and not others from among the thousands of talented individu-

als seeking advancement in the Israeli political establishment and civil service, will rise to the key positions that truly interest us. That said, I must point out at this stage the subject's obvious drive, cool-headedness, lack of scruples, and impressive capabilities as factors that bode well for the rise through the ranks he has promised. Most significant is the fact that the subject has already offered himself to us.

9. I don't think we've got anything to lose by viewing the subject as an investment for the long term. Our financial input to begin with should be modest. We should pay the subject the minimum sum required to preserve the relationship and fuel his motivation to move forward under our guidance.

Duke put his pen down. His draft report was ready. He placed the pages in the small safe in the corner of his office, shut the heavy door, locked it with a key he retrieved from his pocket, and turned the number dial.

On the way home to Parioli, he stopped

outside a café he was in the habit of drinking at almost every day — espresso in the mornings and whisky in the evenings. With a piece of white chalk he removed from his pocket, he drew a small star on the crumbling brick wall on the corner of the street. He had given the signal. And he was now waiting for the meeting.

6

He waited. After alerting his handler of his need for a meeting, William Duke sat for three evenings in succession in the plush bar of the Hassler Hotel, looking out over the city's domes and steeples, sipping exorbitantly expensive whisky, passing the time in idle thought, and casting a bored gaze over the establishment's incoming and outgoing patrons. If he didn't show up tonight, he would have to repeat the same waiting process in precisely one week, and this time at the Grand Hotel de la Minerve, near the Pantheon. Driving by his regular café two days ago in the morning, he had seen a red circle around the white star he had left there on the wall. His signal had been received and confirmed. All he had to do now was to wait. Duke was pleased to be serving in Rome on his own. His wife had chosen to remain in Washington to continue managing her trendy boutique —

a surprisingly successful and prosperous venture, or one that at least hadn't folded like her previous business efforts, which had left an increasingly large hole in their bank account. Their two children were grown up and were both at college — Patty at North Dakota, and Greg at Michigan State. He needed the foreign-service pay to support them and also to finance his wife's rather extravagant lifestyle. His relationship with his wife had long since become a business arrangement. The warmth and intimacy had disappeared — just as the love had before them. Could what they had had really be called love?

He closed his eyes and thought back to their first night together, at that dismal motel along the highway north of St. Louis. He remembered how beautiful she had looked, her blonde hair, her teeth so incredibly white, the sweetness of her smile. She was still dressed in her Lafayette High School cheerleading squad uniform when he picked her up. She looked like a breath of fresh of air. He, a discharged soldier, had just completed six years as an army intelligence NCO, mostly in Darmstadt, West Germany. He was to report in four weeks' time to the CIA in Washington for an additional series of tests, after having already undergone an interview and initial screening at the agency's offices in Frankfurt. Many years had passed since then, he thought to himself, inadvertently fiddling with the knot in his tie and then brushing back his graying hair. His secret, his terrible private secret, warmed his heart and made him feel that here, in his small realm of sin, he was the master of his own fate — far away from his wife, whose teeth were indeed still white but whose smile hadn't been sweet for ages; far away from his demanding children; and far away from his arrogant bosses. He'd been in the service of the CIA for exactly twenty-six years; and for quite some time now, he'd been working under people practically half his age, stuck with the duties of an aide to a department head and watching others take the credit for his modest achievements. He thought for a moment about his father, who had worked all his life at a steel plant in Pittsburgh, and said to himself: For fuck's sake, he helped build America no less so than all the others, and perhaps even more. His father had served in the Pacific for two and a half years during World War II — a Marine, a rank-and-file combat soldier, but trustworthy and spirited. Yes, he, too, deserved credit, no less so than all the others; but what did he get in return?

Duke suppressed those thoughts, which washed through his mind from time to time. He was often haunted by the image of his dying father, riddled with lung disease. During the final months of his life, his father was no longer the broad and solidly built high-spirited man he used to be. Lying there in his bed in their home at 515 Jefferson Street, he cut a pale and thin figure, and appeared to be withering and fading further from one minute to the next. The hospital was too expensive, and the health insurance had disappeared along with the bankrupt steel plant. His father, choking and gasping for breath, was occupying less and less space in the world. He remembered his rage from back then. Hadn't his father done his fair share? Yet it seemed as if the world saw him as a weightless speck of dust. He was thirty-six when his father died. His father was sixty-one, just ten years or so older than he was now. He was buried in the Catholic cemetery, among tall and tightly packed tombstones, green with moss and prematurely blackened with age. He hated visiting the grave, shivering with cold in the shadow of the dilapidated plant, which blocked the sun's pale light and painted the cemetery in dark patches of blue and purple.

As always, his heart skipped a beat when Gunther entered the bar. Night had fallen over the city, and the palely floodlit white dome of St. Peter's Basilica looked like a clear and weightless celestial body hovering in the dark sky. Gunther walked over just as he rose from his chair.

A broad smile lit up Gunther's face as he shook Duke's hand and then, in one continuous motion, tugged him closer and warmly embraced him, his free hand slapping down firmly on Duke's shoulder. "Good to see you, good to see you," Gunther joyfully exclaimed; and Duke, who feared the entire bar — and not just the bar, but the whole world — was looking at them now, remembered what Gunther had told him a thousand times already: Act natural, act like a regular guy. Only if you whisper will everyone listen. Are you happy to see me? Yes? So be happy! Hug me! Greet me loudly. We're two friends who don't get to see enough of each other, and we've finally made time to get together. I love you, he'd say, lowering his voice a little. You know that, right? Our "business" connection aside, I really do feel like we're family — kindred spirits, he'd say, so as not to sound too dramatic or embarrass him too much. And Duke truly did feel that Gunther

36

wasn't simply another handler blindly chosen for him by fate. He had worked with other handlers before Gunther, and he knew that there'd come a day when Gunther, too, would come to see him — in a somewhat celebratory mood, tinged with just the right amount of sadness — to tell him that the time had come for him to move on, that he, Gunther, was being transferred to a different arena or had been appointed to a senior position at headquarters, and that he, Duke, had no choice but to get to know a new handler. But, he would continue to monitor his progress and take pride from afar in his significant contribution, he'd say — because what do we have in this fucking life if not a handful of people we care about and with whom we have a real and heartfelt connection that doesn't fade even if we see less of one another, even if life takes us in opposite directions? He knew all that, but still felt a sense of intimacy and true friendship, and he hoped that the time to say farewell to Gunther lay as far in the future as possible.

Gunther sat down in the armchair across from Duke and let out a sigh of relaxed contentment. "I've had a long and hard day," he said, as if to let Duke in on a secret. "I need a drink," he continued, signaling with his hand to the elderly waiter, ordering a shot of Lagavulin whisky and a glass of soda water on the side, and asking Duke if he'd like something else. Roberts asked for a Lagavulin, too, and an espresso as well; he liked the bitter brew they served at the bar of the Hassler, and he especially liked the plate of small sweets they served on the side. It has to be the most expensive espresso in the world, he thought to himself, but the price included the view, and the ambience was quiet and dignified, and Gunther was paying anyway. That was the cost required to oil the wheels of the revolution, wasn't it, he thought, aware of the wry irony that sometimes trickled into his thoughts uncontrollably, poisoning them.

"So what do you have to tell me, my dear sir?" Gunther asked after relaxing a little and settling comfortably into the leather armchair. "What's happened that couldn't wait for our regular meeting?" he added with a sharpness unfamiliar to his conversation partner. "Just so we're clear on this, when you call me to a special meeting, I have to assume you have good reason to do so. Don't think I'm complaining or anything like that, okay? I'm always at your disposal; I'll come whenever you need me to."

"Look," Duke said, "it may very well be nothing, but something happened that triggered — how can I put it — triggered an instinct of sorts, a sense, I'm sorry to say, that had been pretty dulled thanks to all the crap that those idiots give me to do."

Gunther nodded, and his eyes reflected a kind of sympathy, as if to say that Duke wasn't the only one with superiors who weren't very smart, and that over the years he, too, had worked under people who weren't always the brightest minds of the generation.

Duke continued: "A walk-in showed up last Monday. There was something unusual about him, something that set him apart from the endless and familiar collection of intelligence junkies and frauds who come banging on our door. A young Israeli guy, highly intelligent, cool and collected enough to make your hairs stand on end, an individual who had already made the decision to sell his soul. All that remains to work out is the price. He offered us a long-term arrangement: We're to invest in him, and he'll fast-track his way ahead and repay our investment further down the line, in a few years' time, or perhaps even much later.

"We get quite a few who approach us with the same kind of offer, even if they aren't able to express themselves as clearly and deliberately," Duke added contemplatively, "but this guy gave me the impression that if we manage things properly, we'll be able to recoup our investment. Look, if it's of no interest to you, I'll pass on his details to headquarters in Langley. I'll have to file some kind of a report anyway. But if you want to develop this asset, I can kill the Langley angle."

Gunther signaled to the waiter, who was standing at the back of the bar, his purple uniform blending in with the velvety wall, and ordered another glass of whisky. He appreciated Duke's gut feelings, but wanted a better understanding of where his faith in the walk-in was coming from. His organization would take on the operation only if its potential value was assessed to be particularly high. Not every Israeli who was willing to work with the Americans would be willing to work with the East German intelligence service, too. In fact, the chances were very low. Establishing a relationship with such a walk-in and developing him into a real agent would require costly and complex handling under a foreign identity, an American identity, and making such an investment would be worthwhile only if the future promised a real return. He asked Duke to elaborate on his encounter with the young man, not to spare any details, and in particular, he stressed, he wanted to hear his insights and impressions with regards to the man's character, with respect to his motives — and also Duke's view of the future, of how he saw the operation in five years' time, in ten years.

Gunther was adept at doing what Duke's CIA superiors had long forgotten. Unlike them, he didn't see Duke as an old, worn-out dog that couldn't learn new tricks, but knew instead to seek his advice, appreciate his opinions, and listen to him. He sincerely valued his judgment. And under such conditions, in this type of atmosphere, Duke flourished. He presented his case in a detailed and well-organized manner, distinguishing between facts and assessments and allowing his imagination to run free. He drew on his experience to paint the bigger picture with broad and bold brushstrokes, yet took care at the same time not to omit the finer details, the subtle areas of light and shadow, the translucent dabs of color. He was an intelligence officer, and in the presence of Gunther, and together with Gunther, in fact, he was also an artist of sorts, perhaps even a bit of a poet, one who could cast an eye into the future.

Gunther waited for several minutes after Duke had completed his report before speaking again. "I'm going to advise taking it on," he said. "Headquarters in Berlin will have to make the decision, of course, but I'll strongly recommend it. It may take time," he warned, "and you'll have to handle things delicately from your end. File a brief and banal report to Langley. Tell them you got the impression that he's nothing more than a money-hungry fraud, with symptoms of a slight intelligence addiction. But note explicitly that the final decision is theirs to make. And one more thing," Gunther added after a moment's thought, "send them an incorrect phone number in the report. Jumble two digits in his phone number. You can always blame the typist in the cypher office. . . . With a bit of effort, they can always locate him if they want to, via the parliament's telephone exchange or simply by knocking on his door at home," he said with half a smile, "but if they have no particular reason to be eager to get their hands on him, their idleness and workload will win the day. You know, of course, that I won't be able to inform you if we've decided to pursue the matter with him. When it comes to operations that could turn into something special, the need to maintain a high level of confidentiality from the outset is particularly important. But we're going to need real-time updates from you — if your guys decide to do something with him after all. It's best for the mistakes to be made elsewhere, and not by us, my friend," Gunther said in a cheerful tone, his eyes suddenly moist. "You really are something special. It's a shame that too many of our officers can't match you for intelligence, experience, and the ability to understand the human psyche. It's good to have you on our side."

Gunther stood up, approached Duke, and embraced him warmly. "It was good to see you; we don't do it often enough," he said as he stepped back a few paces, moving away from Duke and toward the exit, waving absentmindedly to say good-bye, good-bye and see you around.

7

Stasi Headquarters, East Berlin, 1983

Gunther — christened with the name Werner, but referred to by his ops name by almost everyone in the Stasi who knew him — burst into the bureau of the director of the Stasi's foreign espionage division, the Main Directorate for Reconnaissance. He hung up his wet jacket in the entrance hall, warmed his hands with undeniable glee over the noisy radiator, winked at Hannelore, the young office clerk who was sitting behind her desk in the corner like a frightened rabbit, and planted a loud kiss on the cheek of Marlene, the head secretary, mumbling softly as he did so, "You smell so good, Marlene. Lucky I don't work at headquarters; you'd drive me crazy and I'd have to set aside all matters of state just to be by your side all the time." Marlene blushed and lightly slapped his hand. "You're all mouth and no trousers, Werner," she said. "You're a big-time talker and a small-time playboy. Fortunately for you, you're good at what you do. Otherwise your big mouth and the Western mannerisms you've adopted would land you a job in the filing department at best, if not a posting to northern Siberia. And there, as you well know, the winters are very long," she added for emphasis, a stern look on her face. "Enough, enough with the tough attitude," Gunther said with a smile, glancing out of the corner of his eye at Hannelore, who had shrunk back in her chair but whose big eyes remained fixed on him with obvious wonderment. "If only I had a chance with you, I'd do any-thing . . ." he said, allowing his words to fade out, like someone who knows there's no point — because Marlene had never married and, since the age of twenty, had dedicated her life to serving the state and the party. For almost thirty-eight years already, the organization, as immense and intimidating as it was, had been the recipi-ent of her real admiration and loyalty, and her love, if anything close to love actually remained in her dry and withered soul at all, was undoubtedly reserved for Markus, the legendary head of the foreign espionage division. And Markus, who just then stepped out of his office, his face aglow, wrapped

Gunther in a tight embrace. "Sir!" Gunther said; and Markus kissed him on both cheeks, announcing to the room, with Hannelore drinking everything in through her gray eyes and Marlene busying herself again with the pile of cardboard folders on her desk, "I love this man like a brother!"

8

Markus and Gunther sat down on two time-worn and faded armchairs in the corner of Markus's office, a constant source of surprise in terms of its modest dimensions and rudimentary office furniture. Steaming cups of tea stood on the low table alongside them, and each man held a small glass of clear and viscous schnapps in his hand. It was a meeting of two masters. When it came to understanding the human psyche, man's weaknesses and desires, they were artists second to none. Gunther, the long-serving field operative, was blessed with a natural talent he had nurtured and polished through the years on end he had spent identifying, recruiting, and handling agents. Markus, who had started out in fact as a political theorist and was fast-tracked into the high-ranking position he currently occupied at the absurd age of just twenty-four, was blessed with a gift from God. He embodied a rare mixture of sensitivity and cruelty, of compassion hardened by icy determination. As profound as it was intuitive, his understanding of the shadowy world of the agents — spies who betray their countries and peoples — was based less on personal experience and more on a unique ability to get a clear reading of the agents' psyches from the gut feelings and reports of his people. He could always pinpoint the drive behind a particular individual's willingness to sell his soul and loyalty — money, love, or recognition, and sometimes also a desire for vengeance or simply the thrill of adventure. Both Markus and Gunther were senior officers in the secret service of East Germany, which was and still remained not only an ally but also a faithful servant of the Soviet Union. Both bore military ranks, with Markus a general and Gunther a colonel. But they donned their festive dress uniforms, adorned with gold aiguillettes and military decorations, only on a handful of occasions during the year, mostly to party events they were required to attend. Despite their shared hatred of formalities and superfluous pomp and circumstance, they identified fiercely with their country. They both knew that the mighty and historic triumph over fascism could only have been achieved thanks to the endless sacrifice, bravery, and daring of the communist faithful. Despite their gripes from time to time about the party's bureaucracy, about its conservative approach and random brutality, they hadn't forgotten the tremendous accomplishments, the huge progress that had been made, and primarily the immense strength of spirit that had instilled the socialist ideology in the masses, in the common people, who were the very salt of the earth. Above all, however, they loved their profession, which they viewed both as a calling and as a form of complex artistry. They loved the never-ending war of minds with their enemies in the West, dealing constantly with the army of agents they had amassed at their side and with the objects in their secret crosshairs. And thus, at ease and with a sense of camaraderie based on long years of work and true friendship, the two discussed the Israeli walk-in who had knocked on the Americans' door and could be ripe for the picking — if they so desired.

Insofar as Israel itself was concerned, the attitude of the East German leadership was one of indifference, as if there was no connection between the activities of the Palestinian organizations East Germany was funding and the state against which they were fighting. As a result, the East German intelligence services showed very little interest in information about Israel, and an Israeli walk-in wasn't going to make any impression at all on the Stasi itself or the party leaders in Berlin. But both Gunther and Markus knew — the one based on a gut feeling, the other with absolute certainty — that a high-ranking asset in Israel would certainly spark a great deal of interest among the big brothers at the Lubyanka, KGB headquarters in Moscow. Because as far as Moscow was concerned, Israel was already an entirely different story. In all the power struggles waged between the KGB and the Stasi, it was plain to see which of the two organizations was the bigger, the stronger, the more senior. On a professional level, nevertheless, the two organizations were in competition — not openly perhaps, but certainly not entirely hidden. On several occasions, the Stasi's foreign division had reaped success where the KGB had failed. The East Germans were at a distinct advantage, of course, with respect to West Germany. The shared national identity, the common language, family members living on both sides of the border, a single history and shared crimes from the time of the war — these were all factors that gave the Stasi the upper hand in West Germany in the continuing arm-wrestling contest between the organizations. When Markus showed up at KGB headquarters in Lubyanka Square, his character and capabilities weren't the only things that spoke for him. He, personally, was viewed as a man whose opinions and advice were worthy of attention. But the agents his organization had successfully recruited and who were often handled in keeping with instructions from Moscow were his primary assets.

The question that was troubling Markus and Gunther was whether the young and cynical Israeli could indeed become a senior asset at some point in the future. In the company of Markus, Gunther felt at last as if he no longer needed to step lightly. There were moments even when he allowed himself to be Werner and not Gunther, the legendary field operative and recruiter of agents. Settled back now in the shabby armchair, his tie loose and the top button of his shirt open, Gunther spoke candidly:

"Truthfully, after all, Markus, we don't know. How could we possibly know where this guy will be ten to fifteen years from now? Anyone offering a definitive and decisive opinion on the matter would be guilty of deception, and not mere deception, but deception of the worst kind — self-deception. Tell me, can I really know if this guy is going to go the distance in the world of politics, which is nothing more than a quagmire of endless manipulations and unbridled lust for power . . . ?"

Markus cleared his throat and a mischievous glint appeared in his eyes.

"I'm talking, of course, about politics in the West," Gunther said with a smile, utterly devoid of the need to justify himself to Markus, but conscious nevertheless of his big mouth and his, and everyone's, constant need to cover their asses in the event they ran into someone whose sense of humor and tolerance weren't at their best.

"How can we be sure," he continued, "that his abilities and talents and drive won't be redirected toward, let's say, the business world, leaving us with a fantastic agent — a real-estate mogul or wealthy lawyer or investment house CEO — but with zero intelligence?"

"Tell me," Markus said, interrupting Gunther, "what's happened to your professionalism, your hunter's patience? Where's this doubt coming from? After all, once we get in on the act, we also have the ability to influence the manner in which things move forward. We shape the reality with our own hands, and we don't make do with simply gathering intelligence about it. This guy has placed himself in our hands, even if he believes he's in the hands of the Americans. We know, after all, how to manage such operations — very slowly, patiently, thoughtfully. We'll get him accustomed to his ties with us, to the sense of adventure, to the thrill of secrecy, to the money filling his pockets slowly but surely, to the gradual and moderate climb in his standard of living. Just like a frog in a pot gets used to water that's boiled slowly. The frog will allow itself to be cooked alive without even considering the option of jumping out of the boiling water," said Markus, who was known for his descriptive imagery. "Little by little, you'll mold this material," he added in a low and warm voice, "and believe me, it's still soft. Shape it in your image. Or in the image of whomever you send to him. He'll want to please you; he'll want you to be proud of him; you'll be the father he doesn't have; you'll be the person he thinks about at night; and he won't want to disappoint you. For you, he'll work his way into positions we view as significant, he'll forge ties with people who interest us. And even if he's drawn into the world of business, we'll make sure he snakes his way in and out of public roles, as close to the plate as possible. And you and I will be with him, or behind the scenes, all the time; we'll feel him; and without his even knowing it, we'll get under his skin and through to his very soul," Markus said, taking the trouble to dryly add for the sake of required Marxist correctness, "the nonexistence of which is unquestionable."

"You know," Gunther said, still clinging to his skepticism, "that handling an agent under the guise of an American is no light task at all, and a major operation. I'll take charge of the handling to begin with, but further down the line we're going to need to make use of our most valued tools, individuals who've been stationed in the United States for years, as Americans for all intents and purposes, awaiting our signal. We've invested so much in them. Using them for a project that is just now getting started and whose development and outcome we truly cannot foretell is a big risk."

"My dear Werner," Markus responded, addressing Gunther by his real name, "if you're still living under the impression that we're on the brink of a Third World War in which we're going to deploy guerrilla forces to launch assaults on the American enemy's home front, then something really has gone wrong with you. Don't be the last disciple of propaganda that no one else believes any longer. We've built up assets. We've invested years of work in them. And for what? To never actually use them? Is it our ultimate goal to have them forget they are East Germans, to have them think they are Americans off the *Mayflower,* there to plant and water flower beds in their picturesque towns in Vermont or Idaho? Werner," Markus said, leaning toward him in a gesture of affinity and affection, "I have faith in your experience and gut feelings, and I have faith, too, in your agent at the American embassy in Rome. You're the old lions in this dirty game, this wonderful and dirty game," he added contemplatively. "If the two of you feel this guy has something to offer, I'm with you on it. And if our good friends at the Lubyanka want him, we'll do the work for them. Earning Brownie points in Moscow can't do us — you or me — any harm at all. You never know," he added in earnest, "you never know when we may need them."

9

Dresden, September 2012

The cold had taken up permanent residence in Marlene Schmidt's bones. Her layers of clothing were of no help, and the same could be said for the piping-hot heating system in the small public housing apartment in which she lived on the outskirts of the city. At the age of eighty-seven, with terminal bone marrow cancer nesting in her body, feeling warm and comfortable wasn't an option for her that gloomy winter. The coming spring, and the summer to follow, with the apple trees in full bloom and the magnificent flotilla of white swans on the river, wouldn't be hers to see again. Her days on earth were drawing to a close, thus dryly said her sharp mind, and she felt no sadness or sorrow about her dwindling life, only a bitter sense of disgruntlement, like a mild heartburn that rises up from the stomach to the throat. So many years of service and loyalty down the drain, service and loyalty to a country and an organization that were the essence of her life, that were supposed to survive for all eternity and to create — yes, despite everything — a new and more just world.

Marlene lived on the fifth floor of an enormous public housing project, seemingly infinite, put together with concrete and asbestos, one of the many built in keeping with the finest traditions of Stalinist architecture in Moscow and Leningrad, in Irkutsk and Tashkent, in Warsaw and Budapest, in East Berlin and Dresden, and in dozens, if not hundreds, of other cities throughout the Soviet Empire and its allies. Immense structures, eyesores, starkly uniform and utterly devoid of charm, but homes that were certainly habitable, that offered shelter, and in which one could live a complete and full life. Marlene loved her apartment, and she still recalled the intense excitement and deep sense of gratitude she had felt when the Workers' Welfare Association had informed her that finally, after so many years of such dedicated service, she was entitled to an apartment. It wasn't something to be taken for granted, certainly not in the case of a woman on her own, an unmarried woman, going on forty. Moreover, they had given her a state-of-the-art apartment, forty-five square meters that were hers alone, with a modern kitchenette and a small bedroom and a guest room and her own bathroom, just for her. For the first time, she could enjoy the luxuries offered by privacy and didn't have to cram herself into a common bathroom at the far end of the long hall with all the neighbors. True, the apartment hadn't been an act of kindness, not at all. It was given to her on merit, in recognition of her devoted and unconditional loyalty to the German Democratic Republic's security services, which she had joined immediately following the war. After twelve years as a cipher clerk at the Regional Command Headquarters in Dresden, she was transferred in January 1957 to the Special Ops Archives, where she had worked for many long years, endlessly dedicated and loyal, arriving every day at five minutes to eight and leaving after dark, twelve to fourteen hours later, her eyes burning, her body spent, filled with a sweet and comforting sense of satisfaction.

Still today, as an elderly and ill woman, she maintained her small apartment in pristine condition. The clean and tidy residence reflected her character — meticulous, stringent, loyal. Resting on the dark wooden dresser in the guest room were small souvenirs from numerous places around the world. No, she, personally, had never left Germany, aside from just once. To this day, her heart skipped a beat each time she recalled the thrill of that trip to Moscow, where in a secret ceremony she had received a special token of appreciation for her contribution and devotion. The small souvenirs were from her boys, her sweet and wonderful boys from the Special Ops Division of the Main Directorate for Reconnaissance. "Markus's boys," as she called them, never forgot Marlene, working there for them in a small office on the basement floor of the regional headquarters. Markus had been the one to insist, from the very beginning, that the division's archives be based in the small kingdom he had established for himself in Dresden, and not at central headquarters in Berlin. He didn't want everything concentrated in one location; he didn't like the idea of having all the intelligence at the disposal of every novice political commissar with a cushy job in Berlin. And his boys, who risked their lives in the covert war they waged against the enemies of the state and party in every corner of the world, always knew there was someone loving and loyal to safeguard their secrets, their daring operations, as well as the agents they managed to recruit and handle for the sake of the revolution. They had brought her a small Eiffel Tower from Paris and a chubby Buddha from China and a frightening wooden mask from Mozambique, and she watched over those small mementos, those symbols of love, with a joyful heart and eyes that sometimes filled with tears. And in the dresser itself, she kept several bottles of selected alcoholic beverages. She wasn't much of a drinker, and even less so a hostess, but she had a number of bottles of whisky from Scotland and also a few bottles of vodka, not only from Moscow but also from Helsinki and Stockholm, along with a bottle of Grand Marnier from France. The strong, sweet liqueur was her favorite of all; and from time to time, when the loneliness turned particularly acute, she would pour herself a small glass, taking comfort in the pleasant fire that spread down her throat.

Many years after starting out at the Special Ops Archives — more than twenty years down the line, to be precise — Markus summoned her to Berlin. "Marlene," he had said to her at the time, "I want you by my side. The post of head secretary is opening up, and I need someone with whom I can be totally at ease and relaxed. Someone I can trust one thousand percent. Not some high-and-mighty young Humboldt University graduate who has been parachuted in by someone from the Politburo." And Markus had offered an ironic description of the potential candidate — an ambitious young woman whom one politician or other was keeping on the side; after arranging a nice small apartment for her, he was now going to land her a prestigious job, too. And in return, Markus said in a tone that to her sounded wearily and angrily disdainful, "She will have to report back on the bureau's activity and also do a few more things for him that you and I don't even want to think about. No. I need a loyal warrior devoted only to me and the revolution. And not in that order, of course. But someone whose head is filled by nothing but work and who is driven by nothing other than the success of our operations and our ability to screw our adversaries in the West over and over again. Excuse me for speaking in such a manner, Marlene," he had said to her back then, seemingly embarrassed. "But you know that when it comes to our operations, I can get very passionate." Marlene kept her compliments to herself, and for a period of almost four years, she went to work for the division chief in his bureau. She didn't vacate her lovely apartment in Dresden. She'd sleep during the week on a narrow camp bed in a small room behind the bureau, and she'd take the Deutsche Reichsbahn's regional train on weekends back to Dresden, where she'd wrap herself in the quiet of the sleepy city and straighten up her already spotlessly clean apartment. If the weather was warm enough, she'd sit for hours on the bank of the river, watching the endless stream of life it carried — barges, waterfowl, fallen branches, small boats with young lovers.

A small cross — an olive-wood cross made in Nazareth — hung above her dresser. She had found it at a little store nearby the farmers' market that sold souvenirs and religious books and artifacts. Marlene rediscovered the good Lord only in her old age, years after it had all come to an end, years after her retirement from the Stasi at the age of sixty-five. A modest yet moving ceremony was held in recognition of all the staff members who retired at the same time; but the ceremony couldn't hide the fact that the retirement had been forced upon them, just a few months after the collapse of the DDR, the Deutsche Democratic Republic, after huge bulldozers were rushed there from West Germany to begin tearing down everything expendable and rebuilding it all anew.

Marlene closed her eyes and her thoughts drifted back to Gunther. Gunther, the legendary handler from the Special Ops Division of the Main Directorate for Reconnaissance. He was best friends with Markus, the division chief, and Markus alone would sometimes address him by his real name — Werner. All the others, aside from Markus and herself, knew him and referred to him only by his field name, Gunther — until it seemed that even he had forgotten his real name and chose not to remember his mother whispering, Werner, Werner, as she caressed his feverishly hot forehead, when he came down as a child with winter's bronchitis and the thin walls of their tiny apartment were as cold as ice and dripping with freezing damp. Marlene loved all her boys, and she could see their faces flashing by one by one when she closed her eyes. But her love for Gunther (she'd sometimes pluck up the courage to call him her Werner) was different. He was a few years younger than she was, and she knew him primarily through the reports he'd write that came to her for filing. There was something special about his reports, something that allowed even her — so far away from the field, from

63

the meetings with the agents — to sense the agents themselves, to smell the sweat of their fear, to recognize their reckless drunken arrogance, to inhale the fumes of alcohol and coffee that accompanied their meetings. Above all, the reports confirmed that each agent in question, each miserable traitor, was firmly in Gunther's clutches, was being propped up by him, purposefully and lovingly manipulated into doing the things Gunther wanted him to do. Through the reports, she could sense Gunther's strength of character, his self-confidence, the scope of his compassion and empathy, which allowed him to thus take command of another individual and turn him into a secret weapon in the service of the revolution.

On rare occasions, Gunther would show up at the Archives in person, hanging up his heavy coat at the door, a bearish and ungainly figure but exuding strength and inexplicable charm, his blond hair still full but starting to turn silver. And when she saw him, a strange yet delightful sensation that she dared not name — but knew nevertheless could be love — would flutter momentarily through her heart, like an elusive little minnow. A woman's love for a man, different from the love she felt for all the other boys. They spoke sometimes, she and Gunther, though not much. Mostly he'd ask for files that he needed and she'd retrieve them for him, get him to sign the required papers, and say to him: "Tell me if you need anything else." But sometimes he'd share a few words about something he was going through, the terrible train ride from Prague, or some inappropriate joke about his mother-in-law (and Marlene would wonder if he even had a mother-in-law at all). Now and then he'd show her a book he was reading, retrieving a crumpled copy from his jacket pocket and saying to her: "Read it, Marlene, read it, if your soul isn't too delicate for this kind of material," and he'd smile, wrinkles appearing next to his eyes, his good smell, the smell of a man returning from a long journey, would hit her, and she'd offer a smile in return and feel all flustered.

Later on, during the few years in which she served as head secretary in the bureau, she'd see him a little more often, always bursting in like a whirlwind, awe-inspiring, intimidating the young secretaries, joking back and forth with her flirtatiously, charmingly audacious, always in a hurry to see the division chief, his good friend. And she, who had learned to open her mouth a little —

65

after all, you can't manage such a bureau without being able to hold your own with important and arrogant individuals — knew how to respond to her Gunther and to give as good as she got, and it was only the truth itself, buried there in her heart, that she couldn't speak. Marlene knew that the young secretaries gossiped about her behind her back, saying that she was desperately in love with Markus, and that there was a story going around that there was something between them, a long time ago, during the initial years after the war, and that thanks to that fleeting romance from the past, she, an old woman like her, almost sixty, had now landed the position of head secretary. What foolish young girls, she said to herself. Foolish and insubstantial. Yes, she admired Markus a great deal, adored him sometimes, and was willing to serve him loyally with all her heart. But love? Don't be crazy! What nonsense, nonsense and a waste of time.

Everything happened quickly in early 1984. Markus suddenly lost his charm. He was too independent. The intelligence provided by his agents ruffled the feathers of senior officials once too often. The reports filed by the agents indicated a clear change in the West's viewpoint vis-à-vis the Soviet Union and its allies. The image of a militarily powerful Warsaw Pact was now being accompanied by more and more talk of the economic frailty of the Soviet Union and its allies, of deterioration and a loss of control, of a fossilized and detached leadership, of centrifugal forces (Marlene remembered the fascinating and frightening term from the reports) that could end up tearing the Eastern bloc to shreds. That was how the West viewed the Soviet Union, and thus, too, the German Democratic Republic, her country. The agents of the Main Directorate for Reconnaissance reported everything meticulously and precisely. Marlene remembered deliberating fiercely with herself while filing the reports in perfect order. Could there perhaps be a grain of truth in the things they were reporting? Could they be seeing things that Moscow and Berlin couldn't see? Or didn't want to see? In any event, it all turned more and more sour. And Markus managed to get himself into trouble, again, with one of his love affairs, and the rumors reached someone or other among the party leadership, and Markus in early 1984 found himself deposed from his position of significant power and appointed to the post of senior advisor on the Industrial Efficiency Council. Her eyes welled up with tears when she recalled the brief and formal farewell ceremony held in his honor — one of the heroes of the Democratic Republic who had done more for the revolution than all of the dry and stiff nobodies who made up the party leadership. But Marlene didn't allow herself to think like that, a wrong word after all would slip out eventually, and then she'd also be thrown out of the Special Ops Archives in Dresden, to which she had returned, with all due respect, a few weeks later, after the new division chief had assembled his bureau staff to his liking. Still, she had said to herself, she had more than seven years to go before retirement.

Three years before her retirement, one of Gunther's operations was handed over to the comrades in the KGB. Gunther stuck it out somehow, following the ousting of his commander and close friend, and continued to handle his agents, professionally and in earnest, albeit with a sullen and grim demeanor. The operation was one of the most classified under Gunther's control, and she recalled that the seeds had been planted back in the days when she was working in the bureau of the division chief. The agent's name didn't appear in the dossier at all and there was only a code name, the nickname they had given him. Marlene couldn't forget him, particularly in light of what happened later on. They called him Cobra. Gunther was his handler, under the assumed name of Martin for that particular operation. He had explained it to her: "In my dealings with Cobra, I play the part of an American. It's essential. But I chose a name for myself that's also a German name. So that if something doesn't seem right to him all of a sudden, not perfectly American, I'll have a cover story to offer." Gunther would often share his little secrets with her. And from time to time, he sought her advice, too, wanted to know what she was thinking. After all, she was just as familiar with the operations as they were, the handlers, and even a little more so sometimes, precisely due to her remoteness from the field. Because, he explained to her, she saw them through the paperwork, via the reports, with a degree of objectivity they lacked.

And then came the day when Gunther turned up at the Archives in the company of two KGB officers. She had never seen KGB officers at her Archives, despite knowing, just like anyone else with eyes in his or her head, that the KGB was involved in one way or another in most of the operations. Evidence of this could also be found in the dossiers on the various operations, which included all the intelligence communications relayed to KGB headquarters in Moscow. But seeing those officers, those foreigners, in her basement? Gunther was stern-faced, there was no smile for her this time, and that spirit of adventure, that sense of faraway places that usually enveloped and accompanied him, was gone. "Comrade Schmidt," he said to her, "in keeping with orders from the head of the Main Directorate for Reconnaissance, we're required to hand over Operation Cobra and all the dossiers pertaining to the operation to our comrades in the KGB. Nothing must remain in the Archives, not even a single document related to the operation. From this day forward, the operation is no longer ours, doesn't concern us, doesn't interest us. I've already forgotten its existence, and I'm relying on you, Marlene" — addressing her by her first name this time — "and it's an order, to forget entirely about it, is that clear?" Gunther waited, and she nodded, unable to utter a single word. He was so official, stiff and lifeless. From an inside pocket in his coat, he pulled out a printed document bearing the signature of General Heinrich Krueger's bureau chief. The document was a written version of the instructions Gunther had just given her verbally. And she went, ran almost, to the shelves on which the Cobra dossiers stood, and gathered them up, six thick ones, and carried them to the counter. She laid them down, and one of the two foreign officers opened a large bag, resembling a military duffel bag, and placed the dossiers inside without a word. She remembered wondering at the time if bags like that were fashionable in the Soviet Union, and wondering even more about how such foolish and worthless thoughts could be going through her mind at such a time. After closing the bag, the officer attached it to his person with a steel chain that closed in a handcuff of sorts around his wrist, thanked her in German with a hint of a Russian accent, appeared to her to click his heels, turned, and began walking, with the second officer in his wake. Gunther waited for a moment before leaning toward her and whispering: "You see, my dear, that's how it ends. Little by little. They've lost faith in us." He rested a large and warm hand on hers for a moment — and left.

Some two months later, in early October 1987, Marlene heard that Gunther had been hit by a truck and killed on the highway north of Berlin. One of the bureau clerks whispered, at lunch, that Gunther was out walking — yes, walking — by the side of the dark road. There was no way the poor truck driver could have seen him. The driver was in custody, but he was still in shock and wasn't able to offer any information about the incident. The Human Resources Department issued an announcement about Gunther's death, noting his senior rank and providing details of the funeral, which was to be held four days from then. The funeral took place on a gloomy and rainy Monday at the military cemetery in East Berlin. Marlene took a day's leave and went alone, her eyes overflowing with tears, on the train from Dresden to Berlin, and stood at the edge of the small group of people who had come to bid farewell to Gunther for the last time. There were no eulogies, and no prayers were said. From afar, and through her tears, Marlene caught sight of Markus's face — she hadn't seen him for two years, and he appeared cold and angry. A dry whimper grazed her throat, a knife dragged across her heart, and her hands reached up to firmly tighten the scarf around her neck.

10

Dresden, October 2012

Marlene didn't think she'd have the strength to open the church door. A feeble autumn sun painted the narrow street in a yellowish light and long shadows. Reddish-brown leaves were piled up on the edges of the sidewalk. Winter would soon be upon them, without warning; the temperatures would plummet and the trees would stand bare, their branches black and their appearance two-dimensional against the backdrop of an opaque sky. Inside the houses, despite the terrible cold outside, people would get on with their lives, enjoying the warmth of their heating systems, the taste of sweet wine, being close to one another. Christmas by then wouldn't be long in coming, relatives would gather from afar, small families would get together, a glowing aura of light around their heads, bent forward close together in humility and love. She, Marlene, wasn't go-

73

·ing to be around any longer to enjoy it all. Her days were over. She could feel it in her aching bones, in the ever-increasing withering of her soul. Her physician, Dr. Baumberger, had looked at her during her last visit to the clinic with sad brown eyes and said, "Marlene, there's nothing more we can do other than alleviate your pain. If there's anything you need from me . . ." he trailed off, not completing his sentence. "Is there a family member you'd like to notify, perhaps?" he asked, and she quietly responded, "No, no," and could think only of one person she'd like to have with her, by her side, in the same room, having a drink, sitting there quietly or telling her his stories, a young smile that belied the age on his face; after all, he, too, would be old by now, if only he were still alive. But he was dead, had been murdered, to be exact. A large truck had run him down on a rainy night, her Gunther, her Werner, she allowed herself to whisper silently, aware of the fact that her weakness and solitude made it possible for her to say those words without anyone hearing.

Weak and fragile, like wood filed down thin, that's how she felt as she stood in front of the church's large wooden door, pulling it toward her, opening a gap just wide enough for her to press through, wrapped in her heavy coat. The church was empty. It looked larger from the inside than it did from the street. Patches of color cast by the stained-glass windows dotted the floor. A strong smell of wax filled the air, and she, whose sense of smell had sharpened the more her illness ate away at her, could also detect the fragrance of incense, which had survived somehow in the dim expanse since Sunday. Marlene made her way forward slowly, dragging her feet. Nearing the altar, she felt drained of strength. She sat down on the wooden pew closest to her and leaned back, feeling small and shriveled in her large coat. She rested her hands, in their woolen gloves, in her lap. The dull glow of copper implements flickered at the edge of her field of vision, and her head fell forward and rested on her chest.

She didn't know how long she had dozed for when she shook herself out of her reverie and lifted her head. The patches of light on the floor were gone and Marlene saw the priest's face close to hers, his hand resting on her shoulder. "Marlene," he said to her softly, "Marlene. Are you okay? I haven't seen you in quite a while." She looked into the priest's wrinkled eyes, felt his hand weighing heavily on her, and said, "I'm very ill, I couldn't come. But I've come today, I have something to tell you." The priest looked at her, his eyes reflecting sorrow and warmth, and asked her: "Would you like to talk, or perhaps make Confession? Both God and I will listen in any event. Whatever you like." He smiled, a soft expression on his face. He sat beside her on the bench and took her hand. "No, there's no need for Confession," she said. "Like this is good." She released her hand from the priest's grip, removed the glove, and then took hold of his hand again, a large and warm hand. The priest could feel the brittleness of her bones, their fragility, and he knew she was right, that not only was she very ill, but she would be dead soon, in just a few days perhaps, certainly before Christmas Mass.

"You don't really know me, Father Jacobs," she said. "You only know that I'm an old and lonely woman who's been coming to your church for the past few years, always alone, always alone. You know nothing about my past, about the things I did before everything changed . . ."

"Those were different times," the priest said. "We've all been there, we all have a past. No one is judging us, neither you nor me. How can . . ."

"I want you to listen," she said softly. "I

want to tell you about a sin of mine, the sin of cowardice. About someone to whom I wasn't able to say even a single personal word, a single word of intimacy, someone who I wasn't able to show, or even hint of the fact, that my dry heart loved him." She paused for a long silence. "I had a lot of boys," she whispered, pulling herself together for a moment. "They were all my boys. But he, his name was Gunther, and Werner sometimes, too, he . . . ."

And then she told him. Told him about the period of the war, and about the Red Army soldiers who had savagely raped her. But so many women were raped back then, so who was going to grieve about it? Who had the time? You survived, and that was the main thing. So many died. There wasn't a single home that hadn't lost someone. And of her recruitment into the Stasi she told him with unconcealed pride, certainly unapologetically, and although he didn't say a word, Marlene adamantly said, "What's there to be sorry for? After all, we built this country on the ruins of terrible destruction. We had to do so resolutely, without balking, without going astray. Everyone had to do his bit. I wish I had been able to give more." And she told him about her boys, about their quests in faraway places, about the dangers and horrors they confronted. And about the general, Markus Hertz, who instructed her personally to set up the Special Ops Archives in Dresden, so that the cache of the big secrets wouldn't be accessible to each and every political commissioner who happened to pass through headquarters in Berlin. Markus, Markus. She saw him so infrequently during her years at the Archives, but when he did come there, he always devoted some time to her, made a point of sitting down with her, drinking tea with her, and winking at her as he added a kick to both their cups of tea with a shot of alcohol, why not, couldn't the two of them enjoy themselves a little? He then had her transferred to his bureau, and later came the big fall . . .

And then she spoke about Gunther, Gunther who took her breath away, who was their top field operations officer. There wasn't a person out there whom he couldn't recruit, turn into his best friend, turn into a secret soldier in the service of the revolution. Because as she saw things, it was and remained a revolution. No less. And she told him about Gunther's murder, "Of course it was murder, who goes for a walk by the side of the highway on a dark rainy night, in the middle of nowhere? The big bosses from

Moscow show up and take the Cobra dossiers just a few weeks earlier, and all of a sudden Gunther is dead. Just like that? He just happened to be killed? My sweet Gunther."

"What do you know about Cobra?" the priest asked in a whisper, holding her dry burning-hot hand.

"Nothing, almost nothing," she replied. "That was our system. Nobody knew the full picture. Only those who needed to. What did I know? I knew that Werner, Gunther that is, recruited him from nowhere. That his wonderful senses had led him to believe that Cobra was worth it. All the risks and effort. That he would go far. Thanks to agents like him, Markus and Gunther were able to walk tall even in Dzerzhinsky Square, at the KGB headquarters. I didn't know his real name. I only knew he was from Israel, from the Holy City, from Jerusalem. A highly intelligent young man, an aide to a senior minister. Gunther used to say that he'd be a minister himself one day, or a very senior government official. I knew he was important enough for the Russians to take him for themselves and destroy everything that could expose him. We were already at a point of no return when they demanded that we hand him over. At some point, after all, we knew it was all over, right? But why did they have to kill him?" she asked, and her tears streamed silently down her cheeks and dripped onto the hand of the priest that was holding hers. "Why did he have to be killed? Gunther would never have betrayed Cobra. He may just as well have killed himself." She sobbed softly, her breath catching now and then on a quiet whimper. "Why kill him like a dog on the side of a highway, in a dark field, with the rain pouring down on him incessantly, and his eyes staring up at nothing but black skies?" It was plain to see that she had pictured that horrific image in her mind on numerous occasions, and that it remained as distinct as ever. The priest clasped both his large hands around her bare fingers. He stroked her thin hair and said, "Marlene, Marlene, that's enough now, it's passed, it was a long time ago. And Gunther knew, I'm sure, Gunther knew you had feelings for him. Someone like him would surely have known. Only his work, his loyalty, the war he was waging stopped him from telling you that he knew, from telling you that he loved you, too. That's how we were in those days, right? That's just the way things were. Too often," he whispered. He stroked Marlene's head, trying to soothe and comfort her. We all carry a cross on our backs, he thought. A cross and a bag of sins alongside. Living a blemish-free life in those days was impossible. The truly good managed to keep some piece of their soul out of reach, untainted. But the truly good also had to survive, also had to give something in return for their lives. Father Jacobs wondered about the constant compromises, endless small humiliations, uncountable acts of betrayal that had allowed him to go on living, to continue leading his small congregation, small and ostracized, which found sanctuary in itself, comfort and a little warmth in those days, days that one couldn't even term black. No, it was worse. They were days of dreariness, of obscurity, like opaque windows that had been smeared with brown paint and dirt that could never be scraped off.

11

Berlin, January 2013

The Hotel Adlon's elegant concierge raised his eyes and gazed in irony at the elderly man struggling to get inside. The doorman, wrapped in a thick coat, his stately uniform underneath, as if he were an admiral in the Imperial Navy, was patiently holding the door, while the old professor — thus he appeared to the concierge observing him — was trying with his one hand to hold on to his hat, so that it wouldn't blow off in the sharp and icy gusts of wind, and with his other to close his umbrella, which had folded in on itself in the opposite direction, as his body pressed ahead, determined to feel the pleasant warmth that permeated the lobby. And indeed, a huge fireplace was ablaze in one of its corners, and a yellowish light, homely looking, dripped onto the ornate marble floor, from the direction of the bar. The professor finally made it through the doorway, mumbling a word of thanks to the doorman, nodding in the direction of the concierge, and waving his umbrella around as if he were fencing with a ghost, trying with his movements to fold it back to its natural state. His casquette was in his hand now, after almost falling to the floor, and he made his way toward the bar in long and spritely strides, hopping with surprising agility up the two steps, his coat already open and flapping, his gray hair tousled. And there we go, the old man had spotted the man who was waiting there for him, who rose from the plush armchair to greet him. At the same time, he also noticed the young man at the corner of the bar whose muscles seemed to be fighting to get out of his gray suit. The young man went tense upon seeing him and readied to rise from his chair, too, but the man who had already stood and moved toward him with his hand outstretched in greeting signaled to the muscular young man with a glance — it's okay, it's him, you can relax.

The two embraced like old friends. "Walter, Walter, it's good to see you." "Good to see you, too, Aharon, good to see you too. Thank you for coming on such short notice." They looked at each other with affection. Walter returned to his leather armchair,

Aharon dragged a second leather armchair closer, dropping his umbrella and coat on a third. "A cognac, if you please," he requested from the waiter who had appeared discreetly at their table. "A glass of hot wine, please," Walter said, and waited for the waiter to walk away.

"I see you've yet to get rid of your bodyguard," Aharon remarked with a smile. "I, on the other hand," he added in the same breath, "am no longer considered important enough. As you can see, fame is fleeting. Ashes to ashes, dust to dust . . ." he went on, failing as usual to complete the sentence and allowing it instead to fade out.

Aharon Levin and Dr. Walter Vogel — the former head of the Institute for Intelligence and Special Operations, known as the Israeli Mossad, and the former chief of the BND, Germany's Federal Intelligence Service. Vogel had retired a few months earlier and, in keeping with procedure, was still entitled to a security detail, or required one, depending on how you looked at it and who was doing the looking. Vogel had spent his entire professional life in the West German intelligence service, signing up shortly after earning his Ph.D. in law from the University of Goettingen. He had spent his whole career fighting the communist threat. He loathed the KGB, and felt the same loathing for the Stasi, too, which had imposed a reign of terror on the citizens of East Germany, the celebrated German Democratic Republic, whom it was supposed to have protected and whom it was supposed to have served. He reserved respect and admiration, accompanied nevertheless by hatred, only for the Stasi's foreign espionage division, the Main Directorate for Reconnaissance, in which he had seen not only bullying fists, but also artistry, from professional and sensitive hands that knew their craft well.

"Look," Walter said to Aharon, "I'll get straight to the point. It sounds like an old-timers' thing — you and me, and an old priest from Dresden, and an old woman who served in the Stasi and has passed away."

Aharon remained silent and nodded his head. He was a good listener. A log caught alight in the fireplace, casting a sudden glow over his wrinkle-grooved face. Walter continued:

"I was contacted on the very eve of Christmas by a source I used to handle, an East German priest, who also worked at the time with the Stasi, like everyone almost, because let's face it, who had a choice back then? He didn't know if it was important or not, but he wanted to share it with me. Anyway, it's a secret that got someone killed. He doesn't know much, and all he does know he heard from a dying and bitter old woman. And like I said, she did in fact die a few days after speaking with him. I'm giving you the gist of what he told me, and believe me, Aharon, I sat with the priest for hours to listen to the story again and again, from every possible angle. The old woman who told him the story was an archivist for the Special Ops Unit of the Stasi's Main Directorate for Reconnaissance. Listen carefully, Aharon. According to her, the East Germans recruited and operated a high-ranking Israeli asset. They called him Cobra. The KGB was aware of the asset and the Stasi passed on all the intelligence he delivered to them. By the end of the 1980s, Cobra was already a parliamentary aide or perhaps even a ministerial aide, with further advancement apparently to come. The East Germans believed in him. Expected him to go very far. When the ground in East Germany began to shake, the KGB demanded full control over the asset. All the material pertaining to him was handed over to two KGB officers who were sent to collect the dossiers from the Special Ops Archives in Dresden. The archivist, by the name of Marlene, said that she did indeed hand over all the material to them. The order to do so was handed down by the then-director of the foreign espionage division, General Heinrich Krueger, and relayed to her personally by the officer in charge of the operation, who went by the name of Gunther. Gunther dryly told her that the operation was being handed over to their comrades in Moscow, and she said he was left furious and despondent. In any event, Gunther was hit by a truck and killed on the side of a highway north of Berlin less than two months later. The poor driver said he hadn't even seen him before he was thrown under the wheels of the vehicle. According to Marlene, Gunther was assassinated. Cobra was such a high-value asset that the KGB took action to ensure that no one who knew his real identity was left behind. As I understand things, the Stasi handled Cobra under the guise of being Americans, for reasons I'm not aware of and can only speculate on.

"And as you know," Walter quietly continued, "Markus Hertz, the serving division chief when Operation Cobra came into being and moved ahead, died a few months after the unification of the two Germanys, while under house arrest imposed by us. He had more than enough crimes for which to pay, but more so than anything he wasn't a well man, and despite our grave suspicions, we weren't able to prove that he didn't die of natural causes."

"Why didn't the KGB assassinate Marlene, too?" Aharon asked. "Did the priest ask her? Was she able to explain that?"

"Marlene wasn't aware of Cobra's real identity. A fact, according to her, that was plain to see in the dossiers the KGB took from the Archives. That was the explanation she offered for being spared. The priest did indeed ask her that same question. But it's possible, too, that they believed that Marlene would never talk. Or that they simply screwed up. We all make mistakes, right? Even the KGB isn't perfect, and it doesn't kill unnecessarily either. Whatever the case may be, Marlene went on living for many years after the Cobra file was handed over to the Russians, keeping her secrets to herself. Truth be told, even when she chose to tell someone — even when she sensed that her days were numbered, even when she needed someone, anyone, even a priest who knew her as no one but a worshipper in his church, to understand that she had known love for a man in her arid life — even then she was hardly able to say anything at all."

"Tell me, Walter, why have you come to me with this? Why haven't you notified someone currently in office in the BND? Why haven't you approached someone serving today in the Mossad? After all, you're acquainted with our people. I'm retired now, whereas your ties still remain intact, at least as far as I understood things . . ."

"I thought it best to approach you. Honestly, I don't know if the information is important or of no significance at all, but my gut tells me it's important, that we're onto something big here. Marlene was speaking on her deathbed. People don't make up such stories. Not at a time like that. And if Gunther really was murdered, there was a reason for it. If the Russians were intent on shielding Cobra against any risk of exposure, the comrades in Moscow must have viewed Cobra as a particularly high-value asset, an agent to be safeguarded at all costs. Who knows how many more Stasi officers they assassinated in order to safeguard their secrets when everything came crashing down? And if this story about Cobra turns out to be true, that means that no one has a clue regarding his whereabouts today, the material to which he is privy, and the information he is passing on to Moscow, perhaps even to this day. I couldn't risk approaching just anyone; Cobra, after all, mustn't know that someone may be on his trail. Besides, I have the privileges of the elderly now, I don't have to speak to anyone and everyone, only to those I love. And you, my dear, I love. A love shared by old spies, right?"

And thus, in the dimming light of the large fireplace, with the night's dark shadows filtering through the bar's windows, they continued to sit there, fighting back the chill within themselves with another drink, appalled by the thought that they'd soon have to step out again into the street's petrifying cold, into the loneliness that always lies in wait for people like them.

12

A silver Toyota Avensis pulled up outside the heavy ornate iron gate of the President's Residence. It was five-twenty in the afternoon, yet winter's darkness had already settled over the homes of the Talbieh neighborhood, just beyond the tops of the pine trees swaying in Jerusalem's icy wind. Aharon Levin himself was behind the wheel. One would be hard-pressed, very hard-pressed indeed, to say he was a good driver, and as always, it seemed that only a miracle prevented him from crashing into the gate. A security guard armed with an M-16 approached the vehicle, and the electric window slid down silently. "Shalom, sir, I recognize you, and we know you are expected, but I need to see some ID anyway. Thank you, sir," he said on returning the pensioner's card Levin chose to produce.

91

"Straight on and immediately to the right. Park next to the black Volvo."

The president was waiting for him on his own in the main reception room, in the large hall adorned with the ceiling mural by Naftali Bezem. It was strange for him to see the reception room empty and dark, and the figure of the president appeared as a silhouette. Light coming through one of the doors that opened into the hall shone around his host, as if his entire person was aglow. "Mr. President," Levin said by way of greeting. "Aharon, Aharon, good to see you. Come, come, let's go sit down in here, we can talk in peace."

The two men sat down together in a small meeting room, sinking into gold-colored armchairs. An elderly server came in quietly and placed two cups of tea and a small plate of cookies and dates stuffed with walnuts on the small table.

"Mr. President," Levin began, "I've come to you because I don't know who I should take this to."

The president and the former Mossad chief had met for the first time when Aharon Levin took up his position as head of the intelligence agency. They had never crossed paths before then. The president moved back and forth between the academic world and the political sphere, feeling at home in both, and making the transitions between the two with a degree of ease and elegance that left Aharon Levin in awe. Levin had operated all the while in the covert world of the Mossad, recruiting and handling agents, conducting his meetings in luxurious hotels, dingy brothels, and cold and anonymous safe houses in rural towns of distant lands. And because the worlds of politics and academe were so remote to him, he could only marvel at the seemingly effortless and natural manner with which the president conducted himself between the two. As in the case of his predecessors, following his appointment to the position of Mossad chief, he began meeting regularly with the prime minister. Some of the meetings were conducted in private, he and the prime minister alone, the recording devices switched off, the military secretary waiting outside the room. At the request of the president and with the prime minister's approval, he started meeting from time to time with the president, too, updating him on whatever was necessary, talking to him about the trends and upheavals in the Middle East, the activities in the region of the superpowers, and listening to the ideas and thoughts expressed by the president, who was always curious, creative, far-sighted. Over time, a quiet sense of trust developed between them, two somewhat elderly Jews, well educated, contemplative but striving to take action. In this sense, too, the president was no ordinary man. Unlike his predecessors, he wasn't willing to make do with the symbolic and ceremonial nature of his position, and instead felt profoundly responsible for the fate and future of the nation. He had seen a great deal in his life, and the more he saw the greater his concern. He knew that the existence of the state couldn't be taken for granted at all, and he never tired of saying, and believed with all his heart, that if Israel wasn't always at its best, if it didn't have the ability to reap all the talent, creativity, and daring of its people, it wouldn't survive. And thus, on more than one occasion, and entirely discreetly, he would offer the utmost of his abilities for the sake of that campaign, which never ceased.

Levin filled in the president on what he had heard from the former German intelligence services chief. "You know," he said, "there doesn't appear to be anything very clear or of much substance here. It's all inferential, vague. What do we have, exactly? An old East German woman, sick and bitter, whose entire world suddenly caved in on her, without warning. Someone by the name of Gunther. Unrequited love. We don't even know if he really was killed, and even if he was, it's far more likely that it actually was an accident, and not a murder made to look like one. Moreover, the KGB didn't carry out targeted killings very often, and certainly not of its people and its allies. Not in the late 1980s. Nevertheless," Levin continued, pensive, his eyes half closed, "my experience tells me we're onto something big here. Huge. After all, we're never going to get anything more than this, more than a hint, a glimmer, which we may even fail to notice if we aren't vigilant. Mr. President," Levin said, "from this moment forward, we have to assume that the Russians have a spy in the corridors of power in Israel, and that he's an important enough cog in the system to warrant his removal by force from the hands of the Stasi, important enough to warrant the murder of one of the East German intelligence service's top handlers. This has to be our working hypothesis. This has to be our starting point. Only information that refutes this new basic assumption will be able to lay it to rest."

Aharon came to an end. A heavy silence fell over the room, its presence palpable and troubling. The president didn't say a word, his sharp mind processing the information he had just received. He closed his eyes in thought. "But," the president suddenly said in his deep voice, "you can clearly see the problem, right? We have no idea where he could be. He could be in a key position in the defense establishment, the army, the Mossad, even the Shin Bet internal security service. He could be at the Foreign Ministry, the Defense Ministry, the National Security Council. If we open an investigation, he could get wind of it, and then we'll never know. He'll simply drop off the radar and we won't even know that we've walked right by him, right?" The president went quiet for a moment, as if he were talking to himself, his gaze fixed on some point beyond his companion's shoulder.

"No. We have to handle the matter differently — at this stage at least. Listen, Aharon," he said, staring directly into Levin's eyes now, his gaze stern and sharp, "I want you to handle this personally. I, the state president, am charging you with the task of running this investigation. You'll report to me alone. Use and employ whoever you trust. Set up a team, not a big one, to do the work for you. You know what to do and you know how to do it. No one could do it better. There's no one else I could trust like I trust you."

The president paused. It appeared, to the former Mossad chief, that the president wanted to add something, but wasn't really sure how to do so. "Look, Aharon," he finally said, "you're familiar with the big picture, you're aware of the threats we're facing. We're working on a few things. It's all very complex and expensive, and who knows if any of it will work out. All we know for sure is that we have to maintain the element of surprise. If anything is leaked, none of it will be worth a thing. And in this regard, the superpowers are our adversaries, too. Certainly Russia, which is fighting again for its standing and status in the world, and perhaps even the United States, which wouldn't want us to take action in a manner that hasn't been cleared with them. But certainly Russia. Moscow won't take another demonstration of Israeli superiority in the arena lying down. And certainly when we're talking about superiority, that would again be based on American arms and weapons systems. Thus, if they get wind of anything, they'll thwart it. Like me, you know they have many ways of doing so, including the relaying of a detailed and specific warning to our enemies. They could also go public with whatever they reveal, perhaps not in an address by Putin, but in the shape of a well-timed leak to this or the other media outlet, or by means of a thousand other forms of psychological warfare they so excel at. But until we get our hands on the traitor and learn who he is and exactly what he knows and what he passed on, until then, we won't know if our plans are worth anything. Under the current circumstances — and forgive me, my friend, for not being able to elaborate — what I'm asking you to do is critical. Critical and urgent."

Aharon gave the president a look that clearly illustrated his understanding of the scope and significance of the task with which he had been charged. He remained silent. The president continued:

"You'll have one of the funds of the President's Residence at your disposal. I'll have the money transferred to an account you'll open specifically for the purpose of the operation. The fund is earmarked for biotechnology research aimed at boosting crop yields. Seems appropriate, right?" said the president, a momentary glint of mischief in his eyes. They both knew a little humor never hurt, especially at trying times. "We'll meet once a month and you'll fill me in. No one but me. Together we'll know what to do. And of course if anything urgent comes up, when you find something, you'll contact me immediately. You know how."

Silence.

"I'm relying on you, Aharon. Like always."

"Mr. President," Aharon said, standing up and shaking his host's wrinkled hand. He left the room and quietly shut the door behind him. He turned toward the exit and continued out into the dark garden. A large olive tree appeared blackened against the dark sky. The temperatures had fallen, and a cold Jerusalem wind gusted suddenly through the courtyard at the entrance to the residence.

13

Tel Aviv, Ramat Aviv Mall, January 2013

Michael Turgeman rode up the escalator, the aroma of good, strong Italian coffee there to greet him as he ascended. That's just how things were with Aharon Levin. For years now Levin hadn't been his immediate superior; he had left his post as Mossad chief years ago. Even I, Michael thought in a mixture of anger and resignation, even I've been out of the organization for more than a year, but when Aharon Levin calls and asks for something in his typically confusing and apologetic manner, I immediately say, "Yes." Always yes.

"Surely he could have found a better place to meet," Michael grumbled to himself. Arcaffe at the mall. True, the coffee was great, but the prices always annoyed him, and the idea of paying a fortune to serve oneself seemed a novelty bordering on chutzpah. Thinking about the chain's regular patrons, and certainly those who frequented the branch at this upscale mall, filled him with an inexplicable sense of animosity. Restored women, in their fifties and sixties, with the bodies of models, dressed in gym outfits that hid the scars of numerous cosmetic surgeries. In general, Michael admitted to himself, he tended to get angry and agitated quite often these days. Every little thing grated on his nerves. He got grumpy and complained all the time. Certainly not very attractive. It had to be reined in. He needed to focus. Focus on the matter at hand, he concluded to himself, pushing the truly important questions to the far reaches of his consciousness. He wondered what the old man wanted this time. Aharon Levin had called him last night, saying, "Hello, hello, hello," three times, seemingly surprised to have reached him, despite being the one who had called. Typical. "There's a matter I'd like to consult with you about. When would it suit you?" he'd asked, then responding himself before Michael had a chance. "How about tomorrow morning, seven-thirty, before the mall fills up?"

The meeting was clearly a matter of urgency for him, Michael thought, refusing to be fooled into believing that Aharon really did want to consult with him. Aharon always relied only on himself and his vast intellect. He didn't need any advice, certainly not from me, Michael thought with a touch of bitterness, but he probably needed something else. Otherwise he wouldn't have called. That's how it went, a hierarchy of status and age. That's how it worked.

Aside from the workers turning on the espresso machines and laying out the cakes and sandwiches on the display shelves, the café really was still empty at that early hour of the morning. He didn't see Aharon, and Michael, out of years of habit, did a recon of the place, checking to see if Aharon wasn't actually sitting outside for some reason, and then going back inside and selecting a table that would offer him a broad field of vision, not only over the café itself, but also over the entrance to the mall and the expanse leading from the stairs from the underground parking garage.

Aharon, as always, was a few minutes late, his coat disheveled and all his attention on the umbrella in his hand, which had again, diabolically, collapsed inside out. He, too, scanned the café, nodding his head almost imperceptibly on spotting Michael. "You're getting thinner and thinner all the time," he said to him, "you need to eat something. A double espresso?"

He returned carrying a somewhat shaky tray, a cup of espresso and a mug of tea perched precariously on its surface. "We're still waiting for a croissant," he said. "They'll call us."

"Yaakov!" the guy behind the bar called out two or three minutes later. "Yaakov, that's me," Aharon said with a smile, and returned a moment later with a warm almond croissant, his face aglow in triumph. "Eat something, eat. I need you healthy and strong. At your best!" And that's when the former Mossad chief suddenly turned serious and stern-faced, businesslike and focused, the semblance of the absentminded professor disappearing in a flash.

Aharon told him about his meeting with the former head of the German intelligence agency and of his meeting with the president. Not for a moment, according to him, did he consider failing to comply with the president's instructions. "How could I say no to him? And I need you, Michael, as the leader of the team we're going to set up. I know," he continued, not letting up for a second and not allowing Michael to get even a single word in, "that you've just opened your own law practice, but don't fret, you're only in the initial stages after all and nothing's going to happen to you if you put things on hold for a short while. You weren't a lawyer for some twenty-five years, so it can wait a little longer. Avigdor Feldman will go on handling civil rights cases. You'll join the fray in a few months' time, no harm done. Civil rights are important, but let's first get our hands on this awful man. I know he exists, my old bones tell me that he's out there plotting and sowing the seeds of evil. Like a venomous snake. I can hear his scales scratching along the ground, I can feel his venom burning and spreading. We'll take him out!" he declared abruptly, and Michael could feel how the image of the reptile, with its cold blood and the deadly venom in its fangs, became etched in his mind, too. And still he remained silent.

"Tell me," Aharon continued, "how many rooms do you have in that apartment you've leased as an office? Three? Yes, that should suffice. On Nahmani Street? Excellent, excellent. There we go, we have a team leader and a safe house from which to conduct operations. Tell me, has anyone come to mind? Who else should we bring in?"

And thus, without giving his consent, and without actually being asked at all to do so, Michael Turgeman saw his life take another small twist, saw himself being shoved down a new path, the road not taken, he thought to himself with a touch of irony, like in that poem by Robert Frost that he still remembered from his school days. But he didn't say a word to Aharon. There wouldn't be much point in doing so.

And perhaps he had already made his choice some twenty-six years ago, when he first began the Mossad's screening process, his very participation in which offered him a taste of secrecy and sense of vocation that warmed his heart, truly so, and led him to see himself as special in relation to all his friends, other fourth-year law students. While they were planning their integration into Israel's leading law firms or postgraduate studies at the finest American universities, he was at the start of a long road that would end with him joining that world-renowned yet elusive and mysterious organization — the Mossad, the Institute for Intelligence and Special Operations.

A long time had passed since then. A lengthy screening and recruitment process followed by twenty-five years of service. Years and years of dealing with the recruitment and handling of agents. When Michael started out as a young intelligence-gathering officer, a case officer, as the profession was known in intelligence organizations around the world, Aharon Levin was the commander of the Mossad's operations in Europe. There they would occasionally meet and spend time together, long hours and days on end, no less, waiting for an object to fall into their clutches, waiting for an agent to show up for a face-to-face rendezvous for the first time in several months. As a senior commander, Aharon wouldn't of course accompany him on all his operations, but when it came to an interesting one, something different from the other operations, when a particularly high-value and important agent was coming, Aharon would then tag along, taking charge of events with the aid of his experience, wisdom, and profound understanding of the human psyche, and the soul of the enemy they were facing. Some ten years later, after the prolonged hunting season the length and breadth of Europe, Aharon was appointed to the post of Mossad chief. He asked Michael to serve as his senior personal assistant, and as always he said, "Yes, at your command." They worked together for three years, with an intimacy born out of sixteen and sometimes eighteen hours of close collaboration a day, every day. The trust between them was forged from secrets that very few knew, from times of rage and of weakness, from crises as much so as from moments of undisclosed glory. It wasn't a partnership between equals. In terms of responsibility, authority, age, and life experience, there was a distinct gap between the two. And Michael knew that in his own amiable, educated, and highly charming manner, Aharon was using him, just as he had used everyone who had accompanied him on his meteoric path.

When he summoned him now, shaking him without hesitation from the law office he had just started to get off the ground, as if it meant nothing, Aharon was banking on his absolute loyalty. That in addition to his reliability, the high level of intelligence he possessed, and his practical skills. Michael had an uncommonly honest perception of his own qualities, just as they were undoubtedly worded and summarized in the confidential psychological evaluation documents in his personal file. Weaknesses were listed there, too — not few and not to be dismissed. "We're all human," he'd always quote his commander. In any event, the brilliance, the profound understanding, and the leaps of faith they'd need further down the road would stem only from Aharon himself. Such was Aharon's way, and Michael knew so, too. That was the way he had worked throughout the years, and that's how he was going into battle now. Michael was simply his lackey, a loyal and courageous servant, a vital yet somewhat technical component in the compact and efficient machine that Aharon was starting to piece together for the purpose of conquering the objective.

14

Michael called Amir and told him he'd like to see him that same day, preferably in the afternoon, before the eve of the Sabbath. He'd come to his place, to the moshav. He asked Ya'ara to meet him at Café Bueno, just off the highway, on the way from Tel Aviv to Netanya. Now. He'd be there in an hour. Yes, it was very important.

He hadn't seen Ya'ara for several years. Strange, yet the thing that stood out in his memory from their last meeting was the muted sheen of the pearls around her neck. Ya'ara was a combat-trained field operative and part of a special ops squad. She was blessed with courage and composure, and in her own restrained manner was always up for a fight, always came to life when a complex and dangerous mission came her way. She was smart and sensible, dressed in clothing he viewed as conservative and mature for her young age, her light hair

109

meticulously arranged, boasting jewelry that alluded to a refined taste and understated wealth. They had worked together on three or four operations over the years, and she had always performed flawlessly, fulfilling her tasks to perfection. When they needed someone to get his or her hands on this or the other piece of information about the object they were dealing with, when they needed someone to get into places where others wouldn't even make it past the doorman in the lobby, when they needed someone to spend hours on end through a long cold night on stakeout, Ya'ara was just the right person for the job. She was extraordinary, special. Nobody had ever once suspected that she, an attractive and composed young woman, so meticulous about her attire and behavior, could be a Mossad combatant. Michael had never witnessed a display of intense emotion from her — excitement, fear, or elation. Even on one oppressively humid and fragrance-filled night in Shanghai, as he waited for her in an expensive dark car, its lights off and its powerful engine humming softly, even then, when she slid into the seat next to him and slipped the small pistol into the elegant bag in her hand, even then, just thirty seconds after firing three .22 slugs into the head of a

North Korean arms dealer, she hadn't shown any emotion at all. Her breathing was easy and regular, her light hair pulled back. "Everything's okay," she said in a deep and quiet voice. "Drive."

They had last seen each other some four or five years ago. They had met in his office. She walked in, and the first thing he noticed was the string of large pearls around her neck. He got up from behind his oversized desk and gestured toward the comfortable seating area in the corner of the office. He always did this when he wanted to demonstrate a lack of formality and a certain degree of intimacy. Ya'ara had come to seek his approval for a lengthy period of unpaid leave. She wanted to study film, she said, and she wanted to find someone to love at long last. She was tired of the endless string of men who couldn't come to terms with her absences, her erratic traveling, their inability to pick up the phone and call her whenever they wanted. They weren't satisfied with the fact that at strange hours, from remote unnamed locations, dead tired and almost blatantly indifferent, she did them the favor of calling to ask what was up. She couldn't even find the will or strength to say "I miss you."

They spoke about her interest in film, her

love for American movies from the 1970s. She was the first woman, he thought, who had spoken to him with such enthusiasm about the Godfather movies, about the grandiose splendor of breathtaking mob hits to the sound of celestial music, about the deep-seated oath hidden in the Mafiosi's battle cry of "going to the mattresses." With their conversation moving along with such ease and amiability in his conformist, bureaucratic office, he wondered why they had never before discussed such things so freely and directly. Why hadn't the long evenings and nights they spent together — waiting, waiting, pressing ahead patiently and persistently with their mission — led to the same kind of straightforward and simple relationship, a relationship like the one that appeared to be evolving during the course of their conversation about, yes, about all things that weren't work and missions and the Mossad? It was the first time that this young woman, a spectacular oyster in his eyes, had allowed him a glimpse through a small opening in her shell. After all, he had never been able to even guess what she was thinking or feeling at any given moment. Perhaps he hadn't tried. He had always focused on her calculated and efficient ability to get things done, which so impressed him. For the first time perhaps, in the small lounge area of his office, of all places, she suddenly appeared to him as a woman with depth and softness, with youthful enthusiasm and charm.

Ya'ara did indeed go on unpaid leave, a leave of absence that had already been extended every year for the past three years. They hadn't kept in touch, and only on very rare occasions would he hear someone mention her name, or say something about her in passing. Someone once said, "She's happy. I saw her a few days ago; there's a light in her eyes." And now, on the phone, when he said, "Ya'ara? Hi, it's Michael Turgeman from the office," he knew she had recognized his voice even before he said his name, and hers rang with a musical chime he had never heard before. He didn't have to explain. When he said he needed to see her in an hour's time, she knew right away that he was talking about work and that it was urgent.

He's cute, she thought, when he suggested they meet at Café Bueno, near the moshav where she lived. She put on her favorite leather jacket, a biker's jacket, and, collecting her keys on the way, said to Hagai: "I'm going out, darling. Yes, I remember, we're at

113

your parents this evening. I'll be back in time."

15

Seeing him approach from afar, she thought, oh my, he's even thinner than he used to be, and his hair is grayer, yet he still carries himself as if he's the master of his domain. Yes, she said to herself, without doubt, Michael Turgeman is someone who occupies a place in this world. When she stood up to greet him with a smile, he thought, oh my, she's looking very beautiful these days. And he saw shards of light in her blue-gray eyes.

They reached out to shake hands, and then Michael said, "Really? Come on," and tugged her toward him and they embraced. She smelled wonderful, as always; this time, however, despite the January cold and the wind coming off the sea, her fragrance was tinged with passionate shades of spring. He looks like a spy in that long coat, she smilingly thought, and then corrected herself — because one thing she already knew, someone had spoken and she had listened — he looks like a retired spy.

A double espresso for him, a mint tea for her. Michael told her about the new office he was opening and his plans to focus on human rights cases, as soon as he got himself organized and caught up on twenty-five years of legal material. She told him about her final project at the School of Film and Television, about the short film she had already shot and was now in the editing stage of. Two people, she said, a woman and a man, who meet up again after several years and find themselves together in a shuttered apartment in a residential tower in Netanya, and the woman says to the man: It's very simple, you've been in love with me now for a very long time, you've loved me since way back when. They remain in the apartment for an entire week without ever going out, living on coffee and dates they find in one of the large apartment's sterile cupboards, going from room to room and from bed to bed, with the shutters opening gradually all the while to allow light and the smell of the sea inside. Michael recalled their conversation about the bold cinema of the 1970s, about raging bulls and bikers tearing down dirt roads, easy riders. But he didn't say a word about *The Godfather.* We all choose our own individual paths, he thought.

He told her about his meeting with Aharon Levin, and said: "I need you on the team. Three months. We'll finish things up and move on. We'll go back to our lives. We'll get started on Sunday. I need you, Ya'ara, what do you say?"

"Don't turn on your charming face. It doesn't work on me and you don't need it anyway. Hagai's gonna kill me; but if the request comes from Aharon, I'm in."

I'm no fool, Michael thought, and Ya'ara knows so, too. When she said, "If the request comes from Aharon," she was actually telling him, "I'm not doing it for you or because you want me. Your request is up against all the other things I'm doing right now and it may not win out. But if it's Aharon . . ."

And a few seconds later, as if she had read his mind, Ya'ara added, "So how do I address you from now on? Sir? Or can I still call you Michael?" And Michael's heart filled to the brim with warmth, and he said to himself, I've made the right choice. She was one of a kind, this young woman, you offer her adventure and danger and she doesn't even think of saying no. She was up for it from the get-go, the scent of war in her nostrils and eager to play a part. As if she had never really left.

With the details already settled, they continued to talk, and Ya'ara ordered another tea. She told him about her studies and how she had met Hagai and the house they were renting on the moshav, not far from here — but you already know that. And she was still on her endless leave of absence, but she thought it really was time to decide now, and it was pretty clear to her that she wanted out, that this long holiday was going to turn into a permanent break. She was not going to go back now to a life of endless traveling, and there was Hagai, and Hollywood awaited her, too. There it was, a hint of her charming smile, she was already trying to decide which evening gown she would wear when she's called up to accept the Oscar for Best Foreign Film, and her smile was now a glowing one, the smile of someone who was busy making student films but dreamed of international acclaim. "Do you know that that smile, that's something new, you never used to smile like that," Michael said to her. "Yes, I'm not really the same person you once knew," she responded.

16

The avenue of casuarina trees loomed
against the backdrop of the darkening sky.
Dabs of purple and gold appeared on the
edges of the heavy clouds. It never fails to
surprise me how quickly evening falls here,
Michael thought to himself, and not for the
first time. He turned off to the moshav, the
wheels of his Audi skidding over the dirt
and stones that filled the numerous potholes
along the rough road. Solitary heavy drops
of rain fell on the windshield, and he
imagined them falling softly on the fertile
earth around him, too, giving rise to the
smell of winter in the countryside.

Amir was waiting for him just outside the
door, shielded by the pergola that hung over
the porch at the entrance to his home. A
smile, a manly embrace, accompanied by
firm slaps on the shoulder, twice, three
times. Michael took a step back and said,
"So this is what a student looks like, does

it? You do look a little too smart!"

Amir smiled sheepishly, his light-skinned face turning a little red. "Just so you know, it's not so easy for someone my age," he said. "I'm not like all you Ashkenazim, who went to study straight after the army, with your parents paying for everything, including a students' apartment in Talbieh. I had to provide for my parents, too. My father, God rest his soul, was still recovering from the work accident and my mother was still taking care of my two younger brothers."

"I know, I know; have you forgotten who I am? What's up with you?" Michael responded, wondering how with the name Turgeman, he could still be seen as "all you Ashkenazim." The two of them, he and Amir, were still standing on the porch, water dripping down around them and the fragrance of mandarins filling the darkness. "And for the record," he continued, "note that I worked all through university. Doing whatever came my way. I worked my ass off. That's why you do it when you're young, not when you're already a middle-aged old man, like some of us here."

"Come, come inside. Smadar and the children are already at her parents'; I told her I'd join them a little later because my commander's coming to check up on me before the Shabbat comes in. Something to drink? We'll make some nice tea, and we have marzipan cookies baked by Smadar's mother."

The aroma of strong sweet tea. And like the tea, the marzipan cookies also reminded him of the sweet and heart-warming foods his mother used to make. He looked Amir in the eyes and got straight to the point. "Listen. I need you. Yes. Like when we were in Marseille that time. A special task assigned to Aharon Levin directly by the president himself. No one is in on it aside from us, from the team we are currently putting together. Ya'ara Stein is already in. Do you remember her? And I'm also bringing in Aslan, the guy who was a part of the security team, and someone else, a young woman you don't know, Adi, who'll be our intelligence officer. I haven't spoken to her yet, but you can take my word for it. She's on the team, too. That's everyone. An elite squad." He told Amir the little he knew, and he could see that Amir already felt offended, angry, and personally hurt by the betrayal of that long-ago young upstart, who was now at the very least a senior director-general or high-ranking commander in one of the security establishments. Amir wasn't one to outwardly display emotion, and his

121

face remained calm now, too, aside from a resoluteness of sorts that clouded his blue eyes. But Michael had known him for years and had been with him in more than enough complex situations to know that Amir always took things to heart, and that he made no distinction between the personal and the public, which were essentially one and the same for him. If this traitor was screwing the state, then he was also fucking him, Amir, personally, and there were many things Amir could take, but not something like that.

"But," Amir hesitated, "my studies . . ."

"Don't worry. We'll wrap this thing up within three months at most. You'll write up the makeup exams. You'll take another semester. We can discuss it after we catch this son of a bitch, and the office will approve whatever you need. Trust me. I'm looking out for you. I'll do the degree with you if you like. But I have to have you with us now. You're responsible for all the logistics and everything else that only you can do. Watching our backs. Making sure everything is functioning properly, working smoothly and quickly, as it should. When the moment of truth arrives, I want you at my side. I don't want anyone else in your stead. Deal, Amir?"

"I said to you already back then, at the airport in Marseille, that I'll do anything you ask of me. Always. I don't say such things lightly and I don't say them to just anyone. I mean what I say. If not, I keep quiet, you know that. So if you're here to ask something of me, it's clearly something serious and I'm in. I'm just going to have to smooth things over with Smadar. She's grown accustomed to having me at home by now."

"Believe me, she'll thank me. She's used to being on her own, you're probably driving her crazy already. Besides, you know what kind of a girl she is. Charming, charming. Don't buy a lottery ticket, bro, you used up all your luck when you found her. Tell her I was sorry she wasn't home when I came by."

17

"Tell me something," Michael panted, "do you think you could run a little slower perhaps?"

"If I were to slow down anymore, man, I'd be dead." Aslan laughed, but came to a halt nevertheless, to allow Michael to catch his breath a little. The sea's high waves were washing up over the beach, leaving just a narrow strip of soft wet sand on which to run.

"This was a particularly bad idea, meeting you here," Michael grumbled. "It's six-thirty in the morning, freezing cold, and we're alone on the beach. Aliens could abduct us in their spaceship and no one would even know.

"In short," he continued after his breathing eased off a little, a sharp pain still piercing his side and dark waves still threatening to wash over both of them, "in short, I need you. Like in the good old days. Like in the cold of Warsaw and Berlin. This time it looks like we're gonna be freezing our butts off in Russia, if we do actually manage to get on the trail of this son of a bitch. I need you for three months straight, without any kayaking down the Amazon or climbing volcanoes in the Philippines in the middle."

Aslan smiled. He lived his life in keeping with a single guiding principle — a lot, of everything, for as long as possible. After serving in the Shin Bet's and Mossad's special ops units for thirty years, he decided upon retirement to make a point of traveling for six months out of every year. At the age of fifty-three, he was still lean and muscular, in excellent physical condition for his age, his hair gray and his skin tanned. And when he smiled, a set of remarkably white teeth lit up his face. Michael knew that Aslan didn't need much for his subsistence, and that every shekel that he didn't spend on the day-to-day bare essentials was put aside to pay for top-quality travel gear, first-class local guides, and air tickets to the farthest edges of the globe. Aslan, for his part, liked working with Michael and appreciated the serious and thorough manner in which he operated. He had once told one of the case officers that he could spot the tenacity and iron will lurking behind their commander's amiable façade. Truth be told, they shared that same tenacity. Aslan had accompanied him for years to meetings with agents of all kinds, some of them scumbags, some profoundly psychologically scarred, some tough, unpredictable, and thus dangerous. Aslan made sure that the agents turned up to the meetings clean, unaccompanied, and with no one following them. He sat in on the meetings himself when the need arose, and always as Michael's "personal secretary" — a personal secretary who didn't say a word and simply sat there with watchful eyes, bulging muscles, and the unmistakable hint of a weapon under his jacket. Over the years, with Michael no longer simply handling the agents himself but overseeing complex operations involving large numbers of people, Aslan learned to appreciate his calm and authoritative conduct, his composure, the trust he placed in his people, and the freedom he allowed them. He saw how Michael managed to get people to display qualities that even they didn't believe they possessed. They were more alike than met the eye. So how could he say no to him?

"I'm with you. Tell Aharon that I'm in. But don't forget I'm in Africa in April. My son is joining me there, and we're going to climb Mount Kenya. You'll find me there if you make the effort," Aslan said with a smile, before breaking into a run and disappearing into the sea spray that rose like a mist from the incessant violent encounter between the waves and the rocks on the beach.

18

"It could rain at any minute now, and then we're fucked," Michael said to Adi, who was sitting on the bench next to him, her hair tied behind her head and one hand gently rocking the red baby carriage. "Sorry for the way I look," he continued, gesturing at himself. "I was out running with Aslan. Do you know him? He's joining our team. Well actually, he ran and I stumbled along behind him. It's never good to tell lies that don't ring true or make any sense. . . . But," he went on without allowing Adi to get a word in, "I've brought along small compensation for the early morning wake-up call." He produced a cardboard tray with two cups of coffee and a small bag of pastries on the side. "I picked them up on my way," he explained, as if Adi suspected he had baked them himself.

"There's no such thing as an early morning wake-up call when you're the mother of a five-month-old baby girl. And this team you mentioned. Ours, you said. Whose team exactly?"

"Yes, I skipped a few steps," Michael admitted, telling himself at the same time that he had skipped far more than he probably should have. After all, he hardly knew Adi. She had made a very good impression on him the first time they met, with a presentation of her intelligence research paper on members of the Iranian Revolutionary Guards Corps. He noted her passion, enthusiasm, and her impressive ability to piece together details, to weave them into a complete picture. He was left dazzled by her proficiency when it came to managing databanks and computerized research systems. But her most important quality, as far as he was concerned, was her ability to readily and naturally say "I don't know, here we have a gap that can only be filled with an assessment, perhaps only a guess; here we need to wait for more information to come in."

He couldn't help but notice her advanced and very becoming pregnancy at that same first meeting. So that's what they mean, apparently, when they say that pregnant women have a glow about them, he thought. She was wearing an airy, summery dress at the time, and there was something special about her that he couldn't immediately pinpoint. Then he had it. She oozed charm. A pleasant, self-assured charm, accompanied by a certain degree of gravity. He gently inquired back then: "Your first?" And she responded with her eyes aglow, "Yes. A girl." They met again a few times thereafter, during the presentation of various plans of action, and she never failed to impress him all over again. He visited her once in her office, which she shared with two other intelligence officers. Michael wasn't in the habit of making personal visits, and everyone usually came to his large and impressive office, but on that occasion he wanted her to show him something on one of her computer systems, and he descended the two floors and went to her office. Her corner was meticulously neat, and pinned to the corkboard hanging behind her desk he saw a postcard displaying a painting of a beautiful woman, deep in thought, reading a letter in front of a sunlit window. It took him just a moment or two to recognize it as one of Vermeer's paintings. Also pinned to the board were a number of poems that had been cut out from a newspaper literary supplement and a single photograph of cypress trees blackening on the backdrop of a setting sun. It's from my kibbutz, she explained after noticing where his eyes were focused. From before we moved here, that is. Where's here? he asked. Tel Aviv. Just near Lincoln Street, if you know the area. He subsequently retired from the Mossad and they never met up, of course, and now, on a bench in a small park in the heart of Tel Aviv, they were sitting down together again, along with her baby, who stared wide-eyed at the gloomy skies spread out above her. He glanced over at her and said: "What a lovely baby! Her name's Tamar, right?" And she laughed and responded: "Are you kidding? Tamar's two and half years old, meet Michal." And, embarrassed for just a moment, he waved his hand in a gesture of forgetfulness and absentmindedness: "I'm such an idiot. Time passes so quickly, devilishly so, Tamar is a big girl already. For a moment there I was under the illusion that time had stopped. Get a grip, man," he said to himself, and smiled at Adi, whose upper lip was already covered with the foam from the cappuccino and whose eyes now smiled a thousand times more brightly.

He told her about the affair from the beginning and about the team he was putting together. "I want you to be our intelligence officer," he said. "I need you."

"But I'm on maternity leave; Michal isn't even six months old yet."

"That's fine. We aren't going to employ you on a full-time basis. We'll be working from my office, a small apartment on Nahmani Street, in fact. You can bring Michal with you. It'll get you out of the house a little. It'll do you good."

"You know, Michael," she said, "we don't know each other well enough for you to tell me what's good for me. And you have no idea if I want to get out of the house or not. And working with a baby on your arm isn't much fun. I'm sure you've never done so." She inadvertently reached up to her neck and delicately ran her fingers over a gold pendant that remained partially concealed under her shirt. Michael imagined she was tracing her finger along the outline of the piece of jewelry that brushed against her skin.

"Touché." Michael smiled, and then turned serious again. "And that's precisely why I want you. You tell me like it is straight to my face and aren't scared of me. You're right, I went too far. I made assumptions I shouldn't have. I apologize. Will you forgive me?"

"There's nothing to forgive. But you can't speak to people like that. All I can say is

132

that I'll give it a try. That if it works out, great. But if it turns out to be impossible for me, you'll have to find yourself a different intelligence officer. I'd like to catch the bastard, too, after all, so I'll give it a go. When do we start?"

"We've already started, Adi. We've started."

19

Ashdod, January 2013

"Have you spoken to her?"

"Yes, I called her yesterday, after Shabbat. She was happy to hear from me. We worked together many years ago on a Soviet defector, a colonel from their Arctic-based submarine fleet. Quite some gift at the time for our friends in Langley. She's an amazing woman, believe me. As tenacious as a bulldog. In fact, she looks a little like a bulldog, too," Aharon added meanly.

They were heading toward Ashdod in Michael's silver Audi A1, the well-known Sayarim roadside diner flashing by on the right, the oncoming traffic to their left heavy and slow.

"Couldn't you have bought a bigger car?" Aharon grumbled, trying to maneuver himself into a more comfortable position.

"It's the parking in Tel Aviv. It drives me crazy sometimes even with a small car."

The remainder of the drive to Hagar Beit-Hallahmi passed in silence. Aharon had already briefed Michael in general terms on the woman they were about to meet. Hagar had served for almost two decades as head of the Shin Bet's Soviet Espionage Research Department. She joined the Shin Bet immediately after completing a master's degree in Sovietology at the Hebrew University. One of the faculty professors, so she learned many years later, had singled her out and passed on her name. She enlisted in 1960 and went on from there to dedicate her heart and soul to the tough and demanding organization that invited her into its ranks. She retired from the Shin Bet only in the late 1990s, at the age of sixty-seven. Her eyes had filled with tears when she left Shin Bet headquarters for the last time. She returned the car given to her as a department head that same day, and according to Aharon, when the division chief offered her a ride home with one of the car pool drivers, she said, "Thanks, but no need. I may as well get used to it already." She then rented out her small apartment in Maoz Aviv and went to live in Ashdod with the family of her niece. Hagar was a difficult and tough woman, and Aharon could only hazard a guess at why she decided to move in with the daughter of her only brother, who had passed away several years earlier.

Had he asked her straightforwardly, they might have come up with the answer together, but Aharon Levin and Hagar Beit-Hallahmi weren't in the habit of discussing personal matters. "The children are so fond of you, Hagar," her niece had said to her at the time, "you're their favorite aunt. And I'd be happy too, because you're *my* favorite aunt." That's rather a liberal use of the term *aunt,* Hagar thought to herself, but cynicism wasn't going to come in the way of the joy that washed over her, joy and relief to know that she wouldn't have to live alone, without family, without children and grand-children, just her all alone in a public housing apartment filled with thousands of books in Russian and without her Shin Bet job, which she had revered, a job that had long since become a vocation and way of life for her. The Soviet Union and the Shin Bet security service were the loves of her life. Being the descendant of a family of Subbotniks may have been one possible explanation, she had thought to herself on more than one occasion; after all, she had been attracted since a young girl to anything and everything related to Russia, to the Russian language that she learned from her grandfather, who had fought on the Crimean Peninsula, to the greats of Russian literature, Chekhov, Bulgakov, Bunin, and even to the wonderful and terrible Soviet Union, which occupied her dreams. The big dream, the brutal revolution, the huge and awe-inspiring mobilization against the Nazis became her reality. Despite her great love for the nation and its people, she was aware of the terrible catastrophe Stalin had inflicted on his country. And after the dust of the Great Patriotic War settled, the world became polarized, the West versus the East, and because of the Cold War, the Soviet giant was suddenly pitted against the young Israel, the state that had just risen from the ashes of the Holocaust. No wonder Hagar Beit-Hallahmi decided to play a part in the war, on her Middle Eastern front. And she enlisted wholeheartedly in the struggle in the shadows and the intelligence battle that took place in the streets of both Leningrad and Ramat Gan.

She immersed herself in the secret world of the Shin Bet, diligently reading through the dusty cardboard dossiers. Every small piece of information, every hint of Soviet espionage activity landed on her desk, and she, with infinite patience and much love, studied every detail, filed and marked every document, carefully piecing together the big picture, the one that would never be completed. When the Shin Bet got its first computers, she learned to use one slowly but surely, her progress accompanied by suspicion and bouts of hostility. At the same time, she continued to maintain her own personal archive, amassing the thousands of reports and bulletins, jotting down remarks in the margins, drawing arrows to other reports and photographs that had collected in the albums of suspects. Hagar, Hagar. Her unique name, certainly for someone born in the 1930s, was whispered with admiration and respect in the corridors of the Shin Bet. No one knew the true scope of her extensive knowledge. A walking and talking encyclopedia of secrets, they used to call her. Her passion for her work, the manhunts she oversaw from behind her desk for Soviet spies and agents and moles, the tenacious, almost personal, war she waged against the KGB's dark empire, her absolute devotion to the Shin Bet security service that left no time or place in her heart for anything else, all inspired admiration and sometimes even fear among those who worked with her, from the desk clerks in her department, the trackers and eavesdroppers of the Operations Division and through to the Shin Bet chief himself — or more precisely, a line of Shin Bet chiefs, who were frequently required to come to grips with her clear, sharp mind, her unshakable memory, and her fiery tongue.

Now, old and seemingly at peace with herself, Hagar eagerly awaited Aharon Levin's arrival. Very few friends visited her in Ashdod. The people she had worked with at the Shin Bet for forty years, she discovered to her surprise, were work friends, colleagues and nothing more. They hadn't kept in touch when they retired, and she chose to distance herself from those who remained when she took her leave. Time and the distance from Tel Aviv played their part, too. She was happy to be living with Alona and her family. She loved Alona's kids, whom she viewed as her own grandchildren, young and mischievous. Her room was cozy and comfortable. She had given away most of her books, but the hundreds that still remained, which were close to her heart like old friends, filled the room to the brim, spilling over from the bookcase onto her small desk, piled up on the floor, threatening to occupy the spectacular Afghan rug she brought with her from the apartment in Maoz Aviv.

She was sitting on a bench in the concrete

square of the shopping center, soaking up the winter sunshine, her eyes closed in bliss. Her purse rested on her knees and she didn't feel comfortable in the light-colored dress that peeked out from under her thick coat. She had decided to wear the elegant dress only in honor of Aharon Levin, despite the fact that it didn't suit her or the wind-swept square in which she now waited with a sense of expectation and longing, not only for him but also for the world he represented. She listened out of habit to the conversations around her in Russian between new and old immigrants — or at least the bits and pieces she could catch. She knew he'd be there soon. And when they approached, Aharon and the tall man by his side, her face wrinkled into a smile, her eyes opened wide, her arms reached out, and her body swung to its feet with a concerted effort. "Aharon, Aharon, good of you to come to visit an old friend." Aharon clutched both her hands, backed off a little, and lied without balking: "You haven't changed! We all age, even Michael — meet Michael — isn't a kid any longer. Only you, still like a young woman."

"It's been twenty years since we last saw each other, Aharon, and I was already sixty years old at the time. Your smooth tongue

140

never worked on me. You can't fool an old bulldog, my dear. No one fools me," Hagar said. "And don't be shocked, I know I was called bulldog behind my back," she added, taking pleasure in the look of surprise on Aharon's face. "Come, come, let's have a look at you." She narrowed her eyes, tilted her head back a little, her two hands still holding on to his, and then she tugged him gently toward her and buried her head for a moment, just a moment, against his chest.

They sat at the shopping center's only café, which was more of a *bourekas* bakery than a coffee bar. The closest store was a haberdashery, of the kind that no longer graced the streets of Tel Aviv. Next to that was a Russian deli, where dried sausages hung in the window alongside smoked fish, their skin golden and gray, small hooks pierced through their gaping mouths.

Aharon and Hagar sat outside on white plastic chairs on either side of an old Formica table. Michael went inside, to order tea for them and a double espresso for himself, as well as a plate of selected small pastries whose warm odor went straight to his heart and reminded him of colorful, winding markets in remote cities in the Caucasus and secret meetings in crowded, smoke-filled teahouses, steaming cups of

141

sweet tea, with savory cheese pastries on the side.

The two old-timers sat facing each other, leaning over the table, Aharon talking, Hagar silent, his eyes fixed on hers.

"We're chasing a shadow, Hagar. We hardly know anything. We don't know when it started, but it was definitely before 1989, before the fall of the Berlin Wall. In '89, or a little earlier, the Russians took charge of the East German agent. Already then they viewed him as an asset worth killing for.

"I want you to try to remember something that may have happened since then and through to the time of your retirement from the Shin Bet, something that appeared important enough, insufficiently explained, something that bothered you at the time, something that may still be bothering you now, that you never managed to decipher, but noticed nevertheless. Anything, a hint of something that could be relevant."

"Oh, Aharon, there were so many things that defied explanation. Strange phenomena. People disappearing. Leaked information that we were never able to verify. Phone calls we couldn't understand. You know how it goes, that's how the game is played. We always said it's like riding a Ferris wheel. Sometimes you're down and sometimes you're up, on top of the world. And then you drop again. That's just the way it is."

"Everything you say is true," Aharon responded. "But I can see a flash of something in your eyes, Hagar, something you recall, maybe a flicker of memory that seems marginal or insignificant, and yet, it's the very thing that's come to your mind right now. Something I said sparked that particular memory. What is it, Hagar? What are you thinking about?"

Hagar looked at the familiar square as if she was seeing it for the first time, as if the scene being played out in the open expanse was entirely in her honor: Two children, large and colorful backpacks slung over their shoulders, ran past their table, a flock of pigeons took to the wing all at once and rose from the square and onto the roof of one of the stores. Low-hanging clouds moved rapidly northward across the sky, casting a shadow over the white tenement buildings across the way.

"Listen, Aharon. There is something, there is something that lit up momentarily in my thoughts when you were talking. It flashed before my eyes, like a dark fish that you see in a pond, or perhaps it's only its shadow that you see, and then it's gone. I have something in mind, but it's floundering and slipping away, and I need to reflect on it some more, to allow it to return to my thoughts effortlessly. I'm an old woman, Aharon," she sighed, "and I need to rest. How about coming back tomorrow?" she asked ingratiatingly, like a little girl. "I need a little time."

Aharon concealed his impatience. He wanted to move forward, all his senses told him that Hagar could help them, but he knew he had to let her be and allow her the time she needed. He hadn't seen her for many years. He couldn't tell how hard she could be pressed. She was no spring chicken, he thought to himself. He wasn't sure how much of that tough and ruthless bulldog she once was still remained. They were all getting old.

"Need some company on the way home?" he asked.

"No, no, my apartment is very close, it's okay. I'm just a little tired. Old people tire easily, didn't you know? Call me tomorrow morning, and I hope to have remembered by then." She smiled hesitantly at Aharon, and Michael thought about time's ability to have its way with even the toughest people. He watched Hagar as she struggled to rise from her chair before tightening her coat around her body and moving toward Aharon for a farewell kiss. Aharon gazed warmly into her blue eyes; his hands tightened the scarf around her neck as if he were preparing her for a harsh winter. And indeed, just then a cold wind blew through the exposed square, and the gray pigeons retreated as one from the man in the casquette who was feeding them bits of bread, beating their wings and flying toward the tenement buildings. Hagar began moving away from them in small, slow steps. Aharon paced impatiently. "Dealing with that woman requires nerves of steel," he mumbled, perhaps to himself, or perhaps to Michael. "Don't be fooled by her performance — she's as tough as ever," he said, and Michael couldn't tell if he truly believed so or had simply said it in an effort to convince himself. "Come on," he said. "Let's go."

20

Hagar walked into Alona's apartment and took off her coat. A familiar thrill of excitement coursed through her body. She was in a hurry now. She could hear the children playing in their room but went straight to hers, a small and foreign realm in the handsome apartment. She closed the door behind her and turned the key and then bent over with a groan to remove a number of books from the bottom shelf. Concealed behind the books was the small cardboard box she was looking for. She lifted it with both hands and placed it carefully on the small table next to the deep-seated and worn armchair over which a richly colored and decorated stretch of fabric lay carelessly strewn. Hagar liked her room and she was particularly fond of that corner, of the old and comfortable armchair, the beautiful rug, the antique reading lamp, her books, and her secrets. The secrets.

She retrieved a pile of notebooks from the box. School notebooks with brown covers. Just like at elementary school, she thought to herself with a smile. There should be seven or eight notebooks in the box, she couldn't remember exactly, and didn't want to count them just then. She wanted to find what she was looking for, the thing that Aharon Levin had asked her about. The notebooks were filled with her handwriting, small and cramped, in green ink, the same ink she had used for decades in her Caran d'Ache pen to jot down remarks and footnotes and reminders and ideas to be checked out. She also always used to add generalizations and conclusions, abridged versions of cases and summaries of investigations. Her summaries were succinct and purposeful, and included long lists of enemies and suspects. Enemies who might have been forgotten by now by everyone but her. My entire life is in these notebooks, she thought to herself. A complicated and convoluted riddle that makes sense to no one but me. And although the rules and regulations of the Shin Bet required that she destroy her notes ahead of her retirement, her heart wouldn't allow her to do so, she couldn't part with them. And thus, with just a touch of hesitation coupled with

147

adamant assertiveness, Hagar Beit-Hallahmi, a long-serving and loyal soldier in the shadow war, violated the regulations of the all-powerful organization she so loved. She did it knowingly, incapable of letting go, unwilling and unable to shred the code, the cipher of her life. She took the notebooks with her the day she walked out through the fortified gates of Shin Bet headquarters for the last time, without a glance at the young security guards, knowing they wouldn't dare check her large bag, a bag that itself had inspired myths, too, much the same as those told about her. Tales spun together like spiders' webs, silvery strands, slender and sticky, layer upon layer, until they became a veneer of words that offered only a small hint of her character, while she herself, the true woman, gradually faded away and disappeared behind it.

She paged through the notebooks, trying to rekindle that spark of memory that had flashed through her mind while listening to Aharon Levin's story, that elusive inkling that was playing tricks on the edges of her consciousness.

When she got to the fifth notebook, it all came back to her.

21

Ashdod, January 2013

"Since you've come all the way back here again, I'll tell you. It happened in the early 1990s, in the winter of 1992. A year after the Gulf War, to be precise. As always, a team from the Operations Division was monitoring the movements and activities of the usual suspects. They weren't busy with any special assignment, and the team leader was running things at his own discretion, sniffing things out as he saw fit. And it was only the intelligence officer's inexplicable gut feeling that prompted him into action at the time. Based on intuition, he decided to keep tabs on an attractive and well-groomed woman in her forties who was seen leaving one of the locations they monitored from time to time, on a routine basis. They followed her for more than two or three hours, and she did nothing. And the next minute she was gone. Either they lost focus momentarily, a possibility that cannot be ruled out, or she managed to lull them into complacency and then grabbed her chance. The fact is she disappeared. She and the large bag that was slung over her shoulder. A fake crocodile-skin bag, the report said. Seriously? They're fashion experts all of a sudden now, too? They came across her again the following day completely by chance, while combing the area around Arlosoroff Street. The team leader swore not to allow her to give them the slip again. And they stuck with her for four days. Four days around the clock. And nothing. Absolutely nothing. They weren't able to come up with anything on her at all. Apart from the lover!"

The three of them were sitting together again at a round table at the café in the square, but the strong winds had forced them indoors this time. Aharon remained silent and allowed Hagar to remember and recount her story at her own pace. Michael was looking at her, and Hagar Beit-Hallahmi suddenly appeared younger than she had the day before, her old blue eyes open wide and aglow.

"She met up with someone in Bat Yam. An older man. They spent four days together. Talking. Holding hands, like two young lovers. Sitting together in a park, having a picnic on a bench, vodka and cheeses and expensive cold cuts." Hagar spoke dreamily as if she, too, was sitting on the bench with them. And that's just when Michael realized that she was far more cunning and dangerous than she appeared. Hagar Beit-Hallahmi had never been a romantic or sentimental soul. He had met people like her, people who immerse themselves in the finer details seemingly out of a sense of solidarity, only to be able to snare their prey with a single sudden motion. "They went by bus to Tel Aviv," she continued. "Visited used-book stores. Strolled arm in arm along the promenade. Dined three evenings in a row at Shtsupak, holding hands over plates of fish cooked whole on the grill. They slept at his place, his home, a shabby apartment in a tenement building in Bat Yam. Three nights . . ."

Aharon indicated to Michael that Hagar could do with another cup of tea. Go, go, he motioned with his eyes, go get some tea to keep her warm. The wind raged outside, and although it was warm inside the café, a chill went through him, as with the first signs of flu. Aharon stared intently into Hagar's face. She went on, plucking the facts from memory without having to look even once at her notes.

"Naturally, we ran a background check on him right away. Igor Abramovich. An artist, a painter. Immigrated to Israel from the Soviet Union in the 1970s. Widowed a few years later. An only daughter. No ties to anything that could interest the Russians. Not to the military, not to the electricity corporation. Not even to the Egged bus company. His daughter served in the IDF's Southern Command, in a liaison unit of a reserves brigade. He hadn't left the country since immigrating, aside from just two short trips. Once, when his wife was still alive, they went to Cyprus for five days. And on another occasion, in the late 1980s, he went away alone for a week. Border control records showed that he had flown to Frankfurt. His paintings barely sell. He had a small degree of success in Russia, locally, but in Israel — nothing. Igor Abramovich made a living teaching art at a junior high school. He wasn't a rich man, not at all, but he was debt-free. A responsible and cautious individual when it came to his financial affairs. Nothing owed to the income tax or social security authorities. No overdraft at the bank. The apartment was his, the mortgage fully paid off two years before we came into the picture."

Aharon didn't say a word. And Hagar, too,

went silent.

"And . . . ?"

"Abramovich was called in for a talk the moment the woman boarded a flight out of Israel to Vienna. We were still acting on a gut feeling, even though we hadn't found a thing. There's no arguing with gut feelings, as you know. We called it a routine background check, and either he believed us or he simply didn't care. Abramovich came in without a fuss. Someone who grows up in the Soviet Union probably gets used to being summoned for a 'talk' or clarification, and he doesn't even think of asking why. That's just the way it is. He was called in to the Beit Dagan police station — we had use of several rooms there, back then, at least, I don't know if the same arrangement still holds today. We showed him our Shin Bet IDs. I was there and one of the investigators from the division joined me. We asked him about acquaintances, about ties he had abroad, about relatives who were still living in the Soviet Union. He was either a great actor or truly was an innocent and simple man. He answered all our questions. Aside from the death of his wife, almost nothing in his life had changed since his initial interview, some twenty years earlier. Yes, as you know, we checked them out one by one, there wasn't a single immigrant we didn't meet. Everything was recorded and everything was filed. That's how we worked back then. And everything he had told us the first time remained unchanged, apart from a few new acquaintances, neighbors in the tenement building, two or three painters from the Bat Yam Artists Association."

"And the woman, what about the attractive woman who was with him?"

"He didn't try to hide her, but was very shy. He told us about her, too, but blushed like a young boy, and tried to find in me, in me of all people, someone who'd understand the delicate nature of the relationship, who'd understand that it was an affair of the heart, that it needed to be viewed differently, with sensitivity.

"He told us that four or five years earlier, in the winter of '87 — he was more precise after thinking about it for a moment — he met a woman he found very attractive at the Tel Aviv Museum one day. He had been a widower for several years already, he took the trouble to explain, and when he suddenly saw the woman narrow her eyes, tilt her pretty head, take a step or two back to look again, differently, at a painting — a piece by Monet — when he saw her, he told us in a thick accent, his heart was overcome

154

with a sense of warmth that melted the block of ice he had there. Those were his words, that's how he described his first encounter with Katrina Geifman. And that was the beginning of a wonderful romance, he recounted, a romance kept alive from one year to the next via the exchange of letters. No, she couldn't come to see him more than once a year, and no, he wasn't able to visit her in the Soviet Union either. She was married, she had told him, a bad and unhappy marriage, but her husband wasn't well, and it was all too painful and complicated in general, and there was no way out at the time, and she would see him when she visited Israel, and maybe, if she got the chance, she would let him know when she would be traveling to Europe. Paris, maybe London. And perhaps he could join her there.

"All in all, they met up on four occasions in Israel, she couldn't make it the one year, and he went to meet her overseas once, too, in Freiburg, Germany. He flew to Frankfurt and took a train from there to his sweetheart. She was a translator, so she had told him, and she sometimes accompanied businessmen from Moscow, her beloved hometown where she lived with her sick husband and their daughter, who studied at a high

155

school for the sciences.

"Their letters were their only compensation for the distance between them and the time spent apart. Oh, my, the letters she wrote to him. No, she didn't want them to speak on the phone, she didn't like the phone in general, certainly not for very long conversations and definitely not for personal ones. It was also very expensive, he said to me as someone for whom frugality is a way of life. She would pour her heart out to him in her letters, she would tell him all her thoughts, so she had said, and so she did, he recounted, somewhat bashfully. He sent his letters to a post-office box in Moscow and she wrote to his address in Bat Yam."

"You said that a person named Katrina Geifman never entered Israel. That's classic KGB," Michael said. "This woman was obviously using various identities and several passports. But why Igor? What did the KGB want from him?"

"That's just it, apparently nothing. You can take my word for it, Aharon, based on all my experience, all my intuition, Igor Abramovich wasn't a spy. And I can tell you with same degree of certainty that Katrina Geifman, if that was her name, was indeed a KGB field operative. I don't know what she was doing in Israel, and I have no knowledge of her assignment or what she wanted from Igor Abramovich. Who knows, maybe she did really fall in love with him. But it was something we never managed to resolve."

"Didn't you bring her in the next time she came to Israel?"

"She never came back, at least not under any of the names we knew. And she definitely never visited Igor again. They remained in touch via the letters for a few more months, and then she wrote to tell him that things had become complicated and that her husband had found out, and that she couldn't any longer. And that's it."

"And Igor Abramovich?"

"Igor Abramovich is dead. He died on August 7, 1998. I was still working for the Shin Bet, and I remember the date as if it were yesterday. Stomach cancer, he died at Tel Hashomer Hospital. He's buried in the Holon cemetery."

22

"Got it," Adi said, "14 Halevona Street, Kiryat Ono."

It took Adi less than four hours to locate Gal Ya'ari, the late Igor Abramovich's only daughter. A bit of Googling, the websites of the Interior Ministry and Chief Rabbinate, and a little work on Facebook.

"Show me how you do it one more time," Michael asked, and Adi guided him through the process step-by-step, until the Facebook search stage, at which he nodded without really getting it, and Adi, who sensed as much, decided not to make things more complicated for him. "And that's it," she concluded, and Michael breathed a sigh of relief.

"How's your database coming along?" he asked.

"I'm working on it. It would have been a lot easier, of course, to get all the data from the Defense Ministry's Security Authority . . ."

"That's just it, we can't ask for help from anyone at all. Cobra, as far as we're concerned, could be anywhere. He could be the director of the Security Authority himself."

The SA, a department of the Defense Ministry, was responsible for security at the ministry as well as the country's defense industry facilities. Among other things, it maintained a list of names of anyone and everyone who has been privy to state secrets.

Without access to this database, Michael had suggested that they compile one of their own, to include the names of individuals who, in keeping with specific criteria, could be Cobra. His working assumption was that Cobra was privy to secrets to which only someone with the highest security clearance had access. And if the Russians did indeed have such an agent, then the State of Israel had a big problem and a sophisticated traitor in its midst. Michael knew there were several shortcomings to this working assumption: First, someone can be a very high-value agent even if he is privy to only so called lower-level secrets, such as intelligence community secrets or the plans of the IDF's Northern or Southern commands. Second, in light of the Israeli disorder with which he was so familiar, he believed that a relatively large number of people were party to vital secrets even if they hadn't received the required clearance. That's just how things worked. An aide to an aide joins the staff of a senior minister, and somehow no one remembers that the eighth copy of the most top-secret report is forwarded to the said minister's bureau, for his eyes only, of course. But the minister has no intention of opening the double envelopes himself or personally completing the forms to confirm receipt of the material, so the aide to the aide does it in his stead. And on occasions when a multiparticipant discussion is under way somewhere, and they get to the truly classified issue, very rarely does the individual responsible request that those without the necessary clearance leave the room. And even if some of the participants do leave, others remain, and no one really knows who has the required clearance and who hasn't. It's certainly possible, therefore, that although Cobra's name perhaps did not appear on the official list of individuals with the highest security clearance, he still constituted a major threat. But they had no choice, they had to start somewhere.

Michael asked Adi to compile a table of names and particulars of all officeholders in the political establishment and security apparatus who could be considered high-value agents. The table would be put together gradually, and would include, insofar as was possible, names, countries of origin, dates of birth, residential addresses, and the like. It was painstaking work, with piece after piece of information collected in the hope that something they uncovered during the course of their investigation could be cross-referenced with the data in the table. Breakthroughs are sometimes made like this, too, with the help of shots in the dark, no less so than through systematic and orderly office work.

"I want Ya'ara to go see Abramovich's daughter," Michael said. "Amir, tell her please to come here, I'll brief her before she goes."

23

Ya'ara and Gal Ya'ari were sitting in the bright kitchen of Gal's apartment, steaming cups of coffee warming their hands. Her parents named her Galina at birth, and she changed her name officially when she enlisted in the army. Ya'ara recognized the remains of an accent only in the manner in which she pronounced the guttural letters.

"Sorry about the mess," Gal said. "I just got in from work, and with two teenage boys at home, you know. . . . Do you have kids?"

"Not yet, but soon, my boyfriend and I moved in together just a few months ago," Ya'ara responded. "My mother's anxious, too," she added with a smile.

"Sorry, I didn't mean to grill you, I was just asking. They're so messy, my boys, I can't even remember the last time this place was clean and tidy. Sneakers everywhere, jackets thrown all over the place, socks . . ."

162

She ended her mini rant and continued: "So you want to make a movie about my father?"

"Not only about your father. About the Russian Artists Association in Bat Yam. It'll be my final project for school. Like I told you on the phone, I go sometimes to the Bat Yam Museum. It's not really a museum, as you know, but more of a large gallery. And sometimes, alongside the main exhibition, they show pieces by a local artist. Those small side exhibits always move me deeply. They immediately offer one a sense of the loneliness of the artists, their determination, the dreams they're trying to force into a measure of reality. Okay, I'm rambling on. Anyway, I got in touch with the association, and I think there's a story there through which I can shine a light on those people, artists working on the sidelines of the Israeli art scene, and also tackle pertinent questions concerning immigration and life on the margins of society. And the people at the association mentioned your father, and they showed me two of his pieces that are on display in their small office, and rather than begin with the current situation, I thought it could be interesting to start off with the early years, when the association was first established."

Gal was staring at her intently with her

green eyes, which reminded Ya'ara of a cat's. "Yes," she said, "I spoke to Vladislav and he told me you had been to the association. He and my father were friends, many years ago. My father passed away almost fifteen years ago. It seems so far away all of a sudden. She's a very attractive young woman, that's how Vladi described you. How do you like that, even at his age he has an eye for beautiful women."

Ya'ara asked if she had any of her father's paintings, personal documents, journals he may have kept, letters, and the like. Gal showed her three oil paintings that were hanging in the apartment.

"Actually, there are a few more of his paintings that I've simply rolled up and now keep in the storeroom, in the building's bomb shelter. As for documents, papers, I really don't know. I left my father's apartment untouched for months after he died, and then I had to clear it out quickly, because I found a buyer, and I threw away a lot and packed the rest into some boxes. They're downstairs. I haven't looked at them in fifteen years, and thought maybe I'd just get rid of them and that's it. I need the space. If I haven't got to them by now, I'm sure I never will, so why keep things for nothing? People are like that, they like to

164

hang on to things for no reason."

"And tell me, did you know Katrina Geifman? Vladislav mentioned her when we met, he said your father did a wonderful sketch of her, and he thinks it's among his papers that still remain at the association. They have a box there of his stuff, you know? But he started to look for it and couldn't find it, and got a little annoyed, and said he'd let me know if he does."

"I know who you're talking about. I was almost seventeen when they first met, but I wasn't spending much time at home. I preferred to study as much as possible with friends, at their homes. And then I enlisted in the army and only came home on weekends. I hardly saw her, maybe once or twice, and I certainly didn't know her very well. Honestly, I was angry with her and my father to begin with, and I was angry in general. You know how it is, I had a mother, and then she died, and suddenly along comes this beautiful woman, so beautiful and impressive, dressed in clothes I'd never seen in Israel, and so inappropriate, for my father and for our tenement building in Bat Yam, and my father was absolutely besotted with her, like a teenager. It embarrassed me terribly."

"But maybe he really loved her?" Ya'ara

asked softly, playing the part of the student looking for a theme for the perfect film. "It was actually quite a few years after your mother died, right? And I know that he loved your mother dearly, you can tell right away from the painting you showed me, in the study."

"I get it better today perhaps, now that I have teenagers of my own. We don't really exist to them, you know? Just like our parents didn't exist to us. And to actually think of them having a life, falling in love, having sex. Eww, it's hard for me even now to imagine it." Gal smiled. "But I think he really did have something unique with that woman, with Katrina. Even though, like I said, she was so special, or glamorous, it's hard to find the right word for it. I thought back then, too, insofar as I could feel and think through my anger, that she really did care for my father, and loved him as he was. Not because he was rich or handsome or extremely talented, but because he was a good and gentle man, a likeable man with vision. You know something, Ya'ara, it makes me happy today to know that my father had a love story like that."

Ya'ara reached out to touch Gal's hand for a brief moment, before clasping her fingers around her cup of coffee again. "I

166

hope to have moments like that in my film, to be able to show the people whose stories I'm telling, your father, as they were. Without all those things that people dress themselves in to feel more protected. Clothes, layers, thick skin, rudeness. Just them, as they are."

24

Ya'ara smiled shyly and wiped the sweat off her forehead with the back of her hand. She and Gal had finished loading the boxes from the bomb shelter into her car. And she had just caught a glimpse of herself in the mirror in the hallway: Strands of light hair had escaped her ponytail and her cheeks were flushed. Gal looked a little disheveled, too, her hair ruffled but a smile on her face. "Take good care of everything," she said to Ya'ara. "I'm going to go through it all when you return them. What can you do, one has to move on, memories shouldn't remain in boxes. But maybe there'll be a movie now, and that's something, too. I'm sure you'll make a lovely one. You have that way, that special way, of seeing things," she said, warmly touching Ya'ara's hand.

25

Dearest Katrina, my love,

It's with a heavy heart that I write to you now. My darling, I've read your last letter over and over again. I read it and didn't know what to do with myself. I know it's hard, I know it isn't easy to deal with, but why are you so adamant and determined? Why put an end just like that to such a special and rare love story, to our love, which has been nothing but beautiful?

I've come to terms with the fact that our relationship is such a fragmented one. We see each other once a year, always at your initiative, always when it suits you, never for long enough and always too painful. And our letters have been my comfort — as if we're living in a different century, way back when, the seventeenth century perhaps, maybe the eighteenth, with you the unattainable princess, and me the poor poet in a faraway land. And the words bind us, making their way across the sea, over mountains and wide open plains, bearing the fibers of our emotions, the passion of our bodies, the undying yearning, to be together, to sit facing one another, to look into your deep eyes, filled with sorrow and beauty, and to feel so close, so close.

And now all of a sudden, without forewarning, you tell me it's all over. No more! No more meetings and no more writing to each other. As if you've been summoned by the forbidden-love police and ordered to do so. And me, I've never asked for more than you could give, and each time I saw you filled me with the strength for another year, another ten years if need be, until I could see you again. But now you say: We'll never meet again. I won't write any longer, and don't write to me either, my dear Igor.

My beloved, my love, I don't understand what happened, what's happened specifically now. Your husband found out, you say. How he found out — you don't say. I'm sorry about his discovery. It must have pained him. He — yes, even he — must know, as I do, how wonderful you are. But I can't help feeling sorry for myself and for you, for the two of us, my Katrina, sorry that our love has thus been doomed suddenly to die.

I've never pleaded with you, but I'll ask just this one time: Can't you leave him? After all, the hardest part is over. He knows. The secret is no longer a secret. Bring your beautiful daughter and come live with me, with us, here. I can just imagine the kind of life you lead, the comfort and luxury in which a spectacular woman such as yourself must live. Not that you ever showed off or looked down on me, God forbid, your soul is a gentle and good one, but I allowed my imagination to run free. And I, as you know, live a simple and modest life. But we'd have a warm and pleasant home, and the beach is nearby, and the hustle and bustle and chaos of our country also offers a joie de vivre and a sense of festivity and color. Come, my love, come live your life with me. And if you want, my darling, I will come live with you. We'll find ourselves a small apartment, even just a room would suffice. I'll paint and you'll do your interpreting, and we'll live together, a happy life. Whatever you choose.

But if you don't respond, this will be my final letter. And suddenly I think to myself: You're such a selfish scoundrel, so focused only on yourself. You can't seem to grasp the kind of hell in which your beloved is living, you only remember the handful of days spent together. And not all the other days through which she is forced to struggle with life's hardships, with life itself, with all its demands and unfairness. And if your beloved says she can't do it any longer, that all she wants is peace and quiet and tranquility, you have to respect that. If you love me, you wrote, let me go. I could see the tears in your eyes through your written words. And that's what I am doing, my love, I'm letting you go, if that is what you want. You know where to find me, and I have no idea how to get to you. I love you and I will wait. I love you and won't be a burden to you.

Yours,
Igor

26

Ya'ara came across Igor Abramovich's last letter to his lover in one of the boxes. Well, a copy of the last letter actually, as the original had been mailed to Katrina's post-office box in Moscow. Attached to the letter was a photocopy of the stamped envelope in which the original had been sent, and Ya'ara came to the conclusion that Igor was either a very meticulous and organized man or simply couldn't let go of anything connected to the woman he loved. Igor's precise and embellished script appeared on the envelope; Katrina's name and address had been written with a loving hand, using a fountain pen. Along the edge of the photocopy, in red ink, Igor had written: "Sent on 4/22/92. My final letter perhaps?"

Ya'ara translated the letter as best she could, recording the text on a white sheet of paper, and wondering all the while if her Hebrew version was capturing Igor's emotions and archaic style that so touched her heart.

She found Katrina's letters in the same box, inside a small cardboard container. The last letter she sent was the one Igor referred to in his. It truly was a heart-rending letter. She sounded tired and defeated. Let me go, she wrote. I won't write to you again. I can't.

One of the other boxes contained a small sketch pad. Katrina's face adorned its pages, in charcoal, in brown ink, skillfully sketched with love. There were also sketches of a tranquil seascape, a grove of trees, a shaded bench in a public park.

A distinct memory flashed through Ya'ara's mind for a moment. It was so real she felt as if she could bite into it. She and her mother were walking hand in hand through their old neighborhood, the wind was whipping up leaves and plastic bags, the smell of exhaust fumes was drifting in from the main road that leads to Haifa, with its incessant traffic, the low-rise and shabby tenement buildings so like the one in which Igor and Galina used to live, in Bat Yam. She had sat for almost an hour in front of that tenement building, trying to make contact with the ghosts of Igor and his adolescent daughter, preparing for her meeting with Gal, who herself was already the mother of teenage children.

Ya'ara's parents also immigrated to Israel from the Soviet Union, from the far reaches of the empire, from Vladivostok. They arrived in the country in the 1970s, after having had their requests to emigrate rejected by the authorities on three occasions. After the first request, her father was transferred from his position in the laboratories of the large oil refinery to the facility's warehouse. He lost his job entirely after the second request. Their lives went from hard to unbearable, but her father, the stubborn man he was, went on to submit a third request nevertheless. He managed to make a living by working in a local market, at a fish stall. He sold fresh produce when available, but spent most of the time dealing in smoked and salted fish, whose smell permeated his clothes. Ya'ara had no real recollection of it, yet she seemed to be able to feel the slippery and scaly texture of the fish. Her father spent long hours on his feet behind the counter, in the freezing cold, in the filth. Her mother survived the first two requests, but she, too, lost her job at the municipal library after the third. The winter that year was a particularly harsh one: icy winds blew in from the ocean, the heating system went down after the water pipes

175

froze and burst, the snowplows worked around the clock, spewing diesel fumes, the skin on people's hands cracked and bled, the radio crackled and broadcast reports about large ships trapped in the frozen seas. The sun, even during the few hours of light, was gloomy and gray. A gray sun, her mother said, can you even imagine that? Ya'ara was just a little girl when she heard her mother speak of such things, and her mother's stories came from a different world, a world that existed somewhere but certainly didn't exist there, in Kiryat Haim, where the sun shone warm most days of the year, casting a bright glow, painful to the eyes, over the endless rows of tenement buildings and the sparse trees. She listened eagerly to her parents' stories, which to her sounded like myths from a cruel and frozen land. And she, free spirit that she was, raced to follow the alluring voice of her heart, which pulled her to the sea and the sun and the greenish pool of water in the dark and fragrant orchard that still survived on the edges of their modest neighborhood, on the other side of the dirt road. There, in the shade of the orange trees, she would immerse herself for magical hours on end in books borrowed from the municipal library, thrilling and chilling books, tales of adventure and tales of love, books about unruly orphans (whose hair miraculously turned from red to auburn over the years), books about tough men and books about smart and courageous women. And to go with her perfect Hebrew, her mother taught her to read and write in Russian, too. "There's no need to be ashamed of the language, *maminka,*" she said to her. "It's not just a language. It's an empire." And that word, *empire,* echoed in her head. As a child she would imagine the immensity of the Russian language, the vast expanse it covered between the giant oceans, the millions of people who spoke it, dreamed their dreams in it, and she wandered back and forth between the ancient language that was hers and that other huge language, which was her mother's, and she also read Russian books that her mother would present to her with a touch of celebration. Those books she'd read in bed, enveloped in her soft blanket, her heart filled with an inexplicable sense of longing.

Her name as a young child wasn't Ya'ara. That's the name she chose shortly before enlisting in the army. She had walked out of the Interior Ministry shaking with pride, her new ID document clasped in her hand. Ya'ara Anna Stein. The name her parents gave her was still there, but from now on, she said to herself, she would be Ya'ara. A Hebrew name, literally meaning honeycomb. A symbol of her new autonomy. Her independence. She felt reborn. She was on her own. Ya'ara, Ya'ara, the name filled her with joy, intoxicated her, and she reveled in its fragrance and whispered to herself, so lovely, so lovely.

27

Tel Aviv, January 2013

The team convened at two. Aharon joined them a few minutes late, concluding a call as he walked in, taking off his raincoat, sinking into the old leather armchair left vacant for him.

"Okay," Michael said, "let's see what we have so far." He looked at Adi and asked her to kick things off.

Adi fidgeted with her gold necklace and blushed. "So here's the story," she began. "Shortly before her death, a retired Stasi archivist tells her priest in Dresden that the Stasi once had a high-ranking source in Israel. The source's code name: Cobra. According to her, about two years prior to the collapse of East Germany, the KGB stepped in to take charge of the source, deeming the operation important enough to warrant its commandeering from the Stasi and also the assassination of the officer in charge on behalf of the East German intelligence service, probably to ensure the secret remained unexposed. The priest relayed this information to his contacts in the West German intelligence service, which by then had become the intelligence service of the united Germany. The information eventually reached the former German intelligence chief, the head of the BND, who then passed it on to the former Israeli Mossad chief, Aharon Levin, who sits here now with us dozing in an armchair."

Aharon, whose eyes were actually closed, muttered: "True, sleeping, but not missing a single word. Go on, Adi, go on."

"Hagar Beit-Hallahmi, the Shin Bet's leading expert on Soviet intelligence matters in general and the KGB in particular, managed to dredge up from memory an unresolved affair, one that centers on the character of a woman, presumably a Soviet intelligence operative, who visited Israel several times under different names, and then disappeared. I need to stress that there's no proof, no proof at all, that this affair is tied to the one we're investigating."

Sunk in his armchair, Aharon interjected again. "That's true," he said, "we have no proven connection, or even a circumstantial one, between this woman and Cobra, but let me remind you that this matter in particular, out of all the numerous unresolved incidents related to KGB activity in Israel, was the one that popped into Hagar's mind, and specifically in the context of our affair. Hagar Beit-Hallahmi is a very serious woman. Very experienced. Her intuition is beyond me, but as far as I'm concerned this is something we have to consider seriously and try to figure out as best we can. Besides, we have no other leads. All we have is the hint of an old and faint scent that an aging bloodhound has got wind of and is now telling us to follow."

"No offense — as my kids would say," Amir remarked, and then went silent again, his cheeks turning red.

Adi continued: "Okay, so this woman, who appeared under several names and then disappeared, is our lead. What do we know about her? Almost nothing. She had a relationship with an Israeli man, an immigrant from the Soviet Union by the name of Igor Abramovich, who's no longer alive. And the nature of the relationship? Hagar Beit-Hallahmi says the Shin Bet was sure that Igor wasn't a spy. Ya'ara will elaborate shortly on what she came up with and her thoughts on him. He, Igor, knew the woman as Katrina Geifman. Her real name? Who knows? In any event, she entered Israel in 1992 using a passport with a different name. On her previous visits to Israel — Igor mentioned three others during his questioning — she came into the country under a different name or different names. We're assuming they were different names because the Shin Bet at the time wasn't able to find the ones they knew of in the border control records."

"Katrina Geifman, Katrina Geifman," Aharon said. "What do we know about her? Ya'ara?"

Ya'ara told them about making contact with the Association of Russian Artists in Bat Yam and her meeting with Galina, Gal Ya'ari today, Igor's daughter. She had gone through, in a cursory manner at least, the boxes from Galina's home that contained papers and sketches and small items belonging to her father, who died in 1998, almost fifteen years ago. And she had read the letters sent by Katrina to Igor and the last letter Igor sent to her, a letter he took the trouble to copy and save, several times.

"I think Katrina Geifman is her real name. It may have been a little reckless on her part to write as she did, but her letters rang true to me. They come from the heart. They're touching. Yes, letters like that can also be fabricated. They can be prepared as part of an overall operation. But I don't see any operation here, any reason for the KGB to want something from Igor Abramovich, and even if they were interested in him for whatever reason, why did they invest so much effort in him? I therefore think, like Hagar Beit-Hallahmi said, that Igor wasn't a KGB spy. So what do we have here then? I think we've stumbled upon a love story. Real, intense, naïve, like in the movies. Katrina probably did work for the KGB. We have no knowledge of what she did for them, what her assignments were, but we know she came to Israel quite regularly over a period of several years, using different passports. As I see it, the fact that she managed to give the Shin Bet surveillance team the slip means she was a highly skilled field operative. Don't forget, she was probably on a mission the first time they followed her. The following day, when they came across her again by chance, she may no longer have been doing something she needed to hide. She was busy instead with the private part of her life, her affair with Igor, and not a KGB operation. And that's why she didn't look for a surveillance team and didn't find one either, and as far as she was concerned the Israeli Shin Bet could keep watch on whatever she was doing. If she was hiding her relationship with Igor, she was hiding it from the KGB. And that's the reason — and this is total guesswork on my part — her relationship with Igor ended so abruptly. Igor was her secret. We don't know if Katrina Geifman was married to someone or not, but she was certainly hitched to the KGB. If she was involved in a love affair with Igor, if she did indeed make the mistake that we sometimes make, too" — she paused for a moment and smiled — "and against all the rules she fell in love, it was clearly in violation of KGB regulations. And when they found out, one way or another, she was ordered to put an end to it. Immediately. If not something worse. And that's why she wrote her final letter."

"A real love affair with someone in Israel could actually be an excellent cover story for her trips to the country," Aslan commented with obvious skepticism.

"True, but if it was all part of a plan, if it was part of an operation, she would have given Igor the name that appeared in her passport. Otherwise it wouldn't be a cover or anything at all. Imagine this: She goes through passport control at Ben Gurion Airport as Elena Yampolsky — that's the passport she used, after all — and they ask her, 'What is the purpose of your visit, madam?' And following some persistent questioning, she shyly admits to a love affair with someone, Igor Abramovich, and when they check with him, he innocently confirms it, telling them that he's involved romantically with a Russian woman by the name of Katrina Geifman, and yes, that's really her picture, and boom, the cover story becomes an incriminating one, or something suspicious, at least. No. It was a real love affair, and Katrina, the KGB operative, broke numerous rules in order to follow her heart. The connection between this high-class woman from Moscow and a humble artist from Bat Yam remains a mystery, but you can never tell when it comes to these kinds of things. The letters, in my opinion, indicate that it happened, and that it was real."

"We need to find her, this Katrina Geifman," Aharon said. "She's the only lead we have, even if it's only to rule out the possibility that she's connected to the affair we're looking into. We have to find out if the bloodhound from Ashdod is on the right scent," Aharon added in reference to Hagar Beit-Hallahmi, the "bulldog" who had rarely erred in the past. Rarely. "How do we locate her?"

"I'm working on it," Adi said. "Using the Internet to begin with. Ya'ara is helping me with the Russian, and Michael gave me the go-ahead to seek the assistance of a young Russian guy who's working now with my brother at Amdocs, a boy wonder of sorts, who served in the IDF's SIGINT unit, Unit 8200. I told him to find her for me, that she's someone I need to locate for my master's thesis. Taking into account that our Katrina is now sixty years old or so, we've narrowed down our search to around ten potential women. Let's hope that the woman we're looking for is one of them."

"Igor will be the key," Aharon said. "If we find her, we'll make contact with her on his behalf. We obviously won't be able to hide the fact that he's dead. But we can approach her with a final letter that he wrote to her before he died. And Galina, his daughter, will be the one to take it to her. Meet Galina," Aharon continued, turning to look at the entire team. "Hi there, Galina," he said, gesturing toward Ya'ara.

"But I don't look like her at all, and she's older than me, and I'm sure her Russian is better than mine."

"She'll want to see Igor's daughter. She's all that remains of something that was apparently very deep and meaningful for her,

186

that caused her to violate all the rules that secret organizations impose on their people. Don't forget, she barely saw Galina, her visits to Israel were very brief, and twenty years have gone by since. She won't expect her Russian to be perfect, there's no reason it should be, and she'll see what she wants to see, particularly if some of the things we show to her are indeed genuine, or we present them as genuine to her. The letter, and maybe a sketch of her, which he did at the time. And something personal from among the items that Galina collected from his drawers and packed into boxes.

"Compose a letter written by Igor on his deathbed, and show it to me. Michael will then get one of our forgers to put it into Igor's handwriting, based on samples you'll give to him.

"So let's get on with it.

"Adi, you're finding Katrina. Ya'ara, you're coming up with a letter and you're also choosing a sketch and one of Igor's personal items to give to her. After Adi finds her, Aslan, it'll be up to you to plan the trip. You'll be responsible for ensuring that you and Ya'ara enter and leave Russia safely. Yes, you'll be traveling with genuine documentation, we don't have a choice. We don't have access to the Mossad's capabilities. Remember, unless explicitly authorized by either me or Michael, no one else, no one at all, can know of our mission."

"Come, Ya'ara," Adi said, stretching her back, "let's get a little work done."

28

"It was easier than I thought it would be," Dima, her brother's friend, said, beginning the conversation without any preamble. He really has become so Israeli, Adi thought, and her heart seemed to skip a beat. "The picture you gave me helped a lot, despite you telling me it's from twenty years ago. My search led me to a young woman by the name of Anna Geifman. On Facebook. Obviously. Where else?" The "Where else?" rolled around in Dima's mouth like a piece of candy, with the faint hint of a Russian accent. "She has her entire family tree on Facebook, down to the very roots. Her mother, Natalya, is a chemist at an oil company in a relatively small city, not far from Moscow. South of Moscow, to be precise. Anna, herself, is studying animation at the Academy of Fine Arts in Moscow. She sees her sweet grandmother, Katrina — that's how she describes her, sweet, I'm simply quoting — very infrequently, because she lives in Dimitrovgrad. I checked, it's about a thousand kilometers east of Moscow. A real dump, check out its website, really pathetic." There's that accent again, Adi thought to herself, flavoring Dima's words with a heart-warming spice. "Pathetic," like a tiny melody. "There's a picture of the three of them, Anna and her mother and her grandmother. From last Christmas, a little less than a year ago. The grandmother caught my eye right away. She looks young, not like some old woman of sixty, and she — how should I put it — isn't simply beautiful, *impressive* would be a better word, as if she's emerging from the picture."

"You said the picture I gave you helped." Adi had scanned and e-mailed him a photograph of Katrina that she had found in one of Igor's boxes.

"Yes, for sure. From the outset, she, Anna's grandmother, looked like the picture you sent me. And then I played around a little with Picasa. It's a program that among other things also offers facial recognition capabilities." Dima paused for a moment, to make sure Adi knew what he was talking about.

"Tell me, Dima, how old do you think I

am? Am I also an old woman of sixty?"

Dima laughed sheepishly. "You're Yair's big sister nevertheless. I have no idea how old you are. Oldish. Relatively so. You already have two daughters, right? They're Yair's screen saver. He's a sentimental guy, you know."

"You're digging a hole for yourself, Dima. Didn't you study Tact 101 at the Technion?"

"Okay," Dima said, choosing to ignore her remark and change the subject. He learned, too, at that very moment, that speaking about a woman's age is like walking through a minefield, and actually stepping on the mines themselves, not in the spaces between them. "So I enlarged the faces in the two pictures, ran them through Picasa, and, believe it or not, got a very high degree of likeness, particularly if you take into account the fact that there's a twenty-year gap between the photographs, and they're not the optimal quality for the purpose of comparing faces."

"You're a sweetheart, Dima. And that's coming from an old and mature woman. Mail me everything. With the pictures and all."

"If you'd checked, you'd have seen you already have it all," Dima said slightly condescendingly, and Adi smiled, admitted defeat, and said, "You've done a great job. You've helped me. I'm truly grateful. Regards to Yair and remind him that he's at our place this evening at eight. And not to be late."

29

Ya'ara could hear the hesitation in her voice. After saying, in Russian, of course, "Hello, my name is Galina Abramovich, may I speak to Katrina Geifman," she heard nothing but silence, and then, a slow, deep voice said, "Could you repeat that, please?" And she did. And silence again. Ya'ara proceeded cautiously.

"We met only once, or twice, in our apartment in Bat Yam, in Israel, but my father spoke about you often. I mean, he didn't say very much, but you were clearly very important to him. Dear to his heart," she added, lowering her voice slightly, like someone who felt embarrassed by her invasion into her father's intimate, foreign, space. A sigh came from the other end of the line. "Oh, Igor. It was so long ago."

"Yes, so many years have gone by. I have to tell you, so you know — my father passed away a long time ago, in 1998." Silence. "He loved you until the day he died."

"Igor's dead?"

"Sadly, yes. My father passed away."

"It's complicated, it's all too complicated."

"I . . ." Ya'ara hesitated, "if you're willing, I'd like to see you. I know it's been a long time, and perhaps it was wrong of me not to write to you when my father died. But you weren't in touch with each other at the time, and I didn't know exactly what to do. Mostly I was embarrassed. But I've been going through several of my father's old things recently, and I'll be traveling soon to Moscow for work, and in my hand right now is a final letter my father wrote to you, right before he died, and I thought to myself that these kinds of things don't happen by chance and perhaps we could see each other."

"Russia is a big country, my dear, and I live so far away from Moscow. I won't be able to come meet you there. It's far, the train fare is expensive, and times aren't that easy right now . . ."

"No, no, I thought I'd come to you. I'll take two or three days off after the work in Moscow, and we can meet. There must be a small hotel where you are."

"There is one hotel, but I live a little out of town. There's only a small hostel in our suburb, but anyway, you can stay with me, I have an empty room. I mean, it's full of stuff I've collected, you know, we collect and collect things . . . I'll make room for you. You'll stay with me, Galinka."

30

*Ben Gurion International Airport, February
2013*

"You know that with your real passport and
the story you told Katrina Geifman, you're
going to be in trouble in the event of an
investigation," Aslan said to Ya'ara. They
were sitting at the Segafredo café, close to
their boarding gate at Ben Gurion International Airport. They still had an hour before
their flight to Moscow was due to take off,
and they, one with a cappuccino and the
other a double espresso, and a bottle of
mineral water, were going over the cover
stories, and what they planned to say on
entering Russia, and then in Dimitrovgrad,
and what would happen if someone were to
waylay them, Katrina and Ya'ara, in the very
midst of their meeting. And who they were
to each other, Aslan and Ya'ara, and what
they were doing there together.

"After all, she knows you as Galina Abramovich, and your passport says Ya'ara Stein. How are you going to explain that?"

"The chances of someone taking any interest in the two of us together are slim."

"Don't forget that she, based on our best assessments, is a KGB operative."

"She was. In the past. We believe after all that she's no longer a part of the organization. She's old, and she probably broke every rule in their book. She lives in a shithole in the middle of nowhere. Do you really think there's any KGB in that miserable town, a thousand kilometers east of Moscow?"

"It's 966."

"What?"

"It's 966 kilometers. Besides, it's no longer the KGB. They're the FSB these days, as you know. And the Federal Security Service has offices everywhere throughout the empire. And with a nuclear research institute in the city, I'm not so sure they view Dimitrovgrad as an insignificant town. But, yes, I agree that it isn't very likely at all that they're still keeping an eye on Katrina Geifman. Nevertheless, if she knows you as Galina and you're required by an FSB official or a policeman sent by the FSB to present your passport, bearing the name

Ya'ara Stein, in her presence, what do you say?"

"You know. The usual story. In the event of any confrontation, I'll say that it's all simply a misunderstanding. I'm not Galina. What are you talking about? I'm a friend of Galina, well, an acquaintance, to be more precise. When Galina heard about my upcoming trip to Russia, she asked if I'd contact someone on her behalf, a woman by the name of Katrina Geifman, who her father had known and been in contact with many years ago. I'm simply delivering an old letter and maybe a small memento. I was in Moscow for the purpose of gathering material for my final film school project, and stopped off in Dimitrovgrad on my way to Kazan. There I'm hoping to find the gravesite of my great-grandmother, my father's mother's mother. And if Katrina believed otherwise, if she mistakenly thought that I'm Galina Abramovich, then either she heard wrong, or misunderstood me, or it's simply wishful thinking on her part."

"So who am I then?" Aslan asked.

"You? What kind of question is that? You're my lover," Ya'ara responded, holding his hand for a moment.

198

31

Russia, February 2013

She hadn't properly considered the awful cold of Russia in February. Ya'ara had worked before in cold places, in Sweden, in Finland, but somehow she avoided making the required mental connection between the fragrant, colorful, and wonderfully pleasing winter of Israel's coastal plain and the intense, unyielding cold that greeted them the moment they stepped out of the plane at the airport in Moscow. The years spent at university, without her having to be constantly primed to take off on a trip somewhere, must have had an effect, and her negligence, her failure to take her destination into account, exacted an immediate price. She knew, of course, that she was going somewhere cold, but she didn't remember just how big a difference there is between minus three degrees and minus thirteen. Traversing the short distance

199

between the aircraft's stairs and the wide passenger bus, diesel fumes spewing from its exhaust, was enough for her to feel the cold biting and stinging and encapsulating her body through her thin sweater and the seams of her leather jacket, and her jeans turned stiff, frozen, and coarse, scratching her skin, cooling the flow of blood through her thighs. Aslan, for his part, appeared pleased with himself. He tightened his long woolen coat around his body and with a triumphant smile pulled out a woolen hat, put it on, and pulled it down, his ears protected, his forehead covered, his teeth white and his eyes sparkling. Within seconds, however, he could feel the cold penetrating the wool and seeping inward, into his head and his body. He knew that fifteen minutes on lookout or manning a security position on the street and he wouldn't be able to see a thing, that all he'd be able to do would be to try to cope with the ever-increasing discomfort, before the cold turned into a burning and painful sensation that prevented him from acting as required. He pressed up against Ya'ara, in the bus that was now filled with passengers, and said: "We didn't take cold like this into account. I'm such an idiot. Me, with two treks in the Himalayas under my belt. With thousands of pairs of thermal underwear. Which I left at home, of course. The first thing we're going to do is get ourselves properly equipped. And dress in the clothes that the people who live here wear." And she responded, her scent still fresh and pleasant despite having slept cramped up in the narrow aircraft seat: "Yes, my darling. It's about time you bought your love a fur coat."

32

Katrina, my love,
Katrina. This is my final letter to you. Six years have gone by since my last one. I didn't think I'd ever write to you again. I asked you back then, my dearest — pleaded almost — to be mine. To decide that you are able to take the bold leap of faith with me, to walk away from your previous life, from your husband whom you no longer love, and to live with me. Your letter was so cold, cold and bleak. Even the very letters that made up the words appeared to disfavor me. And the words themselves were like a sword through my heart. You told me you would never see me again. And that I should cease writing to you.

We were so happy, sweet Katrina, and each time we met we shared such a simple and innocent joyfulness. From the very first time, and year after year to follow. Until you decided that you couldn't any longer. You touched my soul, elevated me, transformed me, proved to me that I was not dry and shriveled as others thought, that I could be interesting for the most part, and even exhilarating at times, that there was a spark of life left in Igor, who used to think that his life was closing in on him.

I remember your first glance. Yours was a look touched with surprise yet full of warmth — a secretive smile in the corners of your eyes, your pupils widening suddenly in their lakes of blue. Yours was a look of invitation to an adventure, or so I thought, but I realized the moment I held your hand that it was an invitation of a different kind, a call to a journey.

And we did indeed embark on a journey, my Katrina, a journey conducted in the heart and via words scripted in ink, meeting face-to-face just once a year, just once. But oh, those meetings! The storms that raged through my body and soul, the joy and delight that washed through my very being. And yours, too, my darling. Your soul, too, filled to the brim with bliss and peace, raging storms and tranquility. And I say these words to you now, too, without hubris or pretension. With me, I sensed, you felt liberated, free of the chains of the oppressive relationship shackling your spirit and restricting your every step. With me, all of a sudden, you were a young girl again. Barefoot, laughing, carefree. With me, with me of all people. Because our souls touched each other. Because we found that freedom in each other's arms.

My darling, please don't allow the lines to follow to weigh heavy on your heart. Fate has thus decreed and there's nothing more to be done. And I have accepted my fate, and feel at peace with myself, and whatever transpires over the coming days or weeks won't move me at all. I'm dying, my Katrina. There's no other way to put it. It's my destiny. I have severe cancer, stomach cancer. It's aggressive and terminal, and my doctors have told me there's nothing more they can do. Truth be told, I appreciated their honesty and cruelty. Regrettably, I wasn't spared months on end of chemotherapy, which seemed to spark an inferno and set fire to my insides. I accepted my pain and anguish, however, because they afforded me additional weeks and months through which to think of you, my darling, to recapture and cling to those sweet and lazy days we spent in each other's arms, or walking aimlessly hand in hand, purely for the purpose of being together.

I'm writing to you, my darling, so you will always know just how loved you are, just how much beauty and pleasure you have within you to give, and just how worthy you are of living life to the fullest, with all the force of your emotions and the splendor of the first blooms of the spring.

Yours, only yours,

Igor

33

Dimitrovgrad, February 2013

Silent tears streamed down Katrina's cheeks. She looked like a figure in a Rembrandt painting, Ya'ara thought. Wrapped in a clay red shawl, her light hair turning golden under the reading lamp, as if the light were radiating from the fine strands themselves, her small living room gloomy and dark, Igor's letter stark white in her hands.

"Forgive me, Galina, I know your father passed away a while ago, but it's as if it's all happening for me right now, the letter, his imminent death."

"He loved you until the day he died, just like I told you when we spoke on the phone, and it's so plain to see, plain and simple, from the letter, too. I have to confess, I've read the letter. I couldn't help myself. I have no idea why he chose not to send it in the end. Perhaps because he didn't want to cause you sorrow. Perhaps he thought his words were inadequate and unable to properly capture his true feelings. To express the connection you shared. In any event I read it, and it made me feel a little strange, a daughter shouldn't be exposed like that to her father's feelings, and certainly not to the manner in which he expresses his love for a woman. But I did read it, and in some strange way it allowed me to discover not only him but you, too. A little. A woman who inspires such love has to be someone special. And not only in the eyes of her beloved."

"I sent him quite a few letters over the years, until the one in which I asked him to cut off all contact with me."

"I know, he saved all your letters. I found them wrapped together in one of his drawers, and I packed them just as they were into one of the boxes and haven't touched them since. I didn't open them, didn't read them, perhaps thus preserving his privacy. His and yours. But I did open the last letter he wrote to you, wrote but didn't send, I apologize . . ."

"You have nothing to apologize for, Galinka. Naturally you were curious. And thanks to your curiosity, you're here now, with me. Warming the heart of an old woman."

"Old? What nonsense! And so beautiful, still now, seeing you took my breath away. As if time had stood still since I last saw you in Bat Yam, in our apartment. Back then, however, I was mad at you . . ." Ya'ara said with a shy smile.

Ya'ara had penned Igor's last letter, with a suggestion or two coming from Adi, who remarked, "It's like we're writing a chapter of *Anna Karenina.*" Amir listened to the version proposed by Ya'ara but said he didn't really know much about such matters. Aslan said: "Not bad, not bad. A little too flowery, but similar in style to the last letter he actually wrote, melodic like the things you read to us from his sketch pad, the notes he made about nature's moving beauty and all that." Aharon, for his part, remained quiet after reading the Hebrew version composed by Ya'ara; he frowned, shook his head a little, briefly closed his eyes, and after a few moments of apparent intense thought, he pulled out his fountain pen, an old green and gold Pelikan, erased a word, altered an expression or two, and said, "Excellent, excellent. Great job, Ya'ara. Michael, take the letter now to Sasha. The guy from the language school. Let him read it to check we haven't made any mistakes in Russian.

Don't let him improve the letter, you hear me? I don't want a 'translate and embellish' job. He only needs to check the Russian. And then give the letter to Avraham from the graphics department. So he can put it down on paper in Igor's handwriting. Give him a few samples. And tell him to use materials from the late 1990s. Tell him not to be stingy with his treasures. And not to say a word to anyone. Tell him it's for me and that's all. We've done a few things together, Mr. Forger-Extraordinaire and me. So here's one more thing now, for old time's sake."

Katrina brushed her hand across her cheek and then wiped it inadvertently on her dress. "Come a little closer so I can see you," she said, the letter still in her hand. "Where do the years go, where?" she sighed. "It's so hard. So hard. You know, perhaps it's better that your father didn't see me like this, in this remote city. Come, I'll pour you some more tea."

She stood up and filled Ya'ara's cup from the urn in the corner of the room.

"I want you to understand something, Galina," she said to Ya'ara, looking her straight in the eye. "I had no choice. I had to break off my ties with him immediately. Right away. They didn't give me a choice."

209

"They didn't give you a choice? Who are they?"

Katrina remained silent for a moment or two. And then she said: "Perhaps we should continue later. I'm exhausted. I'll rest for a while. Drink some more. Your room is heated. You can rest, too, if you like. Please forgive the mess. All the booklets lying around there. That's how I earn a living these days, translating technical manuals into Russian. From English or French into Russian. But I cleared away as much as I could, and I put some linen and a nice blanket on the sofa. Rest, my dear, you look tired, too. I'm sure it isn't easy for you either to remember your father like this."

Ya'ara stood up and approached Katrina. She reached out and embraced her warmly. Katrina rested her head on Ya'ara's shoulder, allowing her arms to hang at her sides and losing herself in the touch and lemony fragrance that enveloped the young woman. Ya'ara tightened her embrace for a moment, feeling the bones of Katrina's slender shoulders. She lifted Katrina's head and kissed her closed eyes.

Aslan was outside, standing on the edges of the thick vegetation in front of Katrina's home, his person blending with the shadows and broken branches. His head was covered

210

with a gray fur hat he had bought in Moscow, and his eyes watered from the cold.

34

It was only seven in the evening, or so said the clock in the small living room, but it had been dark for quite some time already. Katrina washed her face with ice-cold water and felt a little more refreshed. She glanced outside, through the living room window, and couldn't see a thing. It was pitch black out, with mounds of dirty snow painting murky white stains in the sea of dark ink that surrounded the house. A reflection of the reading lamp appeared in the window, as did the figure of Ya'ara, who emerged stretching from the study where she had been resting. Katrina grabbed hold of the thick curtain and closed it completely. She went over to the radiator and turned the dial. "I'm turning up the heat a little. It's cozy under the comforter, but the cold gets into my bones like this," she said, tightening her shawl around her. "Come, sweet child, let's sit in the kitchen."

They sat on either side of a small table that was covered with a red cloth. Alongside the steaming cups of tea stood a squat jar filled with black cherry jam. "Have a little. Taste some. Jams I'm good at. It's excellent." Their fingertips met in the center of the table, and Katrina suddenly clasped her two hands around Ya'ara's one.

"I want to tell you something. It's important for me to tell you, because I couldn't tell Igor the truth. And the lie, the lie" — her throat tightened for a moment — "it weighed heavy on all we shared, our true love, our destitute love."

Ya'ara looked into Katrina's face and whispered almost inaudibly: "I'm listening."

"I fell in love with your father, Galinka, out of the blue, in an instant. Without intending to. He wasn't a strikingly handsome or tall man with a particularly impressive physical presence. But you know that naturally. A thin man, not very tall, modest and gentle. After you got to know him you learned of course that he had the eyes of an artist, and a beautiful soul and enthralling passion, too. Perhaps I shouldn't be saying such things to his daughter, but we don't have time for niceties. When I first saw him at the museum, I could see the way in which he was conversing, talking without words, with the painting hanging there in front of him, a work by a Russian artist, I think, or French. Those kinds of things had never concerned me. I was at the museum only for the peace and quiet it offered. And suddenly I wanted — desperately wanted — him to speak to me just like that, too. To be able to listen to me and see me, and to be able to give me things I'd never had before in my life.

"I told your father that I was married and worked as an interpreter. That wasn't the truth. I do indeed earn a living today as a translator, as I've already told you, translating technical material. But that's the present. Back then, I worked for the KGB. I'd been a part of the organization for almost twenty years already when I met your father. I was recruited at a very young age, immediately after I graduated from university. I studied foreign languages and literature. I was very beautiful back then, and adventurous, and I loved my country. Still today, here in this remote location, and maybe even because I'm here in the middle of nowhere, I love Russia. I was assigned to the First Chief Directorate, which was responsible for KGB operations abroad. I was a dedicated and loyal field operative. We worked hard. The things I did! But that's not what I want to talk about. I was never married. The opportunity never arose, and perhaps I never met the right man. Work always came first anyway. And second and third." A small glint appeared in Katrina's eyes. A tired smile. "But I fell pregnant. The result of a brief and whirlwind relationship with a handsome military officer, ten years older than me. He was in the fast lane. And married, of course. He got a slap on the wrist when the story emerged, a letter of reprimand in his file, his promotion put on hold for two years, but he was talented, and well connected, and they didn't want to ruin his career. And me, stubborn me, I rejected the warm offer of those who knew about the affair, to have an abortion and move on. Having an abortion in Russia at the time wasn't a problem, and I don't think things have changed. A woman in Russia has say over her own body, and she and no one else decides what she does with it. She, and sometimes the party. They didn't make things difficult for me, they just wanted the mishap to be resolved quickly. I went on leave for a few months, moved in with my mother, had the baby, and we raised Natalya together, my sweet mother and I. And after four months, my mother continued to take care of my beautiful baby and I went back to work. I used to spend weeks at a time outside the Soviet Union, one trip after another, operation after operation after operation.

"One day, toward the end of the 1980s, just a few months before the fall of the Berlin Wall, I was summoned to a special meeting. I reported to the offices of the directorate's Tactical Planning Division. I learned later that the division was responsible for special, highly classified undercover operations. The division wasn't even based there. It was a cover office of sorts inside the Lubyanka headquarters. I got there and a young man immediately asked me to accompany him. We went down to the underground parking garage and left from there in an unmarked car for a different facility, in southern Moscow. Oh, Galina, I don't even know if any of this interests you, but at my age — who's left for me to talk to? Anyway, we arrived at an industrial building in an area of garages and workshops. That's where I met the colonel. His name isn't important just now. He was dressed, of course, in civilian clothing, and told me after politely introducing himself that from that moment onward I belonged to them. I was a part of them and was now working with them. He told me I'd been drafted into

216

the division responsible for handling a small and particularly classified group of spies working for the Soviet Union in key locations around the world. Top-level agents, he termed them. A special committee headed by the commander of the directorate himself decided which agents were transferred to the division. My job would be to provide cover, security, and operational assistance to the agents' handlers. Every case is a unique case, he said, and my role would be determined in keeping with the special requirements of each operation. And that's how I met your father."

"I don't understand," Ya'ara whispered. "Are you saying my father was a top-level KGB agent?"

"No, no, don't be crazy! Your father an agent? Are you serious? What would he have filed reports about, the deliberations of the Bat Yam Artists Association? Don't get me wrong, my dear. Your father was an innocent and honest man. He was an artist. Period. You knew him better than I did, after all, even though you don't look like him at all. Anyway, my work took me, among other places, to Israel, too, and so, only because I was in your country on a mission that had nothing at all to do with Igor, only because of that did fate bring us together.

"I can tell, in fact, that my story *does* interest you," Katrina said with a bitter smile. And to sweeten it, perhaps, she scooped up some jam with her teaspoon and stirred it into her tea without bringing the fruit preserve to her lips. "I don't know the identity of the agent we were handling in Israel. Compartmentalization was very tightly observed, so if I didn't have to know something, I wasn't told. The agent was referred to as Cobra, that I knew. After all, we had to use some code name in the operational orders, on the expense report forms, on all the endless paperwork that accompanied our operations. Sometimes I felt more like a desk clerk than a field operative. I also knew that he was very important, and that we were investing a great deal of time, effort, and money in him. Even his handler himself was a rare and valuable resource. He was a long-serving KGB operative, who worked very deep under cover, as deep as possible, in the United States. We must have handled Cobra under the guise of being Americans; it's the only way to explain why such a valuable asset was assigned to the operation. Just imagine, an officer living in the United States as an American, for all intents and purposes. Believe me, he really did look and sound like an authentic American. His cover was perfect, as if we had tailored it ourselves, aside from once. I knew he was actually Russian by birth. There's a look in the eyes that only a Russian can have. He went by the name of Brian Cox, but I didn't know his real identity. I'd meet with him during his trips to Europe, in Switzerland or Italy usually. We traveled to Israel together as colleagues. He operated under a Canadian passport, and his cover was that of a professor of the ancient Near East. He truly was an expert in the art of the ancient world, he knew a lot and told me quite a bit during the long hours we spent together, waiting for a flight or a meeting or a final briefing before a round of meetings with an agent. Sometimes we'd visit a local museum together, or even exhibitions of small collections at universities. He was an avid admirer of the art of the Middle Ages, and whenever possible we'd visit cathedrals and churches, where he'd lecture me enthusiastically about the murals and sculptures and ancient sacred artifacts. It was a hobby of sorts for him, he said, and he certainly knew a great deal. Of course, I'm pretty sure it was a lot more than just a hobby. It wasn't simply a cover. He lived the subject, understood it, was a true expert." Katrina's gaze turned distant and Ya'ara could tell that she had never had anyone to talk to about the things she had experienced over the years. Katrina pulled herself together and continued: "Like him, I received my documentation for the specific assignment only once we were in Europe, to carry with me to the operational arena. I operated under a different identity each time we met. French, Swiss, or Belgian. My French is near perfect, which made things a lot easier. Confronted by a Belgian, I'd say I was Swiss; if the person talking to me was Swiss, I was from France — and so on. Look," Katrina smiled again, "can you believe it? You're getting a crash course in espionage. Anyway, when we met, Cobra's handler and I, I'd accompany him as his research assistant, and if the cover so required, I was his mistress, too. All men, including police officers and interrogators, are respectful of affairs on the side, and if they're led to believe they're touching on delicate territory, they'll remain discreet. It's always easier to operate as a couple, a man and a woman. You're spared a lot of questions. My assignments in Israel, or anywhere else we met with him, also included providing security for Cobra, to ensure he got to the meetings unaccompanied, without anyone on his tail. And to make sure that Brian wasn't being followed either. I was also there to act as the liaison with the Russian embassy, but only if left with no alternative. We didn't want to go anywhere near the embassy, because we assumed the Shin Bet kept it under surveillance. I went into the embassy only once during all my visits to Israel. Brian had some kind of a problem with his secret communications system, and I had to get him a new diskette from our representatives at the embassy, from the *Rezidentura.* Just once. And I noticed thereafter that I was being followed and it took me a few hours to put them to sleep, to bore them, and then to give them the slip so I could meet up again with Brian and give him what he needed."

"So you don't know Cobra's name then?"

"I don't know anything about him. I saw him, of course, but never from up close. Slim, average height, smooth, dark hair. He may have been thirty or perhaps even forty. Brian once pointed him out from afar. 'There, you see, that's him, that's him,' he said. That was enough for me. And I also know he has a birthday in late January or early February."

"How do you know that?"

"On one of the occasions when we met with him in Israel, Brian said something about it being his, Cobra's, birthday. He made a point of celebrating it with him. He brought him a gift, a token of his love and attention, pulled it out of his pocket like a magician, and the next thing I saw was an ivory statuette from the Middle Ages balancing in the palm of his hand. It was winter. Cold even in your part of the world. I'm almost certain it was in late January. And I remember Brian telling me they hadn't had such a snowy and cold Christmas in ages. It didn't really mean much to me, we didn't celebrate Christmas, as you know. He was talking about the United States, of course.

"And then, my lovely girl, during one of my visits to Israel with Brian, who was there to meet with Cobra, I met your father. He was so different from all the people I used to work with, so different from any man I had ever known. His entire world was different. Clean and bright. And our eyes met. And I knew, I knew, of course, that developing close ties with strangers was strictly forbidden. A violation of all our rules and regulations. But I said to myself: I deserve something, too. I deserve something unsoiled, something that is mine alone. I hadn't loved anyone in years. Constant vigilance and a sense of self-preservation always overpowered any desire for romance or even a flirtation. I was a mother, I couldn't run around like a fool, and when I had free time, I devoted myself to Natalya. I didn't want her to be only her grand-mother's child. And all of a sudden I was forty, and my beauty was starting to fade, and I had no one other than Natalya in my life, and all the rules and regulations and procedures were so hard to live with some-times. So didn't I deserve a chance at love? How often in life do you run into someone you've been searching and searching for without even knowing, and suddenly your eyes meet?"

"I think I know what you mean," Ya'ara said. "Even though I don't work in an organization with so many regulations and restrictions. In high-tech anything goes, but there's so little time for anything . . . Yet I still managed to meet Eran, my husband." She smiled warmly, and their eyes met. "But what you said about the rarity of love, about everyone deserving true love, about the right to act on an opportunity if one hap-pens to come your way . . . that, I think I get."

"In any event," Katrina continued, "that marked the beginning of those sweet and wonderful years during which your father and I were in contact. And although we saw

223

each other only once a year, for just a few days, we exchanged letters in the interim, and the bond we formed, through the written word, was magical. We sustained and nurtured our love affair at the pace of the eighteenth century. And then we'd meet again. I always told myself that things would work out well in the end. That the impossible situation in which we found ourselves would resolve itself somehow. That one day we'd be able to be a real couple, that we'd be able to live a real life, together."

"Did you meet only in Israel, you and my father?"

"Almost every time. Except for once. Brian had arranged to meet with Cobra in Geneva. I traveled to Switzerland via Germany, and I was due to return to Moscow via Germany, too. I wrote to Igor to tell him we could meet in Germany, if it suited him. And he came, of course. After the meetings with Cobra, my task was to further establish my cover as a simultaneous translator, and to do so I attended a conference at the University of Heidelberg. Brian went on his way, and I returned to Frankfurt and took a train from there to Heidelberg, where Igor was waiting for me in the small lobby of the hotel by the time I arrived. My heart melted when I saw him there."

"Did someone find out about you in the end?" Ya'ara asked. "Is that why you ended the relationship with my father? I mean, did the KGB learn somehow that you were involved romantically contrary to regulations?"

"They're very strict when it comes to such things, relationships like that. It's not viewed merely as a bureaucratic transgression. I can even understand it from their perspective. But I didn't want to see the world only through the eyes of the organization. I had eyes of my own, and I wanted my view to prevail just once."

"What happened? How did it happen?"

"I went ahead and opened a private post-office box in Moscow, so I could receive letters from your father without having him send them directly to my residential address. I told Igor it was because of my husband. So that a letter from him, from Igor, didn't mistakenly end up in his hands.

"The thing I forgot, even though I shouldn't have as a KGB operative myself, was that they carried out random checks on the post-office boxes. The KGB, not my directorate, but the one that dealt with internal security, systematically checked the post-office boxes throughout the empire. Checked who opened a post-office box, how

225

frequently letters arrived to the box, whether they came from inside Russia or from abroad, and so on. The post-office branch managers were working in the service of the KGB, of course, and it was routine work, in fact. Systematic, gray, and carried out by all security services, I'm sure. And they stumbled upon my post-office box one day. I don't know if they simply ran my name through the computer and revealed that Katrina Geifman was one of their own, a member of the KGB, or if the branch manager told them that the box served only mail from abroad. And I don't know if they opened Igor's letters, or if they contacted me immediately on learning I had a private post-office box at the branch. I was told, of course, after being summoned to the Internal Affairs Division, that they were approaching me as colleagues, and that they wanted to hear the explanation from me directly. But I believe they waited things out for a while for operational purposes, and read several of my letters from Igor before they called me in for questioning. Why wouldn't they have? Why forgo such obvious leverage over a subject under investigation? I would have done the same. But that invasion of my privacy still causes me to blush with shame. Can you imagine it?

Foreign hands opened the letters that were meant only for me, foreign eyes read the private words written on the pages. And I can just imagine the comments they must have made to one another, their coarse remarks. Getting hard simply from reading other people's letters. Miserable bastards."

Katrina paused for a moment. The light in the small kitchen suddenly faded. The two women sat there facing each other, in silence.

"And how did it all end?" Ya'ara asked.

"When they asked me about the post-office box, I told them everything right away. There wasn't much to hide, and there was certainly no point in trying. Either they knew already, or they'd get it out of me without much effort. I told them I had met a man and had fallen in love. I swore to them that I hadn't told him anything, nothing about the organization and nothing about the real reason I was in Israel. I told them everything I knew, yet they continued to badger me for days on end. I wasn't arrested, however, and I was released to spend the night at home every evening, but I underwent questioning all day long for days. Initially by one pair of interrogators, and then by others. They brought a woman in, too, at some stage of the questioning, someone of my age, more or less. They must have thought I'd tell her things I wasn't willing to tell the others. She certainly did take a different approach with me, one woman conversing with another. The sessions with her didn't even take place at the offices of the Internal Affairs Division. I could breathe with her. We walked through parks, sat at cafés, strolled along the riverbank. And we chatted. Some girls' talk, some moaning about life, a lot about men, all men, their nonsense, their childishness. I was questioned later by a more senior officer. We went through the same things all over again. They didn't have much to question me about, so they went through the same things time and again. Primarily to verify that my and Igor's story was the entire story, and that Igor wasn't a Shin Bet agent who was on to me, and that I hadn't revealed KGB secrets and definitely hadn't breathed a word about Cobra to him or anyone else. I was summoned a few weeks later to a disciplinary hearing. To this very day I can still close my eyes and feel myself standing there, in that large and magnificent room in the old section of the Lubyanka, which served as a palace in the days of the czar. I walked in and was told to sit down. I sat on the lone chair that had been placed in the

very center of the room. Sitting some five
or six meters from me were the three members of the disciplinary committee. And
hanging on the wall behind them was a large
Soviet Union flag alongside the insignia of
the KGB. The shield and the sword. The
chairman of the committee, a senior officer
from the Manpower and Resources Admin-
istration, addressed me and said: First of
all, Katrina Geifman, you have to promise
to sever all ties with Igor Abramovich immediately. And what if I decide — I asked
on the verge of breaking down emotionally
— what if I decide to leave the organization
and continue my relationship with him, with
the man I love? Look, said the committee
chairman, the heart does what the heart
wants to do. But if that's the case, we will
throw the book at you, Katrina Geifman. As
you know, you've not only violated the
regulations of the organization, but you've
also broken the laws of the state. Moreover,
you've committed a series of explicit criminal offenses, namely maintaining unlawful
contact with a foreign national, conspiring
to undermine state security, breach of trust,
and the illegal use of state property. We
won't be the ones to try you for your offenses, the courts will do that. But we,
Katrina, we want to make it easier on you,

we want to avoid handing your case over for criminal prosecution. You never know how that could turn out for you. And there's another thing." He paused for a moment and cleared his throat. "The matter of Natalya, your daughter. If you are convicted and sent to prison, a very real possibility, who will take care of her? My mother's already looking after her today, I argued. Come now, your mother isn't a young woman anymore, and if you're convicted, the blemish on your record will undermine Natalya's chances of graduating from school honorably and going on to academic studies that suit her talents. Guardianship of Natalya will have to be passed on to the state. With you in prison and Natalya being raised by a foster family or in an institution for young girls, there'll be no justification for leaving your mother in her apartment. Three rooms for a woman on her own? That doesn't sit well with our concept of social justice. But all of that, dear comrade, will be out of our hands and in those of the other authorities, the criminal prosecution, the courts, the social services, and the municipal housing committee. You'll be able, of course, to argue your case. Every citizen, even a criminal, even someone in breach of his duties, has the right to have his say and to be afforded a fair chance to argue the charges against him. You can always try your luck. But due to your long years of service, and because you are fundamentally patriotic and loyal, and because we, the members of the disciplinary committee, are also people, after all, with hearts and feelings, who understand the loneliness you've been forced to live with due to your fieldwork, due to all of that, we want to offer you the easy and considerate way out. Without prison, and without having your daughter, Natalya, taken from you. So what we're expecting is for you to sit down now, under our supervision, and write your farewell letter to Igor Abramovich. Tell him that you will never be in touch again. Of course, you won't be able to remain in your post at the First Directorate. We believe you've gone beyond the point of no return and have nothing more to offer there. You'll be assigned to Border Police Headquarters, here in Moscow. Naturally you can forget about any promotions, and you'll be stripped of your operational bonuses, but you'll have a job, and you'll keep Natalya, and you won't be evicted from the apartment, and you can go on. And perhaps, when the dust settles, you'll find yourself a life partner.

"Give me a pen and paper, please," I said.

"Yes, Galinka, what choice did I have? How could I risk blackening Natalya's name forever? How could I risk losing her?

"They didn't make me the offer out of kindness. They wanted me to remain under their watchful eyes. That's why I wasn't expelled immediately from the organization. They wanted me to remain completely under their control. Oh, my, what a boring job they gave me! The days dragged on endlessly. Day after day after day. Such tedious work. And my longing for Igor. So heart-wrenching to begin with. But the feeling slowly dulled. My emotions became buried under the mountains of paperwork I handled every day and my feelings of guilt. I said to myself: That's it, Katrina, keep your head down, shut off your heart, and take care of what you have, your daughter, your mother, your small apartment — it's more than enough.

"My mother died a few years later, and Natalya left home to go study at the Academy of Sciences. I was then informed by the manpower department that I was being transferred to district headquarters in Dimitrovgrad. I went. What else could I have done? And two years ago, I took early retirement. I decided to remain here. Perhaps out of habit. Natalya had started a family and had built a life for herself far from here. I didn't want my bitterness to have any influence on her and her sweet daughters, my granddaughters. I see them once a year, I spent some time with them just a few weeks ago, over New Year's and *Novy God,* our festive season. And I live my life here, peacefully, without bothering anyone."

"You said earlier that Cobra's handler looked and sounded like an American in every way — except for once. What did you mean by that?" Ya'ara asked.

"Well, okay. I told you already that I have a talent for languages. And I have a particularly sensitive ear when it comes to accents. On one of the occasions when I met up with Brian, ahead of a series of meetings with Cobra, we were held up for a while. Cobra failed to arrive on the scheduled day, and in keeping with procedures we were supposed to wait twenty-four hours to give him a chance to show up. Agents aren't always able to report in on the precise date scheduled for them in advance. Last-minute disruptions can always come into play. In any event, we had to wait. We were in Munich, I think. Yes, without a doubt. I remember the spectacular stained-glass ceiling of the *Vier Jahreszeiten,* the Four Seasons Hotel. We had to pass the time. It was wintry and horrible outside, so we drank at the bar. Quite a lot. Brian and I always spoke English in public. We lived our covers. We only spoke Russian behind closed doors. And even then, never anywhere where someone might be listening in. Anyway, we drank quite a lot and chatted. We spoke English to the barman, too. And suddenly my ear caught the sound of another accent under Brian's perfect American one. A hint of another accent. I told you I'm sensitive to such things."

"What accent?"

"It was just a hint, like a current of warm water that flows through a cold river all of sudden. It sounded like an Australian accent, possibly South African. I didn't catch it again, and didn't give much thought to it anyway. But it was there. I'm sure of it."

Ya'ara remained silent for a short while. And then, with a warm look squarely in Katrina's eyes, she quietly asked, "If you ran away from it all, if you remained silent for all these years, how come you were willing to meet with me? What made you tell me all that you have?"

"I can't really say, Galinka. Maybe to prove to myself that there's still a little life left in me. That I'm not completely dried out just yet. Perhaps to rebel, maybe for the last time. To tell someone finally about those awful officials. Thank you for Igor's letter, and for the sketch. And his tie pin. It was nice of you all to think of me. And anyone who is wise enough to select a woman as attentive and pleasant and lovely as you deserves to be told the things he wanted to know."

Both women went silent and Ya'ara waited, because Katrina appeared to have something more to say.

"Nevertheless, perhaps you shouldn't have underestimated the strength of an old woman's memory. After all, Galina's eyes were green and yours are blue, almost gray. Rarely seen eyes. You probably assumed I'd simply think I was mistaken. That I'd blame myself for not remembering very well. But as you've seen, my memory hasn't faded over the years, certainly not when it comes to matters of significance. Galina had the exact same eyes as Igor. What can I say? You really are very sweet and attentive. And what do I know? Maybe your name really is Galina. Or Natasha perhaps, or Anna? And now, I need to rest a little and you need to leave."

Ya'ara rose from her chair, a sudden dull pain in her stomach. She walked into the adjacent room, and Katrina made her way toward the front door, looking at her in silence. Ya'ara put on her fur coat and tightened the scarf around her neck. Laying her bag on the floor, she walked over to Katrina and embraced her, holding her close for quite some time. Katrina kissed her cheeks, and Ya'ara could feel the moistness of her tears. Their saltiness. Ya'ara then opened her bag, rummaged through it, and retrieved a bottle of her perfume. "It's almost full," she said. "Take it. Something for you to remember me by," and she closed Katrina's hand around the bottle. She stepped out into the icy darkness, and Katrina gently closed the door behind her. The headlights of the taxi Katrina had ordered for her glimmered in the blackness and it chugged toward her. Aslan, still in hiding on the other side of the street, watched Ya'ara get into the taxi and head off toward the city. Minutes later, he saw a large black car approaching, its headlights going black as it drove on in total darkness for a few dozen meters more, before taking up a lookout position nearby the house. Two large and cumbersome figures remained seated in the front of the car, their eyes on Katrina's residence. Aslan watched them for a full hour. When the lights in Katrina's house went out, he began making his way through the thick vegetation and away from the road, reaching the bank of the river a few minutes later. An icy mist hovered over the water, and the current hissed like a giant snake. Aslan picked up his pace and began making his own way toward the city.

35

Tel Aviv, February 2013

"Drama, such drama," Aharon declared to the team members sitting around him. "Ya'ara and Aslan's trip has yielded outstanding progress! Hagar Beit-Hallahmi's gut feeling has been confirmed. Her suspicions concerning a link between the mysterious woman, Katrina Geifman, and the Cobra affair have been verified!"

"Let's do this in an orderly fashion," Michael said. "You've all received a copy of Ya'ara's report. Now let's see what we've learned. Adi?"

"Okay, here goes," Adi began. "In the late 1980s and early nineties, the KGB was running a top-level Israeli agent code-named Cobra. He may still be active today, but that we don't know.

"Cobra's handler went by the name of Brian Cox — or rather, he used a Canadian passport in that name for his trips to Israel

238

to meet with and brief Cobra. The name in all likelihood isn't his real one or even the name under which he lives or operates in the framework of his permanent cover, since Katrina told Ya'ara that after arriving in Europe they'd receive new passports with which to travel to Israel for their mission. Brian Cox is a Russian KGB officer who is living deep undercover in the United States. He has the ability to pass himself off as an American for all intents and purposes. He lived at the time in a region of the United States in which the Christmas period is cold and snowy. He may still be living there today. My guess is that he lived on the East Coast, but that's just a gut feeling. There are several other cold and snowy places in America, but not with renowned schools. So we're probably looking for a professor of ancient history, of the Near East perhaps, maybe even of art history, at a prestigious university in the eastern United States.

"Cobra in the late 1980s was probably in his thirties, or early forties perhaps. Average height, slim, straight dark hair. Katrina's description. It doesn't tell us much. It could fit thousands of people."

"Cobra has a birthday in late January or early February," Ya'ara added. "And we know that he traveled at least once to

Geneva, Switzerland, to meet with his handlers."

"Cobra was in Geneva in late March or early April of 1989," Adi said.

"How do we know that?" Michael asked.

"According to Hagar, Igor Abramovich traveled abroad just twice after immigrating to Israel," Adi responded. "Once with his wife to Cyprus, and once, in the late 1980s, to Germany. That second trip corresponds with the time and place of Brian Cox's series of meetings with Cobra in Geneva. Katrina met up with Igor in Heidelberg, Germany, immediately after Geneva. I found Igor's passport in one of the boxes Ya'ara received from his daughter. Based on the stamps, he left Israel and entered Germany on April 5, 1989. He returned to Israel a week later, on April 12. The meetings with Cobra took place just before then, either at the end of March or the beginning of April 1989."

"Anything else?"

"Yes," said Ya'ara. "I think the feelings Katrina displayed to me were authentic. I think that she really tried through me to touch on that deep love she shared with Igor Abramovich. It appears in the operational report. Katrina knew from the very first moment that I wasn't who I had said I was.

She knew right away that I wasn't Igor's daughter. She even said so in no uncertain terms."

"And what does that tell you, Ya'ara?" Michael asked, as if to test her.

"That we were lucky. Katrina had her own reasons for speaking to me — revenge or anger, perhaps a desire to make amends. In any event, I think it tells us that we're in a race against time. At some point, very soon, the Russians will learn that we're after their man. It could already be happening as we speak. I'm not saying that Katrina is going to speak to someone about me, about us. But she herself knows. It's like the gun in Chekhov's play. It has already appeared and will be fired in one of the coming acts."

"I can see that your theater studies have had an effect on you," Aharon remarked dryly, and Ya'ara remained silent, choosing not to remind him that she was studying film. "But you do have a point."

"And don't forget the black car that showed up in operational mode to stake out Katrina's residence," Aslan said. "That only reinforces what Ya'ara's been saying. Although we did manage to leave Russia without any problems, making sure, too, that no one was on our tail. Sticking to our cover story, we went on to Kazan and then returned to Moscow. We checked ourselves in both cities and we were clean. It may take them a while to check all the facts, Katrina may not be helping them, things may move slowly there. But if they have started to sniff around, they'll realize eventually that something is going on. If they're still in contact with Cobra, they may warn him. We need to move fast."

"So what are we doing now?" Michael asked, his gaze taking in the full team.

"I'm making progress with the database of potential suspects," Adi said. "Theoretically, we can now start checking the names against dates of birth. Late January, early February; I'd say from January 15 to February 15, 1950, through to 1960. Remember, Cobra, according to Katrina, was thirty to forty years old in the late 1980s. We can also check who left the country during the two weeks leading up to April 5, 1989. After all, we know Cobra was in Switzerland at that time."

"What do you mean by being able to start running the check in theory? Why only theoretically?"

"Only theoretically because we don't have access to the Interior Ministry computers. We're undercover, remember?"

"It may be less theoretical than it appears," Amir said. "I have a friend, not really a friend, more like a contact, at the Interior Ministry. He'll do my bidding, or he'll try to at least. After all, we're two Tiberias boys who served together in the army in a support company." He smiled.

"Excellent, excellent," Aharon Levin declared, appearing to suddenly shake himself from another world somewhere. "Very important. And I think the time has come for a short trip to the U.S. The American side to the story is critical. We have to try to get to this professor, Cobra's handler. This Brian Cox guy. Maybe the CIA has a lead that's linked to our case. I'll meet with Bill and we'll take it from there."

"Who's Bill?"

"It's a long story. A single evening wouldn't nearly suffice to tell it all. In short, however, Bill is William Ahab Pemberton. He was the CIA's station chief in Moscow in the 1990s. He served for more than a decade at one station — unprecedented. He subsequently served in other positions, including as head of the Psychological Warfare Unit. His final post was head of the Russia Division at CIA headquarters. He retired just a few months ago. He was rumored to be too old and too extreme for some people's tastes. A somewhat strange man, an odd man for sure. A fanatic, belligerent. Very devout, American style. A confirmed bachelor. Interested only in his agents. And ancient religious texts. A self-taught aficionado, but very knowledgeable on the subject, and a real expert in early Christianity. That may also have been something that connected him to us. Anyway, we ended up working together on several occasions. He had a great deal of interest in a certain contact of mine in the Soviet Union. We spent many nights in each other's company, the two of us and a bottle of Wild Turkey, of which nothing much remained come morning. The Soviet Union fascinated him, but he was strictly a bourbon man when it came to alcohol, not vodka. Yes, we need to meet with him as soon as possible. Ya'ara and Michael, I want you to come with me."

They nodded, their faces serious.

"And Amir. Find out if your contact can run a check on the list of names Adi's compiling. How many do you have so far?"

"Several hundred. It's a shot in the dark. I'm trying to draw up a list of people who could fit the definition of a top-level asset in Israel. It's a list, actually, of officeholders. I'm then adding the particulars I find on the Net. It's pretty disheartening, to be honest. I have no idea of my chances of coming up with a hit. Cobra, after all, could also be an aide to an aide of someone on the list. And if so, he won't even show up on the list at all."

"But then you'd hardly call him a top-level agent."

"We don't really know how the KGB defines its agents. Or how the head of the First Directorate selected the agents to be run by the Tactical Planning Division."

"True," Aharon said, "a lot of what we're doing is guesswork and supposition. But A, without any additional concrete information, we have no choice. And B, the intuition of experienced and wise individuals is something I hold in very high regard."

"QV Aharon Levin," Michael mumbled.

"I heard that," Aharon said, raising his eyebrows theatrically. "But yes, even the intuition of an old man like me still counts for something. Don't underestimate us old folk." He said "old folk" in a somewhat shaky voice, and Michael couldn't tell if he was joking or had simply decided to adopt a new manner of speech to befit his status. "But I really mean this," Aharon continued, "I look at this team I've selected, and I know we can do it. We're on the scent now and it will lead us forward, until we get our

245

hands on that piece of filth. And the scent is now taking me to Virginia."

And a few minutes later he announced to everyone: "I've spoken to Bill. He's expecting us. I told him to put out two extra glasses. The bourbon's on us."

36

Dimitrovgrad, February 2013

They made her wait for almost an hour. It was already five to nine, and the meeting had been scheduled for eight. FSB headquarters in Dimitrovgrad were located in a relatively small three-story office block. It looked ostensibly very much like the neighboring buildings, which were fronted by small businesses offering tools and spare parts for agricultural equipment. Aside from the guard post at the entrance and the barred windows on the first floor, it wasn't readily distinguishable from the adjacent structures. The flag of the Russian Federation flew unobtrusively on the wall of the building.

Katrina could guess what was coming next when the phone rang all of a sudden on Thursday afternoon. No, no, said a courteous voice, it isn't urgent. A routine inquiry, standard procedure. They hadn't been in touch with her for some two years, and now, immediately in the wake of a visit from someone who had presented herself as Igor's daughter, she was called in for a routine talk. Or a routine inquiry. It didn't really matter what they called it, especially since everyone clearly knew it was going to be an interrogation by the security services. Katrina tried to think who could have seen the young woman who had visited her and who had reported them to the local FSB office. She knew from experience that it could have been anyone. The taxi driver who had driven the young woman to her home, the neighbors across the street. Anyone could have reported seeing Katrina the recluse getting a visit at her home from a pretty young woman who could hardly have been her daughter or granddaughter. True, gone were the days when every second individual throughout the empire was an informer. The KGB's iron fist had been gloved in fur and leather. But Katrina wasn't a rank-and-file citizen. She had been banished to that remote city and had no doubt that the security organizations, even if they had changed their names, were keeping an eye on her. She didn't think she was under round-the-clock surveillance, that would surely be an unnecessary expense. But her phone was probably being tapped, sporadically at least, and the little mail she received was probably being checked, too. And the neighbors must have been instructed to report anything out of the ordinary in the life of their quiet neighbor.

She waited without a fuss. No one took the trouble to keep her posted on what was happening or to apologize for the delay. At nine-thirty, she noticed a man walking toward her. She knew him by name, Alexei Volkov, from her years spent working at the local office. They had never exchanged more than a few polite words, when passing one another in the corridor or standing in line at the cafeteria. He was fat and unkempt, his hair greasy and in need of a cut, his shirt crying out to be ironed. "Good morning," he said to her, not missing a stride, his right hand clutching a steaming cup of tea, a cardboard dossier tucked under his left armpit. "Come with me, please." They walked into an empty dusty office, and Alexei gestured for her to sit down. He circled the metal desk and sat down across from her with a grunt, his oversized stomach pressing against the edge of the piece of furniture and pushing it toward her. He opened the dossier and said, "Yes, yes. Katrina Geifman. Well, how's life been treating you since your retirement? I envy you. I still have a good few years to go before I can retire. And then only if the powers that be grant me permission. Anyway, you aren't here to listen to my problems." With an air of exaggerated importance, he retrieved a pen from his shirt pocket, reached for a notepad, cleared his throat, and said, "As you've already been told, this is merely a routine inquiry for some clarifications. We received a report last week about a foreign couple who had checked in to Hotel Lenin. Dimitrovgrad isn't a small town and it gets its fair share of visitors, but they were the only foreign couple staying at the hotel at this time of the year. Two guests from Israel. We'd have been guilty of gross negligence had their presence not caught our attention. We checked with our usual sources, the kind you're familiar with — you worked here for years, after all. And we learned via the taxi company that the woman had been to see you. You, Katrina Geifman. A stranger, from another country, comes to see you, a former employee of the Federal Security Service. She comes all the way to Dimitrovgrad in the dead of winter to see you. That's unusual. And it certainly warrants a report, Katrina. And you didn't make one."

"I haven't had a chance yet to report it,"

Katrina responded apologetically. "And there really is nothing to report. She's the daughter of someone I once knew. It's all there in my personal file, there isn't anything new to add. But the issue is classified. In any event, the man died years ago. His daughter contacted me only now. She was coming to Russia anyway. A business trip to Moscow. Something concerning her family in Kazan. I was happy to see her, we reminisced about her father. That's all."

"Did she tell you anything about her partner?"

"Not much. They're coworkers and they're involved with each other. I don't really know her very well at all. I knew her father. I wanted to hear about him. I've wondered for many years what became of him."

"Is there anything else I should know? Did she want something from you? Did she offer you anything? Did you make any arrangements with her, another meeting at some point in the future perhaps?"

"No. We spoke in general terms about keeping in touch. Of course she didn't ask me for anything. What could I have to offer her? A pleasant young woman, polite. That's all."

Alexei scratched his head, scribbled a few lines on the piece of paper in front of him, and said: "Okay, Katrina. But the next time you make contact with a foreigner, or a foreigner contacts you, make sure you inform us before we come to you. I realize that you don't view such things as matters of urgency, but procedures apply to pensioners, too. You know that and have signed all the relevant documentation accordingly. Have a good day, and if you remember anything I may need to know," he said, before pausing for a few seconds with a stern look on his face, "if you remember anything, call and let me know. I'm sure you still remember the central telephone number."

37

Virginia, February 2013

Michael drove. Ya'ara was in the front next to him. And Aharon dozed at the back, his head against the window. The road narrowed after they turned off the freeway, embracing the contours of the hills, densely packed gray, bare trees rising skyward along its edges. Patches of pure white snow shone from time to time from within the woodland, but the earth was brown and muddy. Strange not to come across any other cars, Michael thought. A sudden curve caused him to turn sharply to the left. He could feel he'd been driving a little too fast. The car's tires lost their grip for a moment, and the vehicle began drifting to the right. Michael pressed his foot down on the gas, and the car accelerated and straightened out. He exhaled, his eyes now fixed on the road. "Good driving," Ya'ara remarked. And from the back Aharon mumbled something like,

"There'd be no need for good driving if you were going a little slower. What's the rush? Do you think he's running away? We've got the whisky, don't forget."

"I wonder what this Ahab is like," Ya'ara said.

"Bill. His name's Bill. What's he like? You'll see soon enough."

The woodland gave way to fruit orchards. "Apples or pears?" Ya'ara wondered out loud. "Apples," Aharon responded. "The blossoms in April and May are spectacular. This entire valley turns white." And then the trees were back, closing in on the road again. A raccoon raced across the narrow stretch of tarmac. Michael had cracked open his window and cold, clean air was blowing into the car. If it weren't colorless, it would surely have been a light shade of blue, its unadulterated crispness like fire in the lungs.

"Some people retire to an estate buried in this beauty while others aren't allowed a moment's peace," Aharon grumbled from his comfortable position at the back, his eyes still closed.

"How can you see anything if you're sleeping," Ya'ara taunted him.

"Don't start with him, do me a favor."

William Ahab Pemberton received them dressed in a dark blue Chinese silk robe. He embraced Aharon and then backed away a little, still holding on to his visitor with both hands. "You haven't changed a bit, my dear friend. Was the drive okay? Come, come, don't be shy! Welcome to my humble abode."

Humble it wasn't. Michael and Ya'ara volunteered to make coffee for everyone, while Aharon and Bill went to sit in the den. A fire was burning in the fireplace, casting tongues of light over the bookshelves that covered all four walls of the room. A large computer monitor displayed the image of an ancient manuscript, but the language in which it was written was impossible to distinguish from afar. Open books with yellow Post-it notes poking out from among their pages lay strewn across the large desk. Just like the battlefield — the antique desk — of my first coach, Michael thought, suddenly remembering his internship under the Supreme Court president. Memories of the chill of the stone walls of the old building in Jerusalem's Russian Compound came back to him, and he could almost smell the dust and pine resin. There weren't many Moroccan interns at the Supreme Court at the time, he thought to himself. I wonder if it looks a little different today. He pushed his memories aside and returned willingly to the icy cold of Virginia in late February, to the dimly lit den and its bookshelves glowing in the light of the fire.

"Here we go, I'm putting the tray here," Michael said, bending over a low table that was standing alongside the leather armchair in which Bill was sitting.

"We raided your kitchen," Ya'ara gleefully declared. "Nut cookies."

Aharon reached into the duty-free bag he was holding and pulled out a cardboard box containing a bottle of Laphroaig, a single malt Scotch whisky. "Ten years old!" he announced. "Not bourbon. Whisky distilled on the remote island of Islay."

"I think I'm up for the challenge," Bill responded.

"Michael, do a little more raiding and bring us four glasses and a bucket of ice. You're drinking with us, right?" he asked, turning to Ya'ara.

"Of course I am. Laphroaig is my middle name."

Aharon gave her a look of admiration mixed with irony. "Where did you find this girl?" he asked Michael, who had returned carrying a tower of heavy glasses.

"No one finds Ya'ara. She's a free spirit," Michael replied.

"Umm, hello," said Ya'ara. "I'm here, right here."

"I'm waiting," Bill said to Aharon, who promptly began pouring the amber-colored liquid into his host's glass, its smoky scent delightfully filling his nostrils. Groaning slightly, he then turned his attention to the ice bucket in an effort to trap a cube between the silver tongs.

"Here, let me help you," Ya'ara said, and the glow from the flames in the fireplace illuminated the unpolished pearls around her neck.

"So that's the story," Aharon concluded, forty-five minutes later. "You now know all we do. We've come to you to see if there's anything that maybe, just maybe, rings a bell from your perspective. Like I said, there's an American side to this Cobra affair. Cobra's handler is a Russian intelligence official who is living very deep undercover in the United States. He may have been born here, in America, or he may have come here at a young age. He appears to have an Australian or South African background. Whatever the case, the KGB entrusted him with the handling of one of its top-level agents. What do we know about him? Next to nothing. He's able to pass himself off as an authentic American, his cover is that of an academic, an expert on the ancient Near East. Knowledgeable on the subject of ancient art. His Canadian passport identifies him as Brian Cox, but that of course means nothing."

Bill remained silent, his eyes closed, the fingers of his right hand tapping on the armrest of his chair. "You've assumed from the outset that Brian is American," he then said. "But theoretically at least he could also be Canadian. I'd like to consider that possibility, too. From my experience, however, Brian's Canadian passport suggests in fact that he's from the United States. It fits the Soviets' modus operandi — disconnection and misdirection, and the more the better. If this Brian guy is based in the United States, his operational passport will probably be a Canadian one. And vice versa. Your Katrina also said he was from the United States. She didn't say why she thought so, but she probably came to that conclusion based on the various indications she received, and despite their stringent compartmentalization procedures. So Brian in all likelihood is from here, from the United States, that's the first thing. Second, he probably really is a professor. Field operatives typically go for a cover story they find easy to live with. They only change the particulars that could expose them. So where in the U.S. is he from? Yes, several regions experience snowy winters. But, just like your intelligence officer, by the way, my money's on the East Coast. The newer universities in the U.S. have indeed started to develop faculties dealing in classical studies and the study of the ancient world in recent years. But if Brian really is an expert on the subject of the ancient Near East, he's far more likely to be from Yale and not the University of Nebraska. And this is where I have something that could tie in with your story. It may be a little out there, a shot in the dark of sorts, but it ties in with something you said. And as a rule, never underestimate the instincts of an old bloodhound."

Silence fell in the room. And although Aharon remained motionless in his armchair, Michael could tell he was on edge. He recalled their drive to Ashdod, and the way in which Aharon had described Hagar Beit-Hallahmi in the same words, as an old bloodhound. He thought about all those bloodhounds in the service of intelligence agencies around the world, mythological figures in modern-day secret orders. Oh, my, the countless tales and legends that were woven around them. Tales passed on in a whisper. He himself had felt so at home in his secret order, and only now, in recent months, had he dared to poke his nose out and catch a whiff, cautiously but with a sense of euphoria, too, of the air of the real world. And Aharon Levin, the bastard, was dragging him back in now by the hair. Just look at what you've escaped from, Michael, he thought to himself, this is what happens to someone who wastes his time in the secret services, all the bloodhounds grow old eventually, and they withdraw to some real or imaginary estate, eagerly awaiting the arrival of pilgrims who come to drink from their fountains of experience and wisdom. And those pilgrims are so few and far between, Michael ruefully thought. And their numbers will dwindle further, and the world will close in on those old bloodhounds, and get increasingly smaller. He shook off his thoughts and listened attentively. Ya'ara was also looking intently at Bill Pemberton, her eyes open wide.

"You know," Bill began his story, the hint of a didactic tone in his voice, "even professional spy organizations make mistakes sometimes. And we earn our keep to a large extent from the mistakes of our adversaries. We wait for them patiently, for years on end. The trick is to be able to spot them. The KGB — or SVR, as Russia's foreign espionage service is known today — also makes mistakes. True, not very often. But it does make them. And a few months ago, just before my retirement, we stumbled upon one of them." He gave Michael a look that said it was time for a refill. Michael obliged, adding two cubes of ice. Bill continued. "More than a year ago, the Canadian Security Intelligence Service, with which we have a close working relationship, exposed a Russian agent in Montreal. How they got to him isn't important right now. Something to do with identifying the source of technological know-how that was leaked and found its way to Russia. The man in question is a Canadian who emigrated from Czechoslovakia at an early age and arrived in Canada as a young refugee. He was believed to be a KGB officer who had been planted in Canada under a false Czech identity. On the other hand, he may have been a real refugee who was recruited by the Soviets only after he'd been living in Canada for years. Whatever the case, he studied electrical and computer engineering at McGill University, graduated as an honors student, and was hired by a Canadian avionics — aviation electronics — company, whose clients include among others the Canadian National Defense Ministry and also our Pentagon. The Russians very rarely meet with their agents. Every such meeting, and certainly one that takes place in the country in which the agent is permanently based, puts the said agent at risk. But sometimes there's no alternative, you need to maintain direct contact with the agent so that he can hand over documents, so that you can pass on money or materials, so that you can thoroughly debrief him, so that you can keep his motivation at a high, preserve his courage, prevent him from acting in haste and doing something stupid. You know it as well as I do — an agent isn't a robot. He's an individual who requires human contact. With his handlers, too, especially with them.

"Like I said, meeting up with an agent in the country he calls home is risky. In our case, Canada would be the worst place in the world for the Russians to meet with this engineer, who was spying for them. Canada, naturally, is the Canadian Security Intelligence Service's home turf. That's where it is strongest. There it can put its capabilities to full use. Canada is also a dangerous environment, because there's always the risk of someone else being privy to the meeting: Colleagues from work, neighbors, family members, they all know the agent, they all see him on a daily basis and could notice a deviation from his regular routine. The Russians therefore wouldn't stage any of the lengthy, in-depth operational meetings in Canada itself. Certainly not in Montreal. The SVR would wait for the agent to travel to a trade conference, in Paris, let's say, or go on holiday with his family, to the Caribbean, for example. It's easier for them to operate outside the agent's natural territory, far from the watchful eye of the company's security officer and the national security service. They can then create significant windows of time in which to meet face-to-face, for lengthy periods, with their man. But at some points it seems they had no choice, and they needed to contact him in Montreal itself. They could do so sometimes indirectly, and that's usually preferable in terms of operational security, and sometimes they needed to make direct contact. Indirect contact can be facilitated by means of a drop point, or what we call a dead letter box."

Ya'ara wondered why he was talking to

them as if they were children, and explaining things they'd learned years ago. Perhaps it's a syndrome that affects all retired secret service officials, the desire to emphasize at all costs just how much better they are than their younger successors. Bill Pemberton continued: "A concealed drop point under a shrub in a public park, or a wall in which one of the bricks is loose, something like that. Somewhere you can hide something — a letter or list of codes, even money — and then leave a signal to let the agent know that something is waiting for him at the prearranged drop point. Even if you haven't read any John Le Carré — and I most certainly advise you to do so — you must have seen the BBC show *Smiley's People,* in which a yellow chalk mark on one of the trees serves to initiate contact with the agents. Moscow Rules, he calls it. And they really were put into practice. By the Russians, and also the British, and maybe even us, too. Who knows?"

Bill Pemberton broke off suddenly, guarding his secrets, and appearing to have lost his train of thought for a moment. But he hadn't. He sipped on his whisky and went on, his voice lower and his eyes half shut. "But as I said, this type of indirect contact isn't always enough. And it, too, involves a

264

fair amount of danger. The operation sometimes requires a meeting in person with the
agent, even if a very brief one. To this end,
the SVR maintains a network of, how
should I say, perhaps *couriers* is the right
word. We call them operative agents. Anyway, these couriers are trained to conduct
brief rendezvous with their agents. In a
crowded supermarket perhaps, on a park
bench, at a train station. The courier and
agent recognize each other, walk by each
other, sit momentarily on the same bench
maybe, something is passed from one hand
to another, rolled up in a newspaper perhaps, maybe in a shopping bag filled with
oranges. The courier is also sometimes
required to convey a verbal message, because the agent needs to hear a friendly
voice. So they do that, too.

"For reasons of operational security, the
SVR assigns a courier to each of its agents.
So that if an agent is exposed, or the courier
is exposed, they'll bring each other down
and that's it. Compartmentalization, as we
call it in the professional jargon, or hedging.
But when they're pressed for time, or when
a specific courier isn't available or the
particular mission is an urgent one and the
commanding officer is eager to get it done
and doesn't give a shit about some theory

that dictates how an agent should be handled — mistakes happen. Sometimes simply due to carelessness or negligence, or as a result of improper risk management. There'll always be a reason, and it'll usually be a good one even, and things work out in the end in general, because in most instances even when you make a mistake you don't get caught.

"Until you do. And that's just what happened in the case of our Canadian engineer. The Canadian Security Intelligence Service suspected him, followed him, and saw him meet with a young man on a park bench in the center of the city. Not far from the Prudential company's building, if you're familiar with it. A few minutes' walk from his firm's offices. In any event, the engineer got to the park and, according to the team on his tail, appeared tense and jittery. A few minutes later, a young man showed up and sat down next to him, without saying a word. And it was actually that lack of communication that caught the attention of the surveillance team. Usually if you want to sit down on a bench next to someone, you say something to them. You ask: Is this spot free? May I join you? Or you say something banal about the weather. In this instance — nothing. Not a word. Being antisocial or shy isn't a crime, but the surveillance team deemed it suspicious, and that's what counts. They filmed and photographed the encounter and then decided to abandon the engineer and follow the young man instead. After all, they could always go back to the engineer. He had a home. He had a job. They knew where to find him again. Anyway, a few minutes later, the young man got up from the bench and walked away. Again, without a single word to the engineer. The surveillance team wasn't able to see if the two men had exchanged anything. They were too far away, and an analysis later of the photographs failed to yield anything concrete. The engineer had come and gone in the possession of a brown paper bag, probably containing a sandwich or a piece of fruit or something. And the young man had arrived empty-handed, but of course he could have been carrying something in the pockets of the light coat he was wearing."

"And then what?" Ya'ara asked, after Bill paused and then remained quiet for a while.

"Nothing. Nothing at all. The team maintained its surveillance on the young man. He wandered around the city for a while, went into a café, returned to his hotel, and then remained there. Later that evening he went down to the bar, ordered something to eat, a club sandwich, fries on the side, a pint of beer. And that's it. The following day he took a cab to the airport and boarded a plane to Amsterdam. End of story.

"But it wasn't the end. The Canadians had photographs, and a visit to the hotel was all it took to get the young man's name and the details of the credit card he had used. The airline and Border Control provided them with his passport details as well. Thomas Langham. British. An inquiry with the Brits revealed that a Thomas Langham did indeed appear in their records, but they had no additional information on him. They would check. Strange that he arrived from the Netherlands and then returned there, but it's possible, it's legit, it's not a criminal offense. There are tens of thousands of Brits, and maybe even more, who don't live on their small and crowded island. And the Canadians ran a check with us, too. They passed on the name and the photographs. Both to us and to the FBI. And it's always an aging spinster on the desk who comes up with the goods. And that's exactly what happened this time, too."

Ya'ara lit up, seethed inside, in silence. Who the hell does he think he is — that chauvinist? Do I really have to travel halfway around the world only to run into smug, self-satisfied, judgmental, condescending men here, too? She didn't know why she was so angry. Why she could feel tears boiling in her eyes. After all, it wasn't as if she was hearing such things for the first time. And what had he actually said? Nothing terrible. Simply disrespectful. She could see that Michael had his eyes on her, and the look on his face told her that he knew exactly what was on her mind. He placated her with a concealed smile. She calmed down and remained silent. Bill continued.

"Maggie, one of our longest-serving desk officials, made the guy. The young man. She picked him out from a photograph of a class of cadets on an officers' training course of the Red Army's, Russian army's, Special Forces, from June 2008. Refusing adamantly to make use of any facial-recognition software, she picked him out using a magnifying glass. My eyes are the best software, she kept on saying to us. As stubborn as a mule. But she was right; no man-made software was going to spot him in the second row, fifth from the left. Presumably he was handpicked by the SVR recruiters and transferred from the army to them. Young, daring, just starting out. And that's how he spent his initial years in the organization. Doing rookie assignments. As a courier for a more important and senior agent. That's how everyone starts out. So far, no mistake. A bit of bad luck perhaps. Anyway, that's not the mistake I want to talk about. Agents do sometimes get exposed. Yes, the revelation that the young man was a Russian pretty much tied things up insofar as the case against the Canadian engineer was concerned. From an intelligence point of view at least. Our Canadian colleagues were left with the task of gathering sufficient evidence to prosecute and convict him in court. But that's not the interesting part of our story. What's interesting is the mistake the Russians made thereafter.

"They gave the young man another assignment to carry out. Unrelated to the Canadian agent. They had no idea that he had been uncovered, and they couldn't have known, because the Canadians' covert investigation into the engineer had yet to go public. Meanwhile, this so-called Thomas Langham, the Russian courier's assumed English name, as you recall, was added to our list of suspects at all our border crossings. The instructions were clear: Encountering a man by the name of Thomas Langham, date of birth such and such, at any American border crossing requires an immediate report to the nearest FBI field office. The FBI has offices, and even operational squads, at all the major airports. When it comes to the smaller border crossings, a report has to be made to the local field office. Don't detain the man, don't touch his luggage, don't take him aside for a customs check. Don't do a thing. We don't want him suspecting anything. Simply notify the nearest FBI office. If we're lucky, we'll be there and we'll be able to follow him. If luck isn't on our side, we'll try to locate him via alternative means. If we don't find him, we'll wait for the next opportunity. Most important, we don't want him to feel at risk and to cancel his plans.

"And we got lucky. The man who called himself Thomas Langham arrived in the U.S. via Boston's Logan Airport, where we have a surveillance team on hand on a permanent basis. Fortunately, too, the Homeland Security officials weren't as dumb as usual, and everything went smoothly. Langham landed, waited almost an hour in line, his name popped up on the blacklist, they asked him the usual questions, stamped his passport, and off he went. FBI officials were already waiting for him by the time he got to the baggage carousel, waiting and ready to follow him. Tracking him became a lot simpler from

271

the moment they saw what car he got into. It may be pretty easy to spot a tail when you're driving a car, but not if you're being monitored from the air. And the FBI had a drone. I told you we got lucky. Because the drone was in working order. The weather was good. And Thomas Langham set out in the direction of Rhode Island."

38

Moscow, FSB Headquarters, February 2013
"Names, names! The moron didn't ask for names!"

Captain Viktor Demedev was tearing his hair out — metaphorically speaking. His hair was so short that no amount of trying would have allowed him to get a proper grip on it anyway. Demedev was a desk chief at the so-called Credibility Department, the department responsible for preventing both current and former FSB employees from leaking secrets. The department's name, Credibility, was a remnant from the Stalinist period. Back then, they still opted for awe-inspiring names that only die-hard cynics dared to secretly term pompous, archaic, or pretentious. Whatever the case, despite the upheaval experienced by the Soviet Union, and despite the changes the KGB itself had undergone, the name, Credibility, still remained in place. However, even

273

though its name remained a constant, the department's methods had changed significantly. Its members during the darkest days of the empire were viewed as the KGB's butchers. And the widespread purging operations, to which the security services, too, were subjected, were carried out within the KGB by its very own people. Arrests in the dead of night, harsh interrogation methods, psychiatric and psychological manipulations, secret trials, and when necessary — a bullet in the back of the head. Over the years, these all gave way to bureaucratic, systematic, and well-organized intelligence work, to tenacious yet pertinent and humane interview sessions, and softer and more contained resolutions than in the past. There were those who longed in whispers for the days when things were put to bed at lightning speed, leaving no loose ends at all. The work the department did, however, remained professional and thorough, accompanied by a stringent, sometimes zealous, sense of duty. After all, who's going to protect the FSB, this huge and magnificent security service, if not the members of the department? With infinite patience and endless determination, only they had the wherewithal to identify the risks and weed out the rogue employees whose individual weaknesses posed a threat to the strength of the whole.

Demedev was holding the brief report that had come in from FSB headquarters in far-off Dimitrovgrad about the surprising visit paid to retired comrade Katrina Geifman. Yes, the system works, Demedev said to himself. At some point in her distant past, Geifman committed a serious violation of the organization's security procedures, and she was dealt with wisely by means of a transfer to a remote city, far from the real secrets with which she had busied herself previously, to a desk position of little significance. She remained there under the watchful eyes of her superiors and the Credibility Department's local representative. Until she was pushed a few years ago into early retirement and became a potential "person of interest," someone whose behavior and actions were monitored from time to time. The FSB's network of sources on the ground had been instructed to report anything out of the ordinary insofar as she was concerned. She was also required to report for a briefing once every two years. And her telephone line at home was subject to random tapping. And lo and behold, the moment something unusual did in fact occur, the system had functioned smoothly.

The hotel reported its foreign guests, the informer at the taxi rank made a report about the foreign woman who had gone to Geifman's residence, one of the neighbors added a report about an unusual visit to the house, and within two days Katrina was called in for questioning, defined as usual as a routine talk. All okay thus far. But that idiot Alexei Volkov, that moron, hadn't even asked Katrina Geifman for the name of her guest, the daughter of that man she had known in the past, that man whose name Volkov hadn't bothered to check out either.

Demedev did that himself. Okay, not really personally, but my means of his secretary, who identified herself as a desk clerk at headquarters. She didn't say she was from headquarters in Moscow, Katrina was supposed to believe she was from local headquarters in Dimitrovgrad. "I'm calling simply to fill in a detail or two, so that the report can be properly filed away. I'm sure you understand." Yes, Katrina certainly understood. She herself had filed thousands of documents during her years in exile, with a separate copy for every name that was mentioned, because every name had its own dossier. "I simply wanted to know the name of the young woman who visited you."

"Galina Abramovich."

"Are you sure her name is Abramovich?"

"Of course. She's the daughter of Igor Abramovich. Actually, she told me that she's married and has two children, with the eldest about to finish high school. Her surname may have changed, assuming she took her husband's and didn't keep her maiden name."

"Did you meet with her husband, too?"

"No, him I didn't see, and I'm not really sure she was with him anyway. I think she said she was traveling with a colleague from work. They were in Moscow on business, and then went on to Kazan. They stopped here on the way because she wanted to see me. But I don't think there's anything sordid going on there, she came across as a good woman. I'm sure they're just friends."

"What's going on between them is really no concern of ours. Okay, thanks, Katrina. You've helped. If I need anything else, I'll be in touch, okay?"

"Certainly. I'm happy to have been of assistance."

Demedev sat down and stared at the papers on his desk. Ya'ara Stein. That was the name of the woman who had visited Katrina Geifman. Not Galina and not Abramovich. Ya'ara Stein. Thus said the records at the hotel in Dimitrovgrad, and that was the name that appeared in the passport she showed to border control officials at the airport in Moscow. Born in 1979, thirty-three years old. Even if her eldest son were only sixteen, that would mean she had him at the age of seventeen. Unlikely. But possible. And yes, Amnon Aslan probably wasn't her husband. At the very least, they didn't have the same name, and in terms of their ages he could be her father. Demedev didn't like what he was seeing. He didn't like inconsistencies and he loathed particulars that didn't add up. He knew life had its oddities, but things that appeared out of place required a thorough investigation. An in-depth probe. Never assume extenuating circumstances, and always carry out a detailed check into anything and everything that people tend to pass off as a slight unpleasantness. He pressed the intercom button and asked his secretary to bring him Katrina Geifman's personal file. He wanted to recall why she had remained under suspicion and surveillance by the organization she had served for so many years.

Wrapped in a woolen blanket, Katrina sat down in her favorite armchair, her Dimitrovgrad home in darkness, all its lights turned out. The call from Alexei Volkov's clerk was troubling her. She had sounded a lot less stupid than he had. She hadn't called on a whim.

Katrina had already exacted her great revenge. She had told that beautiful young woman all she knew about Cobra — the little that there was to tell. Now she only had to wait. She had paid them back and she was going to have to pay the price.

39

They listened with bated breath. Thomas
Langham was on his way to Rhode Island.
A drone was keeping watch over him from
above. And an FBI surveillance team was
waiting for him meanwhile on the outskirts
of Providence, the capital of the tiny state.
Michael could already tell where the story
was going, and how it tied in with their
Cobra mystery from Bill Pemberton's perspective. But he allowed Bill to tell his tale.
Ya'ara was sitting next to Michael, and his
fingers brushed inadvertently against her
hand. She squeezed his hand for a second
and then let go, her eyes fixed on Bill's face,
over which shadows and tongues of flames
from the fireplace appeared to be dancing.
His eyes were shining. Aharon was slumped
back in his chair across from their host, his
eyelids almost closed. But the fleeting touch
of hands between Ya'ara and Michael failed

to escape his vision.

"Okay, then," Bill continued, in a show of the power of his memory when it came to even the smallest details, "the FBI team continued to monitor Langham. He settled into a small motel nearby Providence and didn't leave his room until the following day, apart from a visit to a diner across the street for a pizza and two cans of beer. He didn't call anyone or meet with anyone. Nothing. He left the motel the following day at around ten, after having already checked out. He had no intention of returning. At the request of the FBI, a police team, allegedly on the trail of a drug dealer, checked the room. You can be sure they turned it inside out, but they found nothing. Langham hadn't left anything behind for someone to pick up. He drove from there to Brown University, without any wrong turns or hesitation. Either he knew the way very well or he was using Sat-Nav software. We learned subsequently that he had indeed used a GPS device, thus reinforcing our assumption that his visit to Brown University wasn't a routine mission. The Russians were improvising — and when you improvise, you also make mistakes.

"He appeared far less familiar with his

281

surroundings once he got to Brown University campus. He stopped several times to read the signposts indicating the way to the various faculties, and he also asked students and staff members he encountered for directions. He eventually found his way to the Institute for Archaeology and the Ancient World, a small, three-story, brick building, with ivy-covered walls. On display at the entrance to the building is a splendid Greek marble statue, the half-turned torso of a muscular man, probably swinging a sword or wielding a dagger, on the offensive. But you can't tell for sure, because his arms are missing. Anyway, the closest member of the surveillance team saw Langham enter the building and walk up the stairs. He emerged again a few minutes later. The team then continued to follow him, leaving two of its members behind. Langham walked quickly back to his car, delayed his departure for a few minutes, presumably to activate the GPS device and enter his next destination, and then drove straight to Logan Airport in Boston. Like I said, we examined the GPS device and Langham did in fact enter only two destinations, Brown University in Rhode Island and the airport in Boston.

"And now," Bill said with the self-satisfaction of a gifted storyteller rather than the dignified demeanor befitting an espionage official, "we return to the surveillance team members who were still at Brown. As you recall, both had remained outside the Institute for Archaeology and the Ancient World. Two young team members, a guy and a girl. Their instructions were very clear. Zero friction with their surroundings. So they didn't enter the institute, didn't make any inquiries, and didn't check who was in the building. But they did exactly what they were supposed to do. They verified that the building had only one exit, and then took up a position on a bench some distance away from it. They sat there holding hands for three hours and looked just like any other student couple on campus, he in his sweatshirt and she with her red baseball cap and blonde ponytail, and they photographed everyone who either entered or left the building. They then called in a second couple to replace them and continue to monitor the entrance to the institute. The objective was to then analyze the photographs and pick out the people who were in the building at the time Langham had gone in. The photographs of the people who entered the building were intended to rule out some of those who were also captured leaving it. Only those who left the building but weren't caught on camera going in were marked as suspects, as they were already in the building when Langham went in. We ruled out a group of eight young men and women who were indeed in the building when Langham went inside but were subsequently identified by the university's chief security officer as students who were attending a seminar class in a lecture hall on the ground floor. You recall Langham was seen going up the stairs immediately on entering the building. In other words, whatever he did there, it wasn't anything on the ground floor. The professor giving the seminar class at the time was also thus removed from the list of suspects."

Bill was telling his story as if he had been a member of the surveillance team himself. Michael was sure he must have met with the team at least two or three times before arriving at an exact understanding of how everything had gone down, until he felt as if he himself had been there on the shaded lawn in front of the institute and until he had a clear grasp of the surveillance operation down to its very last detail. Someone like him surely went to Rhode Island himself to feel the campus slowly seep into his bones. That's what he would have done, anyway. The place, any place, tells you its story. Teaches you things that are impossible to learn from afar.

Bill continued. "The results were surprising. Aside from the lecturer and the eight seminar students, there were only four other people in the Institute for Archaeology and the Ancient World at the time of Langham's brief visit. Three researchers and the institute's legendary secretary, whose name, if I'm not mistaken, is Mrs. Ascot-Giles." He wasn't mistaken. "The three researchers were two professors, Professor Julian Hart and Professor Linda Baer, and a doctoral student, a young German man by the name of Kurt Assenheim. From Darmstadt originally."

"So what do we have?" Aharon asked, and then immediately answered. "On the one hand, Cobra's handler, a man, in his fifties at least, a Russian intelligence officer deep undercover, an expert on the subject of the ancient world, or so he purports to be, who's been living in the United States for a very long time, probably on the East Coast, or some other cold location, where it snows at Christmas. And on the other hand, a courier for the Russian intelligence service who meets briefly with someone from the Institute for Archaeology and the Ancient

World. One of four possible suspects flagged by the FBI and the CIA. Probably someone in the service of the Russians. But we're obviously groping around in the dark. It's nice after all to tie loose ends together, but we all know there's no definite link between the Cobra affair and the Russian agent in Rhode Island, and Cobra's handler could very well be at Yale or Harvard or the University of Chicago or in Ann Arbor at the University of Michigan or a thousand other places whose names I don't even know."

"Before you rush into a summation, dear Aharon, you'd be wise to listen to the rest of the story," Bill said. "Look, we have just four suspects. Two women and two men. A very simple process of elimination: You're not looking for a woman, as Cobra's handler is a man. And of the two men, only one can be relevant, since the German is too young. We conducted a thorough inquiry, the FBI and ourselves. Because we were convinced we had stumbled onto something big. Think," and he turned to look at the three people sitting in the room, "we know that Thomas Langham is working in the service of Russian intelligence. We know that he came to the United States to carry out an assignment of some kind at the Institute for

Archaeology and the Ancient World at Brown University in Rhode Island. He did nothing else at all between the time he arrived at Logan Airport and the time of his departure from there, less than forty-eight hours later. His destination thus was clearly Brown University. They didn't even bother to fabricate a cover for him: He didn't participate in a conference, didn't engage in a prolonged meeting with one of the scholars. He went in, left, and that's it. Something took place there. Let's assume he relayed an urgent instruction or received certain material. We have no evidence to indicate what he may have done there. Sometimes you have to make do with probable assumptions. We also don't know why the SVR chose to assign a courier of another agent in Montreal to the mission in Rhode Island. He arrived in Rhode Island and appeared very unfamiliar with the territory. That's unprofessional. The assignment in the U.S. was new to him. But, as all of you sitting in this room are well aware, intelligence agencies, even the very best of them, make mistakes. And the Russians made a mistake and led us to another of their agents. We exposed not only the engineer from Canada, but also another one of theirs at the institute at Brown University."

Pausing at that point for dramatic effect, Bill Pemberton took a deep breath, gulped down the last sip of whisky in his glass, and waited as always to allow those around him to marvel at the extraordinary powers of his memory. Groaning, he then rose from the deep armchair in which he was sitting, his hand inadvertently reaching for a painful spot in his lower back, and took a few steps toward his large desk. He retrieved a key from a small silver box that was on the desk, and groaning again he bent over to open one of the drawers on its left side. From it he pulled out a leather-bound notebook, and then began browsing through its pages after returning to his armchair, stopping at one page and resuming his story in a voice that had become somewhat gloomy and slow.

"We poured all our efforts into the four suspects, and carried out an in-depth background check into all of them, a complete life history," he continued. "We had two blue-blooded American women, Mrs. Ascot-Giles and Professor Baer. Not that we've never had blue-blooded spies before, and not that the Soviets and then the Russians don't have the ability to recruit our finest sons and daughters. But when we checked out all four of the people who were at the institute, only one appeared to have a hole in his record. When it came to the lives of the two women, both from established upper-class families, we knew everything about them from the day they were born, through to the schools they attended, the colleges they went to, their family members, all well known, everyone eminent. The grandmother's buried in the cemetery of a small church in New Hampshire, the father fought with General MacArthur's marines in Korea, that kind of thing. We asked our German colleagues to carry out a similar check into Kurt Assenheim, the doctoral student. Waiting for those Germans to actually get moving can drive you crazy; but when they do something, they do it properly. In any event, Kurt Assenheim also checked out from day one. But when we looked into Professor Julian Hart, that's when the bells started ringing.

"Julian Hart came to the United States in the early seventies, 1972, in fact, from New Zealand. He was twenty-two years old at the time, with a BA cum laude from the University of Canterbury in Christchurch. Ancient languages and classical studies. He received a scholarship for postgraduate studies at Columbia University in New York and went on to do his doctorate there, too.

289

He was at Brown already when he did his postdoctoral fellowship, and he stayed on there as a staff member, initially as a junior lecturer, then as a senior lecturer, and finally as a full professor. Toward the end of his studies at Columbia, he met his future and now current wife, Frances Green, who grew up in Oregon and moved to the East Coast after being accepted to college there. They have three children, two daughters and a son. The girls have already left home, while the son is a student at Brown and still lives with his parents. We made inquiries in New Zealand. A very discreet inquiry, handled personally by our station chief there, in cooperation with the New Zealand Security Intelligence Service. Yes, a man by the name of Julian Hart does appear in the records in New Zealand. The records actually show several such individuals. But only one with the same date of birth as our Julian Hart. Hart was born in Auckland. His family must have emigrated from New Zealand when he was a young boy, because the Hart family stopped paying taxes there in 1953. We weren't able to locate any relatives. According to an old and not very lucid neighbor whom the local security service managed to track down, the family may have moved to Australia, or maybe somewhere else, he couldn't be sure. The old man, as I said, wasn't at his best, to put it mildly. Early dementia, and plenty of alcohol in his blood. In Hart's admissions file at the university in Christchurch we found certificates from a high school in Cape Town, letters of recommendation from two enthusiastic teachers, a photocopy of a New Zealand passport issued by the consulate in Pretoria. In a letter attached to his application for a living allowance, Hart noted that his parents had been killed in a terrible car accident a year earlier. We tried to make inquiries in South Africa. Our capabilities there are somewhat limited. The relationship with the local security service is very problematic, and we chose not to involve them in such a sensitive investigation. Our efforts to conduct the inquiries in Cape Town independently yielded only partial success. The high school Hart had attended no longer existed, and no one could tell us what had happened to all the school's records after it was shut down, and we failed to locate the teachers who wrote the letters of recommendation. But we did manage to find a small report in the *Cape Town Herald* about a couple by the name of Hart who were killed in a traffic accident. The name of the man who died matched the name of Julian's father, Jacob

Hart, as it appeared in the records in New Zealand. The woman's name was different, so we can't be sure if she was Julian's mother. She may have been the father's second wife, or perhaps the reporter made a mistake. Who knows? In any event, the report noted that Jacob Hart had been a member of the Cape Town branch of the Progressive Workers Front, which we knew better at the time as the cover organization for the South African Communist Party. And that's where we hit a dead end. We weren't able to come up with anything else, but we didn't like what we had found. The story of the early part of Julian Hart's life troubled me a great deal. Too many loose ends, a biography lacking continuity and coherence. And from our perspective, the link to the South African Communist Party certainly raised an alarm or two. How were we to know if the Julian Hart who was born in Auckland, New Zealand, was really the same Julian Hart who turned up to study in Christchurch some eighteen years later? And maybe Jacob Hart, who was very conveniently killed in an accident, and can't be asked even one fucking question, handed over his son's personal papers to the KGB, and thus they were able to manufacture a different Julian Hart? Perhaps wandering around in some shithole in South Africa somewhere there's another orphaned Julian Hart, completely unaware that his shadow twin has risen to greatness in the American academe, and is also a deep-cover Russian intelligence agent in his spare time?"

"Have you met with Hart since Thomas Langham's fleeting appearance under the beautiful skies of Providence?" Aharon asked.

"Not officially. We continued to make discreet inquiries into his past. The FBI put a tap on his phone. We even sent an agent to see him under the guise of an undergraduate student with an interest in going on to do a Ph.D. on the subject of the ancient Near East. He was very welcoming, and willing to help. Meanwhile we weren't able to come up with anything even remotely suspicious on him. And yet I know" — and at that point Bill slammed his fist down onto the small table next to his armchair, violently rattling the cubes of ice in his whisky glass — "I know there's something fishy here! I," he declared, "wasn't born yesterday. When I sense there's something amiss, I know what I'm talking about."

"And how does the Julian Hart case tie in with the Cobra affair?" Aharon quietly asked. "You haven't provided any proof of that."

"You're right. I don't have any proof," Bill responded. "But you said you were looking for a Russian intelligence officer with the hint of an Australian or South African accent who's been living in the United States as a professor of the ancient Near East, and that's exactly what I've found for you. A fucking Russian intelligence officer, with a background in New Zealand and South Africa, a professor at the Institute for Archaeology and the Ancient World at Brown University, where — and you can check this on any weather site — it snows in December."

"Aharon," Ya'ara said, "I think Mr. Pemberton is right. The circumstantial evidence is pretty impressive. And you taught us never to believe in coincidences. I think we should go to Rhode Island. The trail leads there."

40

Dimitrovgrad, March 2013

The light military aircraft touched down at the small airport in Dimitrovgrad just as the sun was setting. The sky had taken on a dark purple hue. It was bitterly cold, and Captain Viktor Demedev tightened his coat around himself before making his way down the stairs leading from the body of the plane. He was accompanied by two additional FSB officers. Waiting there for them on the tarmac, and trying to hide the fact that his body was shivering with cold, was the commander of the FSB's Dimitrovgrad office, Colonel Arkady Semionov. The deputy chief of the FSB himself had called Semionov a few hours earlier to inform him that Demedev and his people were on their way to see him. Keep this completely under wraps, came the instruction; look after them personally and do all they ask of you. Got it? Every single word, sir. And please allow me to wish you good health and success. It's an honor to serve you.

The guests from Moscow got into the backseat of Semionov's car, with Semionov himself squeezing into the front, alongside his driver. They were greeted by the scent of an air freshener mixed with the odor of cheap cigarettes, and Demedev suppressed the gag reflex that threatened momentarily to overcome him.

"Anything and everything you need," Semionov said, "just say the word."

"I'll tell you exactly what we need," Demedev responded. "The interrogation room you have on the basement floor of your headquarters, along with a secluded detention cell on the same level. And you'll also give us a room in the basement to serve as our accommodation. Three field beds, a desk, a safe. A bottle of vodka. One guard per shift, three in all. That's all we'll need. I want our presence here to go completely unnoticed. But if someone does see us and asks questions, simply say it's a routine spot-check by general headquarters. That we showed up unannounced. I don't want others to be privy to the inquiry we're conducting. No one from your Investigation Division or the Credibility Department. And certainly not Alexei Volkov, who somehow ended up here instead of receiving the Nobel Prize in Physics." The irony wasn't lost on Semionov. "Is that clear?"

"As clear as a sunny day in mid-August," Semionov responded.

"Make the arrest at three-thirty in the morning. I want a low-profile operation, without any fuss or disturbances. Knock quietly on the door, without alerting the entire neighborhood. If necessary, rather than make a noise, pick the lock. Don't break down the door. I don't want any drama. But the moment you're in the house, cuff her hands tightly, so that it hurts, and put a bag over her head. And not a new one, if possible. A bag that others have thrown up in before. You know what I mean, one that's still going to smell even after a thousand washes. And bring her directly to the interrogation room. We'll be waiting for her."

"Everything will be carried out exactly according to plan, Captain Demedev."

"And one more thing, Colonel Semionov. I wish to thank you. I appreciate your efforts and expeditious organization. It's good to see that we have competent commanders of high stature in remote locations, too. Thank you."

■ ■ ■ ■

Katrina Geifman was led into the interrogation room. The bag was still on her head. She was shoved down onto the chair set aside for her, a low chair, its seat sloping forward slightly, almost imperceptibly, toward the floor. "Take the hood off, please," Demedev said quietly to the guard. "Release the handcuffs. And now please leave the room. We'll call for you if needed."

Katrina rubbed her eyes and tried to fix her hair. Her eyes were still puffy from sleep, and she massaged her wrists, which were now swollen, thanks to the over-tight handcuffs. A powerful beam of light was aimed in her direction, and she could barely make out the face of the interrogator standing in front of her, dressed in the middle of the night in a dark and handsome suit, his shirt white, tieless, its top buttons undone. He approached her slowly. "Katrina Geifman," he said softly, almost in a whisper, "Katrina Geifman." He stood behind her, and despite the terrible stench from the bag that had invaded her nostrils, she could still detect the fragrance of his manly cologne. He leaned over her suddenly and reached for her left wrist, gripping it tightly and pinning her palm to the table. With his right hand he then grabbed her forefinger and violently tugged it upward, until the room filled with the sickening noise of a bone snapping and the terrible sound of her screams. Katrina felt as if the screaming was coming from someone else. An awful pain spread through her and she gazed at her broken finger, which now appeared crooked and no longer an integral part of her hand. Her eyes filled with tears of anger and surprise, and she could see flashes of red, purple, and yellow in her mind, as if something had exploded inside her head. Her interrogator sat down seemingly in slow motion, without a sound, on the other side of the table. On the edge of her vision she could make out a second, dark figure, leaning comfortably against the wall in the corner of the room.

"Katrina Geifman," Demedev said in an even tone. "Good evening. My name is Captain Gorodov. View this as a piece of personal advice: Make this process as brief as possible. Because it could also be a long one, and very painful, too. It's your decision. I demand to know exactly, in full detail, what you told the spy who visited you at your home, a spy whose presence you didn't even bother to report to us."

■ ■ ■ ■

Katrina Geifman lost track of time. She couldn't tell if she had been there for an hour or two days or perhaps even longer. And if it was only an hour, then it was a very long and agonizing one. Two men dragged her to the detention cell and tossed her onto the bed like a rag doll. The blood was pounding in her head, her broken fingers appeared swollen and deformed, as if they were no longer human digits. Her entire body was crying out in pain. She asked for water. Air. All she wanted was a brief respite. Just a brief one. A pause before the pain resumed. There were moments when it seemed to her that there was nothing else in the world aside from the pain that sliced through her body, as if it were a lightning rod for all the agonies of the world. At those moments her mind was blank. Her thoughts weren't her own. She told her interrogators everything, absolutely everything. All she knew about Cobra, and every piece of information on him that she had passed on to Galina Abramovich, who, as the interrogators had mockingly hurled at her, was actually someone else. At the edges of her thoughts somewhere, between the explosions of pain and waves of nausea, she asked herself if they were authorized to be privy to the secret. Yes, Katrina, good on you, she mocked herself. Preserving compartmentalization and information security even during your darkest hours. Is that really the thing that should concern you now, in the pits of hell, the inferno of your pain — whether the interrogators are authorized to know your secrets? During the course of her interrogation she hadn't behaved any differently from the tens of thousands of other interrogation subjects whose flesh and bones had been crushed and broken. The human body isn't designed to be torn to shreds with torture. And there was only one thing that she didn't tell the monsters. One detail she had guarded as if her life depended on it. And it wasn't even anything significant. But Katrina knew that if she wasn't able to keep it from them, her soul would be crushed. She had told Galina that Brian, Cobra's handler, was from a place in the United States that gets snow during the Christmas period. But she had kept that from the elegant officers from Moscow who had turned her into a miserable and beaten lump of flesh. They would never hear that from her! That was one more secret, a small one, that would remain hers.

Her pulse pumped shards of pain to every organ in her body. It wouldn't let up. Perhaps the pain would never let go of her. A heavy darkness descended on Katrina Geifman, and she couldn't tell if she was falling or asleep or passing out.

41

The adjutant showed Demedev into the extensive chambers of the deputy head of the FSB.

"Sir, I requested to update you in person."

"And good that you did so. The less on paper, the better. This is" — and here the deputy head of the FSB gestured toward a slender man, dressed in a finely tailored gray suit, who was looking at him from the other side of the enormous desk — "the head of the SVR's Tenth Directorate, the Black-Ops Directorate. We're handling the investigation into the Katrina Geifman affair on their behalf, since the operation to which you've been partially exposed, Operation Cobra, is one of theirs."

Demedev snapped to attention momentarily and nodded his head — in subordination mixed with a sense of pride and self-worth — in the direction of the high-

303

ranking SVR officer. "Sit, please," said the deputy head of the FSB. "We're listening."

"I've completed the interrogation of the traitor Katrina Geifman," Demedev began after sitting down stiffly in his chair. "She told the young woman who visited her everything she knows about Cobra. The young woman, known to us as Ya'ara Stein, although that's surely not her real name, probably works for the Israeli Mossad or Israeli Security Service. There's been a leak concerning Operation Cobra and they've got wind of it, and they're trying to learn more. Thanks to stringent adherence to procedures, Katrina Geifman knows very little about Cobra, almost nothing. But she knows he's a top-level agent, and she knows that we've been investing extensive resources into the operation. Including the assignment of a deep undercover combatant to serve as Cobra's handler. She didn't tell the Israeli woman anything about the handler, apart from the fact that he had a Canadian passport in the name of Brian Cox. I don't think she knew very much more than that about him. Trust me, sir, we questioned her in a manner that left nothing held back. But I am concerned about the things she said."

"Tell me something, Demedev, did she not suspect that the young woman wasn't

Igor Abramovich's daughter?"

"I think she wanted her to be his daughter, and that's also why she didn't confront her on the matter until the end. It was a chance for her to return to her past, to recall the wonderful romance she once had, a love affair that turned ever sweeter in her memory with the passing of time."

"But she told her about Cobra. She didn't have to say anything about him. He wasn't a part of her story with that Abramovich man."

"You're right, sir. I've read her file and my guess is that this sudden reconnection with her past also reawakened her old anger about being forced, and quite rightly so, to immediately put an end to that outrageous love story, which was, in my opinion, a fantasy, for the most part. Seeing each other just once a year doesn't make for a true love affair, does it? What did she have, after all? Love letters and a pile of lies. I'm no psychologist, but I can read people. She was overcome by anger, and she opened her heart and mouth to reveal the big secret to which she had the privilege of being party to the first stranger she saw — who just happened to be Galina, or someone who said she was Galina, it didn't really matter to her."

"Naturally, Demedev, you aren't familiar with the particulars of Operation Cobra. After all these years, it remains a very important and highly classified operation. Don't get me wrong. You've done an excellent job until this point, and now I'm asking you not to take any further action on the matter. If you come across any information you believe could be related to the affair, report directly to me. Only me."

"Thank you, sir. I can't even begin to describe the sense of satisfaction I get from playing a part, even marginally, in a special operation of this kind. Moments like these justify all the endless work we do. Suddenly we see how important it can be. What are we going to do about Katrina Geifman?"

"She's no longer your concern, Demedev. I'm handling it personally. You did some fine and trustworthy work. The head of your department will be retiring in a few months, and I think I've found an excellent candidate to replace him. Take care of yourself and send my best wishes to" — and at that point the deputy head of the FSB glanced fleetingly at the piece of paper on the desk in front of him — "send my best wishes to Olga, your wife."

"Pass on my best wishes, too," the head of the SVR's Tenth Directorate added dryly.

306

"We appreciate the good work you've done."

The deputy chief of the FSB asked to be put through to Colonel Semionov in Dimitrovgrad once Demedev had left the room. "Semionov," he said, exacting a profoundly respectful response from the other end of the line, "put Katrina Geifman out of her misery. I believe that sadist Demedev worked her over good and proper. Oh, well, that's the way things go sometimes in this line of work. We have no choice. Who's going to do it for us? And report to me directly, Semionov. Your efforts don't go unappreciated here in Moscow."

42

SVR Headquarters, Moscow, March 2013
Colonel Dmitry Malenkov, the director of the SVR's Tactical Planning Division, which was responsible for the running of sensitive sources, and the head of the Tenth Directorate walked side by side down the long corridor leading to the bureau of the organization's commander. An urgent discussion concerning Cobra, that's all they were told in person by the commander's secretary, who added that the meeting would appear in the computer logs as a consultation on "personnel matters." They needed no further explanation. The code name Cobra didn't appear in the organization's computer systems. Their footsteps echoed off the sleek marble floor, and Dmitry Malenkov thought: They certainly know how to look after themselves here on the sixth floor. That's for sure. They were ushered into the commander's extensive office promptly and

without delay, and that, too, from Dmitry's limited experience at the lofty heights of the floor serving the organization's top brass, wasn't commonplace.

"I'll get straight to it," said the head of the SVR after the two had settled into their chairs on the other side of the huge, empty desk across from him. "Cobra may have been exposed, or the enemy may be on the verge of exposing him. We're still trying to figure out how it happened, but the fact is that a woman, who probably works for the Israeli Security Service or the Mossad, paid a visit to Katrina Geifman, who once provided security for Cobra's operational meetings. She wasn't there by chance or for any other reason. She asked questions about Cobra and she got answers. I believe we're seeing only the tip of the iceberg here. They've come across something, and there's no reason to assume they have any intention of letting go. So several things. We're going to conduct a comprehensive damage-control assessment. We have to bring his handler into the picture and get him to Europe as soon as possible. If Cobra has yet to be exposed, he needs to be warned and we need to weigh the option of extracting him from Israel. As part of our damage-control assessment we also have to consider the worst-case scenario: Cobra's already been exposed and arrested, and he is now telling the Israelis everything he has done for us throughout all the years in our service. We have to assess whether Cobra's exposure means the exposure of his handler, too. We need to come up with a contingency plan in anticipation of the possibility that Cobra is going to be exposed. There's a good chance the Israelis will respond to Cobra's exposure by expelling our people at the embassy there." He broke off for a moment, a grave expression on his face. "Your thoughts?"

"We definitely have to assume that Cobra's cover is about to be blown," said Dmitry Malenkov. "Our primary concern has to be getting him out of Israel. If they haven't exposed him just yet, the most important thing is to get him on the next flight out. I don't have to tell you what will happen if he falls into the hands of their interrogators. Sooner or later he'll come clean and tell them everything — how much damage he caused, the focus of his reports, the issues he didn't touch. It would be best for all of us for him to vanish. As always, not knowing will be harder on them than knowing. They'll have to assume the worst.

"And at another level, getting him out

would convey an important message to our agents. In terms of prestige and image. All of us in this room know that there's an enormous difference if an agent is exposed, tried, and sent to prison for a very long time, or if a certain individual was under suspicion but managed to get out unharmed and can go on living his life as a free man elsewhere. That sends a hugely significant message to all our agents around the world. It's important for us to show again that the SVR always takes care of its own, no matter what."

"I may be putting the cart before the horse," said the directorate chief, "but Russia itself is the only place where an individual with Cobra's profile could be resettled and given a new life. He won't be willing to live on some remote farm in Venezuela or spend the rest of his days in some dusty town in Angola. We wouldn't be able to protect him in those places, and we have to remember that the Israelis are obsessive and have long memories and impressive capabilities. If we don't bring him here, they'll get their hands on him, and take him out or put him on trial in Tel Aviv."

"There's another issue, too," said the commander of the SVR, "and it's not a trivial one at all. He's been under the impression since the 1980s that his handlers are American, and we've invested very extensive resources to this end. How's he going to react when he's instructed to go to Russia and not the United States?"

Dmitry Malenkov was the one to respond. "First of all, he has no choice. I don't have to tell you, matters like these aren't for the pampered. Second, I'm not so sure it'll come as a complete surprise to him. Yes, from the outset, back in the days when the Stasi were running him, his handlers have always acted like authentic Americans. And yes, we've never met with him on American soil, but we've put that down to security concerns, which I believe he accepted as legitimate. In any event, he's never pressed the issue. Furthermore, the questions we've asked and the assignments we've given him have never been of a distinctly Soviet hue. We've asked him about things that are of interest to any superpower, including the United States. After all, we've had a special team charged with ensuring that our briefings didn't betray our true identity. Nevertheless, he's been a spy for almost thirty years. And Cobra is a sharp guy. No matter how good we are, I'm guessing that somewhere along the way someone has made a mistake of sorts, even a small one. One that should have made him think that maybe we aren't really Americans as we've led him to believe. And there must have been other signs over the years, slipups of some kind by someone. They may have been small things, even the way in which someone drank his vodka, or lit a cigarette. Little things like that, which could give someone away. I have to say that Cobra has never pressed us in this regard, has never asked questions. He may have tested us, but his handler's cover holds up perfectly, not only vis-à-vis an Israeli agent, but also when it comes to FBI investigators. Moreover, the debriefers who sometimes joined the rounds of meetings with him all speak fluent English."

Malenkov looked at his two colleagues and continued. "And another thing, and this may be the overriding issue: I believe that Cobra simply doesn't care. His cynicism and absolute lack of scruples were plain to see from day one. He is a man without values, a worm, concerned only with himself and his own personal gain. I have no doubt he'd abandon the family he's raised in Israel in an instant. Deep down he doesn't care if he's working with the CIA or the SVR. All he cares about is the sense of respect and power. And we can continue to provide him with that. And the money, of course. True, we haven't put this to the test, we didn't want to make things difficult for him, we didn't want to risk overstretching the limits of his betrayal, but I believe this is the kind of man we are dealing with. When the moment of truth arrives, he won't fall apart on learning that he's been working for Moscow and not for Washington."

"We'll move forward in keeping with the points you noted, sir," said the directorate chief. "With respect to Cobra himself and also insofar as the wider circles are concerned. We can meet with his handler the day after tomorrow already, in Zurich. And we'll make every effort to make contact with him by the weekend, too. It isn't easy for a man in his position to leave the country from one moment to the next. He's accountable after all to the people around him. He can't simply disappear for no apparent reason. But we'll certainly impress upon him that the matter is a critical and urgent one. In any event, I don't want to meet with him in Israel. It's too dangerous. If they've already blown his cover, they have a huge advantage over us in Israel. We're on an equal footing more or less when it comes to Europe."

The directorate chief and the head of the

Tactical Planning Division rose and stood at attention in front of their superior. They then turned around and left, both with a serious and determined look on their faces. They were still pacing down the magnificent marble corridor when Dmitry Malenkov turned on his mobile phone and instructed his secretary to convene the Cobra team for an urgent meeting.

"You're wanted back on the sixth floor for a moment," the security guard said to the directorate chief just as they were leaving the building. And turning to Malenkov, the directorate chief said: "Go ahead. Don't wait for me. Keep me posted on your progress."

The SVR commander's secretary was waiting for him at the entrance to the bureau. "Go right in," he said. "The commander is expecting you."

"I've been looking through Demedev's report again," the commander said without looking up. "Katrina did indeed know very little about Cobra, but she did pass on all she knew to that young woman from the Mossad, or the Shin Bet, or wherever she's from. She estimated Cobra's approximate age, she even had a rough idea of his date of birth. And she told her about a round of meetings we held with him in Switzerland, including their precise dates. I didn't want to discuss these issues in the presence of Malenkov, he isn't in the know," the commander continued, finally looking up, "but something's troubling me. I've asked my bureau chief to bring me the Viper dossier. I want us to go through it together. And we'll do some thinking." He stood up, walked over to an elegant antique sideboard in the corner of the room, and retrieved two small crystal glasses and a clear unmarked bottle. He poured out two shots of the viscous, colorless liquid and said to the directorate chief with a smile: "Come, let's have a drink. I don't know about you, but I certainly need one."

43

"I'm too old for these flights," Michael grumbled to himself while struggling to find a good angle for his long body in the cramped economy class seat. He'd managed to get himself a seat in one of the last rows of the jumbo jet, a row that had only two seats rather than three between the aisle and the window, and the arrangement offered a certain sense of comfort, but mostly a small sense of triumph to someone who was familiar with little tricks like that. His sense of achievement, however, didn't last very long, and after three hours of dozing on and off over the Atlantic Ocean, it gave way to despondency. He wasn't at all happy with the fact that several hours of flight time still lay ahead, and his efforts to position his limbs in a manner that would allow him to relax and silence the noise swirling in his

317

mind were to no avail.

He knew they were getting close to him, to Cobra. He knew that Aharon and Ya'ara wouldn't return from Rhode Island empty-handed. They were moving in on their prey in ever-tightening circles, and they would eventually corner him. Michael tried to picture that moment in his thoughts, to imagine the very instant in which they closed in on him and brought him down. He couldn't shake the image in his head of a large gray wolf, injured and bleeding, slowly collapsing into the deep snow, staining it with its blood, its mouth gaping and spewing steam, its yellow eyes dimming and losing focus, and them standing around it in a circle, dressed in heavy coats, the hunting rifles in their hands pointing toward the earth, looking at it in silence, at the dying beast, huge stretches of snow all around them, the air painfully crisp and very cold.

Michael put on the headphones he found in the seat pocket in front of him. And once again he wondered why the airlines — in this day and age, with headphones of wonderful quality readily available — continued to provide their passengers with inferior-quality devices that made every sound that came through them very unpleasantly tinny. "You're cranky," he said to himself in

318

silence, while noticing that it wasn't the first time that same self-analysis had passed through his mind in recent months. "You're cranky," he said, addressing himself in the second person, "and it really doesn't suit you. Make an effort to snap out of it." He could hear, or rather he thought he could hear through the rasping tinny screen, Frank Sinatra singing "New York, New York," and immediately thereafter came a grandiose Italian number, San Remo Festival style. "If you're familiar with the San Remo Festival, you're probably not that young anymore," he said to himself with a fair amount of self-pity, and his thoughts wandered to Ya'ara, "who probably doesn't even know what kind of music you're talking about." And he thought about her beautiful, serious face, about the way in which rays of sunlight trapped and illuminated strands of gold in her hair.

He smiled to himself and then turned serious. Just before falling asleep again he thought about Cobra, pictured him in the interrogation room immediately after being caught. Cobra, shocked to the core at being apprehended, fists pounding on the door of his home, his hair disheveled, his eyes puffy from sleep. They would take him in at a time when a man's walls of defense are at their weakest. They would drag him out in his pajamas, to make him feel ridiculous and humiliated, a terrible dryness, that insipid taste of the night, in his mouth. He would be pushed into the backseat of the un-marked security vehicle, his head would bang against the door frame as he tried to bend down, his limbs would still be stiff from an uneasy sleep. They would move off in a convoy of three vehicles, accelerating aggressively, displaying with their manliness, with his terrified wretchedness, just how fast and far he was falling. Michael drifted into a broken sleep, his head resting on the arm of the seat, imagining the fear gripping Cobra, the sour taste rising in his throat, the sudden sense of thirst that would over-come him, his shriveled cock, the uncontrol-lable shudders that shake his body from time to time. For an instant, just a nanosec-ond, his mind entertained the thought that under different circumstances, in an alterna-tive pattern of revolving doors, he could have been Cobra.

44

Providence, Rhode Island, March 2013
Ya'ara rang the doorbell at the home of Professor Julian Hart. Aharon was standing one step behind her. They could hear the chimes echo through the expanse of the interior. The wide stretch of lawn in the front of the house was covered in mud stains. The shrubs were topped with the remains of dirty snow. The tall trees on the sides of the house stood bare, their leafless branches sketching gray lines on the backdrop of a cold sky. Two cars, stained with splatters of mud and salt water, were parked side by side at the entrance to the home's garage. The taxi that had dropped them outside the residence turned around and disappeared down the windy road.

An attractive, well-groomed woman in her fifties, wearing a light-colored dress and a thin gray sweater, opened the door for them. "Good afternoon," Ya'ara said. "This is

Professor Max Katz," she continued, gesturing toward Aharon, "and I'm Annabelle Eshel. We'd like to speak with Professor Julian Hart. We've just come from the university, where we were told that Professor Hart should be at home."

"Hello, I'm Frances, Professor Hart's wife. It's a shame really that you didn't call before coming. Not to mention not bothering to make an appointment," said Mrs. Hart, clearly agitated, openly hostile, and with more than just a hint of reproach in her tone of voice. She looked every inch a lady, but Ya'ara noticed that her high-heeled shoes and makeup weren't exactly appropriate for such an early hour. Yes, she was definitely overdressed for that time of the day. "Regrettably, my husband isn't home. He was called away in the middle of the night." She glanced over their shoulders, presumably looking for the vehicle that had brought them there, but they had chosen to take a cab rather than rent a car. It wouldn't take more than a simple inquiry with the car rental company for a vehicle to reveal their real names. And the fact that they were there without the option of making a quick getaway served their purpose, too — to spend as much time as possible in Hart's house, even if he was unwilling to see them.

Finding out that he had gone away in the early hours of the morning, perhaps unexpectedly, was in itself significant. And even if he wasn't there, his wife was a worthy target for their efforts. They were clinging to every sliver of information, every little thread. "I take it you came by taxi," Frances continued. Her manners wouldn't allow her to leave them outside. "Come, come in, please, have something to drink. We're quite a way out of town. Tell me," she said while taking their coats, her hands shaking slightly, "what brings you to see Julian?"

Aharon and Ya'ara sat down in the large living room, which was a model of comfort and good taste. A fire burned in the stone fireplace, casting a golden glow over the volumes of books on the shelves, and antique-looking Greek urns that Ya'ara presumed were hand-crafted copies stood proudly in small, well-lit display cabinets. Everything spoke of old money, stability, and refinement. Noticing the two empty wine bottles on the floor, alongside one of the armchairs, Ya'ara looked away. She was playing her part to perfection, as she always did, slipping easily into any and every character, and now she was a loyal academic assistant, serious and altruistic. She sat there looking innocent, her feet together, upright and alert. Frances Hart excused herself and went to the kitchen to make tea. The sound of glass shattering disturbed the silence, and Ya'ara thought she also heard a stifled sob. Then she heard Frances speaking softly. Probably on the phone.

Frances returned from the kitchen a few minutes later, bearing a tray with two porcelain cups and a plate of cookies. Ya'ara thought she looked troubled, but even if she had been crying, her eyes were now dry. Her hands trembled slightly as she placed the tray on the low table in front of them. "I have called for a taxi to take you back to town. Remind me of your names, please," she asked, and sat down across from them, folding her arms across her chest, as if she needed to keep warm. Or protect herself.

"I'm an antiquities dealer from Israel," Aharon introduced himself. "With a Ph.D. in Near Eastern Studies from many years ago," he said, alluding to his advanced age. "Back then already, I ran into your husband's name. I'm aware of his expertise when it comes to ancient texts from our part of the world, and I wanted to interest him in a scroll that came into my possession in one of those ways that are best left untold, as is customary in the field. A scroll that was discovered in the Transjordan region,

324

passed from one hand to another, and was brought to my attention by a colleague from Bethlehem. I was thinking that Professor Hart might like to review the manuscript, check it, verify its originality, and perhaps receive first rights with respect to its study."

"Surely you have experts in ancient scrolls back home. What brings you all the way here?"

"We came over for a series of meetings, at the Metropolitan in New York and at Harvard. Annabelle, my assistant" — Ya'ara flashed a pleasant smile — "suggested that we also pay a visit to the library at your university, believing that it would be worthwhile trying to meet with staff members from the Institute for Archaeology and the Ancient World. Our universities in Israel have limited funds, and the leading universities in the United States have actually been the ones investing in recent years in the acquisition of manuscripts, scrolls, archives, anything related to the ancient and contemporary culture of Israel, and the land of Israel. We were hoping to interest Professor Hart in an item that may turn out to be one of the most significant findings of recent decades."

"I'm sure he'd be happy to meet with you . . . but he had to go away unexpectedly. I'm sorry," Frances Hart said. Ya'ara caught sight of the shadow of worry in their hostess's eyes. And the slight trembling of her hands. And her furtive glance at the wine bottles on the floor.

"Annabelle, can you please give Mrs. Hart one of my business cards?"

Ya'ara reached out to hand her the card, and after some hesitation Frances Hart placed it in the corner of the table. Whether she was going to make use of it or simply throw it away after her guests departed was impossible to tell, but Ya'ara's money was on option one.

"May I use the bathroom, please?" Ya'ara asked.

"Certainly. Just around that corner, second door on the left."

Ya'ara set off in the direction Frances had indicated, then passed by the bathroom to get a quick look further into the residence. Her memory took note of the layout of the house, of the various items on display, of the pictures and bookcases that popped into view from unexpected angles. She then returned to the bathroom, and after stepping back into the living room she said, apologetically, "Sorry, I got a little lost. But everything's fine. I found my way eventually."

326

Frances smiled at her. "Truthfully," she said, "I'm happy you're the ones who came. Julian left in the early hours of the morning so unexpectedly that it got me thinking strange thoughts. He looked so stressed and pale. He travels quite frequently, but this was something really out of the blue, and he wasn't quite able to explain to me what had happened and why the urgency. Something about a colleague in Heidelberg who had taken ill suddenly. That's what he said. But the e-mail he received, I didn't really read it, but I caught a glimpse, over his shoulder, that's just me sometimes" — she smiled, coyly, like a shamefaced teenager — "I saw he received an e-mail to confirm a flight to Zurich. Why fly to Heidelberg via Zurich? Wouldn't one fly via Frankfurt? I asked him, but he just muttered something about airfares and the research budget." Ya'ara knew now for certain that Frances had been drinking, and quite a lot, too, since her husband's hasty departure in the early hours of the morning. A person with her wits about her wouldn't be chatting so freely, certainly not with strangers who had almost forced their way into her home. "Anyway," Frances continued, "when you rang at the door, I thought maybe two Mafia thugs had shown up, *Sopranos*-like, you

327

know." She smiled again, trying to capture Ya'ara's gaze. Ya'ara reciprocated, her gray-blue eyes warm and deep. "I can just imagine what went through your mind," she said.

"Yes," Frances said, "that alarming ring at the door, echoing really loud through the silence all around. And who do I see? Not two killers from New Jersey but a harmless professor, forgive me" — she threw a somewhat embarrassed glance at Aharon, who was watching the scene with wide-eyed innocence — "and an attractive young woman, tastefully dressed. And suddenly it dawned on me that I was simply imagining things, that I've just been telling myself stories ever since Julian got the phone call."

"I'm sure everything's fine," Ya'ara said. "People involved in the world of antiquities and manuscripts are always going to get strange phone calls and have to go away sometimes, even out of the blue. It's a little like being a secret agent . . ."

The sound of an approaching car came from outside, followed by footsteps, heavy breathing, and a ring on the doorbell. "That's your taxi," Frances said. "I'm really sorry that Julian isn't home, but I hope within a few hours to know what's happening with him and when he'll be back. I'll tell him you were here. I'll give him your

328

phone number, sir." She looked at Aharon.

"I'm planning on being in Providence for a few days," Ya'ara said. "I'll be staying at the Heralds Inn. If you hear anything, you're welcome to let me know." She moved toward Frances and hugged her gently. "Everything's okay, you've nothing to worry about. These things happen sometimes, those demons of the night following us into the day." She held Frances's hands. "And thank you for the hospitality. We showed up uninvited, and you were so welcoming. I hope our scroll finds a place for itself at Julian's institute. It deserves to be studied by a scholar of stature. You'll see, Frances, everything will fall into place just fine."

"Well, that didn't go very well at all," Aharon said to Ya'ara, who was sitting to his left in the backseat of the taxi. "I had trouble convincing myself even. An antiquities dealer, come on."

"Look, something's happened. She's upset. She doesn't know where he is, and she's imagining all kinds of things. She must have picked up on his sense of danger or urgency. Otherwise she wouldn't have behaved like she did. After all, it's not the first time he's gone away."

"And what's this Heralds Inn business?

Do you feel like a bit of a holiday?"

"I get the sense that I should stay for a while. I'd like to meet with her again in a day or two. You need the patience of a hunter. You once told us that."

"Yes, spying is waiting. Le Carré penned that, I believe."

"My father likes to read him. He always spoke of him as a master spy, and it took me a while to learn that Le Carré had worked for the British secret service for just a few years and in a junior role. How does that make him an authority when it comes to matters of espionage?"

"Literary fiction can sometimes paint a truer picture of our gray reality. Look at us, an old man and a young woman in a filthy taxi in a city buried in this dreary winter. It's better to be a writer, isn't it?"

"It's better to live life, that's what I say. Anyway, I'm staying for a few days. I'll keep you posted. Are you going back today already?"

"There's someone I have to see in Boston. And I'll meet with Bill again in New York; he'll be there for a couple of days for some conference. We'll have a drink or two together, and then tomorrow, at around midnight, home, on the El Al night flight."

"Yes, you two really didn't drink enough,

obviously. You're full of surprises, Aharon. A woman in Boston?"

"All men have to guard their secrets," Aharon replied with a thoughtful look on his face. He didn't tell her the woman was someone who had worked for him in the United States many years back, and who now lived in an institution about a thirty-minute drive from the city, her memory fading, getting thinner by the day, a chill fixed in her bones, with no one else in the world but him. The office footed the bill without fail, through a branch of an Irish bank, but he was the only one who visited her once every few months, a debt of respect on the part of a veteran combatant.

45

Katrina was in heaven. A soft mattress, clean, crisp sheets, a thick comforter. A gentle hand caressing her forehead. "Sleep, dear, sleep," said the soothing voice of an old woman. The hand caressing her was the woman's hand. The caressing hand was now tightening the blanket around her body. Soft footsteps moved away. The light in the room went out. She drifted again in and out of a light sleep, rocking gently among the waves of slumber.

"How's she feeling today?" Arkady Semionov asked his mother in a whisper.

"She'll be okay, she's a strong woman. We went through far worse during the Great Patriotic War."

Arkady took a deep breath. "I want you to nurse her until she's back on her feet," he said. "And then I'll take her."

"I hope you're not doing anything foolish,

332

Arkady."

"I'm doing only what you taught me. Don't worry."

"I'm an old woman, but you?"

"Mother, who's the FSB commander in Dimitrovgrad?"

"That's exactly what I'm afraid of. You're riding a white horse and telling yourself that you're noble-hearted, a knight in shining armor. Arkady, Arkady, very little has changed in our country. Don't fool yourself. You may rule the roost here in your small, remote kingdom, but don't underestimate those who wield the true power. They'll crush you like a bug. Without a second thought."

"And yet, Mother, you are still helping me."

"I told you. I'm old. There's very little left to take from me. And I'm tougher than you. Don't be mistaken."

"You're right. I'll be careful. But I couldn't just leave her like that. And I don't shoot people in the back of the head. As far as I'm concerned, those days are over. I won't allow them to force us back to places we should never have been in to begin with. We can be humans, too. I don't think that's asking too much."

Arkady's mother clucked her tongue and

went to the kitchen to get Katrina another cup of tea. She was proud of her only son and concerned for him. She hoped that the tortured woman lying in the bed in the small guest room would recover quickly and disappear elsewhere, somewhere better. Later, she approached her again, caressed her forehead and face, saw her eyes open, and brought the cup of tea to her lips. "Be careful, dear, it's hot."

Arkady was sitting in the large armchair in the deliberately darkened room, his eyes closed. He could hear his mother's soft mutterings and felt that he and Katrina Geifman were in good hands. Good, safe, and brave. He had returned to his mother like a young boy with a broken toy that needed mending. He didn't have a plan of action. He didn't know what he'd do with Katrina once she was on her feet again. The instructions had been clear: Katrina Geifman must die. He didn't know how he was going to hide the fact that instead of resting in an unmarked grave in the forest, Katrina was at his mother's house. He'd been given a direct order from the deputy commander of the FSB and he had defied it without a second thought. "Put her out of her misery," he'd been told, and it would be impossible to argue in any way or form that his actions had complied with the intentions of the senior commander from Moscow. Arkady could picture her broken fingers, her swollen face, her one eye closed, bruised purple and yellow. He could still hear her groans of pain, the quiet sobbing that had shaken her thin frame. He could still see the bloodstains on the thin mattress upon which she had lain, long, wet strands of saliva and bloody phlegm dribbling from her lips. What else could he have done?

Late in the frozen night he dragged her unconscious body into the backseat of his car. He removed his coat and draped it over her gently. He opened the trunk and threw a spade inside. His car was covered in mud when he returned to his office the following morning. Pine needles were stuck to its tires. The magazine of his personal weapon was two cartridges short. He instructed his aide to get the car washed and to clean the pistol. He didn't offer any explanations and didn't say where he had spent the night and why he appeared to have returned tired and battle-weary. He then instructed the maintenance officer in person to clean the detention cell in which Katrina Geifman had been held and to make it look as if no one had been in there for a very long time. Once again he offered no explanations, issuing his order with a tired and emotionless look in his eyes. In the early afternoon he informed his secretary that he hadn't been sleeping well at night and was going home to rest. And thus Katrina Geifman disappeared from the FSB's regional headquarters, as if she had never been there at all. No one documented her arrival. No one made note of the particulars of the officers who came all the way from Moscow just for her, no one filled out a release form or a death notice. There was no paper trail. Anyone who might have seen something had forgotten. Anyone who might have heard cries of pain and sobs of defeat hadn't actually heard a thing.

The furnace was ablaze in the home of Arkady's mother. Katrina was asleep under the thick blanket, breathing easily. The elderly mother was sitting in a chair by her side, her head drooping now and then in fits of sleep. The fire died down around midnight. The house fell quiet.

46

Zurich, Hotel Baur au Lac, March 2013
Alon spotted Brian from afar. Following security procedures came to him automatically by now. He'd been meeting with his handler once or twice a year for decades. Sometimes in Zurich, sometimes in Paris. He never felt compelled to account to anyone for his trips, but he always took the trouble to offer an explanation to those around him. Sometimes it was a trip for work purposes that he'd extend for a day or two. "Once I'm abroad, I may as well enjoy the weekend, too. I deserve it, don't I?" he'd say. And sometimes it was a vacation with his wife during which he'd disappear for brief periods of time. "This job is impossible," he'd sigh, and explain how he'd been instructed to deal with some crisis. His wife didn't ask questions. She had long since grown accustomed to the fact that his work was in the habit of invading their private

lives without explanation or hesitation. And she also enjoyed the moments of quiet and sudden sense of freedom afforded her by his absences. Each city required him to operate in keeping with precise instructions — when to arrive, the rendezvous point, which taxi to hail, and when to switch to a different one, which route to take on the subway, where to wait, and where to make the necessary time adjustments and keep himself busy for the exact amount of time set aside to allow his undercover counter-surveillance team to regroup. Once — it was hard for him to believe that so much time had passed since then, almost thirty years — once it was all new to him. The thrill, the anticipation, the meticulous carrying out of the instructions to the letter. His handlers were strict and unwavering, unwilling to cut any corners. He had gone through the same ritual many times, even on cold winter days, even if it was snowing, and he was used to it by now. Alon had grown accustomed to many things. To these meetings, to the excitement that washed through him nevertheless, to the constant fear of being exposed that never left him. When he wasn't able to sleep he'd imagine fists banging on the door of his home in the middle of the night, and him being led out in shackles, handcuffs around his wrists, two burly plainclothes policemen dragging him from his home, neighbors who had woken up peering through half-drawn curtains; his son, who still lived at home, waking up in fear; his wife, her hair disheveled, the rude awakening of the night exposing her vulnerability, mumbling, "Alon, Alon, what's happening?"

They had always followed procedures, and now this urgent call out of the blue. It had happened just once before, in 1996. He was instructed back then to follow the security procedures in place for Tel Aviv, and a windowless van showed up to collect him. Brian was waiting for him in the van, which pulled up for just a few seconds and then took off again right away. He shook his hand warmly, taking care not to stand up to greet him because of the violent rocking of the vehicle, which was switching from one lane to the next and making sudden sharp turns at very high speed. It was a meeting of the utmost importance and urgency insofar as they were concerned, due to tension along the northern border and concern regarding the possible outbreak of war. They needed to know what the prime minister really had in mind, what was being said during the cabinet discussions, where the red lines were being drawn, whether Israel would make do with a massive aerial bombardment or whether it would put its bigger plan into action. Alon had already told them about the plan — to move eight divisions into Syria, to lay siege to Damascus, and to move into Lebanon at the same time, along its eastern sector, with the purpose of getting through to the Beirut–Damascus highway, and from there to maneuver eastward, to complete the strategic encirclement and bring the Syrians to their knees.

The instruction this time had been a different one: Get to Zurich as soon as possible. It had come to him in the form of an encoded message on a website disguised as an international real-estate site offering opportunities to purchase land at attractive prices. He smiled wryly despite the sharp pain in his lower stomach. His communication with his handlers used to be a lot more primitive. It had started out in the form of letters written in invisible ink that became legible only after undergoing a special chemical process. The invisible marker was replaced over the years by special printer ink. He refused back then to allow his handlers to relay messages via shortwave radio transmissions. "I'm not going to close myself off in a room," he said to them, there's no way I'm going to lock the door and write down groups of letters to be deciphered thereafter like some kind of spy in World War II. That's not for me, it's dangerous and unnecessary, he said to Brian, who put up some resistance to begin with but eventually saw it his way. They came to an arrangement whereby he'd receive his missions once or twice a year during face-to-face meetings. Moreover, he liked those meetings and had no intention of making do with random letters as a rather pathetic and humiliating substitute for personal encounters.

They could now communicate online with complete confidence. That's what they told him, at least. But if they wanted to relay a message to him, they could also always revert to the age-old method of the chalk markings, which they still maintained as a backup. Each city had a unique sign. The code that alerted him this time was a simple one — a star drawn in red chalk, surrounded by a white circle, on the wooden fence of an apartment building on one of the small side streets leading off Ibn Gvirol. He made a point of passing by the fence almost daily, usually driving slowly in his car, and sometimes on foot. His handlers were sticklers when it came to routine and planning. No phone calls, no conspicuous e-mails. He had received just two calls from them over the past twenty years, both alleg-edly wrong numbers, and both intended to let him know that they'd left a sign for him down that small side street that he needed to go and see right away. One call every ten years. Alon couldn't help but marvel at the restraint and professionalism of his han-dlers. He loved them for that, too. For their serious attitude, for their sense of responsi-bility toward him. For their levelheadedness and self-confidence. And now this alert. Both online and in the form of the marking on the fence. Alon couldn't ignore the fact that this was the first time he had been sum-moned abroad, the first time in thirty years. His stomach had tightened, but his heart warmed and widened now as he spotted Brian from afar.

They embraced. Warmly. Genuinely happy.

"I'm sorry you had to wait for me," Alon said. "I needed some time to get organized. I couldn't just drop everything and leave the country right away. I had to wait until Thursday evening, and fly out only then to Vienna. I flew Austrian Airlines to Schwechat and went on from there with a Swiss ticket that I purchased at the airport. According to the drill. Like always. And here I am."

Brian and his men had waited for three days for Cobra to arrive. For three days the security teams took up positions in the hope of seeing him emerge from the northern gate of the Hauptbahnhof, the central train station. And only on day four, at the fixed time, at precisely two minutes past three, did they spot him. A slim figure, wrapped in a long coat, a casquette on his head, his eyes hidden behind sunglasses, emerging from the gate and turning right in the direction of the taxi rank. He walked slowly and joined the line, knowing they had eyes on him and were in position around him.

"No problem," Brian responded, "we always operate as agreed. We have patience and we have time. You have to do whatever suits you best. Don't forget, your safety comes first. Let's go to the bar, we'll have a drink, warm up a little."

Cobra and Brian were sitting on two antique leather armchairs in the dark corner of the bar, on the table in front of them polished crystal glasses filled with an amber gold liquid. Aged Calvados brandy, infused with the scent of apples, steeped in the rich flavors of Normandy, encapsulating, as Alon always imagined it, the commotion of the invading soldiers, the thunder of the land-ing craft crashing against the raging foam of the sea, the barrage of artillery shells, the assault charge, wave after wave of brave fighters, onto the beach. For some reason he thought all of a sudden about Martin, his first handler, the first one he met after walking into the U.S. embassy in Rome back then, so many years ago. He couldn't recall the name of the embassy's CIA officer, the one who had amusingly and clumsily insisted on introducing himself as a consular employee. He could only remember him appearing old and tired and even a little shoddy. But he could never forget Martin. Martin was the one who taught him to love Calvados. He taught him so much, and made him into the man he was today. Alon didn't love many people in his life. His mother, perhaps, but for her it was mostly concern, and the concern far outweighed the love. Yes, he loved Naomi and Nimrod, his children, but that was the love of a parent. Based primarily, from his point of view, on a profound sense of duty and responsibility. But Martin he truly loved. From the bottom of his heart. The love of a young man for an older one, a strong man, full of charm. Not an erotic love — although the question of where one draws that line between loves had crossed Alon's mind

344

more than just once — but a love that meant a desire to be with, that sparked yearning and pining. Martin, Martin. And then came Brian. He'd known him for twenty-five years already. Maybe more. They'd been together for a lifetime. Oh, how time flies.

They sipped their drinks, and then another one each. Brian had yet to explain the nature of the pressing urgency. Why they had summoned him in such a hurry. But he knew it was coming. Precise timing was of the essence insofar as Brian was concerned. Alon had learned that a long time ago. "Let's go outside for a while," Brian suggested. "We'll take a walk by the lake. A bit of clean, cold air won't do us any harm."

"So here's the story," Brian said. The dark water of the lake lapped at the shore. Alon was walking to his right, wondering who of all the people he could see around them was a member of the security team.

"I'm afraid that moment has come," Brian said. "That moment at which the relationship between us is facing a very real risk of being exposed." He looked at Cobra to see his reaction. He had taken him outdoors intentionally, so that if he was going to react in an unexpected or unrestrained manner, then at least he would do so in an open area with few onlookers rather than in the hotel. He needed the space around him. The space and the ability to respond accordingly. But Cobra as usual was cold, and his narrow eyes looked straight ahead, and not at him.

"There's been a leak. Something out of our control. Something that appears to be tied to the distant past. And it's risen to the surface all of a sudden. We believe, we know in fact, that Israeli security officials are on the hunt these days for an agent high up in the government establishment. They're in possession of solid information that is causing them to look, to leave no stone unturned. And if they persist, they're likely to get their hands on you. But we can preempt that. We want you to come to us. Now. You'll be safe with us."

Alon felt his balls tighten and shrink. The tremor that shook his body traveled from his scalp down to his anus. He hoped it was merely an inner sensation, and that Brian hadn't noticed.

Brian had.

A bitter taste filled Alon's mouth, and he sensed a foul odor on his breath. He asked Brian if he had a mint.

"Let's sit down for a while," Brian suggested, and he led the way to a bench overlooking the lake, which appeared to be darkening, as if black ink had been poured into its waters. Their security detail, a young man and woman who were following them, stopped and took up a lookout position some distance away. The young man retrieved a pack of cigarettes from the pocket of his leather jacket, lit one, inhaled deeply and with obvious pleasure, and said: "It's going to be a long night." The woman tightened the scarf around her neck. A cold mist was coming off the lake.

Appearing to have guessed his need ahead of time, Brian took out a box of strong mints and handed it to Cobra. "Look, Alon," he said in a soft yet distinctly resolute tone, "now's the time for some quick decision-making. The danger is real. But there's no need for hysteria or panic. You know how important you are to us, and we'd do everything to keep you in place. The information you've been feeding us is of enormous value, and you know that we've expressed our deep appreciation for your contribution through deeds and not just words. You've helped us, and in doing so you've added to the stability of the region as a whole. We admire your courage and perseverance. But you, Alon, you are more important to us than anything else. We don't want your cover to be blown, with all its implications. And you know what I'm talking about. So here's what I'm saying to you: Come with us now. Don't return to Israel. We'll take care of everything that needs to be done. You'll be joined within a few months by your wife and children, or at least your son who still lives at home. You'll have a good life in Moscow. Among friends. Completely secure. We can keep you safe there."

Alon wasn't sure he had heard correctly. "Moscow?" he asked suddenly, his voice cracking.

Brian decided not to go easy on him. Convey the message as clearly and unequivocally as possible, and Cobra wouldn't be able to deny or suppress it. "Yes, Moscow. Or St. Petersburg. Wherever you like. And you'll also get a summer house, a dacha. On the shores of the Black Sea. With weather just like at home, right?"

Alon was confused. What was this about Moscow all of a sudden? Or St. Petersburg? A dacha? He felt strange, as if he had detached from his body and was now observing himself from above, his shadow lengthening. He caught a glimpse of himself behind his eyelids, which he had closed for a moment — a young and headstrong man, ringing the bell of the U.S. embassy in Rome. How had he gone from there to Russia? He stared at his handler, his eyes dark and cold. "What are you telling me, Brian? What are you saying?"

Brian began telling Cobra the cover story he had prepared for this very moment. "Look, Alon," he said. "It's long and complex, and we're still going to talk about it a whole lot more, and in depth. But I'll fill you in on the main points right now. At some point in the past, the superpowers — the Soviet Union, Russia today, and the United States — came to an understanding that may appear surprising on the backdrop of the Cold War. But that makes absolute sense when you think about it. The supreme interest of both countries, from the 1980s onward, at least, has been stability. Stability with no decisive outcome. The price of instability is simply too high. Unbearable even. And the developments we have witnessed over the past twenty to thirty years have only reinforced this principle. Stability and a balance of power. To avoid any deterioration in the situation, any loss of control that would lead to a disaster. Yes, there were those who, for a brief and inconsequential moment in time, announced to the world that the conflict had been decided, and that there was only one superpower left in this world. There were idiots who spoke of the end of an era. Ignorant intellectuals, foolish and irresponsible. It remained clear all the while, or it should have remained so, at least, that what we really needed was a fine and well-monitored balance between Washington and Moscow. The conflict that emerged after the Great Patriotic War couldn't be allowed to end in a decisive victory. That would spell certain disaster for both sides. High-ranking and responsible officials from both countries have worked in earnest to ensure the preservation of this balance. On all levels."

"What does all this have to do with me?" Alon asked.

"You showed up at the American embassy in Rome some thirty years ago. You offered to do all you could for the good of this stability, and if possible — for the sake of peace in the Middle East. You said you'd go far, that you'd rise to positions of influence, and you've kept your promise admirably. You've become a significant player. With the courage of a soldier in civilian dress, you've worked to prevent your region from dragging the planet into a third world war. It's been thrilling to observe you. Making the right choice, choosing you, gave us a sense of pride. But for the sake of that crucial, that essential, that indispensable balance, the powers that be decided consensually that we would assume responsibility for maintaining the relationship with you, sharing all the intelligence and insights you pass on to us with our colleagues in Langley."

Brian went silent. And Cobra didn't say a word either. Brian had voiced that same explanation, the one he had just given to Cobra, dozens of times before. To himself and in numerous conversations with his superiors at the directorate. He had always asked himself if there was any logic at all to the crazy story. Would Cobra see it as a likely explanation for the fact that he'd been in the hands of the Russian SVR and not the American CIA, contrary to what he'd thought all through the years? And he had always told himself that even if the story was far-fetched and not very convincing, Cobra would prefer it to the truth. Because the true story was worse, a lot worse. A story of betrayal upon betrayal. Cobra, who was betraying his country, and his handlers, who were betraying him. That could be too much to handle even for a man of no scruples. Cobra would rather cling to the fantasy and believe he was part of a huge web of considerations and forces working to promote stability and calm and not some idiot who had fallen victim to manipulation for the past three decades.

Alon tried, despairingly, to argue. "Well, if that's the case, why don't your partners in Washington put me up, in San Francisco or Boston or Chicago? And I'm not going to say anything just yet about the fact that you could have shared your thinking with me, this concept of yours of the global balance."

"The moment we assumed responsibility for the relationship with you, Alon, the responsibility to offer you a quiet and safe place in the event of your exposure became ours, too. Ours and no one else's. And the only place where we can ensure your security is with us. Security and a good life and people who appreciate you. That's what I'm offering you now. You'll be a hero, Alon. But you must understand that we are serious. We need to act immediately. Trust us, just as you have trusted us all these years. We've never let you down. You know that. The sums of money deposited for you over the years — they'll also help you to acclimatize. Not that you'll need the money. We won't let you down now either, now that it's time to decide quickly and take action."

"Listen to me, Brian," Alon said quietly, almost in a whisper, dead tired all of a sudden. "I'm getting up and leaving now. I need some alone time. Quiet time. You can't drop something like this on me and expect me to simply accept it, without questioning myself. You've been like a big brother to me for so many years, and now I don't know who you are. You can't even imagine the danger you've put me in. I'm not a piece in a game. You, and your partners, if any part of your story is actually true, have treated me like a puppet on a string. What a cliché. Who do you think you are?" He raised his voice. "I'm a personal senior advisor to the prime minister, not some pathetic informer! I meet with presidents and heads of state! I'm authorized to read documents from the Mossad and Military Intelligence and the Shin Bet and the Atomic Energy Commission. You can't treat me like some kind of pawn, someone of insignificance that can be moved from one place to another like a package."

Brian put his hand on Cobra's arm, but the latter pulled it away as if he'd been burned. "Alon, Alon, I understand you. I understand your emotional turmoil. Being a covert fighter for so long isn't easy. Yes, you're right, you need some time to yourself. You need some quiet. We'll accompany you to your hotel. Have a good night's sleep.

353

We'll see each other tomorrow. We'll talk. You'll see things differently. You're dear to me like a little brother. I won't let anything happen to you. No one will touch you, Alon. Come, come let's go." He stood up and Cobra did the same, swaying a little, clutching his arm. Night had fallen. A chill was blowing onto the shore from the lake. They started walking. At a distance of a few dozen meters the pair of bodyguards set out in their wake.

47

Alon was sitting on a chair on the small balcony of his room, which overlooked the black waters of the lake. He had left the room in darkness and had wrapped himself in his coat. Wisps of smoke rose from the cigar in his hand, a Punch Double Corona, which glowed a dull orange. He sat there and thought.

Again he could picture the young man, filled with conviction, who had rung at the door of the U.S. embassy in Rome all those years ago. Sometimes he recognized him, remembered who he was. He recalled his unbridled ambition, his deep-seated desire to go as far and as deep as possible, all the way into hidden, smoke-filled rooms that required presenting a tag or ID before the security guards would allow you in. And no less so, Alon recalled his fear of poverty. He saw his mother sitting at the small table in the kitchen, bent over a notebook, doing the math with a sharpened pencil, counting out the meager pile of banknotes and coins, counting and making notes, carefully slipping the money into the various compartments of her wallet. He felt a yearning for his father, whom he barely remembered. His hatred of the uncles who'd visit them on the rare occasion and disappear into his mother's bedroom, until they stopped coming altogether. The thing that had saved him already back then was his unquenchable thirst for knowledge. Everything interested him — dates, details, names, well-known sayings by famous people, verses that begged quoting, algebraic formulas, programming languages. He remembered the initial battery of tests for the Israeli naval commanders course, the second testing phase, the excitement when the course started, the sense of disaster and shame when he was dropped, his insistence on embarking on an officers' course nevertheless, the white uniform, the gold insignia of his rank, the small base he commanded. And despite his success, he remained envious of anyone who was better looking, smarter, richer.

He thought again about Martin. One night, and he still a young man at the time, they finished off an entire bottle of vodka

together, while eating Beluga caviar with a
soup spoon from a large tin. Martin looked
very pleased with himself when morning
broke — not a drop left in the bottle, the
tin shiny and empty, the two of them drunk
and kings of the world. That night, as if to
shed a heavy load off his chest, he told Martin about Israel's strategic energy reserves,
the quantities of oil and gas in the underground reservoirs, and the rationale underlying the calculation of those reserves, how
many days Israel could survive without support and provisions from the outside. He
was serving at the time as the young and
brilliant aide to the minister of energy and
infrastructure, and the minister, a former
general, gray-haired, a long scar running
from his right eye down to his chin, said to
him back then, You see, Alon, someone here
needs to be serious, and the seriousness
starts here with us. We'll hold out for as long
as we have to, and we'll have the courage
and the perseverance and the patience, and
if we're pushed into a corner we'll take
everyone with us. Get it? I don't mean
another Masada, or Bar Kokhba revolt, or
like Saul falling on his sword. I'm talking
about the end of the world. And he told
Martin not only about the reserves, but
about everything else the minister had said

to him, too. And Martin sought his advice, asked for his opinion, asked if he didn't think the numbers had been intentionally exaggerated, and if the minister's sentiments weren't somewhat grandiose, and how it all fitted in with his perception of the geostrategic reality. And Alon, who had yet to sink into the embracing fog of the vodka, talked and talked, and Martin allowed himself to take out a small notepad and write some things down, so as not to forget, and rest a strong, fatherly hand on his shoulder.

Vodka and caviar? Alon asked himself, staring into the blackness of the lake. Just like any good old American, right? But Martin was the last person you'd think was a Soviet secret agent. His openness, humor, no-holds-barred criticism, the scope of his education, his range of knowledge, his love of baseball, for fuck's sake, the perfect English, with that unique New England accent. Alon had always felt, even if he didn't really know for sure, that he had a good grasp of Martin. He was a good American, he was willing to bet that he collected baseball cards as a kid. Martin, after all, was an avid admirer of American literature, and would even quote entire lines from Walt Whitman's *Leaves of Grass* when the mood took him. How could he have known? He couldn't have been from the KGB. Alon tried to figure out where it had all gone wrong. Perhaps the transition to the KGB occurred only with Brian? But Brian was a professor and the son of a professor from a prestigious East Coast university. That is, if he wasn't a CIA officer. But it was the same Brian who was now offering him refuge in Russia. Something here didn't make sense at all. He had a throbbing pain in his temples and the acid again rose from his stomach and burned through his chest and throat. He inhaled again and the cigar only made things worse.

48

It was early evening and Ya'ara was overcome once again by that familiar sense of
discomfort, that nagging boredom, that
yearning to do something, to be outside, to
breathe in fresh air, anything but remain
closed up in a standard hotel room, with its
wall-to-wall carpeting and a double bed and
small desk and an armchair in the corner
and a television with nothing on except the
incessant drivel of CNN and Fox and ABC
and a million other equally tedious stations.
She picked up her book again, an old
Somerset Maugham novel, and laid it down
again a few minutes later. The small, tightly
packed letters danced before her eyes. Spying is waiting, apparently, but it drives you
crazy sometimes. Waiting, waiting, waiting.
For how long? When was something going
to happen already? She lay down on the

bed, her one bare foot hanging over the edge of the mattress. She stretched and drew her left hand across her breasts. Her other hand slipped into her panties, indifferently stroking the small mound, the mound of Venus, feeling its sweet softness over the hard bone. She could feel the familiar wetness, but she didn't want to continue. Not alone. She got off the bed and took a shower. She then dressed herself in a pretty, light-colored outfit, put on her pearl necklace, and went down to the bar.

With a glass of Jack Daniel's in her hand she went out to the freezing indoor patio, wrapping herself in her coat. The air was cold and crisp just like she wanted, and she felt revitalized. The bourbon warmed her and she felt good all over. Her cheeks were flushed when she went back inside, and the sparks from the fire burning in the large fireplace reflected off her light hair. She asked for another glass of bourbon, something light and pleasant swirled in her head, and she sat down in a huge armchair, one of two positioned on either side of the fireplace. She still sensed she needed to remain in Providence for a few more days. She needed to be patient. She would pay another visit to the Hart family's home two or three days from now. Ya'ara knew: If she got her timing right, something would transpire. She had sensed the connection that formed between herself and Frances against the backdrop of Frances's concern and fear for the fate of her husband, who had gotten up in the middle of the night and disappeared without any real explanation. When she held Frances's hands, when she soothed her with the look in her eyes, she discerned a response of sorts from that elegant, hard, and miserable woman. And now she had to wait. To wait for the right moment. Not yet, she said to herself, a little longer.

She looked up and smiled at the young man who had sat down in the armchair across from her. She liked the look of him. His hair a little disheveled, a handsome face, a strong chin, a large, straight nose. He ordered a cognac from the waiter who approached him, settled back in his chair, and stretched his legs.

"It's nice here, isn't it? Just like this, doing nothing," Ya'ara addressed him.

"I love this fireplace. Yes. What a day I had. You have no idea. I hate lawyers. Hate them."

"No offense, but you look a little like a lawyer yourself. That's what I would have guessed anyway."

He sighed. "You're right. That's why I can't bear them. Being with them in endless meetings. Going through clause after clause after clause and constantly squabbling. I'm Don."

"Annabelle," Ya'ara said. That was the name she had registered under at the hotel. Annabelle Eshel, just in case Frances Hart, or Julian Hart perhaps, came looking for her.

"And what about you? You don't look like a lawyer to me. Academic researcher? A spy?"

"A spy only in my free time. But most of my days are taken up with classical studies, and I'm also a consultant to an antiquities dealer."

"So you're one of those smart young women, right?"

"Spend the evening with me and you'll find out just how smart I am."

Ya'ara rested her head on Don's chest, her light hair, which was partly covering her face, revealing an ever-watchful blue-gray eye. She felt wonderfully relaxed and her body seemed to be brimming with delight. The soft light emanating from the bathroom accentuated her beauty. She rose lightly from the bed, and her body appeared strong

363

and graceful as she walked across the floor. Like a dangerous tigress, Don thought. "It was a wonderful evening," she said to him. "I'm gonna take a shower now, and then I want to get some sleep. Alone. I hate not getting enough sleep. Good night." As he made his way to the door, a clearly astounded Don could hear the powerful jet of water splashing against her body. A fragrant mist filled the room.

49

Brian walked past the car in which the two counter-surveillance agents were sitting. A young man and woman, who had spent the entire night outside Cobra's hotel. The woman recognized him and got out of the car. Brian stopped alongside a bench farther down the street and she joined him. He offered her a cigarette, and she took one, along with his offer of a light, both his and her hand shielding the small flame, touching each other momentarily.

"Nothing," she said to him. "Since parting company with you and returning to the hotel, he hasn't gone out at all. Vasily did a walk-through of the lobby and also had a quick look into the dining room about ten minutes ago, but he wasn't there. They'll be serving breakfast for just another twenty minutes, and if he doesn't come down he'll miss it."

Brian looked at his watch. Eleven minutes past ten. The breakfast was the least of his concerns. "I'll go in now," he said. "If he doesn't come down to the dining room, I'll wake him. We can't leave him on his own. He's had a rough night, and if he's falling apart, we'll have to pull him together again. That's what we are here for. You're doing a good job, Natasha Petrovna. When are your replacements coming?"

"At twelve. Don't worry, we're keeping an eye on him and won't let him disappear. In the event of anything out of the ordinary, we'll let you know. If we spot or sense any danger, we'll get you out. We'll get you to the safe house in Geneva and take it from there. In keeping with procedures."

Procedures, procedures, procedures. Everything in keeping with procedures. Brian was well aware of the importance of procedures, of the experience and collective wisdom they embodied, yet he couldn't bear them. Sometimes he'd look at himself from the outside and struggle to recall what a professor of ancient world history at Brown University was doing among all these spies and procedures. It was good of them to afford him a secret trip to Moscow once a year, albeit just for two days — but even that was better than nothing. It was his way of refocusing. He would go off to a conference at the University of Vienna, stay on a few days for meetings and archive work, meet with the courier who gave him a passport and air ticket, and disappear. Forty-eight hours during which he wasn't Julian Hart or Brian Cox or anyone else. Simply himself. And they welcomed him with open arms on those visits! They spoke to him only in Russian, and he was always amazed by how well he remembered, but felt, too, that his language was a little behind the times. And the meetings with the head of the directorate and the SVR chief. They appreciated his sacrifice. The huge burden of living under two identities. In two worlds. The loneliness. And at the division, at the division he would be briefed and brought up to speed. And there was also the refresher course on how to operate the secret communications system, despite the fact that he'd been using it for years already without any mishaps.

And the firing range, they always took him to the firing range, shooting practice with a SIG Sauer 9mm pistol. That was the type of pistol they had given him years ago; he kept it stashed away at his home in Rhode Island. Not that you couldn't purchase a gun in the United States. You could buy yourself a tank or fighter jet as well. But headquarters didn't want there to be a record anywhere, not even at some remote guns and fishing gear store, of Professor Hart owning a weapon. He was not supposed to use it anyway except in an emergency, and exactly what would constitute an emergency, if one ever arose, wasn't very clear. As unlikely to actually happen as it was, if called in for questioning or arrested, his explicit instructions were: Your cover is your weapon. It's so deep and tight that it would be impossible to incriminate you. A cover story and lawyers of the highest order. Don't ever put up a fight and don't ever turn your weapon on the American law enforcement authorities, not the police and not the FBI. You'll achieve your victory by way of the secrecy and the cover. So why a gun then? For unforeseen circumstances, in which the good old gun could offer a more appropriate response. In any event, he enjoyed the ritual of the firing range. He and the hard-assed instructor alongside his handler, all alone at the range. The three of them shooting. And he was not bad, not bad at all, particularly considering the fact that he didn't do any shooting practice and wasn't all that young these days. He was steady and composed, and in good physical shape, too, the instructor told him. And after the range, after cleaning the weapons and ensuring again that they were unloaded and the chambers were empty, the instructor would give him a rattling punch on his right shoulder and then embrace him and tell him to take care. See you next year.

He saw Cobra exit the elevator and turn toward the dining room. He looked pale, and there were dark circles under his eyes, but his composure remained intact. Clean-shaven, his clothes pressed. An unstoppable glint of joy flashing through his narrow eyes on spotting Brian. That's good, he still wants to see me, Brian thought. As long as he's not falling apart, that's the main thing, and if he does so, then let it at least happen when I have him under my control.

"Good morning, may I join you? I've eaten already, but I'll have a cup of coffee."

"Good morning. And go ahead. You're paying in any case."

They sat at a small table in the corner of the dining room. An elderly waitress poured them coffee and orange juice. Cobra went to the buffet and returned with a half-empty plate.

"I'd like to take a walk with you for a while," Brian said. "There are two or three antiquities stores that I need to visit, and I think we should go see the Paul Klee exhibition. A wonderful show. We can talk there and on the way. And then in our basement. Beer, sausages, and rösti, just like civilized people should eat."

"I'm going back tonight. The flight leaves at eleven. I'm all yours until then."

"That's what I want to talk to you about. I don't think you should go back. It's too risky. The name of the game at this stage is speed. Who's quicker. Who's more decisive. We know they're looking. We don't know where they are in their search, or if they're about to get to you. But believe me, if they have something to go on, their motivation is sky high. They won't stop at anything. And we have to be one step ahead. To act fast. Not fast. Right now. Immediately." He paused after realizing he had raised his voice. Brian continued, trying to radiate authority and restraint. "We have to ensure that when they do get to you, all they find is a ghost. You'll be elsewhere by then, safe, out of their reach. Think about it. About their frustration. About outsmarting them once again. About outdoing them again."

"Brian, how we ended up in a situation like this was all I thought about all night long. About the fact that you don't know how to safeguard your secrets. About the fact that you've screwed up with respect to safeguarding me. That you've been deceiving me all these years."

"I could tell you a different story," Brian responded. "One about how we've been looking after you for thirty years. How now, too, we can make sure you aren't caught, and can go on living a good and secure life. I could remind you of your enormous contribution to the fact that the volatile region in which you live is still in one piece. The Middle East could have sparked three world wars by now, but the balance we've managed to create, and the cooperation between ourselves and the United States, have prevented them. We've had the wisdom to draw the lines in the right places, to keep tensions in check, to ensure that no one gets too powerful. And you, we, our work together, have played a significant role in doing so. It's not something I'd belittle, or erase, Alon. You've enjoyed tremendous achievements. Historic. Of near epic proportions. Not to mention the financial reward you stand to gain. Eight million dollars await you in an account in Lausanne, not to mention the other accounts. Where's that money come from? I'm not saying you haven't earned it or don't deserve it, but

I'm allowed to remind you, now and then, that it came from us. We've never failed to keep our promises to you. We've always kept our word. So now, in a time of crisis, I think you should listen to us. Listen to me. We want this story to end well. I'm looking out for you, Alon. I value you. I love you as if you were my brother. So listen to me, listen to me."

50

Tel Aviv, March 2013

Michael and Adi were standing in the kitchen next to the small espresso machine. Michael had brought the red machine to the office just a week ago and everyone was already hooked on it. The clear glass bowl standing on the granite countertop was filled with colorful, shiny capsules, like a collection of assorted candies, enveloped by the strong aroma of fresh coffee.

"Tell me," Michael said, "does the database now include all the material we received from Amir's friend at the Interior Ministry?"

"That's exactly what I'm working on now," Adi responded. "I'm almost done. I took a coffee break and I'm now adding the remaining data to the Excel spreadsheet. Essentially it's just a big table, not some sophisticated system. But we may be able to learn something from it. When does Aharon get back?"

"He's back already. Arrived yesterday, in the early evening. Still recovering from the flight. He should be here soon."

"And Ya'ara?"

"She stayed on in Providence. I spoke to her early this morning. Before my run. She's hanging around there for a while. She didn't say exactly why, and it's never really a good idea to say too much over the phone anyway. But there's still something she wants to do there."

He inserted a green capsule into the machine and continued: "Amir is working his ass off at school, waiting for us to rescue him and summon him to work. And Aslan is killing me, pestering and pestering, wanting to know when this whole thing is going to end, because he needs to arrange some rafting trip down the Amazon or something like that."

"When is it going to end really? What do you think?" Adi touched the pendant on the chain around her neck.

"From the little I got from Aharon, I think we're getting close. He didn't want to elaborate on the phone. And that's just the way he is, too, you know, a man of mystery. He has his ways. Anyway, based on what Bill Pemberton has told us, Julian Hart, who they believe to be a Russian intelligence officer living deep undercover in the United States, could be Brian, Cobra's handler. And it appears that Hart was summoned suddenly by his handlers a few days ago and has now disappeared. A sign that we've stirred the pot, and things are starting to happen. And I'm telling you, if Brian did go abroad all of a sudden, there's a very good chance that Cobra has done the same, presumably to meet with him. Perhaps they sense we're onto something."

"How could they know?"

"Via Katrina perhaps. They may have found out that we met with her, and that she said something to us about Cobra. It seems a bit of a stretch, but it's possible. I don't know how efficient they are, but don't forget they have a tradition of investigations and surveillance operations dating back to 1917. They know the job. I asked Ya'ara to call Katrina, as a personal gesture of sorts, a follow-up to her visit as Galina, Igor's daughter. But no one's answering there. Ya'ara tried contacting her at various times of the day. Either Katrina's gone on holiday, to her granddaughter, perhaps, or they've already got their hands on her and know we're on the chase. Let's complete the table and see if we learn anything we don't yet know."

They moved to the room in which Adi was working. Michael settled into the armchair in the corner of the room, closed his eyes, and tried to figure out how instead of working on the law office he wanted to open he was now caught up in this Aharon Levin–orchestrated adventure. As always.

Adi worked diligently and quickly. Michael marveled at her skills. He could see the serious look on her face, her focused eyes. An almost imperceptible bluish vein throbbed in her forehead.

"Let's see," she said to herself and him, some twenty minutes later. "Let's see what we've come up with."

Michael got up from the armchair and stood behind her.

"It'll be easier if you sit next to me," Adi said. "Pull up a chair. There you go, here. I'm cross-referencing based on the few particulars we have on Cobra," she explained. "Remember — and it's important — that Cobra may not appear in the table at all. He could be someone we haven't even thought of but, insofar as the Russians are concerned, who still warrants the title of top-level agent in terms of his access to information. It's their definition, after all,

376

not ours. In any event, based on the way this country works, there could very well be people with access to the most important secrets even if they're not official cogs in the system."

Michael was familiar with Adi's prudence and remained silent. And as she typed he saw the tables changing before his eyes.

"Here we go," she said. "Look! We have five results!"

Michael moved closer and looked at the monitor. Staring back at him were five names, and five role descriptions: the industry and trade minister, the deputy director of the Defense Ministry's political-security division, the prime minister's political strategy advisor, the head of the Shin Bet's counterintelligence wing, and the chief of the IDF's Northern Command headquarters. Those were the five, out of a pool of hundreds of officeholders with access to sensitive state secrets, who matched the criteria Adi had determined for the purpose of cross-checking the data — date of birth between 1/15 and 2/15, between the years 1950 and 1960, and a trip abroad in 1989 at some point between 3/20 and 4/5.

Michael reminded himself to heed Adi's words of caution. Yes, there was a good chance Cobra wasn't even on the list of names that were included in the database. But a thrill of excitement coursed through him nevertheless. He affectionately caressed Adi's head, as if he was ruffling the hair of a small child, and said, "Wow, Adi. This is wonderful. We're close, sweetheart, we're close. I can feel it!"

He then called Amir. He heard the sound of passionate conversation and Amir yelling, "Hello, hello!" Amir must have stepped away from the group because suddenly he could hear him. "Hi, sorry. We're on a break. You know what these youngsters are like, savages. What's going on?"

"Listen, I need something urgently. Take a short break from your doctorate and call your friend at the Interior Ministry. By the way, the two of you have done a great job. Well done. Now give him these five names, and ask him to check if any one of them has left the country recently, in the last seven days. Okay?"

"Aye, aye, sir," Amir said, and he started writing down the names and ID numbers of the five suspects offered up by Adi's table.

A wave of energy washed through Michael. And just as if he were traveling in a particularly fast car, he saw the road flash by under his feet, leaving a blurry trail in its wake, and a bright horizon up ahead.

51

Michael left the apartment and headed for the bar at Hotel Montefiore. It was early afternoon and the sun still caressed the street. On display at the entrance to the hotel stood a broad-rimmed ceramic bowl filled with pale lemons. Pieces of silverware gleamed in the pleasant dimness of the place. He ordered a double shot of Lagavulin. The drink's strong, smoky aroma burned his nostrils and, as always, gave rise to a yearning for foreign and faraway lands. His thoughts carried him back two years. To Anaïs. She had remained a constant fixture in his subconscious from the moment they met. As if she had taken up permanent residence there, just below the surface, rising to the top from time to time, flashing an enigmatic smile, disappearing for long stretches, her underlying presence accompanying him nevertheless, like music that only he could hear. To say he knew her would be a bit much, he told himself. He knew only what she chose to show him, after all. Highly professional. The best in the business. They met for the first time in Hamburg. It was a cold and gloomy evening, and he had sought refuge in the bar of the Hotel Atlantic. She was already sitting at the bar, a dark beauty, her skin a velvety deep brown, her eyes black, huge, her hair cropped very short. In her mid-thirties, he guessed. The ring on her right hand drew his attention. A large green stone, an emerald, perhaps, in an unpolished yellow gold setting. "That's a beautiful ring," he said to her, unable to restrain himself, and she responded, absentmindedly twisting the ring around her finger: "Thanks; a keepsake from the Old World. The Austro-Hungarian Empire, no less." She spoke American English, he was sure of that, but he thought he detected a hint of a foreign accent, too.

From that moment onward he broke every rule in the book. He was on operational assignment at the time, a series of meetings with an agent who was in Hamburg as the chief mate of a Finnish ship that sailed regularly along the Europe–Eastern Mediterranean line. He had few opportunities to meet with the agent during the three days when the ship was docked at the city's enormous port. And those meetings were devoted to final briefings ahead of a mission in Tripoli, to a tiresome evening at a shady nightclub on the Reeperbahn, Hamburg's infamous red-light district, and to further instruction on the photographic equipment the agent would be using. The instruction itself was superfluous in light of the agent's obvious high level of proficiency, but doing things methodically and by the book was an absolute must. And instead of remaining focused on his agent, Michael's head was constantly elsewhere. Anaïs. Anaïs. The lawyer from Chicago. He fell in love even with the unique name her father had insisted on giving her when she was born, in honor of the French writer he loved. By now Michael had identified the hint of a Czech accent that accompanied her sultry voice. Yes, she was born in Prague. She told him quite a lot about herself during those sweet, lazy hours they spent lying sleepily in the oversized bed in her room, between one bout of sex and the next, drinking black-red Barolo wine he purchased and smuggled into the hotel room. He told her about himself, too. About his work as a personal and discreet consultant to several business tycoons. He was a troubleshooter when necessary, a friend when needed, and he also told them the truth to their faces, that's what they paid him to do. He didn't tell her about the Mossad, of course. He didn't tell her about his family, who were waiting for him back in Tel Aviv. But despite all the masks, he spoke about himself in a way he hadn't with any other woman in a very long time. They both traveled frequently and arranged to meet again, if and when they happened to be going to the same part of the world at the same time. No, she said, Chicago wasn't a good place to meet. Yes, she was still involved in a relationship that should have ended long ago, but it was complicated, and they'd just met, after all, so they should bide their time and allow various other things to run their course. If they ran into each other again, if fate brought them together once more, that would surely be a sign. Don't look so serious, honey, she had said. Come, come here a minute.

When he emailed her a few months later to tell her he was traveling to Delhi, she replied: You're not going to believe this, but I'm going to be in Mumbai and Bangalore at the same time, and I'll come see you in Delhi. We'll get just one room this time, okay? He didn't give a thought to the coincidence and delighted in the fact that destiny would have him see her again, and together in the same wonderful room at the Kempinski Hotel, no less. He postponed his return to Israel by two and a half days, and she managed to clear her calendar in Chicago, too. After all, I'm a senior partner, she said.

Come with me, she whispered to him on the second evening. I want to show you something. They set out in a small, cramped taxi in the direction of the airport and came to a quiet residential neighborhood, as quiet as anywhere in India could be. The neighborhood appeared dotted with luxurious homes. Groups of security guards and drivers and random loiterers stood at the gates to all the houses. Despite the magnificence of the structures, the streets themselves were dusty and filled with potholes. Dogs with their tails between their legs and scrawny cows roamed freely. The taxi stopped at a small commercial center that reminded Michael of remote shopping centers in development towns in Israel. Anaïs forged a path for them among rickshaw drivers who were sitting around on small chairs, waiting for customers who might or might not show up, and made her way toward a locked iron door. She sent a WhatsApp message, received a number in response, and entered the digits into the keypad lock. The door swung open with a hiss and they climbed the dimly lit staircase to the second floor, where they were greeted politely by a young man. Anaïs led the way in without a word. And the moment they entered he felt as if they had time-traveled to a different world. Antique leather armchairs, greenish in color, furnished the room. A large wooden ceiling fan spun lazily above them. Bottles of expensive beverages stood on one of the dressers that were inlaid with mother of pearl, and resting atop a low table like an old lion was a large humidor, made of polished red wood. Like a display case for expensive jewelry, its glass lid revealed an array of spectacular Cuban cigars. Covered with plush wallpaper adorned with intricate patterns, the room's walls displayed black-and-white photographs of famous cigar smokers, from Che Guevara and Churchill to Sean Connery and Robert De Niro. A handsome young waiter quietly poured them each a shot of single malt Scotch. Anaïs went over to the humidor and selected two cigars for them, Cohiba Siglo VIs. "You smoke cigars?" Michael asked, somewhat taken aback. "I do a whole lot of things you don't know about," she replied with smiling eyes, and Michael's heart was gripped by a yearning still to come, a longing for Anaïs even though she was sitting there right in front of him at the time. Sitting at the tables in the relatively small room were two pairs of men and another group, two men and a young woman. Everyone was speaking in soft tones. A cloud of bluish smoke filled the room. A sense of calm and lethargy spread through his limbs, and they spent several minutes puffing on their cigars without any desire or need to talk. Michael gazed at Anaïs and was struck again by her beauty. In the dim light he could hardly see the scar alongside her left eye, which he had come to love and would sometimes gently caress, with their faces almost touching each other.

"I want you to meet someone," she said to him. "After you told me about your consulting work, I thought the two of you may have some shared interests. Only if you want to, of course. He's a childhood friend of mine who's in Delhi for a few days, and he told me he could join us. He manages a huge investment fund in Atlanta. We represent some of his companies, and he's someone special. Not your ordinary millionaire, if there is such a thing at all. But then again," she added, "you aren't just an ordinary guy either."

Despite wanting to erase it, not only from

his memory but also, and primarily, from the depths of his consciousness, Michael couldn't forget the conversation he had that evening with Chris Bentham. Nothing, absolutely nothing could have performed that absolute delete that Michael so craved.

There was something amiss about the conversation, but it was impossible to pinpoint anything concrete. And Michael had certainly tried to do so in hindsight. They were speaking about business and about the world and about the craziness of India, and naturally Chris showed an interest in the Middle East and Israel, and its red-hot high-tech companies. And Michael asked questions, mostly to be polite and maintain his cover story, and showed an interest in Chris's work, and without making any commitments they even broached the subject of meeting again, maybe even the following day, in Delhi, but if it didn't work out then soon, perhaps, on one of Michael's trips to Europe. And he'd be very welcome to visit of course if he ever got to Atlanta, but Europe was more or less a midpoint, so it would probably be the most convenient for them both. But it wasn't all that noncommittal talk that was bothering Michael. What was really troubling him immensely, like a near-inaudible high-pitched shriek, the thing that seemed so strange to him, was the thought that he wasn't hearing Chris but himself instead. Chris sounded exactly how he must have sounded during the hundreds of conversations he'd conducted over the years. That was how he had conversed, fishing for things from his objects, those individuals introduced to him in discreet bars, hotel conference rooms, aboard luxury yachts by Arab headhunters or beautiful women. Surely, he thought, Chris can't be trying to recruit me, because that would mean that Anaïs had initiated the contact with me precisely for the purpose of getting to this point in time. But I was the one to approach her, he thought. After all, she was already at the bar when I walked in. She couldn't have known I'd be going to the bar at the Atlantic. Unless, unless they've followed me before and have seen that that's where I go to seek refuge, to pass the time, to somewhat dull all the thoughts racing so chaotically through my mind. Surely not.

Essentially, Chris wasn't saying anything any other businessman wouldn't have said. But the way in which he was speaking, his pace, the timing, the implied offers, the casual references to the riches that were just waiting for those who dared, the wonderful adventure just waiting for someone made of the right stuff, for the select few who had the power and energy to act and not simply wait for things to happen to them — that revealed more to Michael than anything else. The pain that coursed through his body was so real, so focused, that Michael looked down at the pure white shirt he was wearing to make sure he didn't see a thin line of blood seeping through the fabric, spreading and becoming a sticky and disgusting stain. He could actually feel a sharp knife slicing into him. But he knew it was the pain of parting ways with Anaïs that had yet to come, the pain of forgoing the leap he wouldn't dare to make, a leap of devotion, reckless abandonment, and betrayal.

He so wanted to say to Chris, Yes, sure, we'll meet in three or four weeks' time, let's set it up now. But only on condition that Anaïs would be there, too. She had to remain in the picture. Had to. He wanted her so badly, in a way perhaps that he had never wanted any other woman before her, so passionately, so desperately. He was ready to lose himself in her, to drink in the velvety sweetness of her dark skin, to see her looking back at him with wide-open eyes, to sit together with her for hours without saying a word. Not for the first time, he imagined himself with her in a simple domestic setting. He knew he could spend all his life with her, but he knew that it wasn't going to happen. He was so close to that line that should never be crossed. He had to block his ears to that false song of the Sirens. You can be such a fool, he said to himself. You're such an idiot. And pathetic, for the most part. You're at a dangerous age at which men do foolish things, but not as foolish as this. Really not like this.

And that's how it ended. A polite farewell from Chris, and yes, yes. We'll be in touch. Take care. You, too. And a final night with Anaïs, together in the huge bed, with as much space between them as possible. He was feeling weak. Probably some Indian virus, he said. It'll pass. Never mind. They would surely meet again. Soon. In the thick darkness that had descended on the room, the curtains remained closed. Not a drop of light from the Indian night found its way through them, and he could hear Anaïs crying quietly — and when he reached out to her, large teardrops that trickled silently from her eyes collected in his hand.

52

Brian and Alon left the Bernhard & Sons antiquities store, which lay hidden, discreetly, along a narrow alleyway in the city's Old Town. Alon liked stores like that — quiet, plentiful, unobtrusive, with the scent of fine tobaccos and polishing materials perfuming the air. It was a store for aficionados, not for the nouveau riche who were fooled by decorative designs. Concealed, yet modern and very effective lighting illuminated the beautiful items that filled the store with a bounty that had surely characterized the establishment when it first opened to the public in the mid-nineteenth century — in 1847, to be precise. Brian had disappeared earlier with the owner into a back room, probably to haggle over a small wooden statue from the Middle Ages that had caught his eye and wouldn't let go. Brian would sometimes drag Alon along on his browsing and purchasing quests. He had a real passion for all things old and beautiful. His field of expertise, insofar as Alon had managed to learn over the years, was ancient manuscripts, but he had a good and loving eye — and sometimes even a covetous one — for objets d'art from various periods, and this wasn't the first time Alon had seen him show an interest in a European piece from the thirteenth or fourteenth century. He had taught Alon what to look for in a piece, how to distinguish between a forgery and the genuine article, but Alon, despite having learned a thing or two, wasn't able to match Brian's discerning eye, and it had never before mattered to him. By the time they tightened their scarves and put on their gloves again, the temperature had plummeted below zero. And suddenly Brian appeared not only revitalized but also content and happy.

"Did you buy it?" he asked.

"Yes, and at an affordable price, too. So much beauty in that one statue! Did you see? A pure expression of suffering and humility and sacrifice. A masterpiece. No less. Made by a great artist. Who may be anonymous today, but who has achieved immortality thanks to his work of art. And within twenty-four hours it'll be in my home. Thanks to DHL."

"Your home in Moscow?" Alon cynically asked.

"Don't get all heavy on me, Alon. I realize it's on your mind, but bitterness won't do us any good."

"Look at the irony here. You're offering me refuge in Russia, and you're going back to your comfortable life in the U.S. Don't you find that a little strange?"

"Yes," Brian responded philosophically, "God works in mysterious ways."

"Are you allowed to believe in God, or do utterances of that nature still get people sent to the torture dungeons at the Lubyanka?"

"You're angry, I know. And rightly so."

"You have no idea just how angry I am," Alon said, his tone soft but sharp. And despite the bitter cold, he loosened the buttons on his coat.

"Come with me to the art museum. We'll warm up a little, have something to drink, look Paul Klee in the eyes."

"Like I said, I'm all yours until this evening. Don't you have a small Klee at home?"

"Believe it or not, I do. Not an oil painting, of course. I'm a civil servant. But a signed reproduction. It also cost me a fortune."

"Oh, Brian, Brian. In a different world we could have been friends. Not spy and handler."

Brian gave Alon a friendly elbow in his side. And then he embraced him, brought his head closer, and kissed him on the cheek. "We're already friends," he said. And the cloud of concern on Cobra's face lifted for a moment and he looked happy.

53

Tel Aviv, March 2013

"Write this down," Amir said to Michael, a distinct tone of excitement in his voice even over the phone. "Two of the five names you gave me are abroad right now. Alon Regev and Oded Leshem. Does that tell you anything?"

"It tells me a whole lot! That was quick, man."

"That's the way it is, when the books are calling. I need to go into a seminar class now, otherwise they're gonna kick me out and Amir will have to spend another year at university."

Michael smiled. Amir tended at critical times to refer to himself in the third person.

"God help us. Get moving. We'll talk tomorrow, at the apartment."

Adi looked at him, on edge. He showed her the two names he had written down on the piece of paper he tore from the notebook. Alon Regev, the prime minister's political strategy advisor, and Oded Leshem, the head of the Shin Bet's counterintelligence division. They both remained silent. Michael was pale and grave-faced. Adi appeared to be trying still to comprehend what she was seeing, or perhaps she had chosen not to at all. Michael could see the questions and dismay on her face.

"Call Aharon Levin right away and ask him to come here, please," he said.

54

Providence, Rhode Island, March 2013
Their meeting this time was arranged ahead of time. Ya'ara called Frances Hart and asked if she'd like to get together. Frances agreed readily, happily even, and suggested they meet that same day, in the afternoon perhaps, if Ya'ara was free. They could have a light snack together. "I'll come get you in a taxi," Ya'ara said. "No, no, we'll stay here at my place," Frances insisted. Ya'ara chose not to use the call to find out if Professor Hart had by chance already returned from his unexpected trip. She wanted to be sitting face-to-face with Frances, to look her in the eyes, to stand next to her and cut the salad vegetables together or wash the lettuce or whatever. Being with someone, doing things together, it brought people closer, it opened the heart sometimes.

Frances opened the door with a smile on

her face. The yellow taxi pulled away and disappeared around the corner. The front yard of the house was still covered with a layer of snow, which was dotted here and there with dark islands of brown grass. Never mind, Ya'ara thought, spring is just around the corner. And it always arrives with a bang, like an unstoppable force. And then everything will blossom again, and the grass will turn green again, a light hue at first, shiny, and then dark and deep when the summer comes. Her head was filled momentarily with all those thoughts, though it wasn't as if she had ever taken much interest in gardening or the state of lawns. She approached Frances, kissed her on both cheeks, and suddenly embraced her warmly. "Come in, come in," Frances said, and Ya'ara walked in as if she was one of the family, removed her coat, and shook out her hair, which had been hiding under her hat.

They sat this time in the spacious kitchen, the coffee bubbling in the *macchinetta,* and talked. No, Frances explained, Julian wasn't back yet, she hadn't spoken to him either. But she appeared at ease now; the anxiety that had gripped her during their previous meeting had disappeared without a trace. Ya'ara was on edge. She had to figure out what had transpired since her last visit.

What had caused that frightened woman, who couldn't even hold on to a plate without dropping it, to now appear calm and relaxed? She waited, knowing her opportunity would arise. And Frances, meanwhile, showed an interest in the antiquities trade in which her guest was involved, with that older man, Max.

"He's quite a character, that Max, isn't he?"

"You should only know," Ya'ara responded. "Lucky I'm good with numbers. As for him, his head's in the clouds. And he chooses to be a dealer. A dealer! He's a professor who's lost his way, that's what he is."

Ya'ara glanced at Frances, but she couldn't discern any unusual reaction to her words. Something's put her mind at ease, she thought to herself. She isn't jumping at every little thing. She knows her husband is okay.

They made a big salad together and ate in the handsome dining area overlooking the home's backyard, both sipping on Californian wine from large glasses. And a ray of sunshine shining directly onto Ya'ara's glass through the large window appeared to shatter its crimson contents into slivers of sparkly red. When Frances went to the kitchen to pour the coffee, Ya'ara called out to her: "I'll be back in a moment, okay? The wine's gone to my head. I'm just going to splash some water on my face."

55

Tel Aviv, March 2013

"Well, Aharon, what do you say?"

Aharon Levin leaned back, his eyes closed. Adi had shown him the database and the criteria based on which the list had been narrowed down to five names. They knew Brian had traveled abroad from the United States, and they were assuming that Cobra was outside Israel somewhere. Of the five people from the table, two had left Israel in the past week. One of them could, possibly, be Cobra. Adi remained dumbfounded. The prime minister's political strategy advisor and the head of the Shin Bet's counterintelligence division. To Adi's surprise, a brief online search had revealed that they were both connected to the Knesset in their youth. That was significant, too. The former BND chief, Dr. Walter Vogel, had told Aharon Levin that Cobra was once a parliamentary or perhaps even a ministerial aide. Alon

Regev served as a parliamentary aide as a young man. Oded Leshem used to work at the Knesset Research and Information Center. All records pertaining to him disappeared shortly thereafter. Oh, well, obviously, he had joined the Shin Bet.

"You know," Aharon said, "it could be bad and it could be a whole lot more horrendous."

"What do you mean?" Adi asked.

"Look. If Cobra is Oded Leshem, it's bad. He's the head of the Shin Bet's counterintelligence wing. His job is to catch spies, including Russian ones. And lo and behold he's a Russian spy himself. He's at the top of the pyramid, he could provide cover for each and every SVR or GRU intelligence operation in Israel. He knows everything the Shin Bet knows about the operations of the Russian intelligence services in the country. And that would mean that the Russians know everything that we know. Worse even, everything we don't know. For someone in the spy game, you couldn't find a more important asset than the very person who heads the entity that's tasked with apprehending you."

Michael's head was about to explode. The notion that the head of a Shin Bet division, and the one responsible for thwarting espionage activities in Israel to boot, was working in the service of a foreign and hostile superpower was too much to take in. Adi appeared stunned.

"But," Aharon continued, "if Leshem is Cobra, we could still consider ourselves lucky. That's the simple scenario. If Alon Regev is Cobra, we're in serious trouble."

"What does the prime minister's political strategy advisor actually do?"

When Aharon responded, Michael and Adi couldn't help but notice the air of tension his voice had adopted. "That's just the thing. The title itself is insignificant. I don't know if you're familiar with Alon Regev's career. He started out as a parliamentary assistant, and very quickly — in tandem with his studies, in which, as in everything else, he excelled — secured the position of aide to Daniel Shalev. A general in the reserves, and a hero from the battles on the Golan Heights during the Yom Kippur War, Shalev was serving at the time as the minister of energy and infrastructure. Regev then left the Civil Service a few years later and was appointed to a very senior managerial post at the Israel Electric Corporation. Just imagine that, he gets parachuted into the post of deputy director-general of business development at Israel's largest company at the age of thirty. Following his stint at the IEC, he served in various roles in the private business sector for the most part, and then returned to a position at one of the government ministries, always with Daniel Shalev, time and again. Once as a bureau chief, once as a director-general, once as a personal advisor with this or the other title. And all the while, he made hay while the sun shone. I hate that expression," Aharon remarked offhandedly. "But he's undoubtedly talented, intelligent, levelheaded, and calculating. People who've met him say he oozes personal charm. A seasoned manipulator, aggressive and forceful when necessary, but always perceived in the end as a good guy." Aharon took a deep breath.

"And like I said," he continued, "he worked with Minister Shalev at all the stations Shalev went through — the Ministry of Energy and Infrastructure, the Foreign Affairs Ministry, the Defense Ministry, and finally the Prime Minister's Office. There wasn't a single forum in which he wasn't present, sometimes to the left of his boss, sometimes to his right, sometimes behind the scenes. He's had access to every single classified document in this country. Certainly during the periods in which he served in a governmental post, but probably dur-

ing the times he worked as a private businessman, too. Then, too, he served as an
unofficial, sometimes semiofficial, advisor
to the minister. And then fate dealt its blow
to Daniel Shalev. And at the time he slipped
into a coma, Alon Regev wasn't at his side.
Back then he was spending long periods in
Beijing as a partner in a Chinese investment
group, and the new prime minister summoned him to serve as his right-hand man,
and gave him some meaningless title, political strategy advisor, or strategic political
advisor, or something like that, the title is
really insignificant. If Alon Regev is Cobra,
we're well and truly fucked. It would be an
absolute catastrophe. Let's just pray that
Cobra's simply some Shin Bet division
chief."

No one said a word, and Aharon planted
his fist silently on the table. His face looked
tired, his wrinkles had deepened, and his
true age was plain to see all of a sudden.
The muscles in his right cheek trembled
with rage. He's truly angry, Michael thought
to himself. That's the look he gets when he
wants to kill someone. And not in the
metaphorical sense of the word. But for real.

His phone rang.

Ya'ara. She sounded worked up. "Michael,
hi, it's Ya'ara."

"The three of us are here together — Aharon, Adi, and me."

"Put me on speaker, please. I want all of you to hear this."

"Ya'ara, honey," Aharon said, his voice no longer shaking with rage, "is everything okay?"

"Everything's just fine. Listen. I've just come from another visit with Frances Hart. Yes, I'm still in Providence. You remember, Aharon, how on edge she was when we went to see her a few days ago. Well, she was completely at ease today. I got the feeling that she knows her husband is fine. That he hasn't disappeared without a trace. And indeed, on my way to the bathroom I saw something that wasn't there on our previous visit. An antique wooden statue, from the Middle Ages I think, but I can't say exactly when."

"That's not really important, the exact date. I'm still pretty impressed. Go on, go on."

"Anyway, it's a beautiful statue. So when I returned to the dining area to rejoin Frances at the window overlooking the garden — you remember? — I said to her, Your new statue is amazing. Such a heart-wrenching expression on its face. And Frances says to me, Yes, it arrived this morning, just before you called. To be honest, it scares me a little. That expression. Julian bought it in Zurich and sent it home. He didn't write anything, there wasn't a note or a letter for me, but it's his way of telling me he's okay, that I've got nothing to worry about. Otherwise he wouldn't have sent it with DHL. He would have sent it by regular mail, like he's always done when buying something he wasn't able to carry with him. After so many years of marriage, he knows me and knows his odd departure must have worried me. So he sent me a greeting in the quickest way possible other than by phone or e-mail.

"And Frances Hart explained to me that her husband almost never calls or corresponds via the computer when traveling. Cyber abstinence he calls it, according to her, good for his soul, he tells her. How do you know it's from Zurich? I asked. Here, here's the address, she says to me, and shows me the receipt sent with the piece. An antiquities store in Zurich. A relic itself. Founded in 1847. Bernhard & Sons."

"Ya'ara, you're a star," Michael said.

"Yes, yes, good job," Aharon muttered. Michael could clearly tell his head was already elsewhere, in Zurich. "Come home now, okay? We're going to need you here. I'll ask Bill to get his people to check if Hart

406

is listed as having a reservation on a return flight to the United States. I'm not sure if he'll return directly from Zurich. He's probably broken up his route. My money would be on Frankfurt or Vienna. And we'll make sure they have a look around his house, too. Good work, Ya'ara. Have a safe trip back." He motioned for Michael to hang up, and then said: "I wonder if his handlers will allow him to return. They sense we're onto Cobra, or that we're at least on a hunt that could expose him. I don't know if they're assuming that Brian's cover has also been blown. That Frances," he said with genuine sadness, "such a beautiful woman. An alcoholic, poor thing. I wonder if she knows anything about what her husband really does. Who he actually is. Or if he's deceived her as well."

"What do we do now? Wait for Regev and Leshem to get back?"

"Ask Amir to get his friend at the Interior Ministry to do some more work for us. I definitely want to know when they're getting back to Israel. But I want us to do something else, too. I want us to leave tonight for Zurich. The former chief of the Swiss Federal Police is an acquaintance of mine, and there are things that can only be done in a face-to-face meeting." He fixed his gaze on both of them. "They don't have a security service like ours. There's an entity within the Federal Office of Police that's responsible for counterterrorism and counterespionage activities. A little like the FBI. We worked together many years ago. We were on the trail at the time of a faction of the Baader-Meinhof Group that wanted to wipe out the Swiss capitalist pigs — the bank directors, in other words. We provided them, the Swiss, with names, codes, and the location of a hidden cache of Kalashnikovs and pistols and, you won't believe it, two shoulder-launched antiaircraft missiles. Apparently, as the investigation revealed, they thought it would be a good idea on this festive occasion of their war on the capitalists to bring down an El Al plane at the same time. We spent several very intensive days together, and we've kept in touch ever since. I want him to take us to Bernhard & Sons, or show us the establishment's security footage. There's no substitute for legwork," he sighed, feeling sorry for himself, and Michael stole a glance at Aharon's shoes and saw that they were indeed well-worn, and that the laces on his left shoe were undone.

"Adi," Aharon asked, "are you able to join me? Would that work with your son?"

"Not a son. A daughter. Two daughters,

Tamar and Michal. And yes, it'll be okay. I'll speak to my husband and my mother and the nanny and we'll work it out. Provided we get back quickly."

Aharon, of course, had no idea how you work things out with a husband and a mother and a nanny, let alone two young children, so he simply offered a perfunctory mumble of satisfaction, and then asked Adi to purchase tickets for them on the Internet, or "however it is that you do it," he said. "I'm going to call Thomas," he announced. "Thomas Mueller, the Federal Police chief. Former chief. Former for sure. Like some of us here — on the junk heap," he added somewhat bitterly, resigned to his fate. He disappeared into the other room and then returned to rummage in his bag and retrieve one of the three cell phones he carried with him everywhere. Needing quiet, Aharon closed the door behind him again. "Hello, hello," they could hear him saying, his voice muffled but oozing vitality, turning on the charm for Thomas in Switzerland, a charm still warm and captivating even though its wielder was well into retirement.

Ya'ara packed methodically but swiftly. She was traveling light, so all she had with her was a small trolley and an elegant black and

409

brown Louis Vuitton bag. It had cost her an unbelievable sum, but she loved it. It made her feel special. She checked every drawer, every closet, made sure she hadn't left anything in the bathroom. Nothing would happen even if she left something behind, but years of training and fieldwork took charge. This was how you did your stuff. This was being professional. And right now she was in the most important operation of her career, even if it was unofficial, even if she was loose, on her own. Totally deniable. A cab would pick her up from Heralds Inn in fifteen minutes. She would take it directly to Logan Airport in Boston. Expensive, but she wanted to make good time. She had to be back in Tel Aviv as soon as possible. She had a strong feeling things would start happening very quickly from now on. And she had to be there to make sure that they responded accordingly. She knew Aharon Levin was vastly experienced and extremely intelligent. She admired Michael's sensibility and clear mind. Yet, for too many years they had been off the streets. And she suspected that sometimes the high command positions that they held drove them to oversophistication, where decisiveness and ruthlessness were required instead. She told herself she was being vain, that she probably didn't know everything better than the others, but then something inside her revolted: Why? Why? Why couldn't she be smarter than the others? Why couldn't she know better than them? Because they were older? Because they were men? Fuck them.

In the cab she calmed down. The scenery was dull and gray. The highway was open, and the driver was focused and confident. She liked his driving. He was around fifty, he had both of his hands on the wheel, and he shut up. She did not lose her sense of urgency, but now she was moving, she was doing something, she felt in control. Finding the details of the antique shop in Zurich validated her stay in Providence. She knew she had to hang around and wait, and she was right. The patience of the hunter now gave way to the energy from a burst of action. She was now on her way back home. They were getting close. An old Bob Dylan song was playing in her mind, and she let it continue, as they grew swiftly closer to Boston, to the huge planes taking off, disappearing in the low clouds, burning fuel and gaining altitude, flying to distant places.

56

Brian and Cobra had drunk a couple of beers and eaten quite a few sausages, and Brian leaned back, sighed, and asked: "So, Alon, you're sticking with me then?"

Alon took his time before answering. "Look," he said. "This isn't an easy decision. And that's an understatement of British proportions. The truth is that it's the hardest decision of my life. Yes, harder even than my decision to do what I chose to do. In Rome." And as he spoke, Alon was hit once again with the realization that the people he had wanted to work with from the outset, in Rome, were Americans, and that his fate now lay in the hands of the Russians. He hadn't quite grasped from Brian when the handover had occurred so unobtrusively. And in a few moments of absolute self-honesty he wondered if he really had realized only now that he'd been

412

working for the KGB and its successors. Hadn't he known, or at least suspected so, for years already? His uncertainty riled him, and his anger and mistrust toward his handler rose to the surface again. "I'm not entirely convinced that I have to make that decision right now. If I run, there'll be no way back for me. A move like that would be irreversible. And self-destructive, from my perspective. It's my understanding that you, too, don't know how close they are to me, if at all. If what you've told me is even true, then they know there's a top-level source somewhere high up in the Israeli government establishment, those are the words you used. I get it that they are motivated to find the source, I also get it that their motivation is extremely high. I know them. When the Shin Bet really wants something, it leaves no stone unturned. It has the bite and tenacity of a pit bull. But I'm hoping that you know what you're doing, too. You haven't explained to me how the fact that there's a key agent high up in the Israeli establishment was leaked. But I'm hoping that you have been able to keep my identity under wraps. And if you've done your job the way you should have, there's a chance they won't get to me. As opposed to assured exposure and disgrace, in the event I openly cross the lines, there's a chance — if I go back now — I'll be able to go on with my life as usual. Maybe I'll even be able to continue working with you. I don't think they have any proof against me. Certainly not legal evidence. Without a confession, they can't touch me. And they won't get anything out of me. Don't worry, Brian. You look uptight all of a sudden . . ."

"I'm worried because you have no idea. You're not a kid, Alon. 'They won't get anything out of me.' Do you know how many people have said the exact same thing before going on to sign a full and detailed confession? Why do you always think you're better than everyone else? That you're different? You have no idea what they're capable of doing to you during the course of an interrogation, even in a democracy, which you aren't really — and I apologize if I've hurt your feelings. And even when it comes to high-profile suspects, there's no immunity and no holding back. Two or three days in their hands and there'll be nothing left of you. After not sleeping for seventy-two hours, and after having no choice but to piss your pants, and after realizing that the high-pitched tones they're going to subject you to incessantly in your detention cell are driving you out of your mind — and that's only the beginning — after all of that you're no longer going to think that you're the senior advisor whom no one can touch. You'll be a nothing. A rag. And after two weeks of the same, you'll be willing to tell them everything — if only they will stop. If they'd just let you sleep like a human being. If the shrieking in your head would just end. If they'd simply let you shower properly. You're not the hero you think you are. You'll go back and you'll never know if you're really home and free. You'll never know if and when they'll come knocking on your door in the middle of the night. Already now, even without being arrested, you'll never have a good night's sleep again. Unless you're with us, under our support and protection. Think, Alon, think."

For the first time in their relationship Brian was losing his composure. He was careful not to raise his voice in the busy pub, but Alon noticed nevertheless that his cheeks were flushed, and not merely from the beer. And the more stressed Brian appeared, the calmer Alon became. He had wormed his way out of quite a few tricky and dangerous situations in his life. He would escape unscathed this time, too. And in a calm and almost tranquil tone he said, "I don't buy your scenario. You've told a

415

horror story, and throughout my life, I've refused to act in keeping with the worst-case scenario. If that's your approach to things, you leave yourself paralyzed."

"It's not the worst-case scenario, my dear. What I've just described to you is the likely scenario."

"I hear you, Brian. You know I admire you. And that I love you. But you have to give me time. I need to think. And I can't make the decision on my own either. My wife has to know what's going on with me. Na'ama has no clue at all about our relationship."

Brian wanted to ask what exactly Cobra's wife thought with respect to the money at their disposal all through the years and where it had come from, particularly when they were students and during Cobra's time as a junior civil servant — one with promise, but still, just setting out. But he restrained himself.

"I'm leaving tonight," Alon said, "and I'll be doing some serious thinking for the next little while. I suggest we meet again in exactly four months. Here, in Zurich, in keeping with normal procedures. If I decide I want to cross over to you" — he was still avoiding the word *defection,* acting as if all his options remained open — "I'll come prepared. I'll make all the necessary arrangements, below the surface, obviously. Discreetly. And I suggest I suspend my covert activities until then. No more copying of computer files, no more copying of documents, nothing out of the ordinary for the time being. Nothing at all. I won't convene strategic discussion forums, I won't make requests for theoretical papers, background papers, position papers, unless I'm instructed to do so by the prime minister, at his initiative. And even then I'll insist that my time is very limited due to my other activities. A low profile. And if I get the sense that there's a real threat, an imminent one, we'll put the predetermined escape procedure into motion. And I hope it will in fact be available to me in the event of an emergency and is not merely theoretical."

Cobra was referring to the procedure they'd always reviewed in fine detail during each and every round of meetings, pertaining to a scenario in which he'd be unable to leave Israel officially. Both parties, he and his handlers, could initiate the emergency procedure, by way of an encrypted message on the Internet and also by leaving a pre-arranged sign as backup. Once confirmation was received, also via the Internet and by means of a second marking on the wall, they'd have a twenty-four-hour window in which a getaway remained possible. Cobra would have to make his way at least one hour after sunset to a natural harbor at a prearranged location on the coast between Ashdod and Ashkelon, where he'd be met by a rescue team with a motorboat. As soon as they made contact, following the exchange of passwords, he was supposed to surrender to them and they were supposed to deliver him safe and sound to a larger vessel, a fishing boat or yacht or merchant ship — he wasn't told which it would be — that would take him on board and carry him to safer shores.

"The plan remains in effect. We conduct regular drills, and it is fully operational. And the rendezvous point on the coast is reserved for you alone. We don't have any other asset who knows about it. Come, I'll take you to your hotel and you can go on from there to the airport. My only suggestion is that we leave just two months rather than four for the meeting option. Things can change, and quickly."

They drove in silence to Cobra's hotel.

Sitting later at the airport, at the bar overlooking the tarmac, after having already checked in, Alon watched as a large Swiss jet touched down on the runway, its wheels spraying up the rain that had been falling incessantly for the past hour. He saw the promise offered by the aircraft. It had come from somewhere far away, Canada, perhaps, maybe South America. And from Zurich it would fly out again to a different destination. To another continent. Alon could buy a ticket, get on board, and disappear. No one would know where he was. Not Brian and not Na'ama or anyone else. But Alon knew it was impossible to truly disappear for any significant length of time in this world. Certainly not without assistance. He forcibly erased the image of the lush green island surrounded by white beaches and a turquoise sea that had popped into his head. Feeling agitated, and with a bitter taste in his mouth, Alon began making his way to the gate for the flight to Tel Aviv. Less than an hour after he was due to land, former Mossad chief Aharon Levin would take his seat in the economy section of the very same aircraft, inching forward like a bloodhound on the scent, determined to capture his prey.

57

Zurich, March 2013

A bearish man, broad and large, his blond — almost white — hair cropped short, Thomas Mueller greeted Aharon at the terminal with a firm hug. Aharon and Adi had just exited through the green customs channel, and Adi picked up on the genuine warmth in the embrace shared by the two elderly men. When Aharon introduced him to Adi, Thomas said she reminded him of his daughter and almost hugged her, too. It was morning in Zurich, but the sky was a steely opaque gray, and Aharon and Thomas used the drive from the airport into the city to catch up on each other's exploits, mixing personal gossip with chitchat from the world of international espionage. They reminisced about the nights they had spent together on stakeout in an ice-cold car with only the coffee prepared for them by Thomas's wife on hand to save them from freezing completely. And Thomas talked with obvious pride about his two grandchildren, to the accompaniment of some indistinct hems and haws from Aharon. Adi sat in the back, looking out the window, wondering what was inside the large trucks that Thomas's BMW flashed past with a low growl.

"You're staying for at least one night, right?" Thomas asked. "You're welcome like always to stay with us, in Bern. But being a little familiar with you, Aharon, I've reserved two rooms for you at Frau Adler's hotel that you like so much."

Aharon almost took offense at his friend Thomas's assumption that they'd need two rooms, but was quick to recognize, all by himself, the absurdity of such a reaction. "Most appreciated!" he said. "How's dear Frau Adler? Still helping you from time to time, with your operations?"

"I've been out of the game for a long time already, and I thought, mistakenly I guess, that the same went for you. So I'm not really up to speed on operations, and Frau Adler isn't either any longer, I believe. Things were different back then, right? Those meetings we conducted at her hotel! She's a very discreet woman, and I think, too, that she had a thing for me," he said somewhat bashfully. "She used to be very beautiful, like a movie star. Today, like all of us, she's falling apart a little."

They reached the city, and the BMW began making its way up toward the mountain overlooking the lake. "Let's go for a little walk in the forest. The cold air will clear our heads, and we can discuss the matter you're here for. I promise we'll end up at that charming café in that cabin — remember, Aharon? The one that looks as if it could have come from a particularly frightening fairy tale? But their coffee is excellent, and they're happy to add a kick to it even in the mornings. And for the young girl, a hot chocolate," he added with a smile.

"Hot chocolate with ice-cold vodka works for me," Adi responded, and Thomas said, "I apologize, Fräulein. You've put me in my place, and rightly so."

"Frau, not Fräulein. I'm a mother of two small children. But I'll take it as a compliment." Nothing fazes her, that young woman, Aharon thought to himself with pride.

They reached the summit. Gray clouds hung below them, and they were enveloped by the pure fresh scent of pine trees. Thomas and Aharon walked side by side along the path that wound its way through the trees.

Adi followed a short way behind them, overwhelmed by the sudden sense of freedom that filled her.

Their cups of coffee stood on the table in front of them, a bottle of clear schnapps in the middle. The early hour meant the café was still empty. And the fire ablaze in the fireplace added warmth and a pleasant aroma to the expanse. Aharon briefed Thomas in general terms about the hunt he'd been orchestrating in recent weeks. He told him about the Israeli person of interest, whose crimes he refrained from labeling explicitly; he focused on the American lead, who had turned up all of a sudden at the Bernhard & Sons antiquities store, here in Zurich. That was the lead he wanted to follow, to see where it took him. Thomas listened intently, a thoughtful look on his face.

"I can still ask for a few favors here in Zurich. The police chief of the canton used to work under me, and he could be of assistance. It would be wise to refrain from doing anything rash like approaching the storeowner directly. We need to check first if he appears anywhere in our records. He may be connected to some sort of criminal activity or something else. And your American — Hart, right? — may not have turned up at that particular antiquities store by chance. Perhaps Herr Bernhard is involved somehow in Hart's covert activities. Maybe he's a courier of sorts himself, a contact, or maybe his store is a secure location at which Hart can leave something for someone else to pick up. If that's the case, we wouldn't want Bernhard's first move to be a message warning Hart.

"To begin with, we can ask Bernhard for the store's security footage from the past week, with a cover story about an antiquities forgery affair that's currently under investigation by Interpol, in which we, the Zurich Police, that is, are providing assistance. We're looking for someone who appears to have visited several antiquities stores in Zurich in the past week, and we're trying to identify the individual by comparing images from the leading stores in the city. This will require the police to request security footage from a number of businesses, and concerns regarding forgeries will convince them to cooperate. In their line of business, reputability has a significant bearing on sales," Thomas said. "They obviously speak to one another, all those antiquities traders, and Bernhard can't know that we're focused on him alone. Hmmm," Thomas hummed and added, "it'll take some doing,

424

but Alexander owes me one. I hope he remembers who awarded him his promotion."

Adi was sitting in her small room, on the second floor of Frau Adler's hotel. It was early evening, and the dim light of a street-lamp illuminated the cobblestone alleyway across the way, but Adi wasn't tempted into keeping an indifferent eye on the view from the window. Frau Adler herself had greeted them on arrival, flirting shamelessly with Aharon Levin, her makeup thick and over-done, or so Adi had thought to herself, and her voice deep and raspy from decades of smoking. She had insisted on referring to Adi as Aharon's "niece," and Adi couldn't figure out if it carried an insult of sorts, and she also failed to comprehend the narrow-eyed look Frau Adler had given her.

Either way, Aharon and Thomas had dis-appeared and she was sitting with her laptop open on the desk, and next to it three flash drives containing all the security footage from Bernhard & Sons from the past week. The screen was split into four sections, but one was black and displayed no data. A review of the initial images indicated to Adi that the store had two levels, each covered by a different camera. A third camera

425

scanned the street, outside the entrance to the business. The images from the upper level also showed a door that led, she assumed, to Mr. Bernhard & Sons' private office. Her guess was that the fourth camera covered the office itself, and she figured that with all due respect, Herr Bernhard wasn't going to provide his good friends at the Zurich Police with the footage from the office without a court order. That probably explained the fourth, black, screen. She was going to have to work and come out on top with what she'd been left with, three screens in shades of gray and white. And that's exactly what Adi was bent on doing.

The hours dragged by. Adi had seen a photograph of Julian Hart on the university website, and had committed it to memory. She was hoping to find him in the footage she'd been given, although in theory he could have purchased the statue through a catalog or online. She was no expert in the field, but assumed that one doesn't purchase an antique wooden statue from the Middle Ages without first seeing it in person. She didn't know what she was going to find, but she, too, was a believer in what Aharon and Michael termed "legwork," and in her line of work, as an intelligence officer, that meant wading through more and more material, without getting tired, without losing faith, to press on with more, and then a little more after that. And that's what she did. She studied the images from Bernhard & Sons until she could barely focus any longer. And then she went to the shower and ducked her head under the running water. The shock of the cold took her breath away. She dried her hair and returned doggedly to the small desk and her laptop. Everyone must be fast asleep at home. She brushed the images of her two young daughters from her thoughts. The earphones from her music player were in her ears, an old Oasis song, and her eyes were again fixed and focused on the screen in front of her.

It was two-thirty in the morning when she finally caught sight of Julian Hart's face in the footage from the camera that covered the store's upper level. She was surprised she hadn't seen him in the footage from the camera at the entrance, and she backtracked a little. Yes, that was him. She hadn't recognized him due to the heavy coat and scarf he was wearing. Entering the store with him was another man, wearing sunglasses and a casquette. He appeared familiar, but she couldn't identify him, both due to the hat and sunglasses and because most of his person remained hidden by Hart. She continued now, very slowly, her pulse pounding in her temples. She returned to the images of Hart inside the store, appearing relaxed and at ease. He took a close look at one of the pieces, it was hard to see if it was a chalice or statue, and then gestured to someone outside the frame, motioning for him to come over. And that someone did so. Alon Regev, the advisor to the prime minister of Israel. If Julian Hart was Brian, then Alon Regev was Cobra. And there they were, forever immortalized in the security footage from Bernhard & Sons, together, speaking to one another as friends. Without even a momentary glance at the time Adi called through to Aharon Levin's room. She woke him and asked him to come to her room right away. Aharon groaned a little and said, "I'm just going to wash my face and I'll be right there. You've done it, Adi, right? You've identified Cobra! Is it bad news or very bad news?"

"Come and see, Aharon. You're not going to like it."

58

Michael's thoughts drifted to the past. He was back in Tokyo, high above the endless maze of streets. The city was dotted with billions of lights. Tiny glittering specks in a plethora of colors filled the expanse. From street level and reaching up to a height of hundreds of meters, on the uppermost floors of the skyscrapers. Lights of aircraft coming in to land, losing altitude on the approach to Haneda Airport, lights of huge ships in the bay, endless strings of lights snaking their way along the multilevel freeways, bridge lights hanging over the river.

From afar, it was simply one of the billions of dots of light that gave the city its shimmering and flickering dimensions. But if, as in a movie, you were to zoom in on that particular dot superfast, you'd find yourself on the thirty-fourth floor of the hotel, your face pressed against the huge glass wall, while on the other side of it, exposed to the entire city, stood Michael Turgeman, muscular and slim and naked, water washing over his body in the extremely spacious shower cubicle with its black slate floor and black marble wall tiles. The water flowed freely, and the city lay spread out before Michael to the west in all its immensity and glory. Tears ran from his wide-open eyes, their saltiness swallowed up by the stream of water that washed over his face and body, mixing with the lemony fragrance of the shower gel. Anaïs, Anaïs. His body ached with longing.

59

Their meeting on this occasion took place in the president's official chambers. Outside, the Jerusalem spring preened in all its glory, with the intoxicating scent of flowers in full bloom and pleasant light gusts of wind. The sky was blue and mostly clear, the occasional white clouds sailing by, sketched by an artist's hand. The window of the president's office that overlooked the beautiful garden in the backyard was open, the drapes were flapping in the breeze, and the Jerusalem air flowed in. Aharon Levin had already met with the president twice since being entrusted with the task of finding Cobra, but his report this time was more dramatic and significant than ever.

"We've got him, Mr. President. And just as we feared, we're dealing with the highest-level, the most terrible spy ever to operate

431

in the state of Israel."

"Simply unbelievable," the president commented after listening to Aharon's detailed briefing. "All our secrets, all of them, at least since Daniel Shalev first joined the cabinet, have been passed on to Moscow. And God only knows where else from there. And now that vermin's in the Prime Minister's Office. I just can't get my head around it!"

"You know, of course, that damage assessment in this instance is meaningless," Aharon said. "Let me remind you that we have no definite information on what was passed on to the KGB and what wasn't. But we have to work on the assumption that everything Alon Regev got his hands on ended up in their hands, too. And if this assumption is correct, the catastrophe is so immense that there's actually nothing we can do. We have no way of limiting the damage, containing it. The only thing left for us to do is to prevent any further damage and to allow the damage that has already been caused to become outdated. And that will be a lengthy process. Certain fundamental intelligence can remain relevant for years."

"What about the option of beating the Russians at their own game?" the president asked. "We could arrest Regev and offer him a deal, under which he'll feed his handlers with misinformation, with the aim of gradually undermining the genuine intelligence he's been passing over to them all these years, of leading them to believe that the old information is no longer relevant, and that the new intelligence is valid and current?"

"That would require allowing him to remain free," Aharon replied. "And we'd have to come up with a very convincing charade that appears to indicate that he's still tied very closely and firmly to the centers of power. If we simply play along — allow him to report daily to the Prime Minister's Office, but put him in an empty and secluded room until the end of each day — the Russians will figure it out. We won't be able to keep it under wraps. And for a ploy with a seemingly good chance of remaining unexposed, we'd have to recruit several confidants in the Prime Minister's Office. But then, because so many individuals will be party to the secret, it'll leak. And how will the prime minister and the people around him be able to function at all knowing that a Russian spy, or former Russian spy, is working there alongside them in the very next room? Mr. President, the notion is a tempting one, and it's sophisticated and has potential in theory, but I'm afraid it isn't practical."

The president wasn't convinced. "I think you're talking from your heart and not your head," he said. "You loathe this Cobra. I do, too. I can barely mention him by name. Dirty traitor. Piece of filth. That's who he is. But all you can think about is exacting revenge. And I'm trying to figure out how we can limit the terrible damage he's caused." He fixed Aharon Levin with a weary look, the look of someone who has seen too much already. "But there is something to what you're saying. Unfortunately, in practice, in the real world, we probably won't be able to sustain a counterintelligence ploy of the kind I thought of for any length of time. It would be too complicated, someone will make a mistake, and the SVR will pick up on it. Those Russians aren't amateurs. Not at all."

"Under such circumstances," Aharon said, "revenge isn't such a bad thing at all. But we still have a way to go before making a decision. What we have thus far is a collection of circumstantial evidence only. We're one hundred percent sure, but we have nothing that actually incriminates Regev. My advice, Mr. President, is that we allow the Shin Bet to assume responsibility for handling the entire affair. Because we now know Cobra's identity, and since we know he's not a Shin Bet official, I can meet discreetly with the Shin Bet chief. The Shin Bet can handle things with caution, as they know how to do, without alerting Cobra before they decide to move against him. The Shin Bet has all the tools needed to deal with an incident of this kind. They have an excellent investigations division. If anyone can get a confession out of that man, they are the ones who will do so."

"Aharon. You convinced me earlier that the idea of turning Cobra into a double agent isn't a good one. Now I'm convinced that your idea to allow the Shin Bet to handle the investigation from here onward is problematic. We're dealing here with an unprecedented situation. Handling the affair through the official channels would exact a heavy price. Our hands would be tied in terms of the courses of action at our disposal, and the public exposure would be terribly costly for us, for the country as a whole. It would be impossible to keep the affair quiet for very long. Shame and a slap in the face aren't legal grounds for secrecy and a gag order. And in today's world, if the story is a good enough one, it'll come out anyway. If not here, then abroad. Gag orders or not. Nothing can be kept a secret in the world of the Internet and cyberspace. If there will be official documentation, it would simply be a matter of time."

"We could argue that publication of the affair would undermine Israel's foreign relations, and lead to a crisis of faith between ourselves and our allies, and the United States first and foremost. There you have cause to justify casting a cloak of secrecy over everything."

"We could argue anything and everything, and even rightly so in that regard. After all, the Americans would lose all faith in us if espionage of such proportions were to come to light. Who knows how many American secrets have found their way to the Russians via Cobra? That's all we need. And the Americans won't forgo an orderly process of damage control. They will want to know about every classified U.S. document that has ever passed through Regev's hands. There'll be no end to it. It'll be a nightmare, a nightmare for generations to come."

"Well, there you have your reason for imposing the gag order."

"Aharon, Aharon, there's one thing no one's ever accused you of. Naïveté. Do you really think the story can be kept quiet?"

Aharon conceded. "If we bring more

people into the know and if we initiate official proceedings, then you're right. There's zero chance of keeping the affair under wraps. None whatsoever. Not in today's world."

"And so," the president responded, "I want you to listen to me carefully now. I want you to have a talk with Alon Regev, with Cobra. To hear what that snake has to say. True, we won't be able to do damage control with respect to all the intelligence he's passed on over the years. But it's vital that we ascertain what he knows about the main project that we're currently working on; and if he does know something, we have to find out if he's passed on anything, even suggestively, to his handlers. It's critical, Aharon. It's our biggest problem right now, and you have to clarify this matter. You can bring another two or three former Shin Bet investigators into your team. That I'll sanction. I don't want any formal process. No official documentation. Get to the truth on this. We have to know. And you'll brief me again word for word. And then I want you to take care of him as you see fit. Do whatever needs to be done."

"Mr. President." Aharon stood, a stern, grave look on his face. The president appeared to be reading through some document on his desk and didn't look up. Without shaking the president's hand and without bidding him farewell, Aharon exited the office and headed toward the staircase leading to the dimly lit entrance hall. The courtyard outside the residence was bathed in the afternoon sunlight, and Aharon squinted his eyes against the glare.

60

Aharon stood up when he saw Alon Regev enter the hotel and start walking through the lobby. Aslan and Amir were keeping an eye on him from behind, from the street outside. Aharon approached Alon and shook his hand.

"You wanted to meet with me," Alon said, a smile on his face, his eyes icy. The last time they had met, Alon was serving as aide to Daniel Shalev.

"I have a few things to tell you, and I have several questions, too. I think you'll find our talk interesting, and certainly important. Let's go upstairs. I have a room where we can talk undisturbed."

Two hours earlier, Amir and Aslan were getting into position outside Alon Regev's home in Tzahala. They used their vehicle to block the driveway to the home's parking

439

garage and made sure they also had a view of the gate to the residence. There was one car in the garage, a silver Audi TT, with two mountain bikes standing by its side. The Regev family's second car, a dark blue BMW 730, was parked on the street. Someone had been too lazy to drive into the garage, Aslan remarked to himself. He and Amir had a wager on which car Alon intended to use. Amir emerged victorious following a stakeout that lasted an hour and a half. Alon opened the gate and walked toward the BMW. Aslan and Amir got out of their vehicle and approached him. They moved up very close to him, and Alon felt trapped between them and the door of his car.

"Alon Regev?" Aslan asked in a pleasant tone of voice.

"And who are you?" Alon asked with a degree of belligerence he didn't feel he truly had in him.

"Good morning. I'm Eitan, and this is Eli," Aslan responded, glancing briefly at Amir. Aharon Levin you surely know. He'd like to talk to you."

"So why doesn't Aharon Levin take it upon himself to call and make an appointment?"

"Mr. Levin would like you to accompany

us and to join him for a meeting right now. It's important and urgent, and he wanted us to inform you in person that he expects you to come, and will be very sorry if you refuse to do so."

"Do I have a choice?"

"Yes, you have a choice. We aren't here in an official capacity, and Aharon Levin isn't on official duty either. We thought that would be better for all parties involved."

"Good on you for thinking," Alon retorted cynically.

"It's best if you come with us. We'll give you a ride back later. It's not far. Aharon Levin is waiting for you at the Dan Accadia."

Aslan opened the door of the rented car with exaggerated courteousness. Alon slipped quietly into the backseat.

Aharon and Alon were sitting opposite each other in the living room of the hotel suite. Between them stood a low table boasting an ostentatious fruit bowl. The large window offered a view of a shimmering blue sea. Michael, Ya'ara, and Adi were in one of the nearby rooms. Ya'ara had come straight from Ben Gurion International Airport. Adi had managed to stop off at home on the way, to kiss her girls and convey instructions to the nanny. They were sitting in front of a large monitor and could hear and see what was happening in the suite, thanks to the admirable handiwork of Aslan, who had rigged the rooms ahead of time. A laptop was recording everything.

"Alon Regev," Aharon Levin said with a grave expression on his face, "let me begin in fact with the bottom line: For thirty years now you've been a spy in the service of the KGB, which following the fall of the Soviet Union became an organization known as the SVR. Your current handler, who's been running you for quite some time already, goes by the name of Julian Hart, and you know him as Brian. He may look and talk and behave like a bona fide American, but he's a born-and-bred Russian. He was probably christened with a different name at birth. You and Brian met less than a week ago in Zurich. There hasn't been a single state secret to which you've been privy that you haven't passed on to your handlers. We're talking about an alarmingly large number of secrets that people have guarded with their lives. And you have placed them in foreign hands without giving it a second thought. This betrayal," Aharon sternly said, "ends here and now."

Alon remained silent. Michael thought he

saw the color drain from his face, but it could have been the monitor playing tricks on him. Alon was sitting stiff and upright in his armchair, fixing Aharon with a cold, sharp stare.

"Do you have even a shred of evidence to support the utter nonsense that just came out your mouth?" he finally asked.

Aharon turned toward the laptop that lay open on the table. "Come have a look at something," he said, and Alon leaned forward to glance at the screen. It displayed an image of himself and Brian in conversation in that damn antiquities store in Zurich.

"What am I supposed to be looking at?"

"You're supposed to be looking at a picture of you and your handler, Brian, in an antiquities store in Zurich six days ago. That's what you're supposed to be looking at."

"I don't know that man. I think I may remember him from the store, but I don't know him from Adam. He wanted to purchase some antique statue and asked for my opinion on the piece."

"And what were you doing in Zurich?"

"Aharon, my friend, I don't think I should be answering your questions, not that one and not any at all. You aren't here in any official capacity, and I agreed to come here

443

only out of respect for you. And here you are hurling the most awful and unfounded accusations at me. Under the law, if there was someone else here to bear witness to what you've just said, you'd be guilty of slander."

"I spoke the substantial truth," Aharon replied, using the wording of the law to which Regev had alluded.

"You don't have even a single piece of evidence. If the best thing you can show me is an image of me and a stranger in some shop in Zurich, you aren't exactly excelling, to say the least. And I, so it seems, can sleep easy. My conscience is clear."

"From this moment onward you will never sleep easy again," Aharon said, unknowingly echoing Brian's sentiments. "And as for your conscience, you, the traitor that you are, lost that a long time ago. I have no idea what drives you. Greed, a sense of frustration, megalomania, loneliness. I used to handle people like you myself. And when push came to shove, regardless of their rank and no matter how high they had climbed, they were nothing more than wimps. People who sought to find in me the things they lacked in themselves. You're just the same."

"Your insults, Aharon, are pretty pathetic. They're simply an expression of your frus-

444

tration. Perhaps your retirement is the reason? Has it caused you to lose touch with reality?"

"You know that if the Shin Bet were to interrogate you, instead of this pleasant chat we are having, things would be looking a whole lot different right now."

Alon thought for a split second that Aharon and Brian must have spoken beforehand to coordinate their positions.

"Is that the worst thing you can threaten me with? A Shin Bet interrogation? And you think a veteran KGB spy couldn't handle that?"

Aharon tried a different approach. "Perhaps you can tell me how it all started?" he asked. "How did you end up in the hands of those Russians? How did they fool you so?"

"As I said, I have no idea what you're talking about at all. But I want you to know something. For almost thirty years now I've been sanctioned to maintain secret ties with official representatives of the United States."

"Sanctioned by whom?"

"Daniel Shalev. Are you familiar with him? He was once the prime minister of Israel. A well-schooled and crafty individual. No less a tactician than a strategist. He initiated the ties for me, told me where to go and what

445

to do, and all through my years with him, when we wanted to pass on confidential messages, when we wanted to reveal our true positions to the Americans in an unofficial yet trustworthy manner, the plans we've made for this or the other development in the region, or the positions and plans we wanted them to believe were genuine, we did so by means of the ties I maintained with them. We pieced together an irreplaceable shunt the significance of which can't be overstated. If anything, I deserve the Israel Defense Prize, for the double life I've led for the sake of this country, the Israel Defense Prize," he raised his voice, "and not the insults of the former Mossad chief, an old and frustrated man."

"Are you trying to tell me that you spied for the Americans at the behest of Daniel Shalev, and that in practice it wasn't espionage but a private initiative by a man who went on to serve as prime minister?"

"You can ask him yourself!"

They both knew that wasn't an option. A stroke he had suffered some four years ago had left Daniel Shalev in a vegetative state, or something like one.

"And how did the Russians come into the picture?"

"I have no idea what you're talking about."

"Do you know that as we speak, Brian, despite himself, his hands cuffed, is our guest in the cabin of a merchant ship currently making its way from northern Italy to Tel Aviv? He needed some persuasion to join us on the trip, but after the doctor administered the shot, he became a far more agreeable individual. And by the way, when he cursed, he did so in fluent Russian. Not in the English of a professor from the East Coast. It's going to be interesting to hear his version regarding his ties with you, and how he fits in to the fantasy you've just now tried to sell me."

To the people sitting transfixed in the other room, Alon Regev appeared to have had the wind knocked out of him by a punch to the gut. But he held firm, didn't fall to the canvas, and his breath returned, albeit short and rapid.

"Aharon, my friend." That Aharon, my friend, again, Ya'ara thought to herself in anger.

"Aharon, my friend. I'm getting up and leaving now. And I'll pass on the ride your goons offered me. I'll take a taxi. I thank you for your time and am sure you now realize what an embarrassing mistake you have made. I'm not vindictive when it comes to aging spies, but you should know that you've crossed the line. Stay away from me. Touch me again, you or your people, and the best attorneys in Israel will come down on you like a ton of bricks. You're walking a parapet. Be careful, Aharon. That's the advice of a friend."

Alon stood and headed to the door. He struggled a little with the security chain, and eventually freed it and walked, uneasily, toward the elevator. Ya'ara called Aslan from the nearby room. "He's on his way down to you. Good luck," she said.

Aslan started the car. Amir was in the front seat next to him. And from a distance of some fifty meters, they kept watch on the hotel's entrance, waiting for the figure of Cobra to emerge.

61

The entire crew had gathered in the apartment, the one that could perhaps go on to serve one day as Michael Turgeman's law firm office. Aharon was sitting in his armchair, alert and raring to go. "Let's start with Aslan's report," he said.

Aslan cleared his throat. "Cobra left the hotel looking tense and as white as a sheet," he began. "He looked around — maybe to find a taxi or maybe to see if he was being followed, I don't know. But a taxi pulled up next to him, and he simply didn't see us, me and Amir. He must have been stressed because the taxi took him straight to Tel Aviv without any stops or maneuvering that would have allowed him to try to spot us. He got out on the corner of Ibn Gvirol and Manne and immediately headed down Manne, in an easterly direction. He then stopped for a short while, just twenty seconds or so, alongside the concrete fence of one of the buildings. And after standing there briefly without moving, he hailed a second taxi to his home in Tzahala. We checked, but there was no marking on the fence."

"Do you think he intended to leave a sign there for his handlers?" Aharon asked. "The age-old technique of chalk marks on the wall?"

"Perhaps," Aslan said. "But as distressed as he may have been, he must have realized that we may have him under surveillance and chose not to do so. Someone like him has other ways of reporting his situation, even if he's reluctant to use them to begin with."

"Thank you, Aslan. Great job. So what do you have to say," Aharon asked the team, "about my meeting with Alon Regev?"

"What astounds me," Michael said, "is that he used the meeting to try already to sell you the ultimate cover story, a story that appears impossible to contradict or refute. Yes, he has maintained secret ties with a superpower, the United States and not the Soviet Union, and these ties — despite their conspiratorial nature, and perhaps even because of it — were in fact a covert channel for passing on messages and sometimes disinformation, with the entire operation initiated, ordered, planned, and authorized by none other than Daniel Shalev, who obviously can't be asked a thing."

"We can ask all we want, but we aren't going to get any answers."

"Why do you think he did so?" Michael continued. "Why play such an outlandish story so early in the game, when it could have been his trump card, in the event he really finds himself with his back to the wall?"

"The explanation for that, I think, is a complex one," Aharon said. "First of all, he's already under terrible stress. His cover's been blown, and he knows it, and he's fighting for his life. Second, I think that already at this stage he wanted us to know what awaits us at the end of the line. He wanted us to know that he has a trump card. A story like that could explain almost everything that he's done that appears to be espionage. And to top it all, with permission and authorization that can't be verified. We could of course ask him to see a document or piece of paper or something that proves he did indeed receive his instructions from Daniel Shalev, but then he'll simply say no. Matters of this kind don't and could never be allowed to leave a paper

451

trail." Aharon took a deep breath.

"But the crux of the matter is that Regev doesn't require exoneration," Aharon continued. "He needs to avoid a conviction. All he wanted to do — over and above the fact that he was stressed and felt an inner need to confront me, and not just sit there like a punching bag — was to show us how complicated things are going to get. And this entire discussion is theoretical anyway, because the Shin Bet won't be involved and there won't be an official investigation."

"The thing that really freaked him out," Adi said, "was the story you gave him about Brian being in our hands and on his way to Israel. That could really put paid to his entire preposterous cover story. Because the moment we have evidence from the Russian side, he's finished."

"Yes, he heard that and decided to end the conversation immediately. That undoubtedly put him under terrible strain, but don't forget," Aharon said, "that threat, as if Brian is in our hands, will hold water for just a few days. Or even less, if the Russians manage to relay a message to inform him that Brian is okay. To win this battle, we need to take advantage of this brief period of uncertainty, during which the complete picture remains obscure to all. Which reminds me that I need to speak with Bill. I want to suggest that they go public with their investigation of Brian, who may already be on his way back to Rhode Island. Unless the SVR has decided to bring him back to Moscow. They don't know for certain that Julian Hart's cover has been blown, but they may have picked up on signs of danger."

"So where do we go from here?" Adi asked.

"I need to do some thinking. To compile all the information we have in an orderly fashion. You'll help me with that, okay?"

"Sure," Adi responded, "no question."

"I'd like us to have a stay of exit order against Alon Regev. Right now, all he has to do to escape is to board the first plane out of Ben Gurion Airport and fly away."

"I think I can sort that out with my friend at the Interior Ministry," Amir said.

"Wow, he must owe you a lot, this friend of yours," Michael said, genuinely impressed.

"It's a little frightening, what your friends can do," Adi added.

"If you had served with me in the support platoon, you'd be doing things for me, too," Amir said.

"I don't even want to think about being with a bunch of paratroopers coming to the end of their service. It gives me the creeps," Adi fired back.

"That's enough, children," Aslan interjected in a fatherly tone. "Stay focused."

Ya'ara was sitting to the side a little, silent and withdrawn. Lost in her thoughts.

"Tell me, Aslan," Michael asked, "can you put together a team of sorts to keep watch on Cobra's home? To make sure he doesn't flee?"

"I can assemble a group of former comrades and tell them we're conducting a drill on behalf of the VIP Protection Unit, or something like that. But they're guys with brains in their heads. They'll start asking questions."

Aharon opened his eyes, which had been closed for a few moments. "I don't want to bring additional people into this story. There are several issues we need to iron out with Mr. Regev. If Amir's friend can block his access to the airport, I'll feel more at ease. The Russians may have an exit strategy, but it will take them at least twenty-four hours to set it in motion. If we move fast, we can stay ahead of them. So no more people in the know. We'll run the risk. For now, we're not bringing in any reinforcements to keep track of Cobra."

At that moment, everyone turned to look

at Ya'ara, who had just dropped the pen she was holding, causing it to clatter loudly on the floor. Only then did they realize that she hadn't taken part in the conversation.

"Aharon," she said, "I'd like to speak to you for a moment, in private."

62

Tzahala, April 2013

Alon Regev was sitting in the large leather armchair in the den of his home. The room was his private realm, frequented by no one but himself and the maid who came to their house three times a week. Not that his family members were prohibited from entering, but it was clear to everyone that the den was his alone. A large work desk, a comfortable antique leather armchair, an elegant humidor filled with Cuban cigars, a bookcase overflowing with volumes on strategy, security and philosophy, a sophisticated sound system, a small Jerusalem landscape painting by Anna Ticho, a marine navigation instrument from the eighteenth century, an ornate silver box.

Fauré's Requiem played clearly and hauntingly over the expensive audio system he had installed in the room. Alon closed his eyes and wondered how he had ended up in his current position. Some two hours earlier, he had opened the real estate website and had clicked on several images of building lots, thus signaling to his handlers to put the escape plan into motion. Following confirmation that his request has been received, he'd have twenty-four hours in which to get to a deserted strip of coast south of Ashdod and board a dinghy. Stripped bare, like a criminal on the run, he would abscond from Israel, never to return. He would cut himself off from his entire family and become the subject of endless condemnation and humiliation. He recalled himself as a young man, at the end of high school, during his military service, his first year at university. Those days of innocence preceding his treason. Before he pressed on the intercom button of the U.S. embassy in Rome. Up until that moment, he had been talented, ambitious, and full of promise. But from that moment onward, he turned traitor. Days of innocence? He berated himself for fudging the reality. After all, the contempt he harbored for this tiny, pretentious, pathetic country wasn't born that day in Rome. It had accompanied him for as long as he could remember himself. Ever since realizing that only by chance had he been tossed into this insignificant shithole at the

457

eastern end of the Mediterranean. No, he didn't want a dusty country, with arid mountains scattered with rocks and wind-swept trees, a densely packed and ugly coastline, a country of small and fanatic individuals, perspiring constantly in the heat and humidity. He wanted a big and expansive country, a country of wealth and unlimited horizons. A country of enlightened and strong people, a country with distinct seasons, filled in the fall with red-leaved trees and with a spring that burst forth green and intoxicating. A country that didn't end after two hours of driving, but one that had no boundaries, that went on forever, that you could drive the length and breadth of for days on end, from one stormy ocean to the shores of another deep sea. A country with people of action who were healthy, strong, self-confident, clear thinkers. Not ones who were bent and buckled under the weight of two thousand years of wandering, humiliation, and exile. So where are these days of innocence that you're talking about, he scolded himself. No one had ever accused him of being naïve. Until now, now that the dream had become a nightmare. He had turned out to be the biggest patsy of all. From being a devoted servant of the United States, he had become a contemptuous spy for the Soviet Union. When did it happen? Already at the start? Toward the end? Had he truly not sensed it? Was Brian — who wasn't even Brian at all — the only thing he had left in this life? And a lot of money, which who knows if he'd be able to even use at all. And Na'ama. Would she join him? Alon knew that the love they once shared had long since become a distant memory, replaced by a partnership of sorts. He couldn't imagine her asking to join him. He knew her too well. Na'ama would distance herself from him, say she didn't know anything, express shock, and try to get her hands on as much as possible of the wealth he had accumulated by means of a combination of business skills and treason. He couldn't bear to think about the children. Did Na'ama really not realize where all their wealth was coming from? Had she turned a blind eye? But turning a blind eye was tantamount to knowing, and who knows for how many years he had done the same thing.

He dozed off for a few minutes and awoke with a start. He was struggling to come to terms with the fact that everything in Israel was over for him. He was familiar with Moscow from his business activities, and knew you could live there like a king, provided you had sufficient money. And that he had. But what would he be there? Who would know him, who'd request his counsel, who would seek his company? He tried not to wallow in self-pity and reassured himself that he only needed to get through the coming days, the weeks ahead, and things would begin to fall into place. Brian would look after him. Brian and the huge organization behind him. They knew what he'd done for them. They wouldn't let him sink. And Martin, perhaps they'd give Martin back to me. Maybe he could see him again. Now they could be friends, now that all those years of that secret war were behind them. He downed the shot of whisky he had poured for himself in one gulp, feeling the burning in his throat and the comforting warmth spreading in his chest. His eyes filled with tears, and he allowed them to wash over his face. He closed his eyes again and fell asleep. He'll take a walk down Manne Street in the evening once again, just to see if they happened to have left a sign there for him.

63

Tel Aviv, April 2013

"Listen, Aharon," Ya'ara said to him after they had sat down in the other room and closed the door. "I think there's only one way to end this affair. We both clearly know what can't be allowed to happen. Cobra can't be allowed to get away. The affair has to remain under wraps. Not only would it cause terrible embarrassment, but it would also undermine the trust between ourselves and our most important allies. If one of the Israeli prime minister's closest aides can't be trusted, then we can't be trusted at all. No one else can be allowed into the loop. We have to remain the only ones in the know. And no investigation team from the Shin Bet either. And we also don't have much time. I can sense it. So that means there's only one way out. Cobra has to be thwarted." She went quiet for a moment. "Forgive me," she then continued. "I have

461

to say it straight. Cobra has to be killed. There's no other way."

Aharon looked at her as if he was seeing her for the first time.

"How old are you, Ya'ara? Remind me."

"I'm thirty-three, but that has nothing to do with what we're talking about. Let Aslan and me end this story right now."

"Listen to me, Ya'ara," Aharon said. "We need Cobra alive, not dead. I despise him no less than you do. But we have to clarify a certain matter with him and find out for certain if he's passed on information regarding this matter to his handlers. It's critical, a directive I received from the state president himself. So I don't agree with your proposal. I have reservations about it for other reasons, too, but we're not going to get into a philosophical debate right now. I am not going to sanction your proposed course of action."

Ya'ara listened but her face remained expressionless.

"Did you understand what I just said?" Aharon asked.

"I understood very well. But you're wrong."

"Listen, Ya'ara. This isn't a Godfather movie or the Wild West, and we aren't a gang of outlaws or mobsters. And there's a

462

hierarchy here, too, even in our unofficial team."

"Aharon, Cobra is going to get away. I know it. I know how he feels and what he is going to do. This is what I would do. I would act quickly, cut my losses and get the hell out of here. You always taught us to be one step in front of our adversaries. So we must act swiftly. This is what my instincts tell me to do. And all my field training and my field experience. I know the streets, Aharon. And I can imagine how Cobra feels now. He is surrounded, he is under imminent threat and he will try to flee. He is going to slip between our fingers if we don't act now. Without hesitation. He will disappear, and all you've said is going to remain merely theoretical. We need to be very aggressive. We must act quickly and decisively. Perhaps," she added contemplatively, without masking an element of audacity that was somewhat out of character, "perhaps you and Michael, who adores you, have lost it. Have gone soft."

Aharon's face paled in anger. "Who are you to teach me about being tough and decisive? The subject's closed. You can go now, and for your own good — I'm going to try to forget we ever had this conversation."

■ ■ ■ ■

Ya'ara knew she was right. She respected
Aharon, but she was sure he was wrong.
Whatever information he was hoping to get
out of Cobra, he just didn't have the time.
She actually felt the Russian escape plan
being put into motion. If she, or one of her
fellow operatives, was cornered, in danger
of being apprehended, they would execute
the emergency protocols immediately, without hesitation. Quick, decisive reaction, this
was what professionalism required. And
there was no reason to think that the SVR
was not as professional as the best of them.
Cobra was in imminent danger and they
were going to get him out. Unless she was
faster than they were. Unless she unleashed
her fury without hesitation.

64

Army Radio was the first to carry the report, which was the third item on the list on the midnight news. "Businessman Alon Regev, a close confidant of the prime minister, was killed this evening in a hit-and-run accident nearby the community of Nitzan, north of Ashkelon. Regev was driving a sports car and appears to have been hit by a truck, which fled the scene. An investigation into the incident is under way, according to a statement from the Israel Police's Southern District."

65

They had assembled again in the apartment. Everyone but Ya'ara.

Aharon looked at them one by one: Michael, Adi, Amir, and Aslan. "This won't take very long," he said.

Amir opened the window and the smell of blossoms drifted into the room along with the noises of the city. Aharon gestured for him to shut the window again.

"I want to thank you for the good work you've done," Aharon said. "For your willingness. Your dedication. We were given a job to do and we came through. And it's time now for each of us to return to what we were doing before. Life didn't come to a halt. We simply took a break. Those of you who still need to be reimbursed for expenses can arrange that with Amir. Michael, I want you to be responsible for ensuring that all material related to the operation is destroyed. Including Adi's computer." He paused. "If anyone ever happens to question you about the Cobra affair, you obviously don't know what he or she is talking about. Total denial. If it's someone official, on behalf of the state, refer him to me. Only to me. Without saying a word."

"That's it?" Adi asked. "We're wrapping things up just like that? Without discussing what happened?" Her eyes filled with tears.

Michael put his hand on her shoulder. "Adi. Not now. We'll talk about it. You and me."

"Yeah, sure, we'll talk." The tears streamed down her cheeks. "But it can't end like this. Aharon's thanking us for the good work but we all know things got out of control at the end. We were supposed to have questioned Cobra, and we failed. He slipped out of our grasp and also managed very conveniently to get himself killed on the way. And I don't buy that accident story. Where's Ya'ara? Why isn't she here? What did she say to you here, Aharon, after our previous meeting?"

"You're upset, Adi. I get it," Aharon said. "And yes, it didn't end exactly as we had planned. I didn't tell you that, but the state president called me last night, at about one-thirty. He told me that his military secretary informed him of Alon Regev's death in a

467

car accident. He asked me if I know anything about it. And truthfully I said I didn't. Adi, we did not plan it this way, but we achieved a great deal, and you played a very big part in that. We exposed a spy who caused us terrible damage, and it's over now. And sometimes an accident is simply an accident, even if it appears to be an improbable coincidence."

Adi didn't respond. She gathered herself and wiped her hand over her face, which looked suddenly to Michael like that of a young girl. All the members of the small team stood up and weren't quite sure how to bid one another farewell.

Amir busied himself with tidying the apartment. There wasn't really much to tidy, so he simply moved chairs from one place to another, adjusted the angle of the table slightly, and then returned it to its original spot, picked up a few pieces of paper he managed to find and vigorously put them through the shredder he had purchased at the start of the operation. "Darling," he said to Adi, somewhat embarrassed by her outburst, which had echoed his own sentiments, "I'm taking your computer now. There's nothing personal on it, nothing that you need, right?"

Adi nodded.

He removed the computer's hard disk and smashed it to pieces with a hammer he found in the toolbox in the kitchenette.

"Careful, bro," Michael said. "Don't destroy the apartment. I still have to open a law firm here, unless Aharon decides that we're going to continue working for him."

"I heard that just fine," Aharon called out from the other room. He was struggling with his raincoat, and trying with all his might to remember if he had brought an umbrella with him or had forgotten it elsewhere. The fact that it was a pleasant spring day, bathed in soft sunlight, didn't seem very relevant to him.

"Okay, guys, we're locking up," Michael said. "Get out of my office already. If you have nothing to do, don't do it here." He looked at Adi tenderly and said, "Come, let's go for a coffee on the boulevard. And then I'll take you home." Adi smiled at him gratefully.

Through the window Michael saw Aslan putting on his helmet and starting up his huge BMW motorcycle. Aslan hadn't said good-bye when he left, but he caught Michael's gaze now and waved to him.

"I'm closing, Aharon," Michael called out, and Aharon hurried toward the door. He stood there for a second, looked Michael straight in the eyes, nodded to Adi, who managed to bring a faint smile to her face, and left the apartment. He appeared to Michael to be talking to himself, or making an important point in an argument. He then saw him stop for a moment alongside Aslan and say something to him, but Michael of course couldn't hear.

"She worked her magic on you," Aharon said to Aslan, who was sitting on his motorcycle. "She worked her magic on you."

Without waiting for Aslan's response, Aharon continued walking and disappeared around the corner. Michael heard the roar of Aslan's motorcycle, which accelerated powerfully, pulled into the traffic with another mighty roar, and disappeared in seconds.

"Amir?"

"Right here, sir. I'm just making sure that everything is closed."

"They asked about you at the university, you know."

"Don't you start with me now, too."

A pleasant breeze caressed their faces as they headed off in the direction of the boulevard.

"You know," Adi said to Michael, "I'm sure I'm going to enjoy being with my girls a little. To read them stories about rabbits

470

and balloons. They say that childhood goes by so quickly. I have to go back to work in a month and a half. To start anew."

"Yes, new beginnings await us all. What we did here wasn't easy. If it was up to me, everyone here would be getting a medal, you know."

"Yes." She went quiet. "I trust all of you, Michael. I want you to know. But it's hard for me."

He clasped her hand briefly. "I know, Adi. I know."

66

Julian Hart saw them from the bedroom window, on the second floor of his home. The black van with the tinted windows stopped right on the corner of the street. A second and third car continued slowly toward the house. He knew exactly what he'd see next, in just a few seconds. Two or three men in suits, shiny badges fixed to their belts, would soon be stepping out of each vehicle.

He was right, but only partially. Because two police cars, their lights flashing blue and red, joined the scene unfolding before his eyes, playing out in a strange silence and seemingly in slow motion. The police cars pulled up at an angle in front of his home, and the officers who emerged drew their weapons and took cover behind the doors of their respective vehicles. Men in suits did indeed step out of the unmarked cars, but over the jackets they were also wearing dark windbreakers. He knew that emblazoned on their backs, large and luminous, were the letters FBI. Two of the FBI agents were carrying shotguns. The others moved forward with their right hands resting on the handles of the weapons tucked into their belts.

They're heading into battle, he thought. Advancing in silence, inching forward, with evidently way too much firepower. No, he was not going down that Via Dolorosa that awaited him. He was not going to be dragged from his home cuffed and shamed. They were not going to take Professor Julian Hart and turn him into a media circus, for all to see and shame, a miserable Soviet spy, fighting wars long since irrelevant. They were not going to tear apart the life he had so diligently and painstakingly built for himself. He couldn't do that to Frances and the kids. That he certainly wasn't willing to do. The thought of himself dressed in orange prison overalls, his wrists and ankles cuffed and shackled, day after day after day in the dock, with Frances among the public, sitting there in the courtroom, elegantly dressed, heavily made up, showing her support for her man, the man who betrayed her and deceived her — that thought, those images, were too much to bear. He felt a sharp pain in the side of his stomach, and gastric acid burned its way up into his esophagus. He wanted to throw up, but managed to suppress the feeling. He retrieved his SIG Sauer P226 from its hiding place in his closet. A nine millimeter. Seventeen rounds. He cocked the weapon and went down the stairs leading to the front door. He could hear Frances busy with something on the back porch of the house. She was completely unaware of the scene that was unfolding in the front of her home. He was thankful for that. He glanced through the window next to the front door to see the FBI agents reach the grass line, at the edge of the driveway to the house. He opened the heavy wooden door, gripped the SIG Sauer just as his instructor in Moscow had taught him, got into position, and opened fire at a slow and uniform rate. Round by round by round. He watched one of the FBI agents drop to the ground, like in a dream, and immediately thereafter he felt something slam hard into his torso. The shotgun rounds threw him violently backward, exiting his back in a wide spray of blood and pieces of bone. Then two rounds from a .38 Smith & Wesson slammed into his head, splattering his brains on the wall behind him.

67

Ashdod, May 2013

Alona was standing in the dining room and sorting through the mail she had just removed from the mailbox. Hiding among the flyers, bills, and bank statements was a cream-colored envelope. "Hagar," she called out to her aunt, "you have mail. It looks like a wedding invitation." Hagar Beit-Hallahmi emerged from her room holding the book she'd been reading, her finger marking the page she was at. She grasped the envelope with a shaky hand and turned it over, immediately noticing the absence of a sender's address but spotting the small illustration, a German shepherd in black ink. Another one of Aharon Levin's quirks, she fondly thought. Back in the day he'd sometimes send her memos accompanied by that same odd signature, and she could never quite figure out if the drawing alluded to him or to her. "Thank you, my dear," she

475

said to Alona, and returned to her room. After settling back into her armchair, she put the book aside and opened the thick envelope. An expensive envelope from high-quality paper, she said to herself. He was never short on style. From it she retrieved an old postcard, a photograph of a giant statue of Lenin in a dusty city, somewhere on the outskirts of the empire. If he was willing to part ways with a postcard from his famous collection, she thought to herself, he really was giving it all he had. She pursed her lips. "My dearest," he had written. "You were right. Like always, you were right. You sent me down the right path. But remember, sometimes an accident is simply an accident. Comrade Vladimir Ilyich sends you his warm regards. An old friend is giving you a hug." She returned the postcard to the envelope, stood up from the armchair with a groan, slipped the letter into one of the desk drawers that already contained so many secrets, and made sure to lock it with a small key. She sat down again, the book still by her side. Closing her eyes, she lost herself in her thoughts. She remembered hearing the report about the accident north of Ashkelon. Everything was falling clearly into place now.

68

It was ten in the morning, and there were few people on the promenade. The restaurant owners were sitting idly outside their establishments, and the walkway's benches were dotted with old folk with time on their hands. The French tourists had yet to arrive, and school wasn't out yet for the summer. It was early June, and the humidity was still bearable, but the heat was on. It would be sticky and scorching in just a few weeks. The clear air would turn hazy. The light clouds would scatter and disappear and the sky would take on the appearance of sheet metal. Somewhat out of character, Ya'ara walked along the pedestrian path in a daydream, with a takeaway coffee from the corner of the street in her one hand and her motorcycle helmet in the other, looking for a bench on which to sit, a bench that offered a view of the shipwreck off the coast.

She found one, sat down, and stretched her legs out in front of her, the paper cup clasped between her hands. Tiny gusts of cool air were coming off the sea. Out of the corner of her eye she saw a woman approach her. "May I sit down, please?" the woman asked in Russian. Her voice was deep and lovely, and it sent a tremor of sorts through Ya'ara. There was something familiar about it. She didn't divert her gaze, and with her eyes still fixed on the sea she said, "With pleasure, here you go, there's room for both of us."

"Galina . . . ?"

Ya'ara looked at the woman who was sitting to her right.

"Galina?" the woman asked again. "Or at least that's the name you used back then."

Ya'ara froze. Sitting alongside her was Katrina Geifman, Igor Abramovich's lover, the woman she had met with less than four months ago — it seemed like light-years away — in the icy cold of Dimitrovgrad. She was still beautiful, but had lost much weight, her cheekbones were pronounced, her blue eyes sparkled, and the wrinkles around the corners of her full mouth appeared to have deepened.

"You must think I'm a ghost," she said.

"I tried to contact you," Ya'ara said. "I

called and called and there was no answer. I was afraid something had happened to you."

"They took me," Katrina responded. "I thought I was going to die there, during the interrogation, in custody." She paused, and her eyes filled with tears. "I wanted to die. That's the truth."

Ya'ara took her hand. They were both looking straight ahead, at the sea. White seagulls glided through the air close to the beach.

"But there was someone there who saved me. He smuggled me out. They must have thought he was going to finish the job. To put a bullet in the back of my head. But he took me to his mother's home. I have no idea why he did it, why someone would tempt fate like that. His mother was a partisan fighter during the Great Patriotic War. An old woman who fears nothing. The heart of an angel. And soft hands. They cared for me as you would care for a baby, and I eventually got back onto my feet. He told me I couldn't remain in Russia. That they'd find me and kill us both. He gave me a Czech passport he had made for me and money, too. He accompanied me all the way to the border with Ukraine. He drove through the night, and then the following night, too, and sent me over the border. I

479

can still picture him there, just standing there and not moving, the sun rising over the hills, and him just standing there and watching me. And I went. I think he was the bravest man I've ever met."

"And how did you get here?" And why did you come? Ya'ara didn't voice her second question out loud.

"I wanted to see Galina," Katrina said, answering the question she wasn't asked. "I had to. I wanted to get in touch with the one person who forms a part of the sweetest moments in my life. I didn't know how to find her, but the Bat Yam Artists Association was able to track her down. Someone by the name of Vladislav is still in contact with her. He used to be a friend of Igor. And I wanted to see you, too. To find out where you live I had to remember things I'd already forgotten, and it took a fair deal of patience to learn that you come here at least once a week, to the Bat Yam Promenade."

Ya'ara felt a cold shiver down her spine. She suppressed the fear that momentarily froze her.

"How was your encounter? Yours and Galina's?"

"You know how it goes. Such reunions always come with an element of disappointment. But it did me good. It took me back

480

to those times. And she was a lot nicer than she had been back then. Oh, well, she was a seventeen-year-old girl then, at odds with herself, and full of hate for me for taking her father away from her, and worse even, for taking the place of her mother. That's how children see it. She's a lot more amiable these days, of course. And you must know that she doesn't look like you at all."

"My name's Ya'ara."

"I know. They slammed me with it during my interrogation, time and again, between punching me in the face and forcing my head into a bucket of ice water."

"I'm sorry," Ya'ara said softly. "If you prefer, you can call me Anna. That was once my name."

"It's okay, sweetheart. You helped me to get my revenge on them. It was so easy for them to break me back then. And there are some breaks from which there's no coming back. So I still need to forgive myself. You have no need to ask for forgiveness."

"There was nothing else you could have done. They threatened to take your daughter."

"I don't know . . ."

They sat there together in silence for a short while and the sun warmed their bodies. Ya'ara closed her eyes and allowed the sea breeze to caress her. After what had happened, she knew that even if she wanted to, she would never work for the organization again. Aharon would have made sure she'd been marked as an unstable element. Someone who despite her talents couldn't be trusted. She didn't want to go back to film school. Even the script she had written for her final graduation project had lost its appeal. The future looked remarkably empty to her.

"What are your plans now?" she asked Katrina Geifman. "Do you have enough money? I can help you."

"I don't know yet. I want to stay here for a few months. To wait for the winter. And then I'll see."

"Do you have a phone?" Ya'ara asked. "I want you to have my number. This doesn't end here, on a bench overlooking the sea."

"I know already that Cobra is dead," Katrina said after they had exchanged phone numbers. "I saw a picture of him on an Internet news site while I was still in Ukraine. I wanted to know what was happening in Israel and I searched every day. Killed in a car accident. That's what the report said. He looked just like he did when I used to provide security for the meetings with him. A little older, but exactly the same. I didn't know back then who he was, only that he was someone important. Now I know just how important. I don't know who had a hand in the accident. God, perhaps. I've seen more than enough through the years to learn not to believe in Him, but I don't see any other way of explaining it." She looked at Ya'ara, allowing the silence to ask what she hadn't dared to voice out loud.

Ya'ara didn't say a word. Katrina's question remained unanswered. They sat there on the bench, gazing at the sea. The sun had climbed to a higher point in the sky, its heat more concentrated now, radiating orange. Anyone observing them from the side would have assumed perhaps that they were mother and daughter. But there was no one there to look at them. The promenade was deserted. Strange, Ya'ara thought to herself, as if someone had evacuated the area for the purpose of shooting a movie scene. "I'll call," she said to Katrina as she stood and regathered her hair, which shone in the glare of the sun. She picked up the black helmet that had been resting on the bench next to her and started walking. She could still feel the soft touch of Katrina's hand as she got onto the large motorcycle and headed south with a low growl, which gradually intensified. The wind swept over her face, the blue sea appeared to flash by on her right, and the urban landscape gave way to sand dunes. The sky opened wider, her heart did the same, and she rode on, sucking clean air deep into her lungs. She was on the move.

69

Moscow, SVR Headquarters, June 2013

By nine in the evening most of the workers had already left the facility. The warm light of the long summer day streamed diagonally through the wooden shutters of the SVR chief's expansive bureau. Dust danced on the rays of sunlight, broken up by the straight lines of shade. Sitting as comfortably as their chairs would allow them in the conference area at the far end of the room were the commander of the SVR and the head of the Tenth Directorate. The commander's bureau chief, who had just carefully placed a frosted bottle of vodka and two chilled glasses on the table in front of them, exited quietly to leave the two men on their own. The SVR commander's fine gray jacket was hanging over the backrest of the chair across from his desk, where he had placed it earlier. His severe back pain, the result of a gunshot wound sustained during a shootout in a coastal city in southern England, back at some point during the Cold War, dictated that his bureau be furnished with simple, stiff wooden chairs. Sometimes he'd suggest to a guest in the office that those were the kind of chairs that had stood in his childhood home, in a small and meager village in the heart of the wilderness that lay hundreds of kilometers east of Moscow. But that was simply one of the proletarian cloaks in which he liked to drape his image. He had grown up in fact as the only child of educated and well-to-do parents in Leningrad, his father a professor of Semitic languages and his mother an electrical engineer, both loyal party members, both fierce fighters, albeit painfully young, during the Great Patriotic War. They were the ones who had instilled in him his values and his dedication to the greater cause, which from his perspective had never waned. His steely character wasn't the product of financial hardship and an arduous life in the wilderness, but of a zealous love for the motherland and a constant desire to excel and earn the attention of his parents, and their praise, too, on rare occasions. He opened the top button of his impeccably clean white shirt and loosened the tie knot around his neck. Sitting across from him, on a rudimentary chair, was the head of the directorate, who stretched his legs out in front of him and emitted a sigh of weariness and contentment to mark the passing of a long day.

"We did it," said the SVR commander. "We pulled it off in the end."

"But we took a hard knock," the head of the directorate responded soberly.

"We managed to make the most out of adverse circumstances," the commander said. "Remember our history, it's not the first time we've sacrificed a rook to save the king. And the queen sometimes, too. We can't be greedy, Alexander. It's impossible to win on all fronts all the time. We were facing a catastrophe and we came through. And that's our true advantage. The ability to survive long-term campaigns despite the losses. That's the main thing, don't forget — to always be one step ahead of your opponent. To hang in just one minute longer than he does. To take what you can. To sacrifice what needs to be sacrificed. To know your capabilities and what's beyond them. And to get back on your feet as soon as possible."

Alexander, the head of the Tenth Directorate, gazed at his commander in admiration. He wasn't simply a darling of the party who had been appointed to his position thanks to political loyalty. Although he was indeed blessed with political aptitude of the highest order. It was a prerequisite for all secret service chiefs, unless they wanted to be eaten alive. But his commander was first and foremost a covert fighter, daring, ruthless, cool-headed, who could see several moves ahead, like a seasoned chess player. He recalled how several months ago — as dusk was falling just as it was around them right now, after they had concluded the arrangements concerning Cobra — he had been summoned back to the commander's bureau to review together, in private, the file of a second high-level agent they had in Israel. Although the Israelis were on the hunt for Cobra, there was something else troubling the commander. Something had led him to request the highly classified file pertaining to Viper. And only then was the real operation set into motion. That evening they sealed, for better or worse, the fates of Viper and of Cobra. The one was spared, without ever knowing at all just how close he had come to his end. The other, like the light from a distant star, continued to shine, but was long since dead.

"Let's reconstruct what they know about Cobra," the commander had said to him then. And without the assistance of anyone else, they sat down together and recorded in detail everything that Katrina had told the young Israeli woman who had questioned her at her home in Dimitrovgrad. It wasn't much. A general physical description, an estimated date of birth, the handler's cover name, a round of meetings in Geneva. "Something's troubling me," the commander had said at the time, "and when I'm troubled, I usually have good reason to be so. It's easy to push feelings of uneasiness aside. But I've already paid a very heavy price to learn that those elusive feelings are actually the ones you have to pursue. They usually count for something. Look here. Katrina told them that Cobra's birthday fell in late January or early February. Let's see now," he said quietly, as if he were talking to himself, "let's see." He opened the dossier on Viper, smoothing down the cover with the palm of his hand even though it didn't show a single crease, and focused on a greenish piece of paper, the document that listed the agent's personal particulars.

"Here," the commander said quietly. "Look. Viper's date of birth. February 3, 1961. And there's something else you should see." He began paging through the heart of the dossier, the part that contained the operational reports. "Look — 1989. Viper was still a kid in terms of running an agent. Just starting out. We summoned him to a round of meetings in Lausanne, but we cut corners. We used the same logistics team for both rounds of meetings, both the one with Cobra and the one with him, so that we wouldn't have to fly in a second team. Look, the directive from headquarters: 'For purposes of efficiency, the two rounds of meetings should be held one after the other, while ensuring they are kept completely separate and conducted under different field conditions.' Do you get it, Alexander? We brought Cobra to Geneva and then went on to meet with Viper in Lausanne. Take note, we even made sure that they'd pass through different airports. Viper received explicit instructions to arrive in Zurich and continue from there by train. Cobra's file contains an instruction to fly directly into Geneva. And truthfully, it all seems just fine. Reasonable planning. Legitimate considerations. Professional decisions — different arenas, separate arrival routes, a staggered timetable. All good. But the picture the Israelis see is of a different resolution. They know too little. Only a few general details. And that actually puts us even more at risk. You see:

They're looking for Cobra and they could accidentally get their hands on Viper."

"Do you really think so?"

"You never know. But they're on the hunt. They know they have a spy somewhere high up in the government establishment and they won't rest until they find him. They don't know they have two. They could accidentally stumble upon our man whom they don't even know about yet. We had no way of knowing in 1989 how things would turn out some twenty-four years down the line. You can put it down either to substandard operational planning or simply bad luck. I don't know. But their hunt can't be allowed to lead them to Viper. He is not expendable. That is not an option as far as I'm concerned."

Alexander looked at his commander. He could see his thoughts taking form in the shape of a plan of action. How out of the murkiness of the details a decision was forming in his mind. "Are you going to sacrifice Cobra?" he asked, his tone a mixture of admiration and awe.

"Not sacrifice him. We'll get him out and offer him VIP resettling. But we'll give them something that points definitively in his direction. And thus keep Viper safe. Even if we extract Cobra and he's not in their

491

hands, they'll have evidence that incriminates him. They may also be onto Hexagon, our field operative in Providence. I have no idea how, but they're keeping close to him. Aharon Levin met in Virginia with William Pemberton, that son of a bitch, and then went straight on from there to Rhode Island. Hexagon lives in Providence. That's not a coincidence. There are no such things."

"How do we know where Levin went?"

"SIGINT. We intercepted Levin's call to Pemberton and then tracked his cell phone. Virginia, Providence, Boston, New York."

"So if they're keeping tabs on Hexagon . . ."

"Exactly. We can use him to provide the clue that leads them to Cobra. Instruct Hexagon to arrange for an image of himself and Cobra to be caught on the security camera footage of some antiquities store and to expose the name and location of the store by means of an item sent from there to his home. If they're onto Hexagon, they'll also find their way to the place from where he sent the package, and it won't be long before they have their hands on the security footage. Aharon Levin thinks fast and has excellent contacts. He'll get his hands on the security footage and have all the proof he needs. And even if it doesn't go down that way, the fact that Cobra has fled Israel will serve, of course, as the damning proof. We'll both incriminate and rescue him. But people in the intelligence game like hard evidence. And certainly when it comes to such sensitive matters. So we'll make sure they get the evidence. And most important, Viper can remain unscathed."

Alexander sighed. "Believe me, sir," he said, "with all my experience and despite all the senior positions I've held, I have to confess that I wouldn't have been able to choose between Cobra and Viper. Who to save and who to sacrifice in this game of bloody chess we play."

The SVR commander sat back in his chair. It was the right time for an important lesson, and he was going to take advantage of the time in comfort. Who knows, perhaps Alexander would be sitting in this very chair one day. "Look, Alexander," he said, "as tough a dilemma as it may seem, the solution is actually a pretty simple one. Cobra is the agent whose cover's been blown. They have yet to reveal his true identity, but his story is the story they're pursuing. The clues are starting to appear, and they have to catch him. They have to get their hands on someone. They aren't going to let it slide in this case, just as we wouldn't. We simply don't want them to make any mistakes along the way. Look, you could have said: To protect Cobra, even at the last minute, let's give them Viper. After all, they don't know there are two. We'll give them one and they'll ease off. They aren't going to and won't want to believe that they have more than one traitor at such levels. But when push comes to shove, both you and I clearly know who is more important and who is expendable." He took a sip of his ice-cold vodka and continued with the lecture he was giving, a lecture to an audience of one, a beloved friend and valued colleague.

"As an offensive-minded intelligence organization, your greatest enemy is the one whose task it is to catch you. Therefore, if you've made the right moves and have also been blessed with a great deal of good fortune that has allowed you to run a high-level agent at the very top of your enemy's counterintelligence service, the last person you're going to forsake as an agent is the counterintelligence service chief himself. The person you are up against and who poses a threat to you all the time, every second. All the others are expendable — military sources, sources high up in the political establishment, financial sector sources. But in order to survive, we have to begin by preserving the assets we have in our rivals' intelligence services. We, after all, are the shield and sword of the Revolution. Even if everyone believes that the Revolution ended years ago, you and I know that it isn't over yet. Blood still flows through the veins of this magnificent body. If we crumble, everything around us will come crashing down, too. If we are strong, we can safeguard everyone. And therefore, my dear friend, if we are in control of an asset the likes of Viper, if we were fortunate enough to recruit as a spy the person who now holds sway over the covert campaign against us in a specific arena, an important arena, we will safeguard him at all costs. All costs. I'm sure that's as clear to you as it is to me."

The head of the directorate regarded his commander with admiration. The ability to cut straight through to the heart of the matter, to make brutal decisions that would also prove to be the correct ones, that's what lifted him a notch above his colleagues. Anyone could be ruthless and tough, but only a few were blessed with that kind of foresight, that kind of ability to separate the wheat from the chaff. Alexander himself, like every talented and ambitious senior officer, also wanted to rise to the position of

SVR chief in due time. But he wasn't in a hurry. And he was pleased to have his old and highly capable friend, who had served alongside him in the past as an operations officer in Turkey and South America, as his current commander. He would step into his shoes one day, and until then he was going to learn all his friend could teach him.

His commander was right. The loss of Cobra was a serious blow. The Israelis had exposed and eliminated one of their best resources. Agents like that were few and far between. But agents like Viper were an even rarer breed. Alexander *did* know — you couldn't win every battle. Sometimes you got hit hard, but you still needed the strength and resilience to get to your feet again. The defeat in the case of Cobra was tempered by the impressive achievement of safeguarding Viper. The Israeli security services would rest on their laurels now. As far as they were concerned, they had chopped off the head of the snake, without realizing that another still slithered there among the rocks. His commander loved that imagery, and Alexander had learned to appreciate it, too. The math was simple: Viper would go on spying for them. They would continue, as always, to remain one step ahead of their bitter rivals in the Israeli Shin

Bet. Yes, he thought to himself, this vodka is well deserved.

The head of the directorate and the SVR commander sat there in the pleasant silence, their bodies warmed by the icy beverage. The last bit of light filtering through the wooden shutters gradually died out. The purple shadows darkened. A welcome weariness washed through them. The SVR chief's slender back remained upright despite the unrelenting pain. And only his sharp intelligence fired a spark in his eyes, his brain already planning the battles of tomorrow.

ABOUT THE AUTHOR

Jonathan de Shalit is the pseudonym of a former high ranking member of the Israeli Intelligence Community. De Shalit's next novel, *Cadets,* will be published in Israel in the coming months. His books must pass a rigid vetting process, including the approval of a special Governmental Ministers' Committee. De Shalit has translated into Hebrew the American novel *A Sport and a Pastime* by James Salter, and John le Carre's autobiography, *The Pigeon Tunnel.*